The
DAUGHTER
-in-Law

Fanny Blake

**SIMON &
SCHUSTER**

London · New York · Sydney · Toronto · New Delhi

First published in Great Britain by Simon & Schuster UK Ltd, 2023

1 3 5 7 9 10 8 6 4 2

Simon & Schuster UK Ltd
1st Floor
222 Gray's Inn Road
London WC1X 8HB

Simon & Schuster Australia, Sydney
Simon & Schuster India, New Delhi

www.simonandschuster.co.uk
www.simonandschuster.com.au
www.simonandschuster.co.in

A CIP catalogue record for this book
is available from the British Library

Paperback ISBN: 978-1-4711-9364-4
eBook ISBN: 978-1-4711-9363-7
Audio ISBN: 978-1-3985-1233-7

Typeset in the UK by M Rules
Printed and Bound in the UK using 100% Renewable
Electricity at CPI Group (UK) Ltd

Fanny Blake was a publisher for many years, editing both fiction and non-fiction before becoming a freelance journalist and writer. She has written various non-fiction titles, as well as acting as ghostwriter for a number of celebrities. She regularly reviews fiction in the *Daily Mail* and has been a judge for the Costa Novel Award, the British Book Awards and the Comedy Women in Print Award among others. She was the commissioning editor for Quick Reads, a series of short books by well-known authors. She has written ten novels, including *An Italian Summer* and *A Summer Reunion*.

Follow her on Twitter @fannyblake1 and on Instagram @fannyblake1

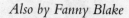

Also by Fanny Blake

The Long Way Home
A Summer Reunion
An Italian Summer
Our Summer Together
House of Dreams
With a Friend Like You
The Secrets Women Keep
Women of a Dangerous Age
What Women Want

A daughter's a daughter all of her life. A son is a son 'til he takes him a wife.

Anon

For Kathryn and Michael
With love and huge thanks

1

Travelling to the island had been a trial for all of them. An early start, a taxi that didn't turn up, the subsequent nail-biting wait for an Uber, Hope's discovery that there were two WH Smiths at Gatwick's North Terminal and she was standing by the wrong one, along with two toddlers and three exhausted adults hadn't made the journey easy.

That had only been the start.

After a six-hour flight to Kapodistrias, they'd boarded the ferry to Paxos, with all the hunger and heat that involved. Everything turned into a combination made in hell, and one that had almost brought all three adults to the point of regretting coming at all. Why were they putting themselves through this?

Then, they'd finally arrived.

A modest, white-washed villa was tucked away off the main road out of Loggos, the small port where they'd arrived. Surrounded by gnarled olive trees, it boasted a glinting blue pool, a terrace dappled with sunlight and a deliciously cool interior.

'Now, which room shall we put Granny in?' Edie sounded as if she was balancing on a tight wire. She adjusted six-month-old Hazel on her hip. The baby had barely slept since they'd set off, and tempers were beyond frayed. Hope had tried to help but Hazel had only wanted her mother.

What could a grandmother do?

Betty – the 22-month-old – toddled in and out of the four bedrooms. 'Gwanny,' she said firmly, pointing towards the prettiest space.

'No, darling. I don't think so.' Edie had followed her into each room to check. 'This big bed's for Mummy and Daddy. Granny Hope can go here.'

'Here' was a more modest room containing two simple wooden beds with thin mattresses, each with a single pillow. Basic. A plug-in mosquito killer flashed quietly in a socket on one side of the room. White-and-blue-striped curtains hung limp in the heat at a small window. The walls were uneven and white-washed, decorated only by a couple of large scenic photos: boxy white houses flanking steps leading down to a harbour; a line of crowded tavernas at the edge of a small port lit up at night, with the moon shining out of a starry sky. Quintessential Greece!

'Does that suit you, Mum?' Paul came in from the hire car. He carried her suitcase and dumped it at the foot of a bed. He straightened up and pushed the hair off his face, shiny with sweat.

'Anywhere suits me, darling.' At that moment, Hope could have lain on a bed of nails and slept.

Already, Edie and the girls had gone off to find their own rooms.

'No, this one has the cot in!' Edie sounded at the end of her tether.

The two of them listened, and Paul gave his mum a sympathetic smile. 'Why don't you have a rest? It'll all be shipshape by the time you wake up.'

Hope had never been so grateful. The early start was beginning to take its toll, and she could feel a sharp headache drilling in above her right eye. Once Paul had left, she took a swig from the bottle of water she'd bought at the port in Corfu, now unpleasantly lukewarm, and lay down on the bed nearest the window. High above it, a small green lizard was poised motionless. She gazed at it, charmed. Outside, she could hear Paul and Edie arguing.

'But I need her to help with Hazel.'

'Give her a break. Let her rest first.'

'For God's sake, Paul! Do I have to do everything?'

'Shhh!'

Hope closed her eyes. This was going to be a test for all of them. Hearing them talk about her behind her back like that hurt. Nothing she did seemed to narrow the distance between her and Edie. The harder she tried, the worse their relationship got. Perhaps she should have refused their invitation, but she could use ten days in Greece. She'd been working hard and needed a break. And what could be better than holidaying with her son and family? In theory. She breathed deeply and tried to rationalize. What she'd overheard was simply the result of a tiring journey, nothing more. This holiday was a chance to strengthen if not build bridges. She'd hold on to that thought.

When she woke up it was to a scream from Betty, somewhere in the villa. 'Swimming!'

Hope checked her phone. She'd been asleep for an hour and a half!

'You have to wait till Daddy gets back.' Edie still sounded as if she was about to snap.

Betty's scream of protest echoed through the villa.

Hope heaved herself off the bed, hot and sweaty. Her hair stuck to her temple and her headache was still there, but no worse. She opened her door and followed the sound of voices to the large open living room, feeling more sleep-deprived than ever. 'I'd love a swim. I'll take Betty.'

'Would you? Really?' Edie gave her a grateful smile of relief. She stood at the kitchen end of the room, drinking from a bottle of Orangina. She'd changed out of her jeans into a cool, floaty dress. Betty was sulking on the sofa, naked apart from her nappy, with one leg in her swimming costume, deflated armbands on the floor. Hazel was nowhere to be seen, presumably in bed.

'Unless *you*'d like to go. I can look after Hazel.' This feeling of having to tread on eggshells when dealing with her daughter-in-law was constant. Hope didn't want to say the wrong thing but seemed to fall into that trap more often than not.

'She's asleep at last, so I'd love a few minutes to myself. Thank you.' Edie put the bottle down with a firm 'chink' as it hit the white-tiled work surface.

4

'Do. I feel much better for a nap.' In fact, she didn't, because now she felt guilty for having had one. Edie looked exhausted. Two kids under two . . . it was understandable.

Betty ran over, holding out her armbands and her sweet candy-striped swimsuit.

'Just give me a second to change, sweetheart.'

Shadowed by Betty, Hope went back into her room and hefted her suitcase onto the second bed. Her packing was efficient, including nothing unnecessary or that might crease, so it took just a second to find her bikini. Slipping into the next-door bathroom to change, she couldn't help wondering whether she was too old to be so underdressed in public. She checked what she could see of herself in the small mirror. Perhaps she had put on a pound or two since she'd last worn it – one of the hazards of her profession. As a professional chef, if she didn't taste the food she was preparing, how could she guarantee its quality to her clients? Besides that, she loved food and the pleasure she could give through it.

'Sod it!' she said to herself. 'If you've still got it, carry on flaunting it. And this is hardly public after all.'

She was less confident when she and a pool-ready Betty emerged from her room and caught Edie's barely disguised surprise at the modest (by most standards) two piece. That lift of the eyebrow was almost enough to send her running back to change. Deep breath. Instead, she took Betty's hand. 'Let's go, then. Race you!'

'We don't do competition. Remember?' Edie's words followed them outside.

Bollocks! thought Hope, taking no notice.

The pool was by the wall dividing them from the next-door villa. Warning signs proliferated. *No swimming between 3pm and 6pm. No diving. No screaming. Try not to splash. Consider the neighbours.* Presumably the ones in Greek echoed the sentiment. They may as well have included one saying: *Do not enjoy yourselves on any account.*

'Sit here while I get in, and then I'll get you.' Hope inched her way down the metal pool steps. With a sharp intake of breath, she launched herself into the pool, flipping herself on to her back to stare upwards at the cloudless sky. A single vapour trail cut through the blue. The water was divinely refreshing, the sun blinding. She shut her eyes. For a second, she felt herself beginning to relax when she heard a shout from the side. 'Gwanny! In!'

Immediately Hope upended herself, feet on the bottom of the pool, and put her arms out for her granddaughter, who hurled herself in, went half under, came up and then clung to her. They took a walk round the shallow end.

'Show Granny how you can swim, Bets.' Paul appeared, carrying two large plastic bottles of water and some bulging supermarket bags. 'I'll just get all this stuff into the kitchen, then I'll join you. It's sweltering.'

Hope let her granddaughter go. She stood in the corner of the pool shadowed by an olive tree, encouraging Betty to swim to her. She had an urge to remove the armbands – they weren't helping at all as Betty floundered in the water – but she didn't dare.

After a while, Paul appeared with Hazel, who looked adorable in a flamingo-decorated swim nappy and a pink T-shirt and hat.

'Edie's gone for a lie down. Can you take Hazel while I blow this up?' 'This' was an inflatable green ring with a seat in its centre.

Hope put Betty on the side before taking her sister. She hugged the chubby baby to her as Hazel looked uncertainly at the water surrounding them. The next thing, she was beaming as her grandmother raised her high then lowered her until her toes touched the water. 'Wheeee!' Hazel kicked her legs in delight.

Once Hazel was safely inside the swimseat, Paul towed her roaring with laughter through the water. Betty begged to be pulled too.

'Daddy! Me!'

Hope grasped her under the arms and swooshed her around so she yelled for more. At that moment, Hope felt a burst of happiness. At last, things were looking up.

Later that evening, Hope put Betty to bed. The toddler had a cot in her own room that was similar to Hope's. Exhausted and in her unicorn pyjamas, the little girl listened while Hope read her a Meg and Mog book, snuggling into her grandmother as if she was the last person in the world. Afterwards, they had another hug and a kiss good night before Hope tucked the sheet over her, making sure she had her dummy and her toy lion. Hope stood, quite content, in the dimly lit room with a reassuring hand on Betty as she settled (the method Edie had shown her). She waited until her granddaughter's breath slowed and she was confident she could leave the room without waking her.

While Edie settled Hazel, a harder task judging from the yells coming from the baby's room, Hope started supper from the ingredients she had asked Paul to buy at the local super-market – a simple lentil-based moussaka (Edie had recently decided vegetarian was the healthy way forward) and a Greek salad. She had quickly made herself at home in the kitchen, the place in any home where she always felt relaxed but in charge. For her, the acts of cutting and chopping and mixing were almost meditative, calming. Then came the aromas from what she was cooking, but most of all she loved serving people a plate of delicious food. Seeing their enjoyment gave her huge pleasure. The bottles of retsina and local white wine (less healthy but holiday essential, Hope suspected) were chilling in the fridge.

Edie eventually emerged from Hazel's room. 'God! What a nightmare. She can be so stubborn,' Edie said, opening the fridge door and taking out a bottle. 'Paul!' She called to her husband, who was sitting on the terrace with a book, having changed from his swimming togs into navy-blue shorts and a pink T-shirt. 'Drink?' When she turned round, she seemed to notice Hope preparing the vegetables for the first time. 'Oh! You're not doing supper, are you? That's so sweet, but I thought Paul and I might go out to one of the tavernas on the harbour tonight. Didn't he say?'

'No. He must have forgotten.' Hope put down the knife. To be relegated to resident babysitter on the first night was a bit hard. She was surprised at Paul.

'I'm sorry, Mum. I meant to mention it.' Paul stood up and came into the kitchen. 'You don't mind, do you? We can always eat this tomorrow.'

True, although she had imagined them eating together on their first night. But no matter. Holidays were all about being flexible and going with the flow, she reminded herself.

'Of course. Why don't you two go and enjoy yourselves? I'll have my supper here and watch the kids.'

To her surprise, Edie kissed her on the cheek before pouring each of them a glass of retsina. 'You're fabulous. Thank you. I know this is going to be a wonderful holiday. I'm so glad you came with us.' She raised her glass in a toast. 'To us. And now, I must change.'

Hope tried not to grimace as the retsina – more petrol than grape – scorched her throat. 'You might have said something, Paul.'

'It went clean out of my head. I've said I'm sorry.' Paul put his arm around Hope's shoulder.

It was funny to think how her little boy she had loved so much had turned into this man whose head was often in the clouds. He had married someone who, as a barrister, had twice the ambition he ever had. A barrister and a carpenter. Hope sometimes wondered what it was they found in common.

'Thanks. Of course, it really doesn't matter. I'm glad to help. I want you to have a great holiday.'

'We will, Mum. How could we not?' He gestured towards the swimming pool and the loungers at one end.

Edie reappeared a few minutes later in a pretty sleeveless dress, her dark blonde updo immaculate. 'Now if either of them wake up, don't bring them out of their room. That's not a habit I want to encourage.' She grimaced at the idea. 'If desperate, you could give Hazel some milk. There's a made-up bottle in the fridge but you'll have to warm it in a pan of water. Betty will probably just need her dummy putting back in. And . . .'

'Don't worry. I'm sure everything will be fine,' Hope tried to reassure her, without pointing out that she had in fact babysat for them many times and knew the rules. 'And if I really have a problem then I can always call you. But I'm sure it won't come to that.'

At last, Edie and Paul drove off through the olive grove, leaving Hope feeling isolated and taken for granted. She scrambled herself some eggs and sat on the terrace to eat them, baby monitor at her side. The surrounding olive trees whispered in the gentle breeze that had sprung up. Otherwise, all she could hear was the constant chirrup of crickets, and perhaps a frog. Somewhere in the distance, a donkey brayed. The silence from the next-door villa suggested it was empty. She sighed. This was balm for the soul, not so bad after all.

After checking on the children, she settled down with the thriller she'd begun on the plane. A skinny ginger cat wandered silently out of the trees and straight up to the house.

She shooed it away, but it seemed to expect a welcome as it threw itself on the ground, offering its tummy to be tickled. Hope obliged. 'My new friend. I should put Bloater on your diet. ' Her own rescue cat was probably about twice the size of this one.

As the evening wore on, Hope realized that she was enjoying her enforced solitude. The tension of the day dropped away and she was free to enjoy where she was without having to watch what she was saying or doing. Betty slept contentedly, and although Hazel had woken about an hour after Edie and Paul had left, she had gone straight back to sleep after half a bottle of milk.

They arrived back late, delighted with the charm of the harbour and the freshly grilled fish they'd eaten, bursting with news about the friends they'd made: Jim and Bernie from Cambridgeshire who had a two-year-old daughter and a baby. What a coincidence! How lucky was that? But no grandmother in tow, Hope noted before she announced she was turning in.

The following morning, Hope was first awake. The early sun flared through her curtains inviting her out to explore. The previous day's exhaustion had left her and she felt refreshed and ready to go. If she was going to be on babysitting duty for the rest of the day, she might as well make the most of her time alone.

Up and dressed, she tiptoed through the villa, but there wasn't a sound from the other rooms. She slipped through the gate, closing it behind her. Walking through the olive grove, she enjoyed this moment of freedom. The two modern houses she passed were quiet. Metal rods stuck up from the top floor, the buildings unfinished. A couple of dogs were snoozing in a fenced run, raising their heads to watch her passing, while hens scratched about in the dust. A couple of bicycles were propped by the closed front door.

As she reached the end of the grove, the olive trees gave way to pines, and pine needles carpeted the path that led towards the cliff and the crystal-clear aquamarine sea glittering in the sun immediately below. To her left, a road leading towards a small car park. To her right, a path that meandered down to a small cove, with white sand and a single rowing boat. Hope glanced about her. There was no one around. She couldn't resist the siren call of the water, so set off down the path as a couple of tiny blue butterflies danced past her. On the horizon, a single yacht was heading towards the island, white sail bright against the deep blue. She held her arms out, enjoying the sun's warmth on her skin. The heat would be ferocious later, but this felt perfect.

The path was getting steeper, stonier and more precarious. Maybe this had been a mistake. Then, as she turned a sharp bend, she felt her left foot slip from beneath her. She reached out, but there was nothing to grab on to. As she fell to one side, her right ankle turned over with a distinctive and agonising 'pop'. Winded, she lay where she was for a few moments, then carefully sat on the path. At least she hadn't fallen over the edge. Small mercies. Her right ankle was throbbing. Looking down, she saw that it was already so swollen the bone was starting to disappear.

'You idiot, Hope,' she said aloud.

Glancing at her watch, she realized she had been walking longer than she'd meant. The others would be up and wondering where she was. As she gingerly got to her feet, a sharp pain shot up her right leg, making her sit back down again. 'Shit!' She reached into the pocket of her shorts then looked about her. Had she dropped her phone when she fell? An image flashed into her mind, showing where she'd left it on the kitchen table. 'Oh no.' She felt like crying.

There was no alternative but to crawl on her hands and knees back up the path to the small car park and hope for rescue. If it had taken her ten minutes to get to where she fell, she guessed that it took three or four times as long to get back up. Stones and grit dug into her palms and knees, the pain excruciating. Sweat poured down her face, tears welled in her eyes, but eventually she arrived and collapsed in the shade of a pine tree, wondering what the hell to do next. But there was nothing she could do, except wait until someone came.

After what seemed an eternity, she heard the sound of an engine, and a red car turned the corner to park in the shade near her. The doors opened and out spilled a family armed with towels, beach games and a picnic basket.

'Excuse me.' How English she sounded.

The woman turned towards her. 'Are you okay?'

Pale-complexioned, friendly faced, a wide-brimmed hat held in her hand, shorts, bikini top and trainers. With a rush of relief, Hope realized they were English too.

She explained what had happened. The woman looked at her ankle. 'That looks nasty. Where are you staying?'

'Down through those olive groves.' Hope waved in the general direction of their villa. 'But I think I should try to get it looked at. I don't think it's broken but ...' Without her phone she couldn't call Paul, but returning to the house as a problem without a solution didn't seem ideal. Better to sort it out herself first. They'd see her phone and realize she couldn't contact them. She'd be back as soon as she could, her ankle strapped up and ready to go.

'Can I take you into Loggos? Maybe we can find your holiday rep if you have one. They'll know what to do.'

Hope remembered Shirley, the talkative girl in a uniform who'd met them off the ferry and escorted them to the villa. She doubted Shirley would be much help in an emergency, but what choice did she have?

'I can't ask you to do that. What about your family?'

'You didn't ask; I offered. And Tom'll take them to the beach. Won't you, darling?'

'Sure,' her husband answered. 'Come on, kids. We'll see you later.' He gave a broad smile and adjusted his reversed baseball cap. 'Go and be a good Samaritan. I hope you haven't done anything too serious.' This last to Hope.

They drove down to the town and found Shirley sitting in one of the cafés nursing a coffee. She immediately let Hope use her phone to call Paul to explain what had happened before supporting Hope to the local surgery.

Thanks to her Samaritan, and then Shirley, Hope was quickly seen by the doctor, who unnervingly doubled as the local butcher.

'He won't chop off my leg by mistake, will he?' Hope made the joke he must have heard a thousand times. Shirley laughed, but the doctor's face remained impassive.

'A nasty sprain,' he said, in halting English. He looked unperturbed, presumably used to careless tourists. 'It needs rest.'

By eleven o'clock, Shirley had found a local taxi for Hope before heading off to the port to greet new clients. With her ankle strapped up, a rusty Zimmer frame on the roof because the doctor had run out of crutches, Hope rode home, dreading Edie's reaction. But when they pulled up outside the house and the driver helped her out, Edie's and Paul's faces were etched with concern as they rushed to help.

'I'm so sorry,' Hope said, hobbling with the help of the Zimmer. She wanted to get in first, before they had a chance to speak. 'I've ruined everything.'

'Don't be silly, Mum. We'll manage. We're sorry for you, that's all.'

'Yes,' echoed Edie, but Hope sensed her displeasure that the holiday they'd imagined was going to be very different. Far from being the help they'd planned Hope would be, she had suddenly become a burden. And, worse, she felt geriatric.

'Why ever did you go off on your own?' asked Edie. 'If you'd waited, we could all have explored together.'

If only she had, then the holiday wouldn't have been disrupted. 'It was such a beautiful morning, I couldn't resist, and you were all asleep.'

Edie shook her head and tutted.

'Never mind,' said Paul. 'What's done's done. We can manage, I'm sure.' He put his hand on Edie's shoulder but she shook it off and turned back to the villa, her annoyance more obvious now. Turning to Hope, he raised his eyebrows as if to say, 'You know what she's like. It'll blow over.' But instead of reassurance, all Hope felt was a stab of sadness seeing that things weren't entirely easy between them.

2

A couple of days after the family's return from Paxos, Edie stretched herself out on Ana's sofa, glass of wine in hand.

The two women had met years earlier at a party thrown by a mutual friend. They'd hit it off immediately – both of them single, ambitious and serious about their respective careers in fashion and law but both making sure that they fitted in excitement and fun, too. Although life had changed for Edie, their friendship had continued.

Back in London, life was infinitely more relaxing. On holiday, she had been constantly on call, looking after the kids, cooking, driving . . . no time to sit down. She reached for a peanut. 'So, she turned up at the house in a taxi, leg strapped up and with an ancient Zimmer frame.' She took a sip of wine. 'Honestly, I'm glad to be back.'

'She must have felt terrible, though.' For once, out of her high-flying role at one of London's leading fashion stores, Ana was dressed down in jeans and a pale blue T-shirt. Her face was alert, quick to read a room, keen to pick up any nuance.

'I know. It was so disappointing for all of us. If only she

hadn't decided to go off and explore on her own.' Edie threw up her hands. If only Hope had waited for one of them, things might have been different. 'The island was heaven. Paul and I had thought we might go out one or two evenings, explore the island a bit on our own, but we couldn't leave the kids with her because the poor woman could barely walk. At least she was a big hit with the local taxi driver. He'd come and drive her down to the harbour for the odd meal with us and the girls. Otherwise she couldn't really help out until halfway through the second week.'

'Can't have been much fun for her.' Ana was separating the tassels that trimmed one of her maroon velvet cushions.

'Oh, I don't know. She just lay by the pool reading, which isn't such a bad holiday.' Exactly the holiday Paul had promised her, she remembered with regret. 'She had us waiting on her hand and foot.' She laughed to cover the sting of resentment.

'What's your problem with her?' Ana asked. 'She's always seemed perfectly nice whenever I've met her.'

Edie pondered, reflecting on why she and Hope had never really clicked. 'For one, she just makes me feel like a totally inadequate mother. She always seems to know what Betty wants. She spends hours playing those games that I find utterly boring after ten minutes. And she has a killer knack for getting Hazel to sleep. And if I hear her comment on Betty being on the iPad again, I'll scream. She puts on a certain expression when she disapproves of something. When I stopped breastfeeding after only four weeks, you'd have thought I was withdrawing life support. Look at Betty! She hasn't suffered. But, oh no! She fed Paul for six months. And, worst of all, she tiptoes round me as if she's frightened I'm going to snap her head off.'

'You probably are.' Ana put the cushion back with the others, such an elegant mountain of comfort.

'I try so hard not to.' But who was Edie trying to convince? That first time, she had been so anxious about meeting Paul's mother. She'd immediately sensed how wary Hope was of her, too.

'But see it from her point of view. She's divorced, she lives alone now, and Paul, you and the girls are all she's got.'

'Hope's had other men in her life since,' Edie countered, 'and she's got friends.'

'I don't get it. Grannies are useful. If you got on better with your own mother, or at least pretended to, she could help you with the kids instead.'

'You don't understand. My mother's just not like that. In fact, she's the exact opposite of Hope. As far as she's concerned, the more distance between us the better. Dad was the glue that held us together, and since he died, we've only drifted further apart.' It wasn't how she had imagined or wanted their relationship to be in adulthood, but she realized now that her mother had always pushed her away. She hesitated before going on, but the wine and a ready listener encouraged her. 'My biggest mistake's been having a second baby. I didn't want one, but Paul was so keen to have another so it seemed a good idea to get the baby thing out of the way and have two close together. I thought my second mat leave would be a breeze after the first. They'd be friends, and I could get back to work. But it's been much harder than I expected. Two sets of nappies, two non-sleepers.'

'You poor thing, it sounds hard.'

'Honestly, it's non-stop, and the sense of responsibility is overwhelming. Worst of all, it feels so bloody lonely. If I'm desperate, I've got Celine, the au pair next door, who's always up for a bit of spare cash. Otherwise, I can get my neighbour over the road or Hope to step in for an hour or so sometimes, but the rest of the time it's just me.'

'Isn't Paul around? And what about the other women you met on that NCT course?'

Edie pulled a face. 'Paul's only about in the evenings and weekends and, as for the other women . . . well, I don't think I'm cut out to be an earth mother, and they sense it.'

'That makes two of us,' said Ana, raising a toast.

'Yes, but I'm in the middle of family life now. You're not.'

'And never will be. Great for others, but not for me. Anyway, at least your nanny's coming back soon. I still don't understand why you gave her so much time off when you needed her.'

'Because Jen wanted to travel and, anyway, I wanted to do it myself: be a mum to my children. This way we both got our chance; she went to the Far East and I've been mothering secure in the knowledge that she was coming back.'

Edie realized that, unless Ana had children herself, she would never understand how Edie had wanted to prove to herself and everyone else that she did have a nurturing side to her, that she wasn't all about her career. She had wanted to be a 'proper' mother in the brief six months of her maternity leave, but the reality had come as an unwelcome and exhausting shock. 'What was I thinking? Anyway, don't worry about me. I'm fine.'

But Edie wasn't fine. The overwhelming guilt she felt was almost intolerable. She was aware that some of the other new mothers she had met thought having a nanny was a mark of privilege, not to mention a sign of her unmaternal feelings.

'How can you bear to hand them over to someone else? Think of what you'll miss,' one of them had said.

When Edie tried to explain her work as a barrister, the demands it made on her time and the impossibility of doing it without reliable help, the woman had looked at her, astonished, and avoided her from then on. She had felt awkward about Jen's presence in their life ever since, but she couldn't live her life without her.

She had thought she was one of those women who could have it all. But the reality was so far from the dream. What she felt for her children was different from the all-consuming baby love that those others in her NCT class claimed to experience. Not that she saw much of them anymore. They only made her situation feel worse. She couldn't give up her career or her family – but juggling them successfully was virtually impossible. She and Paul needed her income but, more than that, she loved what she did and couldn't imagine her life without being a barrister.

Although she had thought she wanted children, now she had them, she found she loved her independence and her career more. She loved the girls in her way, but it wasn't enough. She recognized the truth but was ashamed to admit it or ask for help. Sometimes, when things got on top of her, she had even wished she had never met Paul, never had children. Then her life would be so much less complicated and she could live it on her own terms.

Especially now Daniel had come back into it.

'What does Paul say?' Ana curled her legs beneath her. 'How's he coping? Is he okay about you going back to work?'

'He's happy.' In fact, Edie didn't know what Paul felt about it. Had they even discussed it? Her return was just something they had taken for granted, never questioning it. She drummed her nails against the bowl of her wine glass.

'That's love for you, you know,' said Ana. 'Allowing the other person to be who they want to be.'

'He doesn't exactly "allow" me,' objected Edie as she took a fat olive, biting the flesh from round the stone.

'You know what I mean.'

'I do. If anyone's allowing anyone anything, it's me. Let's face it, without my earnings, we'd go under.'

'And you resent it?' Ana was always quick to point at the truth.

'Sometimes ... Yes, sometimes I do.'

'But he's so good at what he does. Everyone admires his work.'

'I know. But you know he trained in Business Management

at uni before he took up furniture making? Not that I wish he'd stuck at it exactly, but . . .'

She had lucked out when she met Paul, a man who turned heads when he came into a room. Tall, broad-shouldered with a shock of uncontrolled dark hair that fell over his forehead, a look of quiet bemusement on his face as if he wasn't always quite connecting with the world. A man of few words who channelled his creative energies into his wood carving and cabinet making in private homes across the city. As soon as he had walked through the door of her apartment to make her a bespoke wardrobe, she had wanted him much more than the wardrobe. And it didn't take her long to get him. Was it his smile, his quiet intelligence, or the way he looked at her, shy but appraising? She didn't remember which attracted her first.

'And Daniel?' Ana filled their glasses. 'That's going nowhere, I assume.'

Edie tensed. Ana was the only person who knew about Daniel's reappearance in her life, and she had been sworn to secrecy.

'I don't know. I'm going to see him next week.' Her stomach flipped. This wouldn't be the first time she and Daniel had met since Hazel's birth, but the physical side of their affair had been put on hold since the latter stages of her pregnancy. She had heard other women talk about how turned on they felt when pregnant, but not her. She felt like an elephant on heat – big and clumsy, so she pushed both men away. She was well aware that her body hadn't bounced back as quickly as it had after Betty's birth; its firm lines had blurred and softened. When she complained, Paul told her that he liked her even better as she was, although since she'd had the girls, he'd started treating her like a piece of porcelain, something too precious to be touched.

Daniel was another matter. He had been in her life for so long now, since long before she even met Paul. She remembered the three intense and heady years of dating before he took an irresistible position at a barrister's chambers in Newcastle. Going with him was out of the question, unless she gave up the chambers she had worked so hard to belong to in London and the kudos that went with it. They promised each other their relationship would continue despite the distance between them, but in the end it proved too much. Their work was too demanding and unpredictable and they agreed to separate. It took a long, painful time before she thought she might be ready to commit herself to someone else. She was still licking the last of her wounds when she met Paul. They had fun together, they laughed together, they travelled together and eventually they lived together and she thought she was in love. Daniel, her first real love, became someone in her past.

Until he reappeared in London.

She hadn't meant to fall in love with him again. She hadn't got married only to get divorced, but when he re-entered her life after Betty was born, she hadn't been able to turn him away.

Nothing between them had changed. The fact that, after one and then two babies, someone who wasn't Paul found her attractive astonished and delighted her. Daniel still loved her, and she him. He gave her back the sexual confidence that she'd lost, and the exciting, secretive love that Paul couldn't.

'Must you see him? Really?' Ana asked. Surprisingly, in her eyes, fidelity in marital affairs was paramount. 'What's the point of putting everything you have at risk?'

'Don't, please. No one knows and no one will get hurt.' She was absolutely determined that would be the case.

'You might.'

'I won't. Not if I'm careful.'

Ana scoffed. 'Oh please!' She was never afraid to express her thoughts.

'I don't want to hurt Paul. I love him, too.'

'You're lucky to have someone who adores you.' For a moment Ana sounded envious.

Edie sometimes wondered if her friend longed for a different life despite her protestations to the contrary, but if she did, she would never admit it.

'It can be stifling, though. Don't you see that?'

'Not really, no. What happens when you inevitably get found out?'

'We won't. We're incredibly careful.'

Ana picked up the wine bottle. 'It always happens somehow – how many times have we seen that? A text message, a hotel receipt, a train ticket.' She indicated Edie's glass. 'One for the road?'

Edie glanced at her watch. 'Eight o'clock already! I'd better not. Hazel's waking up at four a.m. these days.'

'How grim.' Ana pulled a face. 'The only thing that wakes me then is a lover. Whoever he might be!'

'We take it in turns, though.' Edie drained her glass, enjoying the oaky sharpness of the Chardonnay, preferring not to think too hard about Ana's string of conquests, her enjoyment of her freedom. 'One good thing about the non-breastfeeding thing is that Paul can do his bit.' In her jeans pocket her phone buzzed with a message. She pulled out the mobile and looked at the screen. 'See.' She waved the phone in her friend's direction. 'He's wondering when I'll be back. Supper's been ready for half an hour.' She placed her glass down. 'I have to go.'

The walk home was short. As she crossed the main road into Barnsbury, the air was perfumed with the distinctive scent of charcoal smoke and barbecuing meat with an undertow of exhaust. She loved London in the summer. Her phone buzzed again. She took it out to find a text – not from Paul this time, but from Daniel.

> Can we make it half an hour later next week.
> I've a meeting that may run on. D x

She felt that beat of excitement that always came with a communication from him, with the anticipation of their next meeting. She stopped for a second, so she could reply before she got home.

26

Of course. Can't wait.'

Not long to go. Whatever Ana thought, she wanted the affair
to continue.

3

Hope jumped at the sound of an incoming text.

She was finalizing the menu for Mrs Carswell, a particularly fussy client, whose dinner party was designed to impress
a contact flying in from America with her husband. She had
enjoyed the to-ing and fro-ing between them until they had
settled on something they were both happy with and had
promised to send the menu over that evening so the final
decision could be confirmed. She was relishing the idea of
cooking everything. They'd agreed on a starter of grilled
lobster tails with lemon and herb butter, beef Wellington
or fillet of sea bass with a vegetarian option of caper crusted
spiced cauliflower steak, followed by apricot panna cotta or
chocolate mousse and raspberry coulis, a selection of cheeses
and homemade chocolate truffles. Tempted to ignore the
phone but unable to, she flipped it over to see who was
calling. Paul.

'Mum?'

At the sound of his anxiety, she saved the document she
was working on. 'Are you okay?'

'I'm sorry, but Edie's held up at work and can't get to nursery in time to pick up Betty. Please could you do it? I'll come and get her as soon as I can get away.'

'Okay. I'll leave now and see you later.' What else could she say?

When Betty had been enrolled in a nearby nursery, Hope had been delighted. She had never particularly longed to be a grandmother. Grandchildren meant old age: something she'd been running from as hard as she could. And she certainly didn't want to be called 'Granny'. But . . . As soon as she met Betty in the neonatal ward, there'd been a special place in her heart for the child. When she held her for the first time, and gazed down at Betty's perfect little face, a burst of love ran through her and she was lost. She was pleased to be near enough to be able to help out.

She checked her smartwatch. If she walked quickly, she could be at the nursery in twenty minutes, on time and ticking off some of those bloody 10,000 steps.

By the time she arrived, there were only a few toddlers in the playground with the nursery workers. She spotted Betty over by the sandpit. After a second, the little girl looked up to see her grandmother waiting by the gate. Her face lit up and she raced over, calling, 'Gwanny! Gwanny!' She was such a pretty little thing: button nose, lively blue eyes, dressed in a pink-spotted blue tunic and pink tights.

Hope's heart soared at the enthusiastic greeting. She squatted as Betty barrelled into her and they hugged. She stood up with Betty still clinging to her. The few mothers still there smiled at the two of them.

'See you tomorrow, Betty,' said one of the staff. 'Have you got your castle?'

'Me down.'

Hope let her go and Betty dashed back to the sandpit to collect a blue-painted assembly of loo rolls and small cereal boxes that she proudly presented to Hope. 'Elsa house.'

'Does Elsa live here?'

Betty nodded furiously. 'Yes.'

'Of course she does.' If Hope had watched *Frozen* and *Frozen 2* once, she had watched them a thousand times.

How could Edie bear to miss this part of the day? Hope didn't understand her daughter-in-law's devotion to her career at this point in her children's lives. She had waited until Paul was in school before she began working towards where she was now. Not quite the same of course, but still . . . the principle was there. Edie seemed to rely on her and Paul more and more as her maternity leave came to its end. She wouldn't mind if Edie asked her directly to pick up Betty from nursery or from a friend's, or to take her a packed lunch that she'd forgotten. But every time the requests came through Paul. Was that because her daughter-in-law felt guilty? Unlikely. Edie seemed to think that being a private chef didn't count as work. At least, not when compared with being a family law barrister.

'Come on, Betty,' she said. 'Let's go to the park.'

*

Paul picked Betty up from hers at six. He dashed in, still in his work overalls, sawdust in his hair. Even though he was long grown up, she still felt that familiar pull of love and pride on seeing him.

'Sorry, Mum. Can't stop. Edie will have Betty's supper ready.' He took the cardboard castle with a grimace. 'Another one. Thanks a lot for picking her up. You're a saviour.'

'That's okay. I've given her some supper already.'

His face changed.

Hope read what he was thinking. 'Don't worry, I was very careful. No additives. Just a quick mac cheese and veg. All organic.'

He rolled his eyes. Hope had done the wrong thing. Again. 'Oh, Mum! I've told you a thousand times. Edie won't be happy.'

'The poor child was starving and she loved it.' It was her best defence. Had she not fed her, Betty would have had to wait ages for a lentil stew or some other offering from the repertoire of the perfect modern mother. She sometimes thought Edie tried too hard, as though doing everything a certain way would transform her into the multi-tasking mother of the year.

'I'm sorry,' she said. And she was. The last thing she wanted was to upset Edie. But wasn't it a grandmother's earned indulgence to spoil her grandchildren? A bit of macaroni wasn't going to do any lasting harm.

'You have to respect the way we choose to bring up our kids, Mum. Things are different now.' He sounded just like Edie.

'I do. I just didn't think giving her supper early would be such a major deal.' Honestly, modern parenting! Everything seemed so much more straightforward when she'd had Paul, and he'd survived.

The two of them had left in a flurry as soon as Betty's bright pink helmet was on and she was strapped into the seat on the back of Paul's bike. With a wave and a backwards call, they were off. Hope could barely watch as he cycled towards the traffic on the main road. Only once he texted to let her know they were home safely did she begin to relax again.

That night, Hope sat in her office upstairs refining the menu options and shopping lists for the Carswells, a glass of flinty Sauvignon within easy reach, a fig-scented candle flickering on the mantlepiece. Mrs Carswell had been especially picky over the choice of dishes and accompaniments but, if she liked what she got, she would undoubtedly bring new business by recommending Hope and her business partner Vita to her other well-heeled friends. So it was worth putting in the extra effort. Hope didn't usually drink on her own but, with the menu agreed, she deserved a treat. What was living alone about if you couldn't do that from time to time? And anyway, spontaneity was always better than habit.

She emailed the finalized menu including all the accompaniments and estimated costs to Vita for a last once-over. Her friend had said she'd look out for her email, so while she waited for Vita's go-ahead, Hope printed off a copy for herself and straightened up her office. 'Tidy office, tidy mind' was something she lived by and which she regarded as key for their business, *Booking the Cooks*.

Just as she was finishing off, the doorbell rang. Nine o'clock. She wasn't expecting anyone. She pocketed her mobile, took the Carswells' menu and left the office, shutting the door behind her. Vita would phone soon, she was sure.

She could see the indistinct silhouette of a figure through the stained glass in her front door. Keeping it on the latch (having seen one too many TV crime dramas), she opened it and peered round.

'Serendipity! I've just emailed you.' She took off the latch and pulled the door wide to let Vita in. This took a minute, as her friend had to haul her sit-up-and-beg bicycle into the hallway. Hope was always pleased to see her.

'You don't mind, do you?' Vita took a supermarket receipt from the big wicker basket at the front to stick between the end of the handlebars and the wall. 'I've lost the bloody lock and I couldn't bear it to be stolen.'

'Of course not. Am I expecting you?' It was unlike Hope to forget an arrangement.

'No.' Her friend looked windswept, flushed from her ride. 'I was waiting for the email, but John was driving me mad, so I thought I'd just come round for a bit.' She adjusted the waistband of her wide grey linen trousers and straightened the loose green top until she was comfortable. Very different from the vintage floral tea dress, picked up for a song from one of the stalls in Camden Passage, that Hope wore.

Hope was used to Vita and John's relationship. Time and

again, she had heard Vita out after a row had blown up over something petty, or when one had rubbed the other up the wrong way. But these were the stresses that could be found in any marriage. Vita and John actually had one of the most stable relationships she knew. They understood each other and never ran out of things to say. Just, every now and then, one of them blew.

She only had to think of her own marriage, long over, to remember what that was like. She thought of Martin now with a frustrated affection that she'd developed once the pain of the split had diminished. His younger second family was a cause for some amusement to her. He was still changing nappies in his fifties. Then all those teen rows. Much rather him than her.

'Nothing serious?' she asked all the same.

Vita laughed as she followed Hope downstairs into her kitchen. 'Nah. He was going on and on about how I always put too much water in the kettle. Then it turned into a gripe about my not putting the plastic into the right recycling bin. Can you imagine? I thought I'd leave him to simmer down.'

'Drink?'

'Once we've sent off this menu. Let me have a look. Have you thought about who'll do it?'

'I will, I think. It's important to the Carswells so I want to make sure it's perfect.'

'Don't micromanage. That's your weak spot. Use one of the girls.' Vita sometimes had to remind Hope to use their

small freelance team of cooks more. Hope's love of cooking meant she would happily cater for every job they were
offered had she but the energy and time.

'I know it is. Even so. Here.' Hope slid the menu across
the kitchen island to her. 'Have a look. At the bottom
there's the usual estimate of cost to us against the charge
for the job.'

Vita pulled out a stool, perched on it and skimmed over
the piece of paper. 'Looks great.'

'Good. I'll ask Jean or Marie to help me.' She named
their two best home cooks. 'Let me just send it. Help
yourself to a glass of white. Once I'm done, we can put the
world to rights.'

Hope had two kitchens in the basement: the open plan,
where they were, at the back of the house that led into the
garden for her private use; the other in the street side of the
basement, a state-of-the-art professional kitchen insisted on
by Health and Safety. Vita knew both as well as, if not better
than, her own. They had spent hours together down there,
cooking, testing, tasting, preparing to launch their business on a world where getting a private chef was the new
going out: all the advantages without the hassles of finding
babysitters, arguing over who would drive, cooking or
washing up. All with the guarantee of a restaurant-standard
meal. Hope, Vita and their team did it all, including the
clearing away afterwards. That's how they sold themselves,
with great results. Hope was proud of how the business
had expanded.

After her relationship with Liam (the last online date she'd vowed ever to have) had ended by mutual agreement, she couldn't imagine herself settling down with anyone else again. The thought of getting to know someone new in all those intimate ways was too daunting, so she had thrown herself into the business with even greater gusto than before. The two of them had gone on to add a new service: seven cooked meals delivered to the home, freezer-ready. After that, there'd been a small cookery school which Hope ran two days a week from home. It was full on, but fun, and made possible by the small team of freelance home cooks they employed to help them.

Hope ran up to the office and sent off the email.

By the time she returned, Vita had found the bottle of Sauvignon and had poured herself a glass.

After topping up her own, Hope fetched a storage jar out of her larder. 'You must try one of these. Cheese and pistachio biscuits. I've added chilli for a bit of kick. I'm not sure if it's too much.' She put a few of them in a bowl, the delicious nutty cheesy smell making her hungry, and took them with everything else out to the table outside on the terrace. They sat at it, overlooking the garden where purple and white allium heads bobbed between roses as swathes of zinnias, Amaranthus, rudbeckia and anything else Hope could find a space for held their heads up to the dying sun. The crowds of colour lifted her spirit and gave her such pleasure over the summer months. The scent of roses drifted in the air. There was the creak of wicker as they sat down.

'So.' Hope started. 'What's going on?'

'More of the same. What about you?' Vita was always more interested in hearing about other people than talking about herself.

'I was sailing along until Paul called, and I had to pick up Betty from nursery.'

'Again? Why this time?'

'Apparently, Edie had a meeting. She's getting ready to go back to work. It's not that I mind doing it. I really don't,' she added quickly.

'Methinks the lady doth protest too much . . .' Vita smiled. They had spent hours discussing Hope's daughter-in-law.

'No, really. I'd just like Edie to call me herself. I don't understand why she leaves Paul to deal with me.'

'Paxos was okay, though, wasn't it? You haven't really told me.' She picked up her glass of wine.

Hope laughed. 'Er . . . no. I told you I sprained my ankle?' Vita nodded.

'They were sweet, of course. After all, it was hardly my fault. But it meant Edie didn't have the rest she was hoping for. Looking after those kids is properly exhausting. The trouble with trying to help her is that she makes me so nervous. Then I try too hard and make everything worse. I know I'm getting it wrong but I don't know how to get it right.'

'She is their mum,' pointed out Vita. 'That's what mums are meant to do. Why have kids otherwise?' Spoken by a woman who had brought up four children up without help and happily survived to tell the tale.

'Not if you've brought Granny along to help out. It was meant to be a last hurrah before she goes back to work.'

'Why you and not her own mother?'

'She doesn't seem to have much of a relationship with her. I've no idea why they're not closer and I wouldn't ask.'

Vita thought for a moment. She popped a cheese biscuit into her mouth and gave a small moan of appreciation as she began to eat. Then her eyes widened and she quickly swallowed. 'Christ! Those chillies are hot.'

'Ha!' Hope quickly poured Vita another glass of wine. 'Sorry. I wondered if they might be a bit much.' She took a bite of one herself, relishing the buttery cheesy crumble and then the hit of chilli exploding in her mouth.

'You must have a mouth like asbestos if you can eat those.' Vita waved her hand in front of her open mouth.

'I'll get you a glass of milk.' Hope stood up.

'And spoil the wine? No need. I'll get over it.' She waved Hope back down into her seat. 'So, things aren't any better between you and Edie?'

'It's not that they're bad exactly. We're just not on the same wavelength. And things have got worse since the children were born. At first I thought it must be because she was grieving her father. He died just before Betty was born so he never met her. Paul says her relationship with her mother is distant at best. I felt so sorry for her but, even then, she brushed off my condolences and offers of help. What can I do? She obviously doesn't really like me but she's Paul's wife so I have to be discreet and diplomatic.'

Vita laughed. 'Like that's going to happen!'

'Well, I can try, even if it doesn't come easy. I have to – for Paul's sake.'

And she had tried. Truth be told, when she'd first met Edie, when Paul had first brought her round, they had got off to a bad start. Within minutes he announced that they were engaged, getting married within the next few months. Despite their evident happiness, she hadn't been able to disguise her shock. Why the rush? Was Edie pregnant? But she hadn't dared ask and, as it turned out, that was not the case. Hope had always imagined that she would get to know the girl Paul chose to marry before he took that step. She had imagined a friendship between them, or at least a bond arising from their mutual love of Paul.

In the past, various girlfriends had come and gone, some of whom she'd met, some of whom she'd heard mentioned and no doubt some she'd never heard of at all. But this . . . this was a whirlwind romance. Having recovered from the announcement, she had produced champagne and tried to talk wedding, but any venue she mentioned was dismissed; any florist, the same. The few friends she mentioned inviting who knew Paul well were rejected – this was to be small and intimate with their friends only. It didn't take long for Hope to realize her suggestions weren't welcome. She understood their desire to do things in their own way, of course she did. But it was the brisk, impersonal way that Edie explained it all to her that irked Hope. For the first time in her relationship with her son, she found herself way out of step. Until then, he had always been interested (or polite enough to look interested) in what she had to say, and she felt a sharp nip of resentment that she was losing her son to a woman who didn't like her.

And that feeling had never changed.

4

'I thought you'd told her not to give Betty supper.' Edie bit back all she wanted to say about her mother-in-law despite her kindness in picking up Betty from nursery. She didn't like her routines being thwarted. These were strategies that she had devised from an amalgam of childcare books, her own limited experience and conversations with two mothers she occasionally saw from the NCT course. Having control helped her keep on top of things.

'She was only trying to help.'

Edie watched him move around the kitchen island, seeing again the man she had fallen in love with. Kind, thoughtful, an easy laugh. The friend who had recommended his work in the first place had said, 'He's gorgeous. Have you ever met a carpenter who isn't?'

Edie had never met a carpenter at all before Paul. But her friend was right; he was gorgeous.

The fitted wardrobe was a job she'd wanted done beautifully, nothing more. But once she'd set eyes on Paul, she wanted him too. 'Predatory' was not a word she liked when used about her own sex, but if she was honest, that was exactly what she had been with Paul. She had still been feeling raw, even a couple of years after the break-up with Daniel, but the time had come to move on. So she was the one who'd suggested a drink at the end of the day. She was the one who'd then mentioned her favourite Italian restaurant, conveniently round the corner. And she was the one who had invited him home afterwards. Funny to think of all that now.

'I know and I'm grateful. Really.' She bent over her daughter and hoisted her onto her hip to be rewarded with a sticky kiss on the cheek. 'Come on, Betty. Bath.'

'Love you.' Her daughter kissed her again.

Edie kissed her back. 'Love you, too.' Nothing had prepared her for the occasional explosions of love that she felt for her children. Compensation for all the downsides of parenthood, she supposed. But it wasn't enough. She heard Hazel cry out from the living-room end of the open-plan basement where she'd been left in her playpen. Her NCT group might not approve, but Hazel on the move would make it impossible to get anything done. And Edie was a doer – everyone said so and she recognized it in herself. 'Can you get her?' she asked Paul. 'She's been a pain all day. Teeth, I think.'

'Sure.' Paul went over to her. A moment later, Edie heard him say, 'God! Hazey, you stink. How long have you been sitting here like this?'

Betty blew a raspberry on Edie's cheek.

'I only just changed her,' Edie protested, though it wasn't quite true. Edie couldn't stand to be accused of neglect but, in her heart of hearts, she knew she had been backsliding. The house was in chaos. Every room, apart from their bedroom, felt as if it was being swamped by a rising tide of plastic toys, children's clothing and unwashed dishes. Only two weeks till Jen, her nanny, came back and Edie could return to work – the day couldn't come soon enough.

Paul laughed. 'I'm not accusing you. Come on, you big lump. Let's change you again.' He walked past Edie and Betty and jumped up the stairs, making Hazel chortle with every bump.

That was the thing with Paul. He never read between the lines. He was one of the most uncomplicated men she had ever met and took everything literally. Something she hadn't realized until they were married. Her friends all told her how lucky she was to find a man who worshipped her, who helped with the children and the house, and made beautiful things. What he earned – or failed to earn – mustn't concern them at all. Ana was the only one brave enough to have asked her if she felt resentful . . .

'Where are the nappies?' he shouted down from upstairs.

'I got more on the way home, I'll bring them up,' she yelled back. 'But don't worry now. She can go in the bath with Betty.' She took the bag holding the nappies, went upstairs, Betty still clinging tight, and started running the bath. Having put Betty down, her next job was untangling her daughter when she got her dress stuck over her head.

'No pooey Hazel.' Betty screwed her face up.

'Don't worry, Daddy'll clean her up first.' Edie sank to

the floor by the bath, exhausted. She couldn't face another scene – Betty was the master of them.

'All done,' said Paul, bringing in the offender, all squidgy flesh and round cheeks, her smile revealing two teeth like little white pegs. 'Shall I go and do the milk?' He bent to put Hazel in the bath. She immediately splashed so hard they all got soaked.

'Hazel! No!' shouted Betty before she followed suit with greater effect.

'Stop it, both of you!' said Paul, laughing. 'You've soaked Mummy. Look.'

'I've only just changed from when Hazel threw her supper over me.' Edie stood up and backed out of the door. 'Grrrr.' Her monster impression was good enough to alarm both girls. Hazel's chin quivered.

'Calm down, darling. She's only having fun.'

Calm. Down. The two words that pushed every one of Edie's buttons. Instead of responding, which she knew would only lead to an argument, she headed for their bedroom, where she took off her wet T-shirt and tossed it in the laundry basket. By the time she got downstairs, she felt better. He was right of course; Hazel was only having fun. After a few minutes, she was back up the stairs with the baby's bottle and a cup of milk for Betty ready for story time.

Once the children were finally asleep, Edie sat at the breakfast bar watching Paul put together pasta and salad for them.

'You've been busy with Hazel all day,' he said, 'and you know you can't resist my pappardelicious cooking.'

She groaned at his joke. 'But you've been at work.' How she envied him the escape and the pleasure of returning home.

'What happened to you this afternoon? Mum only just got to school in time.'

She felt a rush of heat rising from her chest over her neck to her face and improvised. 'You know how James hasn't been convinced about my commitment to work. Some of the men I work with are such misogynistic dinosaurs!' She rolled her eyes in mock despair. 'But he was telling me about a recent case that he'd given to Olga. It should have been mine if I'd been back now. She's always been after my cases. I couldn't tell him I had to leave so I could pick up my daughter. It would have confirmed all his worst fears. You must see that.' Her eyes asked for Paul's understanding. 'The sooner I'm back for good, the sooner he'll favour me again.' But, in truth, her meeting with the senior clerk at her chambers wasn't what had held her up. She had left that with more than enough time in hand, but she had gone to meet Daniel. She hadn't intended to, but she'd been unable to resist his last-minute texted invitation. She argued to herself that they worked such unpredictable hours, they had to take the opportunities that presented themselves. Hazel was well looked after by Celine, the au pair next door, who didn't seem to mind.

'I get it, but next time, perhaps call Mum yourself?' He poured the dressing onto the salad and tossed it around.

'I don't like to. I know she disapproves of me going back to work so soon.'

'She's never said anything, has she?'

'No. But I can tell she thinks six months isn't enough. I can't persuade her that the world's moved on from her day.'

'I'm sure you're imagining all this. She loves you.'

'Maybe,' she said, though she very much doubted it. 'Anyway, one of us has to bring in the money.'

He flinched. 'Don't rub it in. I'm doing all I can.'

'I know. I'm sorry.' Sorry that she had let her resentment at being the main breadwinner surface. As if her guilt over wanting to get back to work wasn't enough.

'You're too hard on Mum. She helps us out a hell of a lot.' He put the salad on the table before draining the pappardelle and stirring in the sauce.

Edie sipped her wine. 'And I'm grateful, but she does love it.'

'I know, but we shouldn't exploit her.'

'If you mean *I* shouldn't, actually I don't. You're the one who uses her when I ask *you* to help out.' She could feel them teetering on the brink of a row. 'That's why I asked Celine next door to look after Hazel for the afternoon. I couldn't ask her to collect Betty as well. Surely you could have stopped whatever you were doing a little early for a change?'

'Well, I couldn't, as it happens. Not without the dresser collapsing.' He spooned some pasta on to her plate. 'Is this enough?' His smile had vanished as he looked up and handed her the plate. He loathed it when she devalued what he did just because she earned more.

'Bit too much, thanks. I've got to lose a few kilos before I start. I thought I might persuade Ana to come to the gym with me.' And, it struck her, perhaps she could use some of the sessions as excuses to see Daniel.

'You don't need to. It's your brain they want, not your body.' He ran the backs of his fingers down her cheek then took back her plate to offload some food.

Edie noticed a woodpecker land on the birdfeeder hanging from the apple tree just outside the French windows that led out into their long, narrow garden. *Tap tap tap.*

'I suppose,' she said, still wondering whether she could make the gym plan work to her advantage. Thank God Paul had no idea about Daniel, she thought, and picked up her fork. He would be disappointed if she didn't enjoy his food.

He handed back her plate and held out his glass to chink against hers. 'Let's not talk about Mum anymore.'

He knows, she thought. *He knows how difficult I find his mother – how intrusive.* She realized, ironically, that it was precisely because Hope so obviously tried not to be that Edie found her so irritating. And then there was her well-meaning advice that contradicted all the modern schools of thought. If she heard the phrase 'In my day . . .' or 'What we used to do . . .' one more time, she would explode. But she was as glad not to have to talk about his mother, as she was not talking about her own. Edie's life was wrapped in the here and now, for better or worse.

That reminded her. 'Don't forget Mary's in town this weekend. I've invited her for lunch on Sunday.' Her mother was a law unto herself, her relationship with her children distant at best. Edie's brother, Noel, had avoided all unnecessary contact by moving to New Zealand, where he had married a local girl and worked in a winery. She doubted if he would ever return. However, Edie did her best – not wanting her relationship with Mary to wither entirely. But her mother didn't make it easy, not least by always insisting that she stay in her favourite boutique hotel in West Kensington rather than slumming it at Paul and Edie's.

'I suggested Mum might come over on Sunday as a kind of thank you for her help today.' Paul sounded tentative, as if he had guessed that it would be a problem.

'But we see her all the time,' protested Edie, and her glass hit the table with more force than she'd intended. 'Can't we have one weekend off?'

He put down his knife and fork and stared at her. She was testing his patience, she knew.

'I'm sorry,' she said quickly. She reached out a hand to him and, after a moment, he took it. She knew what she should do. Be the bigger person. 'Why don't we ask them both?' she said, her heart contracting at the thought of both mothers being there together. 'It'll be fun.'

He squeezed her hand. 'That would be great.'

The weekend had come round quicker than Edie would have liked. But a bonus was that no one was coming for

Sunday lunch, after all. Her mother didn't want to; she had other, better fish to fry in the form of an old friend flying in from Dubai. So, Saturday coffee at home it was, despite Hope having to leave early to swim in the Hampstead Ladies' Pond before work that evening. This arrangement had all the potential to work brilliantly. Edie had made a clementine and almond cake (healthy, in its way) the previous evening. Just to show she could. Coffee was so much easier than spending the morning cooking a lunch, and the two grandmothers could entertain each other – win, win. However, if she stopped to think – and she did her best not to – her mother's decision to pay such a fleeting visit was a little hurtful. Why wouldn't she want to spend more time with her grandchildren? After all, she'd only seen Hazel once since she was born. Her social life in Cheshire was often her excuse – another card game or painting class, another party. That or flying abroad to stay with her friends. Her attitude only underlined her absence and the lack of affection Edie had always felt from her. If only her dad were still alive. He at least had been interested in what was going on in her life, in what she was achieving.

Mary swept in at 10.30 a.m. on the dot, just as she had been invited to. She had maintained the haughty air of a woman used to being waited on – despite not having been for years – and of being the wife of a successful man.

'Hello, darling.' Her embrace of Edie bordered on the warm, and her look of slight alarm as Betty approached wielding a red wax crayon a little too close to her cream trousers and peach silk shirt was as funny as it was sad. Edie took a deep breath. She was not going to be irritated by her mother or lose her temper.

When Hope arrived five minutes later, the conversation had barely got beyond a few stilted exchanges and Betty was refusing to respond to Mary's stabs at grandmotherly interest. Through the baby monitor, they could hear Hazel murmuring to herself.

'She always does this. She'll go off in a minute.' Edie held up her crossed fingers. Paul rested his hand on her shoulder.

'Oh, but I do want to see her,' said Mary. 'I've brought her the sweetest Babygro – the shop assistant thought it would be perfect. Bring her down.'

'I hoped she'd go down earlier but she wouldn't,' Edie replied, not wanting her mother to see her inadequacies with Hazel. 'She's so exhausted, she'll just be a pain if she doesn't have a nap.'

'She won't sleep for long,' said Paul. 'You're bound to see her before you go. Don't worry.'

Mary looked put out, but didn't object further.

'I brought this,' said Hope, holding out a plastic container.

Edie predicted that inside there would be a lemon drizzle cake – one of Hope's many specialities.

'Oh, I didn't realize I was meant to contribute,' said Mary. 'Should I have? There's a wonderful patisserie right by the hotel.'

'Of course not,' said Edie, a little too quickly. 'Actually, I made a cake myself last night.'

Hope looked embarrassed. 'I'm sorry, I didn't think. I can take this away.'

'Don't do that, Mum,' said Paul, taking the container. 'We'll eat them both.'

They had enough cake for at least twenty people now. Edie thanked Hope and suggested she sit next to Mary on the sofa looking out of the French windows. Outside, the skies had opened and a summer shower lashed down, knocking the plants sideways.

'The garden's in a bit of a state,' said Mary. 'When does your gardener come?'

Paul and Edie exchanged a look.

'We don't have one,' said Edie. 'Paul does most of it.'

'It's just the rain,' said Hope. 'Normally, it's beautiful.'

Edie felt a rare pulse of gratitude to Hope for saying so.

From upstairs, Hazel had begun to wail. 'I'll go,' said Paul, rolling his eyes towards the ceiling.

'Let me,' said Hope.

She was already up and halfway to the stairs before he answered. 'If you think you can get her off, then do, Mum. Thanks.'

Edie did her best to contain her annoyance at Hope's presumption, knowing she should be grateful. Gritting her teeth, she went into the kitchen area to make the coffee and bring it over.

Not long after Hope had disappeared upstairs, there was silence, and she reappeared to join them. Betty ran to her and hugged her leg. 'Gwanny!'

'You're a baby whisperer, Mum,' Paul said.

'Just luck and timing,' said Hope. But she was clearly pleased by her success. She sat by Mary again, and let Betty climb on to her knee, carrying a fat board book. Trying not to be rude, she started turning the pages in an effort to keep Betty amused while focusing on the conversation.

'I was never much good at that sort of thing,' said Mary. 'But I was lucky in my own way. Where we lived, we always had help. Those local women were marvellous. Especially in Singapore.'

'Read it,' said Betty, bouncing on Hope who began to read quietly.

'Were they?' Hope interrupted the story to ask.

'Read,' insisted Betty, squeezing Hope's cheeks.

Edie supposed some of them must have been. Only one or two of them stuck in her memory. Mini was an older woman who smelt of cooking and bleach who would pinch Edie if she was naughty. Ah Lam had been much younger, and had treated Edie and her brother like her own. She would take them to visit her own parents, who always gave them a warm welcome, pressing small gifts on them. Edie had been heartbroken when, after three years, they had left her behind when her father was posted to the Middle East.

'The gardeners were too, no doubt.' Edie couldn't resist the dig.

The comment sailed over Mary's head as she dug into her bag and brought out a shop-wrapped parcel (a Hamleys sticker was the giveaway). 'This is for you, Betty darling.'

Betty clung on to Hope, uncertain.

'Go on, Betty. See what Granny M's brought you.' Hope felt the weight of Mary's gaze on her.

Betty inched herself off Hope's knee and took the parcel with a shy grin before she went straight back to Hope. 'Gwanny. Look.' Hope encouraged her to rip off the paper while Mary looked on with an odd expression. Hurt at being rebuffed? Relief that she didn't have to do more? Edie would never know. Instead, she watched the interaction between the three of them, struck by how much trust Betty had in Hope.

'Wow! Look at these! But perhaps save them till you're a bit older,' said Hope, passing the present to Edie.

Edie saw it was a jewellery-making set, a see-through plastic box full of gaudy plastic beads. *Age 4 upwards* read the label. Hope was right – again – they were too old for Betty. She tucked them behind a cushion, hoping Betty would forget them now Hope was distracting her from their disappearance by re-reading the board book.

'I remembered how you loved making things when you were a child,' Mary said to Edie, who was pouring coffee while Paul sliced up the cakes.

Edie was surprised that her mother recalled anything much about her childhood. She remembered it as long months in boarding school while her parents lived it up abroad. When her friends went home for half terms, she either stayed in school or went to her aunt's. Her father's sister, Emma, was married but had no children and provided a warm, safe haven for her and Noel, her brother, but it was never the same as having an actual parent to love them. When she did fly out, wearing a luggage label and accompanied by a stewardess, to Dubai, Nigeria or Singapore, her relationship with them remained distant. She and Noel felt like intruders in their ex-pat lives. As a result, Edie had developed a protective carapace at a young age. No one could hurt her if she looked after herself without relying on anyone else, not even Aunt Emma.

'Really?' she said. 'My main memory is peering between the bannisters at the parties you gave, perfumes mixed with cigarette smoke and the sound of voices and music. All sorts of smells coming from the kitchen. And then being dragged away by whichever maid was looking after us.' The idea of doing any kind of painting or crafting with her mother seemed a far cry from the reality of her young life.

'Your adventures sound so glamorous compared with ours.' Hope sounded wistful. 'Life on a farm was very different.'

Edie had envied Paul his childhood life when he had first told her about it. The stability and love. Until their divorce, Hope and Martin seemed to have given him the sort of upbringing that she had craved for herself.

Mary had reclaimed the box of plastic beads from under its cushion and was showing Betty how the pieces of jewellery fitted together.

'Be careful she doesn't put them in her mouth,' said Edie.

'I daresay we were lucky,' Mary replied to Hope, not

acknowledging her daughter. 'David was such a wonderful and clever man.'

Her adoration of her late husband must have been what led to her emotional neglect of her children, reflected Edie. There was no room for anyone else, not even her and Noel.

When Betty's chubby hands tried to fix the tiny beads, they fell to floor. But Mary pressed on undaunted, despite Betty losing all interest. She was rummaging in the box looking for the right colour and shape of bead, then whooped with triumph. 'Yes! Here it is. Betty. Look!'

Betty looked up at her name but returned her attention to her doll that she was making whimper by punching its stomach. Eventually Mary had made a bright necklace, by which time Betty was reading a book again with Hope.

'Betty! Come and try the necklace. Now.' Edie called, eager to get it back in the box before the beads were swallowed or lost. Besides, she wanted her mother to have some appreciation.

Paul looked up at her.

She hadn't meant to sound so stretched.

'This is great cake, Edie. I wish you'd make them more often.'

'It really is,' said Hope. 'You must give me the recipe.' Was she being as patronising as Edie heard?

'The lemon drizzle is superb.' Mary had eaten about a teaspoonful. 'Is that the one you made, darling? I've forgotten.'

'No. That's the one Hope brought.' Her mother didn't mean to be tactless, she told herself. 'Betty, I love your necklace.'

Mary popped it over the child's head, looking pleased.

As Betty reached up to pull at it, the string of popper beads broke and scattered to the floor. Her mouth opened wide with disappointment and her eyes welled with tears as Mary and Edie scrabbled on the floor to rescue them.

'Betty! Can you make me some tea?' Hope brandished the plastic teapot she had given Betty for Christmas, successfully distracting her. 'I'll help you.'

Betty looked at her warily, then forgot the beads and busied herself with organizing the plastic cups and saucers. Mary poppered the necklace together again, a tut accompanying every added bead, her apparent pleasure in the task diminishing by the moment. By the time she had completed it, Betty couldn't be torn away from pouring out imaginary tea and presenting cups to Hope and the others.

'More coffee, Mary?' Paul proffered the jug.

'I should really get going,' she said, clearly upset by Betty's lack of attention. Or perhaps more that the little girl's attention was on Hope.

'What about Hazel,' asked Edie, desperate for her mother not to leave on a bad note. 'You haven't even seen her. I could get her up now.' Although she knew this would cause problems. Hazel hated being woken.

Mary looked at the wall clock. Ten minutes slow, but Edie didn't draw her attention to that. It would only make her rush. 'Well, all right.'

Edie ran upstairs and lifted Hazel out of the cot. The baby was all warm and snuggly until she realized Edie was putting her on the plastic mat to change her nappy. Immediately her back arched and her mouth widened into a piercing scream.

'Shhh. Come on. Be good, please. I want you to make a good impression.' Edie finished unbuttoning the legs of her Babygro.

Edie eventually succeeded in forcing her wriggly baby into a nappy and her clothes. By the time they got downstairs, they were both exhausted, but Hazel at least had cried herself out.

Mary looked taken aback as Edie went over to give her Hazel, but she couldn't refuse. She looked stiff and awkward as she attempted to make Hazel comfortable on her lap. 'Oof! You are a big girl,' she said.

At that, and the fact she was in the arms of a complete stranger, Hazel's chin wobbled, her mouth turned down at the corners – a sure warning sign – before she opened it in a loud wail.

5

As the water of Hampstead Ladies' Pond closed round her, Hope felt an invigorating shock of cold race through her body which she slowly adjusted to. Swimming outdoors reliably made her feel at one with herself, with nature, and soon the tensions of the morning at Paul and Edie's began to ebb away. Iridescent blue dragonflies and bright butterflies darted past her while in the distance a family of moorhens scattered. She spotted a heron on the bank, completely still, observing the scene in front of him. Around her, the water was dark, the bottom unknowable, and the particular leafy organic smell that she associated with the place permeated the air. And, of course, only women were admissible, which gave a very special sense of community. She imagined Mary swimming here and couldn't help laughing to herself. This was a million miles from the warm, clear blue pools her co-grandmother would have been used to with loungers at the side, cocktails on tap and sunshine guaranteed.

Drying off later, Hope reflected on the morning. What a self-centred woman Mary was. No wonder Edie had issues – who wouldn't with a mother like that? Was that why she had always clammed up when Hope asked anything about her background? Was she embarrassed or ashamed? Or even angry and resentful? The only time she had seemed to open up a little was when talking about her dad, whom she had clearly admired, but that was not the same as love. Hope would remember that in future.

'How did it go?' Vita stepped out of the water, larger than life in her flamboyant pink swimsuit. She shook the water out of her hair.

'I made a terrible mistake by taking a cake with me – a peace offering, I suppose – but Edie had made one herself. Immediately, I could tell that I'd done the wrong thing, but it was too late then.'

Vita laughed and took the towel Hope held out to her. They went to the grass burnt brown by the summer sun that was now struggling out from behind the clouds. They found a spot to lie and dry off. Hope loved this place, the vast expanse of water surrounded by trees and bushes, cutting it off from the city. It could be relied upon to make her feel at peace, whatever was going on in the world outside. A flight of shrieking green parakeets flew overhead.

'Then Mary said she preferred mine. I could have died.'

'Ah well, at least Edie made one. I like that in a mum.'

'Me, too. But see how I did the wrong thing again?'

'You know what I think? You need to find another man. You must be over Liam by now. That way you'd have some-thing and someone else to think about.'

Hope remembered the man she had met online and pulled a face. 'Is that really the solution?'

Vita's view was that everyone needed someone else if the world was going to keep turning. 'You don't want to be on your own for ever, do you?'

'I'd rather be on my own than be with someone I don't really like.'

'He seemed okay to me.'

'He was more than okay, but he wanted more from me than I wanted to give and then we grew apart over the years. He was too needy.' To begin with she had enjoyed his pursuit of her, wanting to be with someone who wanted her. But eventually she couldn't put up with another conversation about how he wanted them to live together, share their lives more. In the end, they'd agreed they wanted different things from the time they had left to them, so agreed on parting as friends.

'Not everyone's like that, though.'

'Probably not. But who would I find? Men my age are looking for someone much younger. Liam's moved on to someone in her late forties, he says, whereas I'd have to settle for someone around eighty and then I'll end up having to nurse them until they die. Nah, I'd rather have a dog.' She laughed. 'Joke! Anyway, I'm quite used to being on my own now.'

'My point exactly! You'll soon be so governed by your routines and habits that there won't be room for anyone else in your life. Not even a dog.'

'There isn't now. The arrangement I had with Liam was perfect.' They had been together for six years, living separately all that while.

'You could find someone else to have the same deal with, couldn't you?'

'How? Those online dating sites fill me with dread, and I don't meet anyone anymore. At least I do, but not in that way.'

'You've got to put yourself out there somehow.'

'I'm happy as things are. I like my independence.'

'If you say so.' But Vita sounded far from convinced.

Was Hope really happy? Did she know? What *was* happiness, anyway? Was it something that came from an outside agency? Or was it something that came from inside? Her grandchildren made her happy. Paul had given her so much happiness. Martin too, until their relationship splintered. She pictured the Cornish cliff paths, the beaches and the farm where she had once found such contentment with her now ex-husband. Cooking – that made her happy too. She lived the life she wanted and experienced the joy that came with that, but it could never be absolute. Only she knew that.

Hope and Marie, her co-cook, stepped through Mrs Carswell's imposing front door armed with boxes of provisions. Both stopped in their tracks. They were used to catering for the more well-heeled, but the Carswells' house was something else. The hall was wide and welcoming, parquet-floored, a signed Hockney print on the wall, a large and elaborate floral arrangement on the console table. Mrs Carswell swept down the staircase wearing a silk peignoir, a towel wrapped round her head, hands held out before her so that the blood-red varnish didn't smudge.

'Thank goodness you're here. I was beginning to worry.'

Hope checked her watch. They were five minutes early.

'The kitchen's this way. I'd prefer you to use the back door when you leave, if you don't mind.' She pushed the door open with a hip to reveal a large modern kitchen, which Hope gazed at aghast. The central island was covered in clutter. Leftover breakfast things jostled with lunch plates. Used pans sat on the hob. A pile of dirty plates and glasses stood on the draining board, waiting to be washed. Cupboard doors were left open. How were she and Marie supposed to stick to their timetable with all this mess to work around?

'The children,' said Mrs Carswell, by way of explanation. 'So sorry, but I didn't have time to clear up and it's our housekeeper's day off. It's not a problem, is it?'

How could Hope say, 'Actually, yes'?

'It's not something we usually deal with, so it'll be an additional cost,' she said instead.

'That's fine.' Mrs Carswell gave an airy wave.

Business expenses, Hope assumed as she followed her in, her back pressing against the door so that she didn't drop anything. Mrs Carswell didn't offer to help or show them round the kitchen. Hope disliked working with clients like this. Most didn't treat them like staff and at least made an effort to prepare for their arrival.

Before unpacking, she and Marie spent twenty minutes clearing space for themselves, washing and drying, filling the dishwasher and piling up stuff that had no obvious home. Having done that, they unpacked the boxes and began to assemble the meal. This was a dance the two of them had performed numerous times and they knew exactly how the other worked. Hope loved Marie's meticulousness. No detail was too small. Hope left her co-chef to the lobster tails, while she heated the oven ready for the beef Wellington.

They'd spent the whole day prepping. Each course was cooked as far as possible in advance so that it could be finished off with the least trouble in the Carswells' kitchen, and everything had to be perfect. Three-quarters of an hour before service, they heard the first guests arriving.

Mrs Carswell returned, now wearing skin-tight black leather trousers and a white shirt. She had pulled her hair back into a ponytail, but even the Essex facelift couldn't hide the tension in her expression.

'Are you ready, ladies?'

'The lobster tails will be on the table in five minutes,' said Hope, checking her watch.

'We said 8 p.m.' She rapped a nail on the face of her Apple watch.

'Exactly.' Hope was firm, knowing that once she let a client walk all over her, that marked the end of the relationship.

Mrs Carswell retreated.

'Phew!' said Marie under her breath. 'She's quite the one.'

'Let's just do this and get out of here,' said Hope.

They removed their aprons to serve the food in the red dining room that more resembled a boudoir than anything else. The lighting was dim, two branched candlesticks at either end of the table. The silver shone and glasses glittered. Conversation between the Carswells and their four guests seemed stilted. Hope announced each course as they brought it in, earning wide smiles. She was glad to know that her food had brought some pleasure to the table, at least.

The following morning, Vita turned up at ten, clutching two takeaway lattes.

'You've read my mind.' Hope was pleased to see her, as always. They went to the upstairs office – once Paul's bedroom, but the bed had gone with Paul – leaving the room to become a compact working space where all the admin for *Booking the Cooks* was done. Almost everything was computer-driven, so all they had on the shelves were their favourite cookery books, photos of them at work, cards of thanks pinned to the corkboard, and on the two desks that faced each other, two laptops. The real work went on in Hope's basement kitchen.

'So, how did it go?'

'Fine. Marie did a great job, and they enjoyed some great food. Not that Mrs C was grateful – just took it as a service.'

'One of those.'

'Not the first and certainly won't be the last. I'm glad I went, though. I wouldn't like one of the others to have to deal with her. I told her we'd need to charge more for having to clean up the kitchen before we started. She hadn't made the least effort.'

Years of friendship and working together meant Vita could read Hope's moods as well as she knew her own. She flicked the blinds to keep out the sun and settled on her ergonomic office chair, swinging round on it to face Hope, her loose red linen dress hanging over the sides. Work was clearly not the first thing on her mind today. Vita was brilliant with the customers, particularly the difficult ones, as well as being the most reliable and helpful listener that Hope knew, but she did like a good gossip. As she probed Hope for more information on the previous night's dinner party guests, she got on with sorting out the post that she'd brought upstairs from the doormat.

'This one's for you.' She passed a white envelope to Hope. She didn't recognize the handwriting: sharp, neat, leaning to the right. 'What's this?'

She watched Hope rip it open with a finger and take out a folded letter.

'Well?'

'No idea.'

As Hope's eyes travelled down the letter, she froze. Then she had to stop and go back to the beginning again. This was impossible. After so many years, she couldn't believe what she was reading.

'Are you okay?' Vita stopped what she was doing. 'You're looking peculiar.'

'Fine.' Hope turned away and carried on reading, shocked by the letter's contents.

'What's up?'

'Nothing, really. Just a letter from someone I haven't heard from for a long time.'

Her head was spinning, so she reached for her glass of water. Only the small teddy bear she had pushed to the back of a bedroom drawer knew the truth about what had happened, and fortunately he couldn't talk. But occasionally, when she was on her own, she got him out, and remembered.

Hope skimmed the letter once more.

It's been a long time . . . I wasn't ready to look for you until now . . . I want to see you.

She quickly folded the sheet of paper, making sure the corners all matched and running her fingers along the folds. This was not something she wanted to share with anyone, not even her closest friend. No one knew. Not even Martin, with whom she had spent the best part of her adult life. Maybe he would have understood her better if she had told him. Maybe she would have understood herself.

'Hope?'

She turned to see that Vita was looking at her curiously.

Hope felt colour rush into her cheeks as she pocketed the letter. 'It's nothing.'

Vita didn't look satisfied but carried on with the business post. Hope had made it clear she didn't want to talk, although she was aware her friend would come winging back in when her defences were down. But she would be ready.

The two of them worked silently to the background accompaniment of Hope's Spotify list – Classical up here and

'70s and '80s chart-toppers in the kitchen where they gave her the energy she needed. Surely Vita could hear Hope's heart pounding as she considered the implications of the letter? She had her laptop open and pretended to be reading something when, in reality, her mind was elsewhere. She was grateful that she had to go downstairs to prep the dinner for four she was cooking that evening: salmon coulibiac and chocolate mousse.

Vita helped with the pastry (her speciality) and hung about opportunistically in the kitchen as if hoping for a morsel of explanation about the mystery correspondent. Eventually she had to accept Hope wasn't going to spill the beans so went home, unsatisfied. As soon as the front door closed behind her, Hope went up to her sitting room where she threw herself onto the sofa. The smell of chocolate – she only used the very best – wafted up behind her. She didn't have much time, but she had to read the letter again. The words seemed to have a life of their own, dancing on the page.

He wanted to see her.

She stared at his signature. *Patrick.* Just his name made her catch her breath. She'd imagined she would never hear from him again. They had been separated over forty years earlier, thanks to her mother's interference. She had considered tracking him down, after she and Martin had separated, but something held her back. Would opening old wounds help either of them? It was then that she'd decided she had to forget. But how could she?

And now, this.

She went over the words one more time, trying to read between the lines, imagining him writing them. Why get in touch with her now, after so long? Did he want something from her? Had something happened? And why the formality of a letter? At the same time, she felt a pulse of nervous excitement. Of longing. Perhaps he really did want a relationship with her at this stage in their lives. She couldn't help wondering what he must look like now. Was he married? Did he have children of his own? As much as she was dying to find out, she knew this could completely overturn the life she had made for herself.

She had never mentioned him to anyone, and letting him back into her life now might throw up all sorts of unexpected repercussions. What would Paul say? Martin? She couldn't bear to imagine. What would they think of her? The implications of raking up her past were too huge to consider. She had found a way of living with what she'd done, managed eventually to push the memories out of her mind. Now, those memories flooded back, unbidden and unwelcome. Should she even reply?

Then again, he must have gone to some trouble to track her down. She had a different name now, had done ever since she'd married Martin, and was living in another part of the country. Didn't his persistence at least deserve a reply, even if it wasn't the one he wanted?

She had half an hour before she had to start loading the van. Time enough to write back – or begin to. She would reread and rewrite until she was sure her letter said what she wanted it to. Only then would she decide whether to send it.

6

Edie put the last of the wooden bricks into their box. What was the point? Another half-hour and they'd be all over the floor again. The point was her sanity. While the girls slept (at the same time was a triumph), she could straighten out the house and her brain.

She'd dressed with thought, in anticipation of her meeting with Daniel. Pale blue jeans, a white T-shirt. Nothing to stand out, but neat and clean – provided Hazel wasn't sick on her. Meeting up in the park was a risk, but it wasn't the first time they'd done it, and nobody would suspect two parents in the playground of anything. After all, any of those kids racing around could be his; no one could know his real one was safe at home with his mother.

But why were they meeting at all?

Because she wanted reassurance of how much she meant to him. Of course she shouldn't be risking her family, but the feelings she had for Daniel preceded and superseded those she had for Paul. They were different; deeper-seated. They say you never forget your first real love – and she hadn't. Nor had he. He still loved her, and that was a drug that was hard to give up.

The coincidence of their meeting in that sandwich shop not long since she'd gone back to work after Betty was born was too much to ignore. Their relationship was meant to be, she just knew it – whatever the cost, it was worth the risk.

She closed the roof of the Noah's ark with a snap and squeezed it onto the edge of the toy cupboard shelf, where it teetered then smashed to the floor, spewing animals everywhere.

'No!' She picked up a weary-looking Noah. *What am I doing?* she thought to herself. *Saturday mornings never used to be like this.*

She dreamed of those lazy Saturdays with Daniel, the holiday they'd taken near Toulouse, where the sun had shone and they'd spent long mornings in bed interrupted only by one of them getting out for more coffee or to bring in the fresh croissants that were delivered with the eggs and milk from the farm. Had she ever spent time like that with Paul? She was almost ashamed that she remembered this one holiday with Daniel better than she remembered all those she had taken with Paul. She didn't want him to, but Daniel won out every time.

She was aware their renewed relationship was in part the stuff of fantasy, the attraction of the forbidden, but her love for him was still there – as was the chemistry. No question. If they weren't both tied down by their partners and children . . . who knew what might happen? She hardly dared think.

'What are you up to?' Paul came downstairs, Hazel on his hip. He looked at his daughter. 'Boo! She was wide awake.'

'I thought I'd take them to the park when Betty wakes up.'

He made a face. 'And you want me to come?'

She almost panicked but controlled herself in time. 'I thought you wanted to get on with that lampstand you're making?'

He didn't hide his relief as he sat Hazel down on the playmat. 'I do.'

'Then do that. I'll be fine.' She gritted her teeth as Hazel knocked over the box of bricks, scattering them all over the floor.

'If you're sure?' He came over to kiss her.

'One hundred percent,' she said, thanking God he hadn't insisted on coming too. 'I won't be long.'

From beyond the window, they heard footsteps approach the front door.

'Are you expecting anyone?' she asked him. Edie didn't want anything to delay her outing.

Upstairs, Betty started shouting, 'Daaaa-ddy! Daaaa-ddy! Awake! Awake!'

'No. I've no idea who it is. You answer it while I get Betty for you.'

Seeing the two of them head for the stairs and, realizing she was about to be deserted, Hazel let out a long wail.

'Oh for heaven's sake.' Edie went back, scooped her up and carried her up to the front door. 'I was only going to be a minute.'

71

Wondering if it was a delivery she'd forgotten about, she opened the door, jiggling Hazel into silence as she did so.

Instead of a package, however, she found her mother-in-law standing on the doorstep, a bunch of tulips in her hand.

'Hope!'

'I was passing so I thought I might as well call in,' Hope said brightly, holding out the tulips. 'Aren't these beautiful? I couldn't resist.'

Edie took them and stood back to let her in. 'Thank you. Actually, I'm just going out.'

'Mum!' Paul came down the stairs with Betty bumping down on her bottom behind him. 'This is unexpected.' He seemed almost as put out as Edie by this interruption to his plans for the afternoon.

'I know. It was a spur-of-the-moment thing.' Hope held out her arms so Betty could jump from the bottom step into them. 'Hello, beautiful.'

'Well, it's nice to see you,' said Edie, trying her hardest to be welcoming, almost overbalancing as Hazel reached out to be taken by Hope.

'But you're busy. Never mind. I'll just get along home.' But it was obvious that she did mind. She let Hazel grab at her necklace.

'I've got some work I need to do and Edie's going to the park, that's all.'

'Gwanny, come.' Betty pulled her towards the front door. 'Park.'

'Good idea, Betty. Why don't you go with them, Mum?' Paul pulled out her purple-and-pink scooter. 'Taking this?'

Hope's face had lit up. 'I'd love to. If Edie doesn't mind.' She handed Hazel back to Edie, and took the scooter.

'Of course I don't but I'm meeting Alice from the NCT group.' Edie grasped wildly for an excuse.

'I can play with Betty then, and you two can chat.'

'That would be lovely. Betty will like that.' What else could she say?

As she strapped an uncooperative Hazel into the buggy, she thought how much she'd like to throttle Paul for suggesting the plan. How could she possibly meet Daniel if Hope was with them? She channelled her nerves into bright meaningless chatter, wondering if she'd get a chance to text and warn him.

'I enjoyed meeting Mary the other day.' Hope began once they'd got out of the house and Hazel had stopped reaching out for her.

Betty wasn't getting the hang of her scooter and threw it down on the pavement. 'No like!'

Edie sighed. 'Betty! Pick that up.'

'I'll get it.' Hope swung it by the handlebars with one hand and held Betty's hand with the other. She started again. 'Does she get down to see you often?'

'Betty should really pick it up herself.' The last person Edie wanted to talk about was her mother. She had far too much on her mind at that moment. How was she going to juggle her daughters and Hope as well as meeting Daniel? She didn't want to cancel their meeting but would the risk be worth it?

'No,' she said, however. 'She visits as little as she can. Or at least only when it's convenient to her.'

Hope looked taken aback. 'Oh, I'm sorry . . .'

'Don't be. I'm sure I've told you.'

'I didn't realize things were quite that difficult.' She was so sympathetic that Edie found herself responding.

'She's just not the most maternal mother, that's all. I'd say she was pretty emotionally absent when Noel and I were growing up. I don't remember her hugging or kissing me ever, although she must have, I suppose. Any affection came from Dad or from the maids. He was the one who read to us in bed for instance.' She remembered the smell of cigarette smoke on his clothes, the tickle of his moustache, his rolling laugh. 'And now he's dead, and Mum's all we've got left.'

'Perhaps without him, she'll . . .'

But Edie had said too much already and didn't want to enter into a lengthy conversation with Hope about her parents. She preferred not to spend time thinking too much about them. She would have loved a different childhood, yes, but she'd had to settle for the one she'd got. 'Nothing will change, trust me. That's just who she is.'

Her mother must have some redeeming features but they were hard to see. The fact that Noel had moved to the other side of the world said a lot.

Hope looked perplexed. 'All those exotic places – it must have been quite a childhood all the same?'

'But there was nowhere we really could call home until we finally moved back here. Then they bought Sandy Acres,' Edie pictured the large regency house in Lancashire surrounded by garden, giving it privacy. Inside, it was smart enough for entertaining but, to Edie, it never felt like a family home. But perhaps that was because of the family they were, not the house itself, she reflected.

'Oh yes. Paul's shown me photos. I thought it looked rather wonderful.'

'Perhaps it would have been if we'd been younger. But they moved there when Noel and I were about to go to uni, so it never really felt like ours.'

'What a shame.' Hope was about to say something else when Betty pulled at her hand to look in a toy shop window where a doll was perched on a pile of games. As they stopped to peer in at it together, Edie said, 'I'll go ahead, if that's okay with you. We'll see you in the playground.' Not waiting for an answer, she quickened her pace, aware she was in danger of being late. Perhaps she would be able to meet Daniel before Hope got there and have time for one quick kiss and then warn him off.

7

The playground was busy. Hope parked Betty's scooter with the other ones under an oak tree at the park gates. There was safety in numbers, she supposed, but given that she had ended up carrying it after they had got a mere two hundred metres from the house, she thought Betty wouldn't much miss it if it disappeared either. Edie had walked so quickly, pushing the buggy as if she was in a race, that Hope had almost decided to turn back, but their previous conversation and Betty's desire to get to the park spurred her on. Perhaps those confidences marked a small breakthrough in their relationship.

By the time Hope had found a place for the scooter, Betty had disappeared. Hope gazed around the throng of adults and children, trying to pick her out, but there were so many kids darting about, she couldn't spot her. *Betty, where are you?* Pinpricks of sweat dampened her hands as she tried to stay calm.

Eventually, she spotted Edie by the big slide bending over the buggy. She made her way over, dodging a toddler uncertainly making his way towards the sandpit, mother trailing behind. Hope waved when Edie looked up.

Hope girded herself. 'Have you got Betty with you?'

Edie's eyes widened in confusion. 'I thought you had her with you?'

Hope's anxiety intensified as Edie looked around, frantic. 'Oh, thank heavens. There she is. Betty!'

A familiar little figure hurtled towards them with another child in blue stripy dungarees in hot pursuit. 'Look,' Betty yelled. 'Aliya.'

'Friend from nursery,' said Edie. Hope noticed that her daughter-in-law didn't look at her. 'Hello, Aliya. How are you?' Edie squatted down to greet the girls. Before she got a reply, her face lit up as she spotted something over their shoulders. She leapt to her feet and began waving. Hope turned to see a woman waving from the other side of the playground. 'It's Alice! I must say hello to her. Would you mind keeping an eye on both of them? I won't be a minute.'

'Sure.' Hope took the buggy. Edie seemed to have forgotten any resentment she might have had about the moment's panic with Betty, and Hope watched her walk over to greet her friend. Hazel stirred in her sleep as if she might be waking up. But, if she did, Edie would be within earshot. Hope glanced over, but couldn't see Edie anywhere. Now *she* was the one who'd disappeared.

A cry rose from the buggy and a little fist flailed in the air. Betty was with Aliya, intent on building something in the sandpit. Hope bent down and offered Hazel her water cup but she batted it away, head turned with a furious scream of protest. She shushed her, brushed her sweat-stuck hair from her forehead and tried again, with the same result. Except, this time, the yell had notched up a decibel.

The rattle. The board book. An organic, barbecue-flavour Gruffalo claw. The things these kids had for snacks these days – Paul had to make do with a plain old rusk. But whatever she offered to Hazel was treated with the same disdain and fury. Pushing the buggy back and forth made no difference. If anything, it made Hazel's angry screams even louder. Aware people were turning to see where the noise was coming from, she bent over the buggy to find Hazel's face screwed up, puce with rage, as she let out another anguished yell. Perhaps her nappy needed changing.

Hope looked quickly round for Edie, but again, she was nowhere to be seen. Betty and Aliya had moved to the climbing frame that led to the slide. There was an army of parents standing around it, Hope saw, so the girls should be all right unwatched by her for just a second while she sorted out Hazel.

Hope bent over to wrestle with the lock on the safety harness, and eventually it clicked open so she could lift a squirming Hazel into her arms. *Where* was *Edie?* Hope caught a glimpse of white shirt on the other side of the railings, but that couldn't be her. She wouldn't leave the playground without telling them, surely.

A child's shriek cut through the shouts and chatter, but Hope was struggling to hold on to Hazel, who was arching her back and attempting to launch herself out of her grandmother's arms. She realized now she should have left her safely strapped into the buggy and rounded up Betty first, but she hadn't wanted Edie to see she was having trouble managing both girls. That would only be another black mark against her.

She diverted Hazel's attention by sitting her in the sandpit and giving her a rubber spade, which thankfully worked. The baby's mood changed as if the sun had come out from behind a cloud. Just as Hope was sitting beside her and adjusting her sights to find Betty, Aliya rushed up with a tall, concerned-looking man, presumably her father, in tow. The little girl pointed at Hope, then stood just behind her father's legs.

'Hi, I'm Aliya's dad,' he explained, lifting the little girl up. 'Betty's had an accident. She's okay, but I think you may need to take her to A&E. If it would help, I could drive you.'

Hope was on her feet in an instant, bending down to scoop Hazel up from the sandpit. 'Where is she?'

Hazel was furious at being ripped from her new game, and her mouth open to scream again, but once she was balanced on Hope's hip she must have caught the sense of urgency and stopped.

Hope walked as fast she could. Aliya's father had taken the buggy and was leading the way. Where the hell was Edie? Once Hope reached the climbing frame, she saw a small group of people by the slide, two of them squatting over a small, seated figure in shorts and stripy T-shirt that Hope immediately recognized. Betty was sobbing.

'Excuse me. She's mine,' she said, pushing her way to

the front of the group. Betty looked up at her with tear-filled eyes.

'She was pushed off the top of the slide,' someone explained.

'I want Mummy!'

Hope noticed the stillness of her granddaughter's swollen left arm as she held it protectively, a bruise already forming. 'Poor Betty.' She reached out to stroke the hair off her grand-daughter's forehead. Hazel pitched herself towards the ground but Hope caught her in time. 'I'm going to find Mummy. Wait here.' She turned to Aliya's dad. 'Could you possibly wait with her for a few minutes? Edie's here somewhere.'

'Of course, I'll keep an eye on the buggy too. Aliya,' he called, 'come and talk to Betty.'

Hope half-ran back to the playground entrance where she had last seen Edie going to meet her friend. Perhaps they had gone for a coffee from the kiosk, or for ice creams for the kids. She left the playground enclosure to enter the park and worked her way round the perimeter fence towards the spot where she'd seen the flash of white. In the bushes, she saw a man and a woman standing close together. The woman was wearing a white shirt and jeans, and she had her back to Hope. She almost walked past them, but the woman's dark blonde ponytail made her stop.

'Edie?'

The woman turned abruptly. It was her. As she whipped round, her expression changed from irritation to alarm. 'Hope?'

Hope saw the man take a step back. Her impression was of someone tall, in chinos, check shirt with rolled-up sleeves. She did notice that he was rubbing his mouth, awkwardly – guiltily.

'Betty's hurt herself,' Hope explained, refocusing on the situation.

Edie's mouth fell open.

'She fell off the slide,' she went on. 'I think she may have broken her arm.'

'Oh my God, where is she? I thought you were watching her.'

'I was, but Hazel . . .'

Edie wasn't interested. She turned to her companion. 'I must go. We'll speak.'

'Of course.' He disappeared through the trees into the main park itself, but not before reaching out towards her. It was just the smallest of movements, but Hope couldn't miss the way Edie's fingers instinctively reached towards him. There was an intimacy in the gesture that suggested a multitude of unsaid things.

And then the moment was gone.

Edie grabbed Hazel. 'Where is Betty?'

Hope led the way as quickly as she could. When they got back to the slide, Betty was still sitting on the ground with Aliya and her father on either side of her. As they approached, Edie thrust Hazel into Hope's arms so she could crouch down in front of Betty, who burst into tears again the moment she saw her.

'My pet, what have you done?' Edie kissed her forehead, careful not to hurt her by hugging her. She listened to Aliya's father explain. 'Adnam, thank you so much for staying with her.'

'Of course.' He inclined his head. 'She should have that arm X-rayed. Let me drive you to A&E.'

'That's so kind. Thank you.' She turned to Hope. 'Will you take Hazel home? Paul will look after her. I'll call him and let him know what's happening.'

Her tone of voice! Rage simmered inside Hope. She had done everything she could in the circumstances. If anyone was guilty of neglect, it was Edie. And for what? For that man, that stranger? Why? She didn't want to believe the worst.

The two of them stared at each other as Edie waited for Hope to answer. Guilt flashed across Edie's face. 'Please,' she stuttered.

Hope inclined her head. 'Of course.' As Edie walked away with Betty and Adnam, she wondered what it was that had made Edie feel guilty. Her abrasive manner with Hope, or the fact that she had been found where she shouldn't have been?

8

That night, Edie went to bed before Paul, exhausted. Betty was finally asleep, with a temporary cast on her arm. A displaced fracture. As soon as they'd made it back from the hospital, she'd thanked Hope for all that she'd done ... and asked her to leave. Perhaps she had been too short when she refused Hope's offers of help, telling her Jen had agreed to come back early now she was back from travelling. She could see Hope was hurt and desperate to make up for her attention lapse. But how could Edie trust her with the girls now?

Most disturbing of all, what had her mother-in-law seen? Her and Daniel, together. Would she say anything? What a stupid, stupid risk Edie had taken. Meeting Daniel there had felt chancy but, however wrong, the brief moments they'd had together had been deliciously thrilling. She needed that excitement of him in her life.

Paul was outside in his woodworking shed, so she knew she had at least half an hour without interruption. Propped up on cushions and pillows, she started texting Daniel.

Betty's broken arm. Pushed off slide. Feeling

terrible as shd have been watching her. That
was my mother-in-law. Don't know what to
say to her

He replied quickly.

Say nothing. Hope for best and never risk it
again. Glad you're back in chambers soon

Despite herself, Edie felt a guilty rush of exhilaration. Paul
was without question one of the best men she had ever met,
but Daniel had always had her heart. She realized that now.
He made her feel more than Paul ever would. For a few
hours with him, she felt passionate, alive. She could forget
the reality of her life and experience what they once had
together. She wanted to make her marriage work, but she
needed more out of it if it was to last. Was it so wrong to
find what was lacking with Daniel if it made the marriage
possible? Their affair suited them both and it made her feel
good – as long as she didn't think about the future and what
would happen to them.

why?

She knew exactly why but wanted him to say it. Even after
two years of seeing each other as often as they could, until
the late stage of her pregnancy and Hazel's birth, she needed
that reassurance that he still wanted her as much as she did

him. Of course they had kept in touch and met for the occasional coffee, but now they were heading into new uncharted waters. She could feel it. Her pregnancy hadn't repelled him, just served to make him want her more.

You know very well

He didn't give in to her prompt.

can't wait

She deleted that as soon as she had typed it. This was all wrong. She shouldn't be chasing past dreams, risking everything she had. But, but, but … she couldn't ignore her feelings. Daniel and she had been inseparable until work had made their relationship impossible by separating them geographically. They'd originally met doing their pupillages in London and spent all their free time together. When she was with him, then and now, she felt complete in a way that she never would with Paul. When she met and married Paul, she had told herself Daniel was part of her past. But when he showed up again, some years later, she knew immediately that she had to have him in her life, that she couldn't live without him however much she would be deceiving Paul. So what the hell was she meant to do?

Maybe – she typed instead – see you soon

Paul would be in bed soon, oblivious to anything wrong. He had settled into their changed domestic routine with enthusiasm, whereas she found it utterly draining. Even when she had put on her dark suits and gone back to work after Betty's birth, the clothes felt like a camouflage, disguising the drab weary her that was inside. Childbirth had taken something from her. She no longer felt attractive or sexy, and despite having done one of the main things women were created to do, she'd lost all sense of her femininity. But that was the point. Her body had changed. Her mindset had changed. Guilt ran through her like a seam in a block of marble. Everything was different. Except Daniel. He was the same exciting, sexy, lovable man he had always been. Every time she saw him, she realized how much she missed that and how different he made her feel.

She had been standing in the queue for lunch at the coffee shop in the square near her chambers, soon after returning to work from her first maternity leave.

'Excuse me, but there's something on your shoulder.' The voice came from behind her, and she would have recognized it anywhere.

She swung round and stared, disbelieving. 'Daniel!' Her breath felt as if it had been stolen from her chest.

He looked as shocked as she was. 'Edie! I—'

'What are you doing here? I thought you were in Newcastle?'

'Jesus, Edie. I didn't . . . your hair.'

Of course, the long dark blonde hair he had known had

been cut and tamed. He was the last person she expected to see, and she found she couldn't stop staring at him. He wasn't conventionally handsome, but he had an open face and a seductive smile, she thought as he took a serviette, poured a little of his water over it and dabbed at the back of her shoulder. 'There.' He took a step away, satisfied. 'No one would know.'

'Thanks. The baby must have puked on me and I didn't notice.' Now at the front of the queue, she put her egg sandwich on the counter and asked for a skinny latte with almond milk. When she'd paid and turned round to leave, he was waiting for her.

'So you have a baby?' He sounded surprised. 'I thought you were—'

'Married to the Bar? Still am, really.'

'Shall we find a bench in the square and have lunch together? We've obviously got lots to catch up on.'

Her immediate instinct had been to run back to work, but then she told herself he would be a good sounding board for her upcoming cases. Also, she was curious about him. How had he spent the years since they parted? What had brought him back to London? Perhaps he had a family too now.

'Just quickly then,' she said. 'If we can find one. I've only got half an hour. You still haven't told me what you're doing here.'

'Maggie, my wife, pulled off her dream job in the brain and behaviour research lab at Imperial College.' So, he was married too. Her face must have given away something of what she was feeling. He smiled. 'Don't ask. I don't entirely understand it myself, but we moved here. Luckily for me, a place came up with the Newman Garlake Chambers, so here I am.'

'When did you get married?' She shouldn't be jealous of another man's wife. But she was.

'A couple of years ago. We already had a baby so just sealed the deal.' He laughed. 'She's the sister of one of my colleagues up there. A real high-flyer.' He looked down at the sandwich he was carrying. 'Bit like you.'

At first glance, there were no benches, but they found one when a couple got up to leave, bagging it before another man who was heading purposefully towards it. They laughed together as they sat down and something sparked between them. Did he feel it too?

'So,' he said. 'You're still in chambers here?'

Immediately, the talk turned to their work – the one obvious thing they had in common now. Their families felt like dangerous territory somehow. There wasn't room for other people in their relationship. Daniel soon had her laughing. He wasn't afraid of taking the mickey out of himself as he told her about his new colleagues and one of the most recent cases he'd worked on: a man who'd been found guilty of murdering his wife and child, despite protesting his distress on nationwide TV before his arrest. The half-hour vanished and, as they returned to their almost neighbouring doorways in the square, they agreed to meet for lunch again. For the rest of that day, despite her attention being taken up by a child custody case, her spirits were lifted.

Now, Edie lay back against the pillows with her eyes closed, picturing their bench under the cherry tree where she and Daniel had sat so often before her second maternity leave. She had hardly dared question who Hazel's father really was when she was pregnant with her, but kept the thought at bay. Paul wanted another child and she found herself going along with it. When Hazel was born, her nose and something about the set of her mouth and chin made Edie certain she was Paul's. Relief took over from her guilt and fear. She heard the click of the bedroom door.

'You awake?' Paul whispered.

'Mmmm. Just.' Her daydream evaporated as she rolled over to face him while he undressed and got into bed.

He reached out to stroke back a lock of hair from her cheek. 'Still beautiful.'

At that moment, the baby monitor sprang into life as Hazel started whimpering.

'No, no, no. She can't. Not now. I'm exhausted.' She rolled over in despair. Hazel's cries got louder.

Paul sighed. 'I'll go, then. But I'm starting a new job tomorrow so you might have to take over if she won't settle.' He had gone before she had even thought to ask what the job was, his resentment lying heavy in the air for once. Because he didn't turn the baby alarm off, she could hear him calming Hazel down. Provided he found the dummy and she didn't spit it out in anger, he wouldn't be long. The sound of his shushing and singing snatches of sea shanties was so soothing that Edie felt herself drifting off even before their daughter did.

Hazel screeched her delight at rejoining the world at five a.m. Edie made sure she was the one to get up and attend to her, whisking her downstairs before she woke the others. There was little time to talk as Paul got ready for work. 'I may be late back depending how it goes. It's complicated.'

Edie had by now at least established that his new job was making an elaborate ziggurat-styled bookcase for someone in Finchley – lots of work for relatively little financial reward. The two girls and she waved him off before going back inside and collapsing in front of CBeebies for a while. She knew she shouldn't, that there was a mountain of household chores to be done – clearing up breakfast, emptying the dishwasher, putting on another load of washing, making their lunch, playing ... on and on it went – but sometimes ... well, a person just had to let go. And anyway, Betty was a bit off-colour, although not apparently in any pain. But a whole day spent at home with no relief? It yawned ahead of them.

And yet as she let the bright cartoons flow across the screen, Edie went over the events of the day before. Would Hope say something to her about Daniel? What if she said something to Paul? Edie would have to pre-empt her in some way. *Come on!* she thought to herself, getting up and going into the kitchen. She was a woman used to making decisions, but her capacity for doing so had virtually deserted her since Hazel's birth and her confinement to home. She shoved the laundry into the washing machine before standing straight and stretching. It was time to get back into gear.

She would pay Hope a visit that afternoon. Jen was coming over to see the girls, so that would be perfect. She could get to know Hazel while Edie left them for a couple of hours.

Her phone, lying on the breakfast bar among the debris of breakfast, began to ring. That could wait. Then she saw Hope's name on the screen and picked up.

'Hello? Edie?' Hope sounded apprehensive. 'I just wanted to see how Betty is today.'

'Much better. Bit sorry for herself, of course.' Edie picked at a nail. 'Actually I'm pleased you've phoned. I'm sorry I was a bit tense last night. Could I pop over this afternoon if you've got time?' She wondered whether Hope would think this was odd? But, if she didn't see her, how else would she be sure to shut this down?

'Oh!' Hope sounded surprised. 'Well, yes, do. I think I should be clear by about four. Will you be bringing the girls?'

Was there a note of suspicion in that voice or was Edie reading too much into it?

'I'd better see how things are. Jen's coming over so probably not.'

Betty moaned and held out her water beaker. 'More.'

'I've got to go, Hope. Betty needs me. We'll talk this afternoon.' If Hope didn't suspect something was up, she was wasn't as smart as Edie thought she was. But now she'd gone down this path, Edie had to follow it to the end.

*

Hope's house always struck Edie as being like the TARDIS. Its narrow Victorian frontage gave nothing away of the living space behind it. A small well-tended garden led to the stone steps up the front door, nothing like the chaotic riot of colour that Hope favoured in the back. Through the living room window, Edie could see the large round mirror over the mantlepiece, one or two invitations and cards beneath it, and that strange Scandinavian vase Hope loved so much containing four or five blousy pink and red roses. She rang the doorbell and waited, going through what she wanted to say to Hope one more time.

After a moment or two, she heard steps in the hallway and the door opened. Hope's apron was scattered with flour. She frowned slightly as she welcomed Edie in. The spicy smell of something cooking drifted up the stairs, making Edie feel queasy.

'Vita's upstairs finishing up some admin.'

'Don't worry, I won't take up too much of your time.' Edie was grateful to have been given an excuse for a quick exit.

'No, no. It's absolutely fine. I've just been making a chicken curry.' Hope looked down as she wiped her hands on her apron. 'Look, I really am sorry about what happened yesterday. I was trying to deal with Hazel when I lost Betty.'

'I know you were.' Edie was cautious. 'Hazel can be so grouchy, much more than Betty ever was.'

'I couldn't be in two places at once and you'd disappeared.' She led the way downstairs. 'Coffee?'

'Please.' Edie took a stool at the island. 'I bumped into

a friend from work, you see.' *Keep it as close to the truth as you can, Edie.* 'I would have introduced you, but everything happened so suddenly.'

'I looked everywhere for you. I thought you were meeting your NCT friend so I wasn't expecting you to be outside the playground. That's why it took me so long to find you.'

There it was.

'We did have a chat and then Daniel's dog ran off, so we were trying to find it.' The dog story was the best excuse Edie had been able to come up with.

'Really?' Hope didn't sound convinced.

Edie upped her game, using her skill at manipulating conversations and self-preservation. 'Yes, a sweet little thing. Otto – a grey whippet. Moves like lightning. His son would have been devastated if he'd lost it.' *Don't overdo the lie or you'll tie yourself in knots.*

'But you were in the bushes?'

'I know. We couldn't see him anywhere. We'd been stand-ing by the gate when he ran off, so I simply went out to help Daniel find him.'

'Oh, right,' Hope said, hesitantly. 'That explains it.'

What had she seen? Not the imaginary dog, obviously. *Not the kiss, please not the kiss*, Edie thought.

'I'm glad Betty's okay, at least. And Paul?'

If Hope was changing the subject then presumably she hadn't seen anything that mattered. Relief flooded through Edie.

'He started a new job today.' Talk of Paul usually

smoothed things over. 'A complicated bookcase. He was looking forward to it.'

'I'm glad. I was worried when he gave up business management for something so unpredictable. I always worry that he won't have enough work.'

'Don't,' said Edie. *Because worrying about whether he has enough work or earns enough money is my job now, not yours,* she thought. 'He's always in demand because he's so brilliant at it.'

'Of course.'

Edie recognized Hope felt she was being brushed off. 'Are *you* busy at the moment?' she asked quickly, trying to keep the conversation going.

'Yes, it's all good. I've a couple of dinner parties coming up, more classes, and some freezer fillers. Hence the curry. I'm also working on changing the menus.' She sounded more relaxed suddenly, comfortable talking about what she loved doing.

Edie felt more confident that they were moving the conversation away from Daniel, hoping she had said enough to be convincing but not too much. Meeting Daniel at the playground was sailing too close to the wind and risked everything just for the briefest of encounters.

She stayed as long as it took to finish her coffee, having achieved what she set out to achieve. Her version of events was out there and, with luck, Hope wouldn't question it too hard.

9

Hope stood in her living room, watching Edie go down the path and through the gate. When she turned to close it, Hope raised her hand in farewell as if all was well between them, although she felt distinctly uneasy. The whole thing was most odd. Edie coming round on her own was such a rare occurrence, she must have had an ulterior motive. The conversation about the playground was not one Hope had wanted to have. She had been too obvious, too accusatory, allowing Edie to take control. On the other hand, what could she say? If that ridiculous story about the dog was the one Edie wanted to tell, Hope wasn't in a position to argue. She knew what she had seen. The last thing she wanted was to interfere with her son's marriage, but shouldn't she find out the truth for Paul's sake? And then she could decide what to do with it. Should she tell him of her suspicions? No. There was no point stirring up trouble if she turned out to be wrong.

But this wasn't the only thing on her mind. There was that letter. She went down to make the poached pears, relishing the scents of the cardamom, vanilla and cinnamon from the poaching liquid. Upstairs, her reply to Patrick remained unposted. The envelope sat on her desk, sealed and stamped.

Just as she finished taking the bread rolls out of the oven, Vita came down from the office.

'She didn't stay long. What did she want?'

'She came to give her side of yesterday's story and then left as soon as she could. That's probably the closest she'll ever come to an apology for being so vile to me. I suppose that's something.' She didn't want to go into details with Vita until she knew the truth.

Vita lifted one eyebrow, sceptical. 'I suppose that's something.'

'What have you been up to?'

'We've just had an email from that awful Mrs Carswell. She wants you back on the tenth of next month. What do you think?'

Hope grimaced. 'She was a nightmare. I know, I know, we shouldn't refuse business. Have we much else in the diary?'

'It's pretty busy, but we could fit her in.'

'Then we'd better say yes. But perhaps we could specify that she gives us a clean kitchen this time. Will you do the menu?'

'Will do. That smells delicious.' She turned to go, then paused in the doorway. 'By the way, Martin called. Not urgent, apparently.'

'Really? Why doesn't he just call my mobile?'

Vita shrugged. 'Habit? Anyway, I'll leave that one to you. I'm going back up to finish what I'm doing.'

What could her ex-husband possibly want? They had separated twenty years ago now, and although they were both devastated, they had been unable to see a future together after the affair. There was no point. The damage had been done. After licking her wounds for a year, renting a tiny holiday flat in Polzeath, hoping he'd change his mind, Hope's head cleared and she began to piece together her new, single life.

She'd left for London, where Vita was living, and suggested they set up a business together. Their children were grown up, they were both keen cooks and if not now, when? Of course, Paul had moved to the big smoke too, which was another attraction. By then, Martin was dating Nora – the young vet's assistant who had taken Hope's place in his life. Then, with almost embarrassing haste, they had their own family, two girls. On the rare occasions Hope and Martin spoke now, he couldn't stop talking about how the pair had most recently exceeded all expectations. She had to give him one thing: although his marriage to Hope hadn't survived, he was unswervingly loyal and committed to all his children. They might not have a lot of contact, but what they had was friendly now.

Curious, she called him.

'Hope!' He always sounded pleasantly surprised to hear from her, as if she'd been kidnapped and returned without notice.

'You called me,' she reminded him. 'How is everyone?' She listened as Martin reeled off his children's achievements. She loved his enthusiasm for everything they did. He took equal pleasure in Paul and his family and loved to hear any news. 'Have you seen Betty and Hazel? Actually, don't answer that. I know you have.'

'Did Paul tell you about Betty?' she asked.

'Not Paul. But Edie FaceTimed me, so I could see for myself. Poor little thing.'

'Edie called you?' Hope couldn't disguise her surprise. She had no idea they had become close.

'Yes. Didn't you know? I read to Betty every fortnight on FaceTime now. Edie's idea. And it works a treat. At least, it does for the few seconds that Betty concentrates. But I enjoy it, and it reminds her I exist. It's fun.'

'It must be.' It was not something that had ever been offered to her. *But you live nearby*, said a voice in her head. *It's not the same. You see them.* All true, but the thought that Martin had negotiated an independent relationship with Edie obscurely hurt. What a failure she had been on the in-law front.

'What happened? Edie said you were looking after Betty.'

Of course she had.

'That's not quite right. I was looking after both of them.' She hesitated. Should she tell him the whole story? 'Hazel was throwing a complete strop, the playground was packed and I lost sight of Betty.'

'You shouldn't have taken them both if it's too much for you.'

'Edie was there too,' she protested. 'I don't think it was too much to assume she might have an eye on her own children.'

'Ah. Then, I misunderstood. But she would always

98

keep an eye on them, surely, unless something important stopped her.'

His support for his daughter-in-law over her was infuriating. She remembered how Paul and Martin would take sides against her when Paul was a kid, even over something as petty as who liked broccoli. Not them. Men against the woman. It was happening again.

'Martin! She wasn't even in the playground. I found her in the bushes with some guy, looking very friendly.' There. She'd said it.

'Really?' At last, he sounded taken aback.

She was pleased to have rocked him.

'There must be an explanation.' Of course he wouldn't believe anything bad of Edie.

'She said she was helping look for his dog.'

'Well, then. What's the problem? The main thing is that Betty's okay.'

'I know. But don't you think it's a bit strange?'

'Innocent till proved guilty, I say. She's given you a perfectly reasonable explanation. I can tell that's not what you want to hear.'

Men! So easily swayed. Hope gave up. 'You're probably right. I hope so. Tell me, why did you call?'

He laughed. 'I'm going to bring Amy up to London for an interview at Central Saint Martins. She's bent on studying art there for reasons I simply don't understand, seeing as we've got Falmouth on our doorstep. But I don't want to stand in her way. Could we stay the night?'

'What? Here? With me?' She was astonished. He had never stayed with her since they'd split up. Nora would never have allowed that in the early days. 'Why not with Paul?'

'Nora thought it would be too much for Edie, given she has two small kids and is about to go back to work. Perhaps they could come over for lunch?' Hope noticed he had already assumed her answer would be yes, but she wasn't going to give in to him that easily.

'Haven't you any other friends up here?' It would be odd having them stay with her.

'Not who I could ask. Besides, I thought it would be fun to catch up.' Martin was an innocent. His approach to life had been one of the things that attracted her to him in the first place. He was the kind of person who didn't see the bad in anyone until he was forced to.

'All right. I'd love to meet Amy.' She was curious about his children, having heard about their prowess in all things. She was curious about him, too. They hadn't met up for some time, but they got on well when they did now.

'Her interview's next Monday morning so I thought we could come up on Saturday, perhaps see Paul on Sunday and go home on Monday afternoon. What do you say?'

'Good,' she said. 'I'll get on to Paul and see if they can come over.' Perhaps this was serendipity offering her the chance to make good with Edie through Martin. She was already running through what she might cook, keeping it simple for the kids and for her ex.

'Thanks, Hope. I was sure we could rely on you.'

She bit back the 'Don't be' that almost came to her lips. She didn't want to be that person anymore. Martin should rely on Nora, not on her. But perhaps letting the past back in was a good thing and would give her a chance to put one or two things to rest. Far better to get on with Paul's father than not.

'Let me know what time you're expecting to arrive. If I'm working, I may have to leave a key somewhere for you.'

Arrangements made, they said goodbye and Hope was left with a pleasant sense of anticipation.

As soon as she had finished cleaning up, she went up to the office where Vita was getting ready to leave. 'Don't you want to taste the pears?' asked Hope. 'I made a tarte tatin as well, as a trial.'

'I can't stop. I promised to meet Angie at the park with the kids. Maybe I'll come back later.' She snapped her bag shut, keen to get off to meet her grandchildren and daughter-in-law.

Hope picked up the envelope that had been lying on her desk ... waiting. 'I'll walk with you. I need to go to the postbox.'

'I can take it.' Vita held out her hand.

'No, I'd like some fresh air.'

They walked the length of the street together, Vita's bicycle between them, as Hope told her what Martin had wanted.

'Isn't it a bit odd that he wants to stay?' Vita steered the bike round a rogue dustbin lid.

101

'Thriftiness and *faute de mieux,* I'm afraid. But yes, and maybe – just maybe – he'll be a way to put things straight with Edie. Though I can't quite think how.'

Vita's dubious look said everything.

They stopped at the postbox. Hope slipped the letter into its mouth and held it there for a moment, not quite able to let it go. Once she did, there could be no turning back. The box would be opened, the postman would take it away and the consequences were unknowable. Whatever happened, however, she knew she wanted to see Patrick again, so she let the letter fall. As soon as she heard the rattle as it hit the bottom, she wanted to reach inside and retrieve it, but short of waiting for the delivery van at six p.m. and fishing it out then, it was too late. She could only wait for a reply.

10

Edie poppered Hazel into her newest pair of dungarees, to her daughter's hysterical enjoyment. Nothing brightened the day more than a baby's laugh, she had to admit.

Betty had draped herself over Edie's right shoulder, waving her rainbow and unicorn hairclips in her face. Her plaster cast knocked against Edie's cheek.

'Ow! Sooner that's off, the better. Just let me finish this.' She tucked in Hazel's pink T-shirt and fastened the straps. 'Can you find her shoe?' She wanted Hazel looking her cutest for Martin and Amy, and slipped on her soft leather shoes. They had cost a ridiculous amount, but Edie hadn't been able to resist.

When Paul came in, she was just clipping back Betty's hair. 'Doesn't she look gorgeous? Smile for Daddy.' She kissed her daughter's cheek.

Betty's attempt at a smile was more of a toothy grimace, which made them both laugh.

'My three beautiful girls.' Paul dropped a kiss onto Edie's forehead before looking at his watch. 'Are you ready? I don't want to be late.'

He was pleased to be seeing his father. Although they kept in touch, he often said he would like to see Martin more often. Edie liked her easy-going father-in-law as well as Nora, so had done her best to build a bridge between their two families, most recently instituting the fortnightly FaceTime reading slot. She felt so much more relaxed with that side of Paul's family.

'Did you feel left out once he had the girls with Nora?' she asked.

'No,' he replied immediately, but she saw through him. His father had another family that Paul would never be a proper part of. They all played at Happy Families, but his half-siblings were much younger, had a different mother, and lived too far away for that to be truly possible. And Paul recognized that. That was one of the reasons he felt so responsible for his mum, the one parent who had been devoted to him. It wasn't long after Edie met Hope that she'd realized the strength of the mother–son bond between her and Paul. At the time, she'd been confident that she could loosen it. If only Hope wasn't quite so devoted.

'Let me wash my hands and change,' she said. She felt pressured. Everything was done at such a rush. If she was quick, she might even have time for a dab of make-up too.

By the time she was ready, Paul had loaded the kids into the car. Hazel was tired and fractious, but Betty was content with her *PAW Patrol* comic.

'At last!' He shut the door on them. Hazel's mood had obviously rubbed off on him.

'What do you mean? I've been five minutes at the most.' She got in the car and slammed her door.

He gave a slight shake of his head as he got behind the wheel. 'Whatever.'

'Well, ten anyway . . . I don't want to look like some old drudge who only looks after your beautiful children and not herself.'

He put his hand on her thigh. 'You don't look like that at all. I'm sorry.'

'Thank you.' She rolled up the sleeves of her white shirt. 'How do you think they'll be together? Awkward?' She couldn't help being intrigued.

'Mum and Dad? It'll be fine. Better than when they were together, probably. They were okay at the wedding, remember?'

'Only because they kept to opposite ends of the room!' She turned to check on the ominous silence from the back, but Hazel was fast asleep, her head lolling against her seat. Betty was still engrossed in her comic. 'Sad how many relationships don't stay the course.' Through her work, she had seen so many marriages founder for all kinds of reasons, some apparently trivial and others terrible infringements of a partner's rights. She felt sick, thinking of her own dilemma.

'At least it won't happen to us.' He signalled left.

His confidence made her feel terrible. And yet, why shouldn't she love him and Daniel at the same time, as long as no one got hurt? The French took extramarital affairs for granted. Why were the English so uptight? She couldn't see how anyone could realistically satisfy all of someone else's needs. It wasn't Paul's fault. But neither was it hers. She had known Daniel and loved him for so long. Never mind what her own work threw up, the news was always full of affairs, divorces, murders even. But did she love both men in the same way? These were questions she had asked herself, over and over again.

'I wonder why Hope hasn't found someone else,' she said instead.

'She has. Don't forget Keith. He was knocking around for years. Then Liam.'

'I liked him.' She stared out at the rows of Victorian terraced London houses they were passing. 'Do you think she likes living on her own?'

Paul stole a look at her. 'I guess she must. She told me she doesn't want to try online dating again. Liam was enough. To be honest, I find it a bit off-putting thinking of Mum dating . . .'

'Takes the burden from you, I suppose.'

'What do you mean? Mum's never been a burden.' His eyes were fixed on the road ahead. He sounded offended by the suggestion.

She felt bad. She didn't want to make things difficult for him, but sometimes she couldn't control herself – odd, she realized, in someone who was trained to be nothing *but* controlled. But when she was at home, it was much harder. At the moment, she felt constantly on the brink of losing control, despite the rules she made for herself and the children.

Sometimes she felt that the tension between Edie at work and Edie at home, not to mention the person underneath who was always worried she would be uncovered as an impostor, made her snap easily at those she was closest to.

They pulled up outside Hope's house. They went up the steps, Paul carrying the still snoozing Hazel, while Edie held the bag of baby paraphernalia in one hand, with Betty clinging on to the other. Through the basement window, they could see the gleaming pro kitchen, where everything was thoroughly cleaned and put away.

Amy opened the door. She immediately squatted down to Betty's level. 'You poor thing. Does your arm hurt?'

She was very much Martin and Nora's daughter. Same mouth, but with her mother's wide-apart keen brown eyes and straight blonde hair. She was wearing shorts with a skimpy summer top.

Betty shook her head, mute with shyness.

'It's been a while now,' said Edie.

'Come on in, everyone,' said Amy. 'They're in the garden. I've something for you, Bets. You remember me, don't you? Amy. Do you want to come upstairs and get it?' She gathered her hair and knotted it high on her head.

Betty nodded but, still overwhelmed, looked at Edie for approval.

Edie smiled, touched that Amy had gone to such trouble. 'Go on, Betty. Up you go. Shall I come, too?'

Betty nodded, clinging on to her hand.

The three of them went up to the spare room Amy was

using during her stay. On the bed was a package which Amy gave to Betty. She unwrapped it uncertainly with help from Edie. Inside was a dress with a sparkly bodice and the sweetest skirt made of lots of different coloured layers of net.

Betty gasped with delight. 'Fairy dress! Me wear.'

'There are some wings too. Look.' Amy pulled them from the bottom of the bag.

Edie lifted Betty's dress over her head and watched as Amy put her in the new one.

A smile split Betty's face. 'Wings!'

'What do you say to Amy?' Edie put a hand on Betty's shoulder.

Betty looked puzzled for a moment then, with Edie's prompt, she remembered. 'Thank you.'

'Yes, thank you,' echoed Edie. 'You shouldn't have.' She would rather Amy had given her a game or a more practical dress, but she also knew that neither would give her daughter so much pleasure.

'We heard about her arm and that seemed a good enough reason to spoil her. Besides, we hardly ever see you. I've something for Hazel, too.'

'If you get into St Martins, we'll be able to see more of you,' Edie reminded her, thinking how enjoyable that would be. They followed Betty bumping down the stairs and out into the garden where everyone made a fuss of her, her new dress and her plastered arm.

'Edie, have a seat.' Martin stood up from his. 'Let me get you a drink. Rosé okay?'

'I can't think of anything nicer.' How lovely! A summer afternoon of relaxation with other people to help keep an eye on the kids. Even with Hope around, with luck, nothing would happen to them. She sat down and smiled at her father-in-law. You could tell he worked outdoors in all weathers, his hands calloused, hair thinning. She hadn't seen him in person since the previous Easter when they'd gone down to stay on his dairy farm for a couple of nights.

Hazel had woken up and Paul was putting her in the highchair. Edie got to her feet. 'I'll get her food.'

'No, stay where you are. I'll do it.' He gestured that she should sit down again.

Paul was such a great involved dad. She reminded herself again how lucky she was to have him. Knowing that everyone here recognized that too made her feel faintly inadequate. None of them understood her conflicted feelings about motherhood, her longing to get back to the life she had pre-children. She thought of Ana, wondering what she was up to that weekend. Something glamorous and hedonistic no doubt.

'Let me, Paul.' Hope was already beside him, clearly itching to take the sachet of gloopy broccoli, pears and peas from him. 'Wouldn't some of our lunch, mashed up, be better for her? We always used to give you whatever we were having.'

'I don't think she can wait, Mum.' Paul passed Hazel the pack and she sucked enthusiastically, both hands clinging to it. 'Besides, she's only six months.'

Edie shut her eyes for a second, concentrating on not over-reacting. When she opened them, Martin had returned with her drink, so she asked about Nora and news of Cornwall. She had never been that far west until she and Paul went to visit them, and she had fallen in love with the Lizard Peninsula and its rugged landscape. She had quickly bonded with Nora, too, who was down to earth, no-nonsense and very funny. Not that she'd ever want to live there. London gave her what she needed.

Hope went back into the kitchen and soon brought the dishes outside, helped by Amy.

Edie stood up. 'Can I do anything?'

'No, no. It's all under control.' Hope went inside again to bring out the roast beef and vegetables.

Meanwhile, Hazel was holding court, covered in gloop.

'Paul, why don't you sit between Martin and Amy? And Edie on Martin's other side? I'll go here with Betty. Come on, my sweet, hop up here.' Hope helped Betty on to the cushion that she had put there for her.

'Can I carve?' Paul was on his feet.

'No, no. You look after the drinks and catch up with your dad. Leave it to me.' She began to cut the thinnest of slices that she dished up and passed around. When she came to her daughter-in-law, Edie raised her hand.

'I won't, thanks. No meat for me.'

Hope took a step back, surprised. 'Oh no! I didn't realize it was a long-term thing. I should have asked. This is Martin's favourite. I thought you might . . .' She stopped, embarrassed.

'I don't eat meat anymore,' Edie explained to the table. 'Especially beef. Because of the methane production.'

'I'm so sorry. I can do you something else – an omelette or cheese on toast?' Hope was flustered now the meal wasn't going to be the success she'd hoped for.

'You're not one of those, are you?' said Martin. 'Since when?'

'Since I started caring about the world my children are going to grow up in. Don't you?' Edie could feel Paul's eyes on her, willing her to shut up. 'If we all do nothing, nothing will happen.'

Martin laughed. 'Depends what you're talking about. You'll harm a lot of livelihoods, talking like that. Mine included.'

Paul cleared his throat.

'That's fine,' said Hope hurriedly. 'Let me make you an omelette?' She passed Edie's plate to Paul.

'No, no. I'm fine with the veg. I love them.' Edie tried to pass over her outburst. 'Sorry, Martin. No offence.'

'None taken.' Martin helped himself to the horseradish. 'More for us.'

'I'll cut yours up, Betty,' said Hope. 'Help yourself to everything, everyone.'

'No,' said Betty, pushing her plate away.

'I'm trying not to let them eat red meat either,' said Edie. 'For the same reason.'

'Just this once won't do any harm,' said Hope. 'Look, we can make a face out of it. Like this!' She started to arrange the food on Betty's plate.

'Mum . . .' Paul's voice held a note of warning.

Edie bit back the words on the tip of her tongue. Let her be. She could see the eruption coming.

'No!' Betty's chin quivered. She tried pushing the plate again, upending it so the food flew on to the table, gravy splashing on the bodice of her dress.

'Betty!' Hope started scooping the food back on the plate and forking up a bit of beef. 'Don't do that. Just try a little bit.'

'Don't force her. She's fine without meat.' The words were out before Edie could stop them.

'Poor child's exhausted. Too much excitement,' said Paul at the exact same time. 'Come here, Betty. Let's wash it off.'

Hope looked at them both, obviously put out, her right eye narrowing very slightly.

The little girl jumped off her chair and ran to her father. He lifted her on to his knee where she sat, her head resting on his chest.

'Okay. I'll leave you to it, then. Cheers, everyone.' Hope raised her glass, but Edie could tell how upset she was. So passive-aggressive. *Say something*, she told herself.

'Well, I for one am very happy with what's in front of me,' said Martin. 'Thanks, m'dear, for going the extra mile for us. Have some carrots, Edie.' He passed the platter of vegetables to her.

Edie felt everyone's eyes on her as she helped herself. They must all hate her, even Martin now. But she held firm. Since when was it wrong to express your own opinion? She wouldn't object if someone disagreed with her, but would argue her corner. All the same, she rather wished she had kept quiet and just left the bloody meat on the side of her plate. If only she could be air-lifted out of there.

'A pleasure,' said Hope, her face relaxing as she turned to Martin. 'It's lovely to have you and Amy here with us.' She raised her glass. 'Welcome.'

11

Hope sank into the sofa, exhausted. Martin passed her the cup of tea he'd made. He'd helped Hope clear up after the others had left, while Amy had gone out to have supper with her godmother who lived in Kentish Town. Their talk had turned almost inevitably to Edie.

'She's quite a handful,' said Martin, breaking the silence. 'I haven't seen her like that before. She's always been fine with me.' He leaned back in his chair, resting his feet up on the coffee table. 'Her disapproval of dairy farming's new. And I could see you two weren't on the same page at all.'

'I do try.'

'Maybe it's a rivalry thing,' he suggested, taking a sip of wine.

'Maybe. So, she and I are tussling over Paul. But he's always going to be my son whether she likes it or not.' How possessive she sounded, she thought.

'And she's always going to be his wife,' Martin reminded her.

'I hope so,' said Hope, remembering the scene she had witnessed in the park. But she also recalled the pain and anger that had come with her and Martin's divorce. It had been years before they could sit down like this and have a civilized conversation, before they regained a mutual respect for one another.

'Then why don't you relax when she's around? I can see how careful you're being.'

'I *want* to get on with her. It's just that I don't seem to do anything right.'

'Must be very difficult for Paul.' Martin stared out of the window, musing.

'What about me? I hate feeling I'm always in the wrong.'

He laughed. 'It must be difficult for all of you. Maybe you want too much when you should let go a bit. I'm just trying to help by trying to see it from her point of view.'

'No, you're not! You're implying that I'm at fault.' Hope sprang to her own defence, but wished this was something she could sort out quietly by herself. Martin hadn't been much bothered when she told him about seeing Edie with the man in the park, but whatever was behind that, she didn't trust Edie now. How could any of them know what really went on when she went off to work?

Martin gave a brief laugh. 'Poor old Paul, caught between two warring women.'

'Oh, for heaven's sake!' She pulled herself to her feet.

'Do sit down, old thing,' Martin leant over and patted the sofa. 'I'm not trying to upset you. We'll change the subject.'

She was touched by the old familiarity and sat back down.

'So, what's going on in your life. Got you a man yet?' Martin filled up their glasses.

115

'Not at the moment.' The question took her by surprise. 'I don't know why everyone's so obsessed with me finding someone.'

He cocked his head. 'But why don't you?'

'I don't really know. Work's pretty full on. After Keith and Liam, I wanted a break and it's just gone on.' She had come to the decision that there was no point compromising her independence by living with someone just for the sake of their company. There had to be more to a relationship than that. 'You were lucky to find Nora.'

'Yes, I was.' He smiled. 'But until the affair, you know I was very happy as we were.' How funny that they could talk about it now without recriminations or upset. It had taken so long.

'Me, too. Though I was never really cut out to be a farmer's wife. I hated the wellies!'

'I'll never understand why you like the city so much. It's so busy and polluted.'

'But I work here, and it's full of my friends and Paul's family. I like the buzz still. And being alone here isn't as difficult as I found it in Polzeath, after we split up.'

'That was a difficult time for both of us.' He looked thoughtful. 'But look at us now. Hey! We survived.'

Yes, thought Hope. *But at what cost?* She remembered the letter from Patrick with a feeling of impending doom. Nothing was over yet.

The remainder of their evening was relaxed. They talked about the grandkids, and he told her his news of the farm.

116

Hearing about her old home didn't upset her anymore, she found, nor the idea that another woman was in residence now. Not really.

'Do you have any regrets?' she asked eventually.

'About us? Honestly? No, not now. Nora and I have a good, solid relationship and the girls are grown up. At the beginning it was hard though.' He paused. 'It's good to see you again, Hope.'

She raised her wine glass. 'You too. I'm glad we can do this.'

Three days later, she was finishing breakfast when she heard the slap of the letterbox. She put down her coffee and went for the post. When she saw a white envelope with the same writing as before, her heart started beating faster. The reply.

She sat at the kitchen table and put the envelope in front of her, moving her plate to one side. She examined the writing as if it would give a clue as to what was inside. Briskly formed letters leaned to the right without a flourish of any kind. She lifted the envelope to her nose and sniffed, as though the smell would tell her something. Right. She must stop prevaricating. Her toast knife made short work of opening the envelope, scattering crumbs on the table, a smear of marmalade along the tear. Inside was a single sheet of paper, just as before. Slowly, she unfolded it. For a moment, she stared out of the window where a squirrel was feasting at the bird feeder. She went over and tapped on the glass, delaying the moment of reading. The marauder paused, alert, twitched its tail and scooted up the apple tree where it would no doubt wait till the coast was clear before returning.

She poured herself the last of the coffee in the cafetière, took a deep breath and looked to see what he had written. The note was short and to the point.

Dear Hope,

    Your reply was exactly what I hoped for. Should we have lunch perhaps? But when and where? If you email me letting me know what would suit you, then we can dispense with the formalities of snail mail. See my email address above.

    Yours,

    Patrick

Her stomach turned over. She really was going to see him again. Thank goodness Martin had left before this arrived.

Having stood for too long, her coffee tasted bitter, so she tipped it into the sink and made some more. Today was one of her teaching days. Six enthusiastic amateur cooks would be turning up in an hour's time. It wasn't that she didn't want to; teaching was always a pleasure and a welcome source of income, but today her heart wouldn't be in demonstrating and encouraging them to cook the perfect summer lunch: watercress soup, miso salmon with noodles, and lemon tart. Instead, she'd be obsessing about Patrick, wondering how the years had treated him. How could she not? And where would the best place be to meet?

There was just time to send the email before she organized

the ingredients for the morning class. In the office, she opened her laptop, drumming her fingers on the desk. Once she had a blank email document facing her, she didn't know what to write. Previously, she had written impersonally, formally. Was this the moment to let go and express her real feelings, tell him how much she longed to see him? She hesitated, fingers poised over the keyboard.

In the kitchen, her alarm went off, giving her the fifty-minute warning. If she didn't finish the preparations now, she wouldn't be ready for class. The doorbell would inevitably start ringing at least fifteen minutes before the class was due to begin, so everything had to be set up, and her head had to be in the right place. Somehow. She snapped shut her laptop.

Downstairs, she finished laying out ingredients round the kitchen island so that everyone had space to do their separate tasks. The tang of the watercress, the savoury smell of the miso and the citrussy zest of the lemons took her back to the first time she had cooked the meal. It was one of the first she and Vita had put on their menus, and they both loved it. She usually demonstrated, then divided the work between the group. One pair would be responsible for the soup, one for the salmon and one for the lemon tart. Finally, all of them would eat the lunch and take home the recipes with Hope's tips for that meal.

At fifteen minutes to the hour, as expected, the doorbell rang. She washed her hands quickly, rubbing them dry on her apron as she went to answer it. One of her most loyal students

stood there: Jimmy Forsythe, a balding man who wore cor-
duroy trousers whatever the weather. He had been widowed
a few years earlier and had decided that learning to cook
would be his salvation. Hope suspected he anticipated more
from her otherwise usually exclusively female customer base,
but as far as she knew he had yet to strike lucky. She rather
enjoyed the idea that there was the potential for romance in
her classes. There was certainly potential for friendship, as
people often returned in pairs.

Within a short time, all six pupils had gathered, quickly
aproned up. While some started chopping the watercress
and making a stock, others got going on the miso sauce, or
weighing out ingredients for pastry. Hope was soon in her
happy place. While her thoughts of Patrick wouldn't leave
her, they were forced to take a back seat. Within three hours,
they were all sitting down at the table by the open French
doors, devouring the results and sampling the pairing wines.

When they eventually departed, Hope returned to her
office. She flipped open her laptop, paused, and closed it
again. She went to make a cup of tea. It was another five
minutes before she was finally settled at her desk.

Dear Patrick, she began.

Thank you for your letter. Was that too formal?

*Shall we have lunch at Giovanni's, a small Italian restaurant
fairly near me?* She deleted what she'd written and tried again.

*Thanks for your letter. Lunch sounds a good plan. I could do
next week. Thursday?*

She took a sip of her tea. Did she want to start rebuilding

her relationship with him over lunch – if, indeed, that was going to happen?

What about meeting in Giovanni's, a little Italian restaurant quite near me? It's in Elia Street, a short walk from the Angel tube. Twelve thirty p.m.?

Giovanni's, a small, unpretentious restaurant run by an Italian family who specialized in local Calabrian food, seemed to her perfect. Their 'nduja, a spicy spreadable sausage that Hope loved, was second to none, and the tables were far enough apart to allow for a discreet conversation.

I'm looking forward to it, she wrote. Was that too keen? She crossed it out.

See you then then.

Then then? She deleted the second then.

She typed her name and sent it before she could change her mind. There was much more that she wanted to say and so many questions she would like to ask. But she had no idea how any of them would land. When Patrick was in front of her, she could look him in the eye and ask whatever she wanted. Couldn't she?

12

Edie lay awake, listening to Paul's breathing. A couple of weeks had passed since they'd had lunch at Hope's and she was back at work. As pleased as she was about this, with that fact came the inevitable anxieties that she would make a wrong step in a case, so she went over and over the details. It was good to be tested, to use her brain again, but she was also troubled by the feelings that came with having resumed her affair with Daniel. As hard as she tried to manage her life, she still felt as if her grip could be much tighter.

Guilt, responsibility, temptation, regret ... They were all fighting for space in her mind. She couldn't stop thinking about how reckless they had been meeting somewhere so public when Hope was only yards away. What had she been thinking? Her feelings for him were as genuine and heartfelt as ever. She loved him as much as she did before he went to Newcastle. If Hope was waiting to catch her out, then what would happen to them? She couldn't bear to think about ending the affair, but at the same time, she knew it couldn't go on.

She had to get up for Hazel, who woke at five-thirty a.m. With only a few hours' sleep, Edie looked drawn. However, Jen arrived at eight to take over and Edie was released. After only a few days, Betty's old nanny had already made her presence felt. At first, she had met resistance from the girls, but she had quickly won them over.

That morning she bounced in, as bright and enthusiastic as ever. Her fair hair was dyed a shade of pink, and her clothes were practical; jeans and T-shirt. She loved working with children and it showed. She never seemed to tire of them.

'Morning! What are we going to do today?' She dumped her backpack in a corner, picked up Hazel from her activity centre and blew a raspberry into her neck, then another. Hazel burst into laughter.

Betty ran over, so Jen squatted down to greet her. 'Hello, poppet. Shall we go to soft play today?'

'Yes!' Betty jumped up and down.

'That's settled then. We'll go this morning before your nap.'

'I'll see you all later, then. Thanks, Jen.' Edie made as quick an exit as she could, kissing the girls, knowing they were in the best hands. Her work diary was almost full. She had known it would be worth the schmoozing she'd done before coming back with James, the chief clerk, as well as with Derek, their head of chambers. She was pretty sure she had successfully persuaded them that she was absolutely focused and ready to go.

James had been sceptical at first. She knew he was wondering whether she'd take time off when the kids were ill, that she wouldn't be able to stick with a case. Of course he'd never say such a thing, but she'd had to persuade him anyway.

'You know me. I'll make sure everything's in order so that won't happen. I won't let you down.'

He had pursed his lips. 'I hope not. I don't want to find work's a poor second to your family.'

She had stared at him, open-mouthed. 'Come on! You wouldn't be saying that if I was a man.' She was appalled by any suggestion of discrimination. Some of the men she worked alongside still held views about women that belonged in the dark ages. They should be called out and proved wrong.

He had the grace to look apologetic. 'Sorry, Edie. So, what sort of thing are you looking for?'

'I need something juicy. I want you to clerk me into silk.' The award of Queen's Counsel would one day be confirmation of her expertise in her field and make her the bee's knees of the legal world. The more appearances James secured for her in the High Court, the more judges would witness her capabilities and, as a result, would support her application. 'Really, I do. It's almost time.'

James was eventually persuaded of her continued dedication and had begun filling her diary before her return to work.

That morning, she'd met with one of her new clients, a woman fighting her abusive and controlling ex for sole custody of their two children, together with her solicitor. The husband was rich, influential and clearly had a short fuse going by the reports of his behaviour. Edie hated seeing her client cowed and was determined to do the best by her. They had a date for court but she hoped they might be able to settle out of court. It was always better that a couple agreed about the arrangement rather than a judgment being forced on one resentful and angry half.

With the meeting over, exhilarated by the sense of being back in the game and feeling positive over the result, she went back to the quiet of her room in chambers. She felt comfortable here, with her books on the shelves: various family-court textbooks, reference books and the indispensable Red Book that contained the information that every family barrister needed to know. Updated with all the latest case law, it was Edie's bible. Her desk was clear, save for her laptop and a photo of Paul and the girls, and another of her and him on the day of their wedding. Technology had made paper almost redundant now that so much more of her work was done online.

She sipped her takeaway latte and opened the laptop. She would email Daniel. Despite everything she wanted, she had reluctantly come to a decision over their future. She had seen too many families broken as a result of an affair ...

Dearest D,

We can't go on like this. I'm so sorry to end it now but being caught by Hope was too close. We have so much between us still. I've loved everything we've done together but I don't want to risk my marriage and I don't think you want to risk yours. I thought I'd be able to continue – God knows I want to – but the stress is too much. Let's stop this before anyone gets hurt and we can remember the best of times between us.

E x

The moment she pressed send, she regretted it.

Perhaps she should have thought about it for longer. She read and re-read her email, wondering how he would take it, what he might read between the lines, how he would respond, how angry he would be, how hurt. Then she deleted it so it couldn't be found.

He didn't reply immediately, but when he did, it was not with the reluctant acceptance she had half expected.

> This breaks my heart. Since we've got together again, we've always had our own commitments, I know, but I can't imagine not having you in my life now. I want us to continue. I urge you to meet me so that we can discuss face to face, to see if we can find a better way of resolving this. Please.

This completely floored her. How tempted she was and yet . . .

At that moment, Olga, a fellow barrister, put her head round the door. 'I think James has asked you to take the Renee Adams case?'

Edie could tell by her unyielding expression that her colleague was miffed. The case was the latest high-profile contact dispute to come to the office, and instead of offering it to Olga, James had asked Edie to handle it. She would be representing a well-known actress who wanted to move her children with her to Los Angeles when her ex didn't want them to go. Of course he didn't. And he would fight hard to stop them.

'Yes, I haven't tackled the brief yet.'

'It needs tackling,' Olga said as she stepped into the room. 'Why don't you ask him to redirect it to me?' Her finger-nails were as red as her lips. 'I've been waiting for something like this.'

'I'm sorry,' said Edie. 'That's not how it works, and you know that.'

Olga didn't say anything else, although Edie could feel the force of her fury as she swivelled on her heel and stalked out. Edie took a deep breath, opened the brief and began to read.

'I don't know what to do.' Edie had gone round to Ana's while Jen stayed on to babysit. If she didn't talk to someone, she would go mad. If she met Daniel as he wanted, she was aware how easily her resolve might be swayed. Just one touch . . . a look from those eyes . . . a few of the right chosen words – those would be enough.

'Well, e-dumping's a pretty shitty thing to do, you've got to admit.' Her friend sat up and took a few nuts.

'I know – but it seemed the best way. I don't want to see him in case I change my mind.' The olive she took was sharp with garlic.

Ana shook her head. 'You're tougher than that.'

'Am I?' Just then, Edie didn't feel tough at all. She felt torn between the two men and was devastated that doing the right thing was going to cause her and Daniel such heartache. For the second time. She pictured them together in bed, the pleasure she got from being with him, the years they had lived together and the times they had managed to fit in since they had met again. She couldn't deny her nagging reluctance to bring their renewed affair to a close. But she must. She must. Despite the drudgery of motherhood, she didn't want to lose her family. But, equally, what she and Daniel had was something special that hadn't disappeared in the years they had been apart. Despite loving Paul, she still loved Daniel in a million different ways.

'Yes, you are. You can choose what you do.'

Edie admired her friend's common sense, but perhaps this wasn't exactly what she wanted to hear. She had come hoping for sympathy, to be told she had done the right thing. She wanted reinforcement and support, not criticism. But Ana hadn't finished.

'And now you're back at work, you'll bump into him anyway. Wouldn't it be better to end it in a civilized way, so that you can cross paths without it being awkward? You've had your time with him. You've both moved on, married, got families. Get over it.'

'I can't. It's so easy for you to say but you don't under-stand.' Her predicament and Ana's lack of empathy made her despair.

'Then make me.' Ana challenged her.

'I don't want to drop everything for Daniel, but we're soul mates. If I'm honest, our affair is what keeps me going. We can talk about anything, the sex is great and I feel entirely myself with him. The truth is that I love him. Paul and the children aren't enough. I feel terrible saying that, but it's true.'

'Really? You sound like a teenager.'

'I know. Ridiculously, that's what I feel like when I'm with him. I met Paul when I was still on the rebound. I'd persuaded myself that I'd got over Daniel and I'd never see him again. What the hell am I going to do?'

'You've got yourself into a right old mess. Even so, you know what to do. You have responsibilities now.'

By the time Edie went home, she was still undecided.

She had a quick supper with Paul and excused herself to read up on her client meeting the following day. She went to the small office they shared, put her laptop on the desk, then stared out over the garden. Before anything else, she opened Daniel's reply to her email again. Of course, Ana was right. His words were too heartfelt to completely ignore. Perhaps she should agree to see him. But she had work to do, so opened the case file James had sent her, reading quickly and carefully, making notes for herself when needed. Eventually, she closed the file again. She would get up early to read her notes one more time.

Switching off the lights, she left the room and ran downstairs. The TV was blaring in the living room, so she detoured into the kitchen to make cups of hot chocolate for herself and Paul and put away the supper leftovers that he had ignored. He never quite finished things, she thought. It was as if he hadn't seen the unused cutlery and pepper pot on the table, the crumbs and cup stains on the worktop. They often joked about how pernickety she was by comparison. She found the marshmallows that she'd hidden from Betty in her secret treats drawer, dotted them on the top of the mugs and took them through to the living room.

The cops on the TV were breaking into a council flat mob-handed, but not even the deafening shouts of 'Police! Don't move. Hands against the wall' were enough to wake Paul, who was sprawled on the sofa, spark out.

He looked so peaceful that she didn't try to wake him. His mouth was slightly open, his chest rising and falling. He must be exhausted. The early mornings caught up on both of them. She put down the mugs, trying not to make a sound, then picked up the remote that lay by his hand and turned down the volume. Immediately, Paul opened his eyes and sat up, rubbing his face.

'Sorry. Must have drifted off.' He smiled at her and nodded towards the two mugs on the coffee table. 'Is one of those for me?'

'Well, I'm not going to drink them both.' She put one on a coaster nearer to him.

'I wouldn't put it past you.' He dodged the cushion that she lobbed at him. 'Easy. Come over here.' He patted the seat beside him, and she sat down as he put his arm around her. 'We don't get much time like this anymore.'

She snuggled into him, pulling her legs underneath her so her head could rest on his chest, where she felt the steady beat of his heart. They'd been there for just a moment or two, not talking, enjoying the closeness, when a familiar sound came through the child monitor. Hazel.

'She can't be awake,' groaned Paul. 'Not now.'

'Let's leave her for a bit. See if she goes back off.' Edie picked off one of the melting marshmallows and put it in her mouth. 'Mm hm.' Having sat down, it was as if all the tension of the day was draining out of her. 'It's only teething.'

Hazel's wails grew louder.

'I can't bear it. I'll go.' Paul stood up. 'Stay where you are.' He was out of the door and up the stairs before Edie had time to pull herself out of her seat. On the monitor screen, she could see Hazel reaching up to him, mouth wide in a tear-stained wail. But he found her dummy, laid her down, hand on her chest as they'd always agreed, and began quietly singing the sea shanties that she found so soothing. Gradually she quietened down. Edie watched the whole process propped up on her arm, envious of his ease with their child, and her resolve to devote herself to her family was strengthened.

The restaurant was quiet for lunchtime. Daniel had chosen it because it was a quick taxi ride from their respective chambers, far enough away for them not to be spotted. They'd both found themselves free when their court cases finished at the same time in the morning. Hasty phone calls had been enough to arrange this impromptu meeting.

'You came.' Despite their arrangement, he sounded surprised.

'Of course. I said I would.' Actually, a quick coffee would have been all that was needed, but she had thought she owed him longer, so lunch it was. Now she was here, she felt her resolution weakening as she experienced that deep and irrefutable visceral pull between them again.

Edie nodded towards her phone that she put on the table beside her. 'Sorry. In case our nanny calls.'

'Of course.' He reached out to take her hand. 'I was shocked to get your email. I had to see you. I don't believe you meant what you said.'

She pulled her hand away. 'No. I know you don't.'

Daniel was smiling at her. 'Let me order us a drink. You *are* drinking?'

'God, yes.' *Go easy*, she warned herself. 'Though not usually at lunchtime.'

He summoned the waiter with a crook of a finger and ordered a couple of glasses of Gavi, her favourite.

She ordered rainbow chard with garlic and a simple penne with tomato sauce (the house speciality) to his burrata and roast mushroom gnocchi. Then, they sat awkwardly, Edie not knowing quite where to start, waiting for Daniel. They chinked glasses and drank, the citrussy wine slipping down easily.

'I don't understand,' he began. 'Last week we were glad you were back at work so we could actually spend some proper time together again. I've already booked another room for us at the Smithson, hoping you'd be able to get away.' This was a comfortable and discreet hotel in a narrow street off Holborn that welcomed afternoon guests. They knew it well.

'Things have changed,' she said, wishing so much that they hadn't.

'But why?' He looked mystified.

'Because of what happened in the park. We should never have taken that risk.' She had to keep reminding him how close they'd come to being discovered.

'Just because someone saw us. They won't again.'

'But that someone was my mother-in-law.'

'Even so. She can't have seen anything to make her suspicious.'

'I think the fact we were in the bushes might have been enough.' Why couldn't he see that? 'I should have told you she was with me so we couldn't meet. I didn't get a chance.'

'And you couldn't resist?' The hope was back in his eyes.

'I couldn't resist.' She noticed her wine glass was almost empty already.

'Then why?'

She looked up as another couple was shown to the table behind her. She told herself to stop being so jumpy. No one she knew would come in here, and certainly not at this time of day.

'It made me realize what a dangerous path we're on. I so want to be with you again, but I don't want to lose what I've got. My family.' This was the realization that had been so long coming. Having a family was hard, but it was what she had committed to, even though the reality was challenging. She and Daniel had gone through agony, parting ways. But that was then . . . and now their situation had changed. 'And what about yours?'

'There's no need for this to be a threat to our families. It's quite separate – just the two of us. They'll never know.'

'But they nearly do! Don't you see? We could be found out at any time.'

'Not if we're careful.' He leant back as their starters were put in front of them. 'Two more glasses of the same, please. One more won't hurt.'

She frowned at the order, thinking of the work she had to do back in chambers before she went home.

'You don't have to drink it.' He had read her face.

'My point is, it's all too stressful. And too dangerous.' She toyed with her chard, not hungry anymore. Underneath the table, his leg pressed against hers. She couldn't move it away.

He looked at her with a mixture of longing and regret. Theirs had been the first and only great passion in both their lives. They had split for good, practical reasons, both career ambitious. They couldn't have known that he would come back to London so soon and that their feelings towards each other would barely have changed.

She took a sip of her second glass of wine but couldn't ignore the way he was looking at her – the half smile, the sparkle in his eyes.

'You don't mean it,' he said. 'I know you don't.' His knee nudged her thigh. She still didn't move.

'I do.' Edie spoke so huskily that it hardly sounded convincing. She cleared her throat. 'I do.' She flinched and looked away as someone laughed loudly at another table. She shouldn't have come. The whole situation demanded that she get up and walk away. 'Of course I do. We can't do this anymore. There's too much at risk ... for both of us. Your marriage must mean as much to you as mine does to me. My girls, Finn, your son. We should think of them.'

'I'm prepared to take that risk. I love you. I don't want to give you up. I *won't* give you up.'

'I don't know.' She felt herself wavering, despite her resolve.

'Yes, you do,' he pressed her. 'You do.'

The door of the restaurant opened to admit a late customer, a man on his own who was shown to the booth behind Daniel. He looked faintly familiar. His wavy dark hair was splintered with grey and just beginning to recede at his temples. She tried to place him. He was fit, attractive and his mouth pursed slightly as he looked around, taking in the scene. He was casual but smartish in a plain green open-necked shirt with rolled-up sleeves, dark blue shorts and deck shoes. She couldn't help noticing that his shorts had crease marks from a precise ironing down the centre of each leg. No, she didn't know him. It was just her nerves again. Probably someone she'd seen across a courtroom. She returned her attention to Daniel who was waiting for her to say something. Did she dare? She was so tempted – but, but, but ...

He was holding out a spoonful of gnocchi. 'Try this. It's delicious.'

On all those times they had eaten out together, they had always tried whatever the other was eating. Accepting a taste of his lunch was like taking a step back to that time. In the brief time she hesitated, the restaurant door opened again, this time to admit a woman. Behind her, a helmeted little girl whizzed down the pavement on her scooter. Edie almost choked on her gnocchi. This time the newcomer didn't just look familiar, she was only *too* familiar.

Hope.

Edie shrank back as she watched her mother-in-law scanning the restaurant for someone. She looked on edge, her hands knotting and unknotting. Her eyes lit on the booth in front of Edie and she took a step towards it before they rested on her. Hope's look of greeting was erased by the shock of seeing her daughter-in-law.

What was Hope doing there? Why wasn't she at home cooking? She was looking great in neat trousers and one of the vintage tops she was so good at finding, a brightly coloured necklace, long fringe pulled back behind her right ear. She was also looking extremely unsure of herself.

They couldn't just ignore one another. Edie recovered from the shock first, raised her hand in acknowledgement, then stood and walked over to her. She gave her a perfunctory kiss on each cheek, trying to pretend this was nothing much out of the ordinary. 'Hope! What an extraordinary coincidence! Aren't you working?'

'Not this afternoon. I'm meeting a friend. What about you?'

At that moment, Daniel, who had his back to the door, half stood and turned his head to see what was happening. As soon as he saw Hope, he ducked down again. Too late. Edie watched Hope's eyebrows rise in surprise. She'd recognized him, of course.

'A working lunch,' Edie said.

But Hope's reaction to meeting Edie like this was quite different from the one Edie might have expected. That look of panic that had crossed Hope's face was ... extraordinary.

'How nice.' Hope's eyes flicked to the man she was meeting.

'Enjoy yours.' Edie was puzzled by Hope's obvious unease, but could think of nothing more to say. She obviously wasn't going to be introduced to Hope's companion so returned to her seat opposite a wide-eyed Daniel. Oh, God. This was a disaster. All Hope's suspicions about Edie would be confirmed. Simple as that. But what would she do about them? She wouldn't be stupid enough to tell Paul. Suddenly the sense of danger compounded with risk felt empowering.

Spearing another of Daniel's gnocchi, she put it in her mouth. She slipped off her shoe and rubbed his ankles with her toe as she watched a smile cross his face again.

'You're right,' she said so quietly that he had to lean forward to hear. 'I do know. I just can't let you go.'

13

Since agreeing to meet Patrick, Hope had been building herself up to their meeting. What would he look like? Had time been kind to him? Was he happy? She had spent the morning trying on clothes and discarding them, desperate to create the best first impression. In the end, she had settled on grey linen trousers and a loose green shirt that she'd picked up in her favourite vintage shop in Crouch End. Then, the lightest touch of make-up. She'd deliberately arrived late at the restaurant. She thought he must be the casually dressed man sitting on his own, but was waiting for the maître d' to confirm when she noticed Edie in the booth behind, looking as appalled as she felt. Before she could react, Edie had got up and was standing in front of her, giving her a dutiful kiss. They exchanged surprised greetings and over Edie's shoulder Hope saw her companion half stand, then quickly sit. She immediately recognized him – the man from the playground. But all Hope could focus on at that moment was Patrick.

She wanted to be able to deal with Patrick's unexpected reappearance in her life in her own way, and in her own time. The last person she wanted to witness their meeting was Edie. She didn't want her family to know anything until she was ready.

Released from Edie's embrace, the waiter indeed showed her to the table she had thought must be hers. She managed a shaky hello to Patrick – inadequate, after so long – and immediately requested that they move tables. He had been sitting quietly nursing a bottle of craft lager, looking at his phone, oblivious to the drama of Hope's encounter with Edie. He moved with good grace despite looking somewhat surprised. They followed the waiter to the back of the restaurant.

'I'm so sorry,' she said, once they had been re-seated. 'That was my daughter-in-law, and I really don't want her listening in.' Her heart was thumping, her voice faint. 'I've been so looking forward to this.' But the highly charged emotional moment that she had imagined on meeting him had been hi-jacked by Edie. She wasn't sure how to behave.

'Just breathe,' he said, a slight West Country burr colouring his speech that she found strangely comforting. 'We've all the time. I'll order us something to drink, shall I? What would you like? Wine?'

She was about to say she didn't drink alcohol at lunchtime, but different words flew out of her mouth. 'A glass of white would be great. Should we order food too, and get that out of the way?' Not that she felt like eating a mouthful.

He nodded. 'Sure.'

They quickly looked at the menu. Hope was so rattled she

just picked the first thing she saw. 'I'll just have the 'nduja and fennel pasta and a small salad.'

As he ordered, and as the waiter poured their wine, she studied Patrick. He had an intelligent face, kind eyes that were alert and a mouth that looked as if it was used to smiling. His hands were sturdy and well kept, his nails cut straight across.

'Better?' He smiled across the table at her and raised his glass. 'Shall we start again?' He seemed calm, matter of fact, though for all she knew he was as nervous as she was.

They chinked glasses. What she wanted to do was to hug him, hold him tight to her, but she had missed that initial moment in the confusion of her entry. Maybe it was yet to come.

'Yes.' Suddenly she could barely speak. As the enormity of their meeting washed over her, she felt tears welling in her eyes. 'Oh, Patrick. I'm so terribly sorry.'

He reached out to touch her arm. 'Don't. Please. We've a lot of catching up to do.'

'Have you been happy?' Already, she could feel the tears welling.

His smile was generous. 'Yes, I have. You mustn't worry about that. I don't have any demons – or none that I know of.' He passed her a handkerchief from his pocket. 'I had a feeling we might need one of these.'

'How did you find me?' She blew her nose, aware she was wiping off her carefully applied make-up. But what did that matter?

'You're not that well-hidden, it turns out.'

'I wasn't trying to hide. I've never forgotten you. Never. I've thought about you every day of my life. I can't tell you the number of times I've wondered whether you'd be in touch. Hoped.' The words tumbled out of her mouth.

She remembered the little teddy in her drawer, its fur worn with her stroking.

'You hoped? Really? Then why did you do it?' His eyebrows almost met when he frowned, curious.

There was a loud clatter of plates from the kitchen, followed by a shout.

'Why?' she repeated. But she knew what he was asking. And, once she'd answered, the answer would be out there to do the damage she had always most feared. But she had also always known that if he came asking, she would have to tell him the whole story. She owed him that, if nothing else. And if she told Patrick, there were others who should be told too.

Two plates of pasta were put in front of them, which gave her a moment of respite as they both took a mouthful, aware of the momentous nature of the next few minutes. They were so intent on one another that Hope scarcely noticed that the tables were filling up, the level of noise increasing. The smells coming from the kitchen were enticing, but for once they didn't make Hope hungry.

Although she had gone over what she would say to him a thousand times, she still hesitated.

'Well?'

This was it: a moment on which her whole life hinged.

141

Nothing would be the same from now on. She took a deep breath. 'I was only seventeen,' she began. 'I was living at home with Mum and Dad in Truro and working in a local café. I'd met a boy at school.'

'Is he . . . ?

She held up a hand to shush him. She had to tell this her own way. 'He was in the year above me. All the girls fancied him and hated me because he liked me.' She remembered how Penny Stevens had put fat yellowy brown slugs into her satchel along with a note to warn her off. 'Anyway, when he asked me on a date it was quite the coup, especially as I was a year younger than him. Our parents weren't happy about the relationship when they found out how close we'd become. They felt we were too young, all of that. They wanted me to carve a career for myself, starting with college.' She paused to take a sip of water.

Patrick was nodding, intent on what she had to say. Their pasta sat in front of them, untouched.

'My parents were orthodox Catholics who loved me and my sister in every way, but who were terrified of what might happen if we stepped off the path they'd set for us. Fran, my sister − she's older than me − did brilliantly in school and went off to college at Bristol. Not too far from home. But me, I'd fallen in love. I left school before my final exams and ended up waitressing. A major disappointment to them.'

He was listening intently, observing her too, as if trying to work out the sort of woman she really was.

'What was his name?'

She ignored his question and continued. 'He and I were inseparable, but then he got a place at college. His parents were expecting him to go and it was what he wanted to do. I knew I couldn't stop him, but I was petrified I'd lose him. We only slept together twice. Is that too much information?' She gave a nervous laugh. She could remember both times with perfect clarity, once in a country lane on the back seat of his ancient Triumph Herald – quite the status symbol in those days – and once after the goodbye party he gave before he left. 'It was only after he'd gone that I discovered I was pregnant and I still had another year of school to go.'

'Pregnant . . . With me?'

'Yes.'

Patrick gave a sigh like a soft whistle, but didn't move.

'I was shattered. I didn't want to tell him because I was scared it would change everything between us. I didn't want him to feel he had to do the decent thing. He'd have had to give up his studies and come home to earn a living. He might have resented that forever. And I didn't want to spoil the essence of what we had together. We were so young. We had no money between us. I didn't know what to do. In the end, I told my mother.' She could still see her mother's face, ashen, furious and determined. 'There was no question of an abortion, of course.'

'Glad to hear that!' His attempt at a joke fell flat.

'But, at the same time, I knew if I kept you, I could never give you the life you deserved. I didn't have any money of my own to support us.'

Us.

That's what they had been once. Between his birth and the moment she let him go. An indivisible unit. She looked down at the tablecloth and watched as a tear dissolved into the weave of the fabric. The pain she felt was almost unbearable. But she couldn't stop now, with the story half told.

'So what happened?'

She had to try to make him understand how then, at the age of seventeen, everything was stacked against her having a baby to look after. There had been no guarantees for either of their futures then.

'There really was only one option. Adoption. For the last three months of the pregnancy, I went to a mother and baby home in London where no one would know me. My mother found it and came with me to make sure I got there.' She would never forget that journey, the two of them sitting opposite each other on the train, her mother pale, tight-lipped with disappointment and anxiety; herself, silent, fearful of what the next few months would bring. Awful. Once in London, they had travelled on the Tube, Edie wide-eyed at the experience, to arrive at a forbidding red-brick Victorian building. She was almost immediately handed over by her mother, who walked away after the briefest of goodbyes. She could still smell the mixed odours of the institution – cabbage and disinfectant – and hear the slap of footsteps going downstairs to the dining room. She could feel the pinch of a cold shower and sense again the misery that overshadowed everything.

'Tell me. I want to know everything. At least – if you can.' There were tears in his eyes as he blew his nose, visibly affected by her story.

'I can't tell you everything, although I know that's what you've come for. I came prepared.' She bowed her head as suddenly Edie walked past them on her way to the Ladies, though she must have noticed Hope was crying. However, despite the tears, telling her story for the first time was giving Hope an unexpected sense of relief. What the telling would lead to, she didn't know, but now she had started, she had to finish. Although there was one important detail she was not giving him. She couldn't. Had he noticed?

'It was big old Victorian house in Hackney, run down. I shared a room with two other girls, pregnant like me, and disowned by their ashamed families. I was there for about four months; twelve weeks before the birth and four after. We were allocated chores, from sweeping the stairs, working in the kitchen, cleaning or whatever. It was hard.

'When I went into labour, they sent me alone in an ambulance to hospital. I was absolutely terrified. The nurses were disapproving and not very kind but at least the birth was straightforward. Not that I appreciated that at the time!'

'What happened next?' He leaned forward, rapt.

Their food was all but forgotten.

'We went back to the home where I looked after you until the adoption was arranged.' She rubbed her forehead. 'Now, I wonder what they thought they were doing. Nobody had told me what I would feel when my baby – you – was put into my arms for the very first time.' It came back to her in a rush – that overpowering sensation of love for both her sons – Patrick and, much later, Paul – the smell of their heads, the curl of their fists, their perfect tiny fingers and toes, kissable cheeks and defined mouths. She couldn't put such deep-seated emotions into words. 'I had you with me during the day, then all the babies were put in a room together at night. I fed you. Nobody visited me. It was as if we were entirely alone together.' Her voice caught. She had buried this so deep – that had been the only way to survive. The only way to keep the secret. Her mother had done her bit by her, so she had to do her bit back – but at what cost to herself? 'After three weeks they found a couple who wanted a baby. I didn't want to let you go. Believe me. But if I'd taken you home, I'd have had no support, and I didn't have the means to look after you alone.'

Talking about this for the first time in forty-eight years burst a dam inside her.

He reached across the table and took her hand, just as Edie walked back across the restaurant to her table. Hope barely noticed. She was remembering the day the social worker had come to take him away. Her tears; her screaming; his screaming. The pain in her breasts, the void in her heart. 'All I had to remember you by was a little teddy with a tartan ribbon I had bought for you. They didn't want it, so I kept it, and I've still got it to this day.'

He squeezed her hand. 'That's it?'

'That's it.' Her shoulders dropped and she sat back against the banquette.

'You only knew me for such a short time.'

'Three weeks. I would have given anything to have had longer.' Although they were mother and son, there was only blood binding them together. She would never have the relationship with him that she had with Paul, she knew that. There were none of the crucial building blocks a mother shares with her growing child. She speared some pasta but had second thoughts and left the fork in her plate. 'Who were they? Your parents. Did they give you a good life?'

He smiled. 'I was lucky. I don't think either of us could have asked for better. Gill and Tony Marchant. Not long after they took me on, she got pregnant. They'd been told she couldn't have a baby but I ended up in a family of four kids – Joel, Bruce, Marcie and me. But, you know what? They never made me feel any different from the others. Mum died two years ago but Dad's been very encouraging since I told him I wanted to find you. I couldn't have done it while she was alive.'

Mum. Dad. It didn't sound right. But she was glad he had them.

'When did you find out that you were adopted? That must have been hard.' There had been times when she had tortured herself with this thought over the years. How unforgiving he might feel towards her when he was told.

'They told me as soon as I could understand. They were pretty enlightened.'

Hope couldn't help but remember her own parents, who were so much the opposite. 'What else can you tell me about them?'

'They were teachers; she in the local primary, and he ended up Head of Bristol Grammar. They loved children and knew what made them tick. Lucky for me.' His affection for them was obvious and prompted a squeeze of envy in Hope. 'I can't remember a time when I didn't know, but the point was I knew I'd been chosen because I was special, that I was meant to be part of their family.' He laughed. 'Nobody cared how I'd got there. The fact I was there was enough.'

'Are you married? I'm sorry. I've so many questions.'

'Me, too. You don't need to apologize.' That smile again. She had a sudden glimpse of his father. 'Shall we take it in turns for a while, and then meet again to carry on and decide what to do next?'

'Next?' She didn't want to think about the difficulties that lay ahead of them.

'Well, yes.' He seemed surprised by the question. 'I mean, I'd like to find my father too and I'll need your help for that if you'll give it to me.'

Her stomach turned over.

'But he doesn't know about you.' The thought of telling him terrified her.

'Doesn't? Do you mean you still know him?'

She shook her head, appalled by her own lie. But what else could she do? She had left it too long not to go on lying, however unforgivable that was. It would be too damaging to all concerned. She watched Patrick's face cloud over.

'He did exactly what I'd been frightened of – met another woman at college, and broke off our relationship.' She stayed as close to the truth as she dared, although she was aware she was tying herself in knots. 'I was devastated. My parents, even my mother, who knew everything I'd been through, were relieved. We told no one what had happened.'

'They sound controlling.' But, from the tone of his voice, it wasn't a criticism.

She shrugged. 'They were. Different times. They just wanted the best for us, I know that now. But back then I didn't. As soon as I could, I packed my bags and went to Brighton where a friend of mine had moved to. There was a bedroom in her flat going, so I stayed with her and started a new life, working in cafés and restaurant kitchens. While I was there, I really began to get interested in food and catering, so eventually I did a diploma in professional cookery. I worked in one restaurant after another but after nine years or so, Mum died and Dad got cancer, and despite everything, I felt it was my duty to help him. I saw an ad for a job in Truro so I went back there as a sous chef where I could help look after him as well.'

'So you never told my father that I existed?' His eyes were wide with disbelief.

'I couldn't.' She put her head in her hands, overwhelmed by the situation, by seeing it from his perspective. Opening herself up to him was leading her into deeper waters than she had wanted to go. Why hadn't she thought more carefully about the possible ramifications of her decision to see him? She had been driven by emotion, not reason.

'I do need to find him,' Patrick said. 'At least tell me his full name.'

'I can't.' Her voice caught in her throat.

'But surely . . .' His expression showed what he thought of her reticence. 'This is such a big deal for me.'

'You don't understand. You've no idea what my life was like then. And you know nothing about my relationship with him.' A spark of anger had ignited in her. Who was he to come looking for her, and then criticize her when all she had done – was doing – was to act in a way that she believed to be for everyone's best? She had kept her decades-long secret for a reason, and she couldn't give it up now.

'I'm sorry. I shouldn't have said that.' He raised his hands, conciliatory. 'I haven't come here for a fight.'

She acknowledged his apology with a nod. But . . .

The thought of what she had regretted and been frightened of for years loomed ahead of her. Everyone made mistakes, but some much bigger than others. She was one of those people with the big mistakes. 'You don't know what you're asking. For all you know, this might overturn his whole life.'

'But you have another son.'

'Yes. Paul.' She nodded. 'That's his wife over there, having a business lunch. They've two adorable daughters.' How would Paul react when he discovered Patrick's existence? She couldn't keep her first son a secret from her second any longer.

'I've another brother. Wow!' His face lit up. 'A whole new family.'

His expression buoyed her up. 'Look, isn't it my turn to ask you a few things?'

'Of course. More wine, or coffee?'

'Coffee. Thanks.' Hope was relieved to be given a break while the waiter cleared the table, having to be reassured there was nothing wrong with the uneaten food, while she got ready to ask Patrick some of the questions she had waited all her life to ask and to listen to the replies.

To hear the story of her eldest son's life.

14

As soon as Daniel had set off on his bike, flushed with wine and the success of their meeting, Edie took out her phone.

'Ana. Are you busy?'

Ana's job could be demanding and difficult too. In charge of the women's fashion and accessory ranges, she had high standards to maintain and staff to look after.

'Yeah. What's up? Aren't you at work?'

'I'm on my way back to chambers but was wondering if we might meet for a drink when you've finished?' She couldn't go straight home after what had happened.

'A drink? Sure. I'll be glad to get out of here. Quick one, though.'

'Great. Me, too. I'll meet you at six. At the usual.'

'Don't you want to put the kiddywinks to bed?'

'Not tonight. Paul will and I'll catch up with them in the morning.' As she walked briskly back to her chambers, she reflected on whether it was unnatural not to be drawn home like a magnet, dashing off as soon as she could get away. Truth be told, she would rather meet Ana or network with her colleagues than play bath-time games. Did that make her an unfit mother? However much she loved her girls, perhaps that wasn't enough. If there was an opportunity to escape, she would take it. Following in her own mother's footsteps, she supposed. Her mind elsewhere, she stepped between two parked cars to cross the road, narrowly avoiding a speeding cyclist who shouted something and gave her the finger.

Once her eyes had adjusted to the dim light, Edie spotted Ana at one of the tables round the sunken bar, scrolling through something on her phone. The wine bar was virtually empty so early in the evening. Framed French posters were displayed on the wood-panelled walls and a large station clock took pride of place beside the long bar. The music was so quiet it was almost inaudible.

Ana looked up as Edie slid into her seat. 'What's so important it can't wait?' She scrutinized Edie's face. 'Don't tell me: Daniel wouldn't accept your knock-back?'

Edie took the glass of wine that Ana had already ordered for her. 'It's not about that. You'll never guess who else was in the restaurant.'

'If I'm not going to guess, you'd better tell me.'

'Hope!' Edie couldn't keep the triumphant note out of her voice.

'And?' Ana was impatient.

'With a man. A much younger one.' She could still picture him: tall, dark-haired, slightly greying, lightly tanned and casually dressed for the summer.

'So? He could have been anyone.'

153

'True. But her face when she spotted me! She wasn't happy at all – obviously didn't want to be seen.' Even less so when Edie had walked past them on the way to the Ladies; they'd been holding hands and Hope was teary-eyed.

'So who do you think he was?'

'I'm going to find out.' Edie wondered why Ana didn't sound more interested.

'Does it really matter? He was probably just a guy she knows from work, or a client. I'm more interested in you.'

Edie made a snap decision. If she was going to continue seeing Daniel, this time absolutely nobody must know, not even Ana this time. That was the only way she would be able to keep her marriage intact but still continue their relationship. She couldn't let him go again. That was decided.

'I told Daniel it was over.'

'And?'

Edie twisted her glass in a circle as if she was thinking. 'And he was upset, angry.'

'But not so upset that he cut it short and left?' Ana looked at her curiously. 'Are you telling me the truth? You'd better be.'

'I am. Honestly. We didn't get to the point till after we'd eaten.'

'You kept him hanging on all that time? I don't believe you.' She knew Edie too well.

But Edie was determined to stick to her guns. 'It was difficult. I didn't know how to bring it up, and then I saw Hope. But, you know, I think he was playing for time too.

In the end, he said that he'd come to the same conclusion. He doesn't want to leave his wife and kid.' That much was true. At least she assumed it was, but they hadn't ever really had that conversation. Both of them were too scared of what would result. She felt terrible lying to her friend, but this was the only way she could see of protecting herself.

'So he dumped you, in fact?'

She couldn't allow that. 'No! We came to a mutual agreement. Nice while it lasted but there was too much at stake.'

'Hmmm.' Ana clearly wasn't convinced. 'If you say so.'

'I do.' Edie stamped the lie with authority. 'Neither of us were happy but we've got to accept the situation.' This was awful. She felt more reprehensible with every word.

Ana drained her glass. 'Well done you, then. But listen, I should go. I need to pack for Venice tomorrow.'

'Venice? You never said.'

'I'm off to see some glassware being blown on Murano. Then I'm popping to Florence to see a ceramicist. Both making beautiful things just perfect for the store. I'll be back in two days.' She pulled a face. 'I'm supposed to be organizing my fortieth but what with Italy and then a fortnight in America, I think I'm going to have to postpone it.'

'Oh, don't do that. We all want to celebrate with you. You must have already organized most of it.'

'I've reserved a private room in that new women's club in Bloomsbury, the Firebird, but I haven't finalized the invitations, food, drink or flowers. I just can't see myself getting it done now.'

'Let me do that for you.' At least Edie could offer her friend some support.

'Don't be daft. You're so busy now you're back at work.'

'Not so busy that I can't find time to help you. Let me. It would be fun. You'll have to tell me who to invite though.' She wanted to help, and it salved her conscience about lying to her.

Ana looked uncertain. 'We-ell, if you're sure.'

'One hundred per cent. All you have to do is turn up.'

'That would be amazing. I accept, then.' Her whole face had brightened. 'But I'll give you a budget so you don't go mad.'

Edie laughed. 'You can give me anything you like, but consider it done.'

'Thanks so much. I'll email you the details of what I've done so far.' She stood up to go, bending to kiss her friend's cheek. 'And ... I'm glad you've agreed to break it off. You really have, haven't you?'

'Yes. What do I have to say to convince you?'

'Nothing. I'll take your word for it, and love you and leave you.' Ana held her skirt on each side and did a little wiggle to straighten the dress.

The journey home provided Edie with ample time to think through her day. By the time she opened the front door, she was quite clear. Having an affair with Daniel didn't mean she wanted to leave Paul. She loved both men in their different ways and her relationship with Daniel gave her what she needed to keep her content in her marriage. That was surely enough to justify it. If she made sure no one found out, no one would be hurt. And the only person who had seen Daniel and her together was Hope. She would have to put an end to her suspicions.

That evening, once she and Paul had eaten a scratch supper, Paul disappeared to spend time doing admin. His habit was to leave things until the last minute and then to blitz the lot in a night or two. Edie took him a coffee and kissed his forehead.

'You've no idea how much I hate this side of the business.' He indicated the screen filled with an Excel spreadsheet dotted with figures and names.

'I have every idea. I'm just grateful our clerks do most of it at work.' She laughed and patted his shoulder.

Shutting the door behind her, she went outside to sit on the terrace. She always loved this time of year. Barbecue smells drifted across the ranks of terraced gardens, voices at a party floated over from somewhere down the road, along with the distant throb of music. She inhaled the scent of the roses that climbed all along the trellis they shared with their neighbours. She took out her phone and went over what she wanted to say, then brought up Hope's number.

'Edie?' Hope sounded apprehensive.

'Yes. Did you have a good lunch?' Brisk and business-like, that was the way to do it.

'Yes, lovely thanks.' Hope sounded unsure.

'I wondered if we could meet?'

'Can't we talk now, over the phone?' Hope's voice sounded stronger.

'I thought it might be good to chat again, you know, to clear the air. I'll treat you.'

'Well, okay.' Her mother-in-law's reluctance was obvious. 'I have to go into town tomorrow. Shall we grab a coffee at that café in the Fields in the afternoon?'

'Perfect.' It was good of Hope to think of her working day. 'I'm in the High Court tomorrow but we finish at four thirty. So we could meet at five-ish, say?' She'd be late for bedtime again, but she should get there in time to say goodnight, if not for the whole routine.

They said their goodbyes as Paul emerged from the house. 'What are you doing out here?' He walked across the garden and put his arm round her.

'Just thinking, and praying that Hazel sleeps through tonight. Have you finished?'

'Not exactly, but I'll do some more tomorrow. I just felt like a bit of us-time.'

Despite everything, she felt herself relax into him.

'Shall we sit out here for a bit?'

'I'd like that.' She was right to have lied about Daniel to Ana. This was a boat she didn't want to rock. The cushioned wicker sofa creaked under their weight as they sat down together.

'Good day?'

'Quiet, preparing for tomorrow, going over how I'm going to present the case. A fourteen-year-old boy has asked to overturn the previous court access agreements so he can move out from his mother, who's now an alcoholic, and move in with his dad. She's fighting like a lioness.'

'I don't blame him.' He slipped his arm around her shoulders. 'You haven't been back at work long but I can see how involved you're getting already.'

'I am. I've a huge feeling of responsibility. I have to do my best for people because the courts' decisions can be life-changing and sometimes they're hard to accept.' Anyone must be able to understand that.

'Do you miss the girls? Just a little?'

'Of course I do, but I need to work too. You know that.'

He looked at her and smiled. 'I do indeed.'

'It's not a problem?'

'Not at all. You haven't changed since I first met you and that's the you I fell in love with.' He kissed her fleetingly on the lips. 'I'm proud of your career.'

His being so open took her by surprise. He rarely expressed what he was feeling, unlike Daniel.

'Shall we go out for supper at the weekend to celebrate your return to the working world?' he asked. 'We could try that new restaurant that's opened in Dalston.'

'What about the kids?' Life just wasn't the same anymore.

'Jen might babysit if we asked her. Or Mum.'

The thought of having Hope in the house didn't make Edie happy. 'I don't think Hope's such a great idea. She often works in the evenings so the free ones must be precious. Jen'll do it, I'm sure.' She really didn't want to be in debt to Hope any more than she had to be. The more distance she could put between them, the better.

'Whichever you think's best.' He didn't suspect a thing. 'But she loves seeing the girls.'

'Pity she wasn't a bit more careful the last time.' The words slipped out before she thought.

'We've been through this. It could have happened to anyone. You were there too, don't forget.'

'You're not blaming *me*?' She sat straight, her guilt resurfacing.

'Of course not. Don't be so touchy.' He stroked her arm. 'I'm just saying there's no one to blame. Just be a bit more understanding.'

'I'm sorry. Let's forget it.' But she couldn't, not that easily at least – and not for the reasons he thought. 'Could you book the table in the morning? I've an early start again.'

'That would be great. I need to finish this bookcase by the day after because she has house guests.' He brightened. 'Shall we go up?'

After a strenuous day fighting over access arrangements in another case that should never have come to court, Edie was tired.

Hope was already sitting outside the café, iced tea in front of her, observing her surroundings. There was the *pok pok* of tennis balls hitting rackets from the courts behind the building.

'Edie! Hasn't this been a beautiful day?'

Her friendliness threw Edie off course. She hadn't expected that. Hope's nervousness seemed to have gone. Her strength had returned.

'I haven't seen much of it, to be honest.' She'd been stuck in a court room for most of the day.

'Of course, you're probably dying to get home. So, tell me what this is about.'

'I thought we should talk about what happened. At the restaurant.'

The shutters came down on Hope's expression. 'I haven't a lot to say.' She was doing that withdrawal thing she did whenever she didn't want to talk about something. 'Have you?'

'You seemed unhappy. Are you okay?' She remembered Hope's head in her hands, the man's face concerned, unsure.

'I'm fine,' said Hope quickly. 'Nothing to worry about.'

'You know who I was with?'

'The man in the park.' She paused. 'Was it really a business lunch?'

Hope had successfully turned the conversation to put Edie on the back foot, but Edie was prepared. 'I know what it must look like to you, but I can only say that it was a silly flirtation with another barrister. I'll come clean. He made me feel good about myself. You must remember what's it like after having a baby. You don't feel like yourself anymore. Overweight and unsexy. Your husband's caught up in the baby thing just like you and it's hard to remember each other.'

'It's all a long time ago for me.' Though Hope didn't sound unsympathetic.

'Well, take it from me, then.' She heard from the almost imperceptible intake of breath that she'd crossed a line. 'Listen. I'm sorry. I really am. But what I'm trying to tell you is that I made a massive mistake, even though it got no further than the flirting stage.' She dug her nails into her palm till they hurt. 'I know where my priorities lie.'

'Which is where?'

How had Hope managed to canter up onto the moral high ground so quickly?

'With Paul, of course. That's what I wanted to say to you. I know we don't always see eye to eye . . .'

'I wish that weren't true.' Hope was staring at her glass as she stirred her tea with the long spoon. Round and round, ice cubes chinking.

If only she'd stop interrupting.

'Whatever it was, is over. And I hope we can put it behind us all and move on. I don't want Paul to know and I don't want anything to upset my family. And, of course, you're part of that.'

How she sometimes wished it were otherwise, Edie thought to herself.

'Thank you.' Hope looked up at her.

Edie could hear the effort Hope was making to be conciliatory. But of course she was. She had something she wanted kept secret too. Who was that man? Hope's distracted behaviour suggested something wasn't quite right. But would she confide in Edie now Edie had put her cards on the table?

'I appreciate you telling me and, of course, I won't say anything to Paul. I've other things on my plate.' There was an unexpected catch in her voice as she handed Edie what might be an opening.

'Can I help?'

She gave a short laugh. 'I don't think so, but thanks for offering. There's nothing anyone can do but me. Tell me, how are the girls?' She was trying to sound everyday cheery, but Edie could tell she was covering something up.

'They're good, thrilled to have Jen back I suspect. She's so wonderful with them.'

'I'm pleased.' But she didn't make the expected remark about how she'd never had a nanny, how she loved being at home, being a mum. She seemed strangely deflated.

They chatted on for a little longer before they left. Edie went home exasperated but curious. What was it Hope was hiding? Had Hope believed her? The thought landed uncomfortably. Was there still a chance that she'd say something to Paul? A mother will do anything to stop her child being hurt. That much Edie knew.

15

Hope sat on her sofa, feet up, head back against the cushions. She didn't believe Edie's story for a second. The little she had observed of her and her 'colleague' that lunchtime had far from suggested they were a couple in the throes of breaking up. Quite the reverse. Edie had seemed on top of the world, her eyes bright and her voice pitched high with excitement even when she stood up to greet Hope. But what could Hope say about that now? She could hardly accuse her of something that Edie had denied, and the last thing she wanted to do was upset Paul or disrupt his family if she was in the wrong. Besides, as she had told Edie, she had other things to think about.

Meeting Patrick had left her drained and anxious. Never had she experienced such an array of feelings in such rapid succession. She had been overwhelmed to meet the son she had never expected to see again. She'd wanted to embrace him, and yet ... He was a stranger. Then, telling him her story had shone too bright a light on the past. Over the intervening years, she had almost managed to pretend to herself that certain things had never happened. But, of course, she had never forgotten him. At odd times, the memories of his birth and those few weeks they had together would suddenly hit her like a sledgehammer and she would resort to getting out his little teddy for comfort. She would sit and wonder where he was, what his life was like. And what had seemed like the right, the most selfless thing to do back then twisted into the most selfish act of all. She had deprived Patrick of his real family. She had deprived a father of his son, and Paul of his brother.

How could she possibly make amends?

She went over and over the little she had gleaned from Patrick. He had said his adoptive parents had been the best any child or parent could hope for. They had made him part of their family and he had grown up knowing he was loved and supported. But not by her, his birth mother. Although she was eternally grateful to the Marchants for what they had given Patrick, she couldn't help the jealousy that seeped through her. She had so many unasked questions, ones that only occurred to her now.

Bloater, the fat tabby she had adopted from a rescue centre, strolled in and jumped up beside her. He circled until he found the space he wanted then settled himself, kneading the cushions first before squashing himself as close to her as he could get. The rumble of his purr was calming and she absent-mindedly ran her hand over his back.

'What the hell am I going to do, Bloater?'

Bloater had no answers. He purred more loudly.

'How am I going to explain to Paul that I separated him

from Patrick? Never gave him the chance to grow up with an older brother instead of being an only child.'

She stopped stroking the cat. Patrick wanted to meet his new family, his birth family. Who could blame him? He claimed he wanted nothing from them, just to be acknowledged by the family that was his. She wouldn't – couldn't – stop him, but he had agreed to take it slowly.

She got up and went to the professional kitchen at the street side of the house where she could always find something to do that would soothe her. Cooking was often her best thinking time. She pulled out ingredients and began making the chocolate mousses for the following day's supper. The familiar movements lulled her. The comforting smell of melting chocolate soon filled the room as she whipped and stirred and filled nine cocktail glasses. Always one extra, just in case something went wrong.

She desperately needed to see Patrick again to ask all the questions she hadn't had the chance to ask. Was he married? Children? What did he do for a living? It was incredible that she had failed to establish even the most basic facts about him. But before getting another opportunity, she would have to decide what to do about his father. She owed it to Patrick to tell him who he was, but it meant overturning another man's life after all this time. Was that the right thing to do? If she didn't, though, Patrick might take the reins into his own hands. She had to keep control of this, and that meant confessing. Somehow, she would have to find the right words.

Going into her own kitchen, she found Bloater miaowing

for food. 'Bloater! Tell me what to do.' She poured some dried food into his bowl.

The cat ate a little then wandered past her, tail in the air, out of the doors into the garden.

'Well, if you won't tell me, then I'll have to talk to someone else.'

Vita came over in the morning to help with a dinner for the Melroses, returning customers. When she arrived, Hope took her out into the garden to sit in the sun for a few moments before the working day began.

'Jesus! You look terrible. What's up?'

'I didn't get much sleep.' Hope poured coffee, jug chinking against the cups. In the broad light of day, talking to Vita didn't seem quite the bright idea it had been the day before.

'Hey! Sit down. I can see something's happened.' She patted the seat beside her.

'It certainly has.'

'And you don't know how to tell me, right? So, try starting at the beginning ... If you can't tell me, you can't tell anyone.'

Hope began uncertainly, but when Vita didn't immediately react with shock, horror or recrimination, she gained confidence and told her everything there was to tell: the sex at seventeen, the disapproving parents, the institution for disgraced girls, the birth of Patrick, his adoption – the whole sorry story. She felt her voice catching at various points as the emotion of reliving her past became too much for her.

167

Eventually, she stopped. Her coffee was cold, and Vita sat transfixed. For a moment or two they sat in silence, neither of them sure what to say next. Eventually, Vita broke the silence. 'Wow! I wasn't expecting that. What a story. And you never told a soul! You poor thing.'

'I honestly believed I was doing the right thing at the time.'

'I can see why. But, God! So hard.' She shook her head as if trying to get her thoughts to settle down. 'Any chance of another coffee? And a biscuit or two?'

'I'll get them.' Hope couldn't help smiling. Food was their answer to any problem. It was cool in the kitchen, although the light was already bouncing off the zinc surfaces. She opened the biscuit cupboard while waiting for the kettle to boil and picked out the jar of oat, orange and sultana cookies that Vita loved plus the chocolate and mint brownies she had trialled for a class a couple of days earlier.

Back in the garden, with the tray safely on the table, Vita stood up and gave Hope a warm, enveloping hug. Hope closed her eyes, yielding to her friend's sympathy. Squashed against Vita's capacious bosom, she felt that perhaps, just perhaps, everything would be all right. But as soon as Vita released her, doubts flooded back in.

They took their seats while Vita poured. With a biscuit in her hand, she stretched out her legs so the sun could reach them. 'So, who is he?'

'Who?'

'The father, of course.'

'Don't. You know I can't tell you.' The tea was comforting.

'I don't see why not.'

'Just because!'

Vita crunched a biscuit. 'Okay, don't tell me, but you know what you have to do. Paul has to hear he has a brother from you.'

'I'm too frightened to tell him. What will he think?'

Vita reached for another biscuit. 'No one said it would be easy. He'll be shocked, that's for sure, but I'll be here to pick up the pieces if you need me.'

'This is going to be hardest thing I've ever done.' Not even the blousy brightness of the garden gave her the usual pleasure in that moment.

'But you can do it. And like I say, if I can help, I will. Now, didn't you say Edie was in that restaurant, too?'

'Yes, with the man from the park, I told you about. Then she phoned, insisting we meet, and I didn't feel I could say no. Things are difficult enough between us. She just wanted to tell me it was a flirtation, nothing more, and that it was absolutely over now. Imagine going out of your way to tell your mother-in-law that! Why would you? Why would I ever trust her now?'

'She's running scared.' Vita nodded sagely. 'Do you believe her?'

'Honestly? I don't think I do. But I haven't really dwelt on it, what with everything else going on.'

'Well, I think you should take a step back and leave them to it. Sort out your own situation first.'

'But Paul . . .'

'He's a grown-up, for heaven's sake. His own marriage is his own business.' Vita was a great advocate for keeping out of their children's affairs – too much so, Hope sometimes thought.

Hope looked to the sky, feeling the sun on her neck. 'Oh, God.'

'You know you'll have to tell Patrick's father before Patrick finds him. Because, sooner or later, he will.'

'I know. I wish I'd thought of that before I met him. But when I got his letter, I couldn't say no.'

Vita stood up, signalling they had talked enough. Vita looked at her watch. 'Hadn't we better get on with tonight's supper for the Melroses?'

Hope felt shattered, but work would distract her. Her life might be a car crash, but she would still produce the best meal possible for her clients.

The following morning, she summoned her courage. The longer she left it, the more difficult it would become. Returning to the living room, she picked up her phone, closed her eyes for a moment, inhaled deeply and brought up Paul's number.

Edie answered. 'Hope?' She sounded preoccupied.

'I'm just trying to get hold of Paul.'

'He's getting Betty up. Not urgent, is it?'

Hope gripped her phone tighter. 'No, no. Perhaps ask him to call me later. That would be great.'

'Can't I give him a message?'

'Who is it?' She heard Paul in the background.

'It's your mum.'

Paul took over the phone, breathless. 'Hi Mum, you've just caught me. We're all in a bit of a rush this morning. Running late.'

'I know but I'm wondering if I could see you. There's something I need to tell you.'

'Fire away. I'm intrigued, but make it quick.'

'I can't do it over the phone. I need to see you.' *And not with Edie listening in.*

'Mum, are you all right?' He sounded concerned. 'You're not ill, are you?'

'No I'm—'

'Is something wrong?' Edie asked in the background.

'No, I'm not ill, nothing like that.' She made herself sound much cheerier than she felt.

'You're worrying me now. Has something happened?'

She knew he would come round straight away if she really needed him. But why make this worse than it was already? The news she was going to share had waited his whole life. Another day or two wouldn't make any difference.

'No, no. Honestly, it's nothing like that. Give me a call when you've got time and we'll fix something. Don't worry in the meantime.'

At the end of the call, Hope felt wobbly. She sat still for a while, staring out at the street but not seeing it, lost in the past. Eventually she made herself go downstairs and give Bloater his breakfast. She didn't feel as if she could ever eat anything again, but a strong coffee was definitely in order. Accompanied by the sound of the cat pushing his dry food round the plate, she got out the coffee grinder and began the process, at the same time thinking of what needed doing before her bakery class arrived at ten. This morning it was to be Victoria sponge and chocolate and mint biscuits: at least that would be plain sailing.

16

As they walked along the hotel corridor, Daniel took Edie's hand. The old spark ignited between them, the secrecy of their meeting only adding to the thrill. They had entered the hotel at different times, Daniel waiting for her on the fourth floor by the lift where she'd appeared a few minutes later. They had embraced but had yet to speak; they both knew what they were doing.

Edie was excited but nervous. Although deep down, she knew that what she was doing was wrong, she had convinced herself that it was right too. If this made her happy then she would be a happier person at home for Paul and the kids. It was better for all of them.

The hotel wasn't too far from their chambers, but far enough away and down a narrow lane that no colleagues would be strolling along to spot them. The small foyer was plush and discreet. No one raised an eyebrow at them booking a room for an afternoon.

Daniel took the key card out of its paper wallet and inserted it into the lock, cursing when the door didn't open. Edie felt an overwhelming urge to laugh. The door swung open on his second try, admitting them to a short corridor, bathroom on the right, wardrobe on the left. The door had hardly shut before they fell on each other – kissing, touching, unbuttoning, unzipping, removing each other's clothes as they stumbled towards the bed.

Afterwards, Edie lay stretched out among the tangled sheets, replete. Nothing, not childbirth, motherhood or marriage, had managed to put a halt on the pleasure the two of them had always shared. This, out of everything, had never changed. Daniel took control, was physical and demanding, so different from Paul. She couldn't bring herself to hurt Paul by asking him to change.

Daniel was over at the other side of the room, looking in the mini bar. Physically, he wasn't a match for Paul. His hair was receding now, and he wasn't as fit as he once was, but he made the most of what he had. He turned round. 'Fizz?' he asked, brandishing a small bottle.

'Just a glass.' She stretched her arms above her head.

'We'll be lucky to get more than that out of this.' He smiled as he returned to the bed with the small bottle and two glasses.

She untwisted the sheet and pulled it up to her armpits.

'Now you look like some kind of Victorian matriarch,' he joked as he sat down, poured out their glasses and handed one to her.

'How would you know?' The champagne trickled easily down her throat.

'My imagination.' He got in beside her and manoeuvred his arm round her shoulder. 'I've plenty of that.'

'Pretty inventive, I'd say.'

'But you like it?' He sounded confident of her reply.

'You know I do. Otherwise, I wouldn't be here.' She looked at her watch. 'I should get ready to go. I thought I had the whole afternoon free but a four-thirty meeting has dropped in. Another warring couple.'

'So soon? I thought we might . . .' He put down his glass and snaked his arm under the sheets until his hand was on her breast.

She shifted her position so the pressure of his touch was less painful.

'Next time. I really mustn't be late, although I'd love to stay.'

'I wish we'd never split up in the first place, then we wouldn't be in this position.' He swept his hair back with both hands.

'I feel so torn. I keep making up my mind and then unmaking it, which is so unlike me. Can we really go on like this? With all the lying, the deceit, the damage.'

'I don't know how else we can have a relationship.'

'I always thought when I got married it would be for better or for worse.'

'We should have married, us two.' He took her hand and looked at her wedding and engagement rings. 'I want a life with you.'

'We were too young and ambitious, but I wish we had too.'

'We still could.'

Edie looked at him in astonishment. This was the first

time either of them had even touched on the idea of a proper future together – something she would like more than anything. Except . . .

'The children. I've seen so many messed about by divorcing parents. We can't do that.'

'Can't we? Not all of them are. Depends on the parents. You only see the worst cases. Will you think about it?'

'I'll think about it.' If only she dared.

She showered quickly, his words ringing in her ears. While she got dressed, he followed suit. As he was doing up his tie, she kissed him. 'I'll leave first.'

He returned the kiss. 'Again, soon?'

'Again, soon. When we can.' In the corridor, the guilt came whirling back. If she was caught here . . . She almost ran towards the stairs by the lifts. It wasn't until she was out in the street, on her way to the Tube, that she breathed more easily. If anyone saw her now, they would suspect nothing. As the escalator in the Tube station carried her down, she allowed herself a small smile. Could Daniel have been serious when he suggested they might have a life together? In her wildest dreams, she couldn't think of anything she'd like more. But at what cost?

After an emotional meeting in which her client, a woman whose husband had kicked her out of the marital home and was refusing to pay maintenance, was sobbing in desperation as to how to get him to play fair, Edie went for a quick drink with a couple of colleagues. She had begun her networking again, deliberately showing her peers and seniors how committed she was to the profession, hoping one day to be voted onto the committee of the Family Law Bar Association.

Eventually she was on her way home, drifting on a cloud, remembering Daniel's words. Had he been serious? He had seemed so. Was it really a possibility? Now he had put the idea into her head, she couldn't dismiss it.

She found Ana on the doorstep, about to ring her bell.

'Hey! What are you doing here? How was Italy?'

'Amazing. I found some beautiful things, but I'll show you photographs. I've come to collect your blue and silver dress. Remember? I'm going to the Women in Business Awards and you said I could borrow it.'

'Of course.' She had completely forgotten. 'In fact, you can have it. It's much too small for me now. I wore it when Paul proposed . . .'

'Well, there's no worries about my putting it through that experience again! But are you sure?'

'Of course. It looks great on you. And I was going to call you to tell you everything's ready for the party. I've done everything we agreed.'

'And the replies are coming in. Thanks a million. I couldn't have organized it without you.'

Edie was too late home to make the children's supper but, once she'd packed off Ana with the dress, she would at least read Betty's last bedtime story. While the two friends chatted, Jen had been finishing bath time. Edie could hear them all laughing upstairs.

'What's this mermaid doing swimming here?' Jen's voice carried down to her. 'What's this?'

'Cwocadile,' yelled Betty. 'Help!' Then she screamed with excited laughter.

Eventually Jen brought both children down, warm and snuggly in their Disney pyjamas ready for bed. Once she had left for the night, Edie curled up on the sofa with them. Hazel was half asleep, content to lie and look at what was going on, but once the door had shut behind Jen, Betty became fractious and within a minute of settling down wanted a different book. 'No Gruffalo. Peppa Pig.' Without warning, her objection suddenly morphed into a full-blown tantrum and she threw the book Edie was about to read on to the floor. Nothing Edie said or did would calm her down. She felt like screaming herself. Surely motherhood wasn't meant to be this difficult? She was sure Betty didn't behave like this with Jen. She and Hope had a magic touch that eluded Edie.

'Let me take over,' said Paul, gauging the situation in a flash as he came in. 'I have to go over to Mum's tonight, but I'll put her to bed.'

As soon as Betty saw him, she stretched her arms out to him and her yells became injured whimpers. Edie had never felt less loved.

'You're going out?' She was dismayed. So much for the crab linguine she had been planning to cook for them. Guilt food.

'I know.' He lifted up Betty and kissed her cheek while she wrapped her hands in his hair, head on his shoulder.

'Apparently, it's important. God knows what. She wouldn't say. Come on, kids, you should be in bed.'

'Just the two of you?' She didn't like the idea of that. Could Hope be about to spill the beans, after all? 'Couldn't she come here? Then I can hear, too.'

He looked surprised by her suggestion. 'She wants to see me on her own. I don't know why.' He angled Betty downwards so she could kiss her mother. 'Say goodnight.'

'There's no way she's going to go to sleep now.' Betty seemed to have found a renewed burst of energy with Paul's arrival. 'But Hope could just as easily come here.' Edie repeated the suggestion, already realizing it was a lost cause, but the thought of the two of them together made her uneasy.

'Nope. Not going to happen. She was absolutely adamant. I'll tell you all when I get back.' Why don't you take Hazel up first then, and I can have five minutes with Bets?'

Edie looked down at the baby in her lap, breathing in the sweet smell of her head, a scent guaranteed to make her feel calmer. 'All right. Though five minutes might be pushing it. I'll be as quick as I can.'

The moment she put Hazel down in her cot, the baby's eyes flew open, but despite a moment of panic that she was going to wake up, Edie managed to send her off, hand on chest, shushing and patting her.

When she eventually got downstairs, Betty ran up to her. 'Apple please!' It was as if the earlier drama hadn't happened.

'I did say she could.' Paul put Betty's doll back in its tiny buggy.

'Oh, Paul.' Edie looked down at him. 'What's the point in making a rule if you undermine it?'

'I don't know what you mean.' He leaned back in his chair, showing off his favourite Nick Cave and the Bad Seeds T-shirt – faded from so much wear.

'I've always said they shouldn't eat after supper otherwise she'll know she can get away without eating that.'

'Did I know that?'

'Apple.' Betty grabbed her sleeve.

'Not now.' Edie stroked her daughter's curly blonde hair and repeated her ultimatum, watching Betty's upturned chin begin to wobble, her expression turn from expectation to fury.

'Can't you just relax a bit?' Paul reached towards the fruit bowl. 'For a quiet life.'

'Don't you dare!' Edie smacked his hand. 'If you don't do what you say, then you shouldn't say it. Kids need boundaries.'

Betty looked from one to other of them, bewildered. Her lower lip began to turn down as she burst into loud sobs.

'For God's sake! Such a small thing.' Incomprehension and anger stained his voice. 'I'd better go.'

'Yes, why don't you? Leave me with your children and go home to your mum.'

His shocked expression told her everything about what he was feeling. 'I don't deserve that.'

'I'm sorry. I didn't mean it.'

'You did,' he said, angry. 'And you're right, I'd better

go. I won't be late back, and I hope you'll be in a better mood by then.'

'I'm really sorry. Long day.' She spoke so softly she was barely heard over Betty's wails. *Don't fight in front of the children* – another of their rules had been broken.

'Daddy! Stay!' Betty's plea as she ran round the table to her father was agonized, and shocked Edie. At least Hazel was sound asleep upstairs.

Paul bent over his eldest daughter and kissed her. 'I have to go, baby. Granny wants me for something. Be good for Mummy. Don't cry, now.' He raised his eyes to Edie who saw the sadness in his expression.

'I'll have supper waiting, and we can talk,' Edie suggested.

'I'll probably eat with her. She'll have made something.'

'Okay.' A baked potato for her, then.

Calm was being restored, but Edie recognized that they were pushing issues under the rug where they would lie, not quite forgotten, but ignored and festering until the time was right for them to emerge and cause more damage.

He prised a still howling Betty off him and stood her by Edie. 'See you later.'

Edie reached for his hand and squeezed it, but he didn't squeeze back. As soon as he was out of the door, she turned to Betty. 'Please, stop. Please. What about a story?'

'Daaaa-ddy!' She was inconsolable.

But Edie had to console her, so she picked her up and gave her an apple. She was so exhausted, she didn't even know anymore. What had Paul said? *'For a quiet life.'*

'Noooo!'

The apple landed on the ground with a thud.

'Oh for God's sake! Come on, Bets. You can choose a story. And you can have some bed-time milk.'

To her surprise, Betty's sobs turned to snivels as she turned towards the shelf of books they kept in the kitchen. Edie put her down and made herself a quick cup of tea. By the time she turned back, it was to find her tear-stained daughter with a bitten-into apple in one hand and a Peppa Pig board book in the other.

Edie didn't know whether to laugh or cry.

'Peppa Pig it is then,' she said, sagging inside, but took the book from her and led the way, Betty following her to the living room where they snuggled up on the sofa together and Edie started to read.

17

At the sound of the doorbell, Hope ran upstairs. Paul stood on her doorstep, grinning, when she opened the front door.

'Good to see you.' She hugged him, hoping this wouldn't be the last moment of such closeness between them. Since Patrick's appearance, this was one of the things that had preyed most on her mind. How much would her revelation test their bond?

'So, what's up?' Gently, he pushed back her shoulders so that he could see her face. 'You've got me worried.'

'Come down, so we can talk.' Her heart contracted at the thought of telling him the whole story.

Paul followed her down the stairs to her kitchen where she took out a bottle of wine from the fridge. Two glasses were already on a tray on the island. She put cheese straws (always very popular with her classes) into a bowl, all the time exchanging chit chat about the girls. She wanted to hear if Betty was fully recovered, whether Hazel was crawling, all the news. Eventually, they went out into the garden, where they sat on the cushioned chairs under the pergola at the far end. They put everything on the table between them.

'Go on, then. Why am I here?'

'Just a minute.' She poured them both a glass of wine then closed her eyes and composed herself.

'Mum, please. You're making me anxious.'

The touch of his hand on her arm made her open her eyes. There was no going back now. 'This is something that happened a very long time ago, before you were born.'

'Then why the urgency? What is it?'

She raised a hand to silence him. He sat back in his chair, waiting.

'You need to understand that times were very different then. Where I grew up in Cornwall was pretty remote.' *Come on, Hope*, she said to herself. *Get to the point.* 'When I was in my teens . . . I became pregnant.'

He leant forward. 'Oh, Mum.'

But she didn't want his sympathy – she didn't deserve it. 'You remember Gran and Grandad, what strict Catholics they were?'

'Of course. We used to joke about how you could set your clock by them on Sundays.'

They both smiled.

'And what staunch members of the church they were?' she said. 'How much store they put on their beliefs and how outward appearances mattered so much to them?'

'Are you saying you never told them?' He looked puzzled.

'Oh, no. I had to, of course.' And so she began the same story that she had shared with Patrick just a few days earlier. As she spoke, Paul's expression changed from sympathy to near disbelief. When she finished, the silence seemed to go on forever.

'So, what you're saying is that I have a half-brother ... somewhere?' Clearly, he could hardly get the words out. He shook his head. 'But why haven't you told me before? And why now?'

'He's been in touch.' She put her hand over her pounding heart. She read puzzlement and confusion in her second son's expression. If she didn't press on now, she never would. 'I honestly never thought that I'd hear from him. Especially after all this time. I imagined and hoped he was happy in the life I'd given him.'

'My God, Mum. How are you feeling?' So typical of him to think of her first. She was grateful.

'Reeling. As shocked as you must be, I guess.'

'But didn't you ever want to find out what happened to him?'

'Of course I wanted to. Especially when he was so tiny. I prayed a kind family had taken him in. A family who wanted him and who could give him what I didn't think I could – a decent life. I could have tried to find him once he was eighteen, but as the years passed I didn't want to cause any more trauma. He might not have known he was adopted, or if he did know, suppose he'd rejected me? I couldn't have borne that. Besides, I didn't even know where he was.'

'You could have found out.' He turned his glass on the table, round and round.

'Perhaps I didn't really want to. By then my life was so

different with you and Martin. Knowing where he was and not being able to see him might have been worse. He's only tracked me down now because his mum died.'

'His mum?' He looked confused.

'All right, his adoptive mother.' But that sounded so formal and so far away from the close mother–son relationship they had clearly enjoyed. The relationship she had been forced to forfeit. She couldn't bear the accusation in Paul's voice. He could have no conception of the agony, the self-doubt and depression she had suffered in those early years. He would never understand how hard she had to work to distract herself and continue with her life. At first, she had convinced herself that if she worked hard enough, she might be able to support Patrick when she got him back – but the adoption agency had made it quite clear there was no chance of that. Her baby had gone for good. 'As the years went by, he became part of my past and not my present,' she explained. 'That may sound shocking and, of course, I never ever forgot him, but other things, like you …'

She attempted a conciliatory smile. He didn't return it.

' … took precedence. I pushed him to the back of my mind. I know that must be hard to understand – I don't really understand it myself. Self-protection perhaps. But then I had you – and you were all I wanted. You made up for everything. You were enough.'

A cloud passed over the sun, and for a moment Hope felt its warmth diminish. She watched a plump pigeon forage for nuts under the bird feeder as she waited nervously for Paul's reaction.

Eventually he spoke. 'What about his father? Who is he?'

He was bound to ask. Everyone would when they knew about Patrick. But it was the hardest question for her to answer. 'It's complicated. I'm not ready to talk about him yet. I'm sorry.'

'Doesn't Patrick . . .' He said the name as if it was a new taste that he was trying out. 'Doesn't he want to find him too?'

'Yes, of course he does. He wants to find all his birth family.'

'You mean, me as well?' He took a large swallow of his wine.

'Yes.'

'Then surely you owe it to him?' said Paul, puzzled. 'You can't keep a secret like this for so long and then only give up half the answers.'

'Maybe not.'

'And meanwhile, what about us? Suddenly Betty and Hazel have an uncle we never knew about. Maybe cousins too? Think how different our lives might have been if we'd got to know him sooner.'

She had expected Paul to be hurt, but not judgemental. He made the situation seem so black and white. Tears welled in her eyes.

'Please, don't cry.' He passed her one of the paper napkins on the tray. 'Tell me what he's like? Would I like him?'

She blew her nose. 'I think so, but I hardly know him myself.'

'Do you want to?'

'I don't know yet. You're my priority here, and I know this must all come as a massive shock.'

'Understatement of the decade.' His hands were motionless on the tabletop now. The cheese straws were left untouched.

'Paul, his turning up has been a bombshell for me, too. I was pushed by my own mother into giving him up for adoption when I didn't know what else to do. Now, I don't know the right way to make up for it. I don't even know if I can. All the decisions back then were made for me. I was told it was the only possible thing. I was only seventeen, terribly immature. I knew no better. You have to believe that. Of course, now I've had to re-evaluate everything and see that perhaps things could have been done differently. But they weren't, and I have to live with that.'

'Did you and Gran not talk about it? Later, I mean.' His brow furrowed.

A neighbour's black and white cat meandered through the garden, as confident as if he had been invited. Bloater shot out from behind a bush, hair bristling, tail aloft, and chased him off with a yowl. For once Hope ignored him.

'Never. She boxed up the whole episode, stashed it away somewhere she couldn't reach, and never referred to it ever again. Clearly, the shame she felt over the whole episode was overwhelming. I had let the family down and she thought of herself as complicit, I suppose. I don't think that she even told Dad. Extraordinary as that may seem. He certainly never mentioned it and, if I ever tried to bring it up with her, she would give me the death-stare. Remember the death-stare?'

Paul had been as intimidated as she had been by the stern we're-not-taking-this-any-further look her mother was so capable of. 'But, of course, I couldn't forget him. I'd looked after him for three weeks before he was taken, remember.'

'Oh, Mum. That's so cruel. Why did they make you?' His attempt to understand meant much to her.

'I don't know. I suppose that's what the mother and baby homes did if there wasn't a couple waiting. Who else was there to look after the babies except the mothers?' She felt her eyes brim with tears again. She could remember the screaming and wailing that accompanied the removal of a child from its mother. She blinked hard to hold the tears back. Crying was so useless and stupid and only made this harder for Paul than it already was.

He poured himself another glass of wine. 'A brother. I always wanted a brother.'

Startled, she looked at him. 'Did you? I don't remember you ever saying that before.' Hadn't they been a perfect little unit until she and Martin went their separate ways?

Martin had wanted another child to run around the fields with Paul, making camps in the woods, learning the ways of the farm. But she couldn't bring herself to have another. She didn't have any more love left to share when so much was tied up not only in Paul but in the child no one knew about. And she felt culpable. At the beginning, Paul had merely reminded her of the baby she didn't have. Patrick. Whenever Paul hit a milestone – cutting his first tooth, crawling, taking his first steps, his first word – she was reminded of the baby who was no longer hers. The baby she had never seen grow up. She had always felt brutally torn between the son she had, and the one she didn't.

'Well, I did,' said Paul, with a regretful smile. 'Don't all children want what they don't have? It won't be long before Betty and Hazel want a brother, too.'

'Another one?' She failed to hide her surprise. 'You're not going to, are you?'

'Who knows. I'd love a boy as well. Edie's just back at work and doesn't want another right now, but one day maybe ... We still have time. But Patrick and you are way more important right now.'

She was relieved to hear him sound more conciliatory, as if he was coming round to the idea of a new brother's arrival in their lives.

'Will you keep all this to yourself for the moment, though? I'll have to tell your dad first, and it needs to come from me.' That was going to be even harder than telling Paul. Martin would naturally see it as a monumental betrayal. All those years together with a secret unshared. The truth would change his view of her and of what she was capable. She still minded that.

'Yes, of course. What will Dad say, I wonder?' He pondered for a moment. 'I don't think Edie and I could ever keep such a big secret from one another. You and your mother certainly knew how to. Everything's out in the open with us.'

Hope could say nothing to vindicate herself. Instead, she only thought about Edie and how she was, or almost certainly had been, deceiving him. However much she was tempted to say something about her suspicions, she held back. Their marriage was something she shouldn't involve herself in however much she wanted to protect Paul. Vita was right. Some things were better left unsaid.

'As for Patrick's father,' he went on. 'What's going to happen there? I bet he'll be upset. Fancy not telling him you were pregnant, Mum.'

'He wasn't interested,' she said. 'He'd moved on.'

'Even so. Won't he be devastated to find he's got a child he didn't know about?'

More than you can possibly know, she reflected.

'But life isn't always so cut and dried. When something you've hardly imagined actually happens to you, things can seem very different. The people, the situation, the time, the beliefs – all sorts of things contribute to a decision.'

'But you were seventeen, Mum. Shouldn't Gran have respected what you wanted?'

'Times were very different then and all I wanted was the best for the baby. We agreed on what that was, however painful.' She felt their conversation had gone as far as it could for now. When he had absorbed the situation and perhaps even met Patrick, she would try to answer his questions again.

'So how are you going to put things right now?' He gazed at her, as if he was seeing a person he didn't recognize.

She couldn't blame him.

'In the best way I can.'

18

Edie had just finished painting her toenails when Paul returned. In the end, she had succeeded in getting Betty to bed without more upset. To reward herself, and to take her mind off whatever Paul might be discussing with his mother, she had run herself a bath and lain there soaking and listening to her Bach Spotify playlist. Her toes were the final touch.

Paul, usually so complimentary, barely glanced at what she was doing. He was the colour of putty as he walked past her, straight to the drinks' cupboard. She looked on, amazed, as he pulled out the whisky bottle and a glass. They never drank spirits, apart from at Christmas. He poured a shot and downed it in one, banging the empty glass on the top of the cupboard.

'Paul?' She had never seen him like this. There could only be one explanation. More fool her for trusting Hope. Her mother-in-law's priority was Paul's happiness, though why she would think telling him about Daniel would contribute to that was baffling. She braced herself.

He took the seat opposite her, putting his head in his hands.

'What's happened?' Her stomach was rolling. She would never forgive Hope for this.

'I can't get my head round it.' He stood again and went to pour himself another whisky, this time returning to his chair with the glass, putting it on the pile of magazines on the coffee table.

Edie's instinct was telling her to leave the room, but she felt paralysed. Paul finally raised his head so that she could see his face. His eyes were red-rimmed with un-shed tears.

'She has another child. A son.' The words fell like pebbles into a pond. 'Can you believe that?'

This was so unexpected, Edie sat up to attention, her toe-nails forgotten. 'Who has?'

'Mum.'

There was a beat while she tried to absorb the full meaning of what he had just said. 'Hope?'

'I only have one mum.' He ran his hand down the arm of the chair.

She must have misunderstood, but she tried to link up the words in her mind. 'You're saying you have a brother you didn't know anything about?'

He picked up his glass. 'Apparently so. Can you imagine anyone keeping a secret like that for so long? Mum most of all.'

'But I don't understand. Who is he? What's made her tell you now?'

'Because he's been in touch with her, and they've met. He wants to meet us.' He didn't sound keen on the idea.

Edie's head was spinning with the news. Then . . .

That man in the restaurant!

193

She flashed back to the man who upset Hope and made her act so shiftily. *That must be him. He wasn't a lover at all.*

She had seen him, knew what he looked like. Guilt stabbed at her, remembering her illicit lunch with Daniel and how easily she had dropped her resolution to break up with him. She couldn't possibly tell Paul of the chance encounter with his mother and half-brother.

'But who's his father?' she asked instead.

'Some guy she met when she was seventeen. She wouldn't tell me more than that.'

'Perhaps she doesn't know. Perhaps there was more than one.' The irony of Hope shielding as big a secret as Edie's appealed to her.

'I doubt it. You never met her parents. They would never have given her the chance to sleep around. They were so strict.'

'There's always a window you can climb out of, or a lie to tell about where you've been. Teenage girls are world experts on breaking rules. I was one once, remember?'

He managed a brief smile. 'When it comes to Betty and Hazel, I'm going to be the most jealous dad in history. Doors and windows will be barred.' He crossed his arms in front of him.

They both laughed. 'I know you will,' she said. 'But there's always a way.'

'This means that the girls have an uncle. You have a brother-in-law. We're his family.' He sounded stupefied.

Edie got up and went to sit on the arm of his chair, reaching to hold his hand, enjoying its familiarity, the roughness of it. Having absorbed the announcement, she could relax, grateful that Hope had kept her word. At least none of this drama was about Daniel.

'If he really is who he says he is, perhaps we should be excited,' she said. 'A new uncle for the girls – a brother for you.'

'For a minute I was excited, but now I'm not so sure.' He put his arm around her waist. 'She asked me not to say anything to anyone, not even you. Pfff!' The sound showed how preposterous it was to suggest that he kept a secret from Edie. 'As if I could keep it from you. But she wants to tell dad and Patrick's father first.'

His trust in her made her feel awful that she couldn't say the same for herself but her secret had to stay that way. The thought of Daniel and herself twined together in the dim light of their hotel bedroom flashed into her mind. She blinked, as if to dislodge it.

'So, she knows how to get in touch with him?' Edie's antennae were on full alert. 'Do you think she still sees him?'

He shrugged. 'Absolutely no idea. I think she's still in touch with one or two of her old Cornish friends. But who knows whether it's one of them?'

'How intriguing. I wonder if your dad knows him.'

'Maybe. But even if he does, he doesn't know that she's got a long-lost son who's turned up out of the blue.'

'So it'll be a big shock for him too?'

'I suppose so.' He was thoughtful for a moment. 'It's not the thought of her having a relationship with someone before she met Dad that upsets me. There's nothing wrong in that.

But how could anyone keep such a secret for so long? I understand the why, but not the how. I suddenly feel as if I don't know her at all.'

'You can't begin to track down a child you've had adopted until they're over eighteen. Even then, you have to do it through an intermediary. I can see why she might not have told you. You might have found it difficult to understand as a child, and then when would be a good moment? Surely Martin must have known something.'

'I don't think so.'

'Let's ask him.' She leant to pick her phone from the table.

He grabbed it from her hand before she had a chance to find his number. 'No, we mustn't. I told you . . . Mum asked me not to tell anyone.'

'She didn't ask me not to,' Edie protested.

'You're hopeless,' he said, tucking the phone under the cushion, raising a hand to stroke her cheek. 'I shouldn't have said anything but I had to. I'm just so shocked.'

'I wonder if there are any more secrets bottled up where this one came from,' mused Edie. She remembered the stranger's pepper-and-salt hair, his air of slight bemusement and, yes, his shorts.

'This one's enough,' said Paul, looking at his watch. 'Hazel's quiet. Do you think we've broken the back of the no sleeping thing?'

'Dream on, sweetheart. But we should go up just in case. Coming? We can carry on talking about this in bed.'

*

She had heard Paul move into the spare room in the middle of the night, and the click of the light. They had talked round in circles about Hope and what had happened until eventually they agreed they should sleep. However, Paul had been restless, so he'd taken himself off, for both their sakes. In the morning, he'd come downstairs looking exhausted but resolved.

'I want to meet him. Last night, I thought I didn't – but now, I do.' He poured himself some tea.

'Shouldn't you take your time? Let yourself absorb the news, work out what you feel?' Edie was checking her emails in case any practice direction notes had come in overnight.

'No, no. I'm absolutely sure. I'll call Mum today. No more secrets.'

But Edie understood keeping secrets. Daniel wasn't the first she had kept. There were others that she had held close to her chest since childhood. From where she hid her mother's favourite gold chain to cheating in exams. And then, perhaps worst of all, the abortion she'd had when she was at university. She had been so frightened of being pregnant, believing that Steve, her boyfriend at the time, wouldn't want to know and, worse, that it could ruin her career chances. She confided in one of her flatmates, who insisted she went straight to the student health centre, even coming with her. That secret had stayed between them. Yes, she knew something at least of what Hope had gone through as a seventeen-year-old but, in Edie's case, an abortion was no big deal. Not really. Just an inconvenience. A couple of friends had been through the same thing. There was simply no room for a baby in her life back then. But Hope had been forced to go through with the pregnancy – that was the difference.

The existence of a child! Another human being. That was huge. And Hope had kept it entirely secret. Even now, she couldn't tell Paul who the father was. The fact that Hope had a past shrouded in shame and mystery fascinated her. At the same time, despite everything, she didn't like to see Paul hurting so badly. She wanted to do what she could to ease his distress, but how she would do that, she didn't yet know.

Arriving at court later, she soon forgot about the problem. The latest case was an appeal made by another man fighting for greater access to his children, where settling out of court looked unlikely. His wife was hurt and angry and rich, like a wild cat fighting for what was hers. Expense was no object to her. She didn't want to give her cheating husband anything and was doing all she could to prevent him from getting anything. That included using Helen Treadwell, one of London's most formidable family barristers. Edie wanted to do her best for the husband, but at the same time she couldn't help thinking of Daniel and what their own decision might involve. She was sure she and Paul would be reasonable and come to a fair agreement over access if they ever took that step. She shocked herself by even having the thought.

On her way home, Edie thanked her lucky stars yet again that she'd been able to find such an excellent and loyal nanny as Jen. Thinking of the expense – not that the cost had anything to do with her – Hope had suggested Edie should find a shared nanny or a nursery, but they weren't enough for Edie. Jen might be expensive, but Edie had to have the flexibility she afforded her. Hope hadn't really got a clue what Edie's work involved. She never knew when or where she might be in court. She also needed to be able to network after work, to attend the meetings and conferences she was called on to do. Apparently Hope had managed with a series of local girls earning pocket money who were prepared to look after Paul on an *ad hoc* basis. That wasn't the right solution for Edie and Paul, especially during the nursery holidays. Jen made Edie's life possible. Employing her gave the children the routine they needed, and the freedom Edie craved. She gave Edie the illusion of there being some control in their lives.

Knowing that Jen was staying late that evening gave Edie time to meet Ana. They had spoken briefly at lunchtime and agreed to meet in a wine bar at Kings Cross.

Edie walked up Kings Boulevard. Behind the hoarding on her right, huge white cranes reared skywards, towering over an office building that was under construction. To her left, shops beckoned her with displays of all the things she hadn't needed during the past year ... Designer clothes, make-up, fancy trainers. She hovered outside Space NK but then forced herself to go on so she wouldn't be late. She crossed the bridge over the canal, past all the people sitting on the Astro-turfed steps down to the water, past the kids playing in the waterjets shooting from the ground in Granary Square, and eventually spotted Ana sitting at an outside table at the Brasserie, two glasses of wine in front of her as per.

Sitting down opposite her friend, Edie was aware of the contrast they made – she in her forbidding black work suit, pristine white shirt; Ana in a floaty summer dress that she'd probably liberated from the store's stock room.

'At last, I thought you were never coming.' Ana put down her phone. 'I decided to order anyway. Cheers.'

Edie took off her jacket and lifted her glass. 'Cheers. So what's the news?'

'I'm going to Paris for the weekend. How romantic is that?' Ana was talking about her latest conquest.

'Who with?' Edie couldn't keep up with Ana's liaisons.

'Gerry. The CEO of Samuel Taylor Barton. Didn't I tell you about him? He's adorable . . . and great sex.'

'You probably did. I'm jealous. What wouldn't I give for a weekend in Paris.' A weekend with Daniel when there'd be no rush to get home and no danger of being found out. Food, sex and fun. Heaven.

'Why don't you ask Paul to take you?'

'On his salary?' Edie laughed, pretending not to feel the slow simmering resentment she sometimes felt when she thought about how responsible she was for the family finances. 'You're joking.'

'At least you've kicked Daniel into touch. Well done.'

Edie looked out at the kids racing through the fountains in the square. 'Yes, I can concentrate on Paul now.'

That familiar ripple of guilt ran through Edie. She didn't

want to lie to her best friend, but if that was the only way she could continue her relationship with Daniel then she had no choice.

'That shouldn't be too hard. He's gorgeous.'

'He'd be even more gorgeous if he could keep his mum at bay. But listen to this. I've got to tell someone, though you must swear you won't say a word. Paul would kill me if he found out I'd said anything, but I'm worried about him.'

'OK. I swear. You know you can rely on me. Go on.' Ana reached for a handful of cocktail mix.

'So ... Hope summoned Paul to see her. Just him, not me. When he came back, he was ashen – I mean, literally, in shock. I've never seen him like that.'

She had Ana's full attention now. Edie didn't want to present Paul's predicament as gossip, but she persuaded herself that telling Ana this was somehow making up for her silence about Daniel. Besides, she might have a suggestion as to how Edie might support Paul.

'Turns out that he has a half-brother he knew nothing about.'

Ana's mouth dropped open, eyes wide. 'You're kidding me?'

'Nope.' Edie shook her head. 'Hope had a baby years before she had Paul. The other son was adopted and now he's come looking for his birth family.' She paused to let Ana take it in.

'I can't believe it. Hope, of all people.'

'Imagine keeping a thing like that secret for so long? *So* hard.' Edie could imagine keeping secret something so potentially damaging to family only too well, but this was very different. Hope had always seemed such a direct – sometimes too direct – woman, so sure of herself. Edie couldn't imagine her not sharing the knowledge of her son's existence with someone.

'I honestly can't. I wonder why she did. Surely, Martin and Paul would have understood.'

'Perhaps Martin knows. I'm not sure. Paul says not though. He's devastated.'

'I'm not surprised. And if he's asked you not to say anything . . .'

'I know. But I'm not just gossiping. Paul's upset and I want to help him. I thought if perhaps I could find out more about Patrick's father's identity . . .'

Ana didn't hide her look of doubtful surprise. 'Old Chinese saying,' she said. 'Don't get between a man and his mother.'

'But I *do* want to help him,' Edie protested, remembering the shadows under his eyes that morning. She had to support him through this.

'Yes, but you're always complaining about Hope, and so I reckon there's a certain amount of schadenfreude in seeing her fall from grace. Am I right?'

Edie bowed her head, ashamed. 'Well, a little, maybe.'

'Then take it from me, sister. Step back. Let her sort out her own mess without you making it worse. Surely you can see that's what you might end up doing. By all means ask her if you can help, but this must be such a sensitive matter for everyone.'

'What's happened to you? You're usually the first one up for a bit of news.'

Ana laughed. 'That's true, I am. But be careful or you'll do something you regret. And don't forget that Paul's mum is probably traumatized. Imagine a child you had forty or whatever years ago searching you out – the shock must be massive. Honestly, I feel sorry for her.'

Edie hadn't stopped to think clearly about Hope's feelings. In fact, she hadn't put herself in Hope's shoes at all. They had always been on opposite ends of the bridge, with Paul oscillating between them and their positions had become a habit. When she stopped to consider the situation, however, maybe Ana had a point. 'I guess you're right. I almost do, too.'

'Good. Now I want to tell you where we're going in Paris.'

Edie listened as her friend began to extol the pleasures of the City of Light and which of them her and her new beau were going to enjoy. Ana's excitement could normally be so contagious, but Edie couldn't take her mind off her friend's earlier advice about Hope. She made all the right sounds, asked the right questions, felt the right amount of envy even, but Ana had made her think. Perhaps she really was right and Edie should leave well alone, leave them to sort out the problems that came with the arrival of this stranger in their midst. After all, she had quite enough on her own plate with Daniel and Paul. To her surprise, thinking about what Hope must be going through herself, she found herself softening towards her mother-in-law.

19

The moment she answered the door to Patrick, Hope found herself enveloped in a gigantic hug. She had asked him round to get to know him better and have a little more time with him alone before sharing him with the rest of her family.

'This is what we should have done last time,' he said.

She relaxed in his arms, her head tucking neatly into the dip beneath his collarbone, breathing in his scent – a hint of sandalwood and jasmine. Her arms went round him, one hand gently patting his back, almost unable to believe this man was the son she'd given up so traumatically. She didn't want to let him go.

Paul had phoned a few days earlier, calmer. He'd asked when he could meet his brother. She had prevaricated, knowing she was seeing Patrick now but wanting to work out the best way to introduce them. The meeting between them was too important to arrange on a sudden whim.

She took him downstairs and out into the garden, pouring some home-made lemonade for herself and a beer for him. 'Now, I want to hear more about you.'

'Where shall I start?' He looked at home in Hope's garden,

sitting under the big cream parasol on the terrace. The silver birch at the end of the garden shivered in the slight breeze while an ardent blackbird sang somewhere above them until it was drowned out by a trio of parakeets flying overhead. Patrick leaned back in the wooden chair, comfortable, clasping his hands over his chest.

'Well, what about your family? Are you married? Children?' Hope prompted him.

He smiled. 'I've a wife – Clem. We married three years ago in Lambeth Town Hall and snuck off to Peru for our honeymoon.'

'No children?' The thought of more grandchildren was thrilling to Hope.

'Not yet. But we're hoping.' He raised his beer. 'Cheers.'

'Cheers. I hope so too. Have you been married before?' She immediately wished she hadn't asked. 'Sorry, that was tactless.'

Patrick laughed. 'Because I'm so old, I must have been? But no. I came close in my early thirties, but in the end it didn't work out. Lucy was great, but she was always away working and we saw less and less of each other. In the end, we called it a day. She moved to Hong Kong and I was happily single till I met Clem. She's definitely the one for me. In fact, she's the one who talked me into finding you. I can't wait for you both to meet. Hang on.' He went to retrieve his phone from the linen jacket that he'd slung over the arm of the seat. He scrolled through his photos then stopped and passed the phone to Hope. The picture was of a young woman, sitting in a beach café. Blonde, fresh-faced, smiling at the camera with one eye screwed up against the sun. She wore a loose white top that gave a hint of her bikini underneath.

'She's lovely. What does she do?' Hope passed the phone back, hoping she might have a better relationship with Clem than with Edie. A second chance to get it right.

'She's a set designer. Self-employed and successful. Her last outing was *The Birthday Party* in the West End. Great reviews.' He beamed with pride, glancing again at the photo before putting his phone face down on the table.

'Tell me more about what you do.'

'Of course. We had so much to talk about, there was no way we could cover everything in one go.'

'Over four decades,' said Hope with a smile.

'I'll start. I went to Birmingham to study law. Dad encouraged me. He wanted the best for all of us. I had imagined I'd be a teacher like him and Mum, but he wanted more for me, so I became a solicitor.'

'My dad was a teacher,' said Hope. 'But both my parents, your grandparents, are dead now. It was all a long time ago.'

'I'm sorry. I didn't mean to suggest there was anything wrong with being a teacher. It was just his view.' He shifted awkwardly in his seat.

'I know you didn't. But you must have had Marchant grandparents too?' she prompted.

His face lit up. 'Yes. They were great people. Mum's particularly. They lived in Bath . . .'

She couldn't help wondering what her own parents would

have made of this man who had found his way back to her. Would they let the shame of his origins be forgotten? If only they could have met him. Her father had almost certainly gone to his grave without knowing the truth. Her mother had kept his existence to herself all her long life, just as Hope had tried to do the same.

Aware she mustn't let her emotions overtake her, she switched her attention back to Patrick. She heard him out as he described his family again, but in more detail this time. She became increasingly grateful to the Marchants for the parents they had been to him. They had obviously loved him, looked after him and given him the best chance in life they could.

But it should have been me, she thought.

'I never forgot,' she said. 'Even with the passing of time, marriage, the birth of your brother ... you were always with me.'

'Was I?' He looked pleased. 'I wish we could have found each other sooner.'

In the distance, she heard the unwelcome sound of the front doorbell. 'Who on earth can that be? I'm not expecting anyone.'

'Do answer it. I'll still be here when you get back.' He smiled.

She tore herself away and found Vita on the doorstep, ready to park her bike in the hall.

'This isn't the best time,' Hope tried.

But the front bicycle wheel was already inside the hall.

'I haven't come for long,' Vita said, steering the handlebars past her friend. 'I brought over these knives you asked me to order. I thought you might offer me some of that gorgeous lemonade before I cycle back. It's so bloody hot.'

'I—' Hope stopped. This was her closest friend, after all. 'Patrick's here.'

Vita's glance darted up. 'And you want me to leave? Please, just a few minutes and a drink? I'm dying to meet him.'

Hope wanted to show off Patrick to everyone, but knew she shouldn't before the family had been told. Then again, Vita was virtually family and the only other person apart from Paul who knew, so she caved in. 'Well, all right, but just for a minute.'

'My old friend and my business partner,' Hope called out as Vita swept through the French doors, into the garden. 'She simply can't be stopped!'

'Hi, I'm Patrick.' Her son stood and held out his hand, looking back to Hope for a lead.

'Vita.' She shook his hand vigorously. 'I'm dropping off some knives for Hope.'

Hope's heart hammered in her chest. Would they get on? She was surprised by how much she hoped that would happen.

'I'm so sorry to interrupt.' Vita sat down opposite him, making herself comfortable.

'It's fine,' said Patrick. 'I'm pleased to meet a friend of Hope's.'

'I'll get your lemonade,' said Hope. 'Another beer, Patrick?'

In the kitchen, she put her hands on the worktop and leaned hard, head bowed as she took a deep breath. This had not been part of the plan, but when Vita was determined, there was no derailing her.

When she returned to the garden, Vita and Patrick were deep in conversation. Hope let it flow, glad to see them at ease with one another. Vita was drawing out his whole life story, it seemed, so she got to learn all about Patrick without having to talk about herself at all. After a while, however, she decided to reclaim her new son.

'Aren't you expected back home, Vita?' Hope said.

'John's gone to the cricket, so it was a good moment to pop round.' She registered Hope's expectant expression. 'But, you're right. I'd better make tracks and leave you two to get to know each other better. What a wonderful thing.' She stood up and hugged Patrick when he stood too. 'I'm really glad to meet you, Patrick. I'm sure it will all work out for you all.'

Hope would never hear the end of this when Vita arrived for work on Monday. She let her friend see herself out so she could spend the little remaining time alone with Patrick.

'I should go, too,' said Patrick once Vita had finally left. 'Clem's expecting me.'

'I'm so sorry Vita interrupted. I'd no idea she was coming round.' She didn't want him to leave.

He smiled. 'I enjoyed meeting her. Anyway, before I go, there is one more thing that I wanted to say. Please, don't get me wrong, I'm so happy that I've found you, but . . . I do want to meet my father, too.'

'I know.' Hope swallowed. This was one subject she'd hoped to avoid.

'Well?' His question was hopeful.

'Let's do things one step at a time,' she said. 'I've been thinking about the best way to introduce you. Paul knows about you and wants to meet you. After that, we'll deal with your father.'

'Do you know where he is?' His finger ran round the hem of his shorts. 'Something tells me you're putting this off.'

'You're right, I am. And I do know where he is, yes. It's just that telling him he has a son he hasn't known about in almost fifty years won't be easy.'

He spoke carefully. 'I can see that, but . . . please. You've got to do it.'

'I will. But you must let me decide when.' She was filled with dread. The honesty Patrick was asking for might result in her losing him. Possibly Paul, too. That might satisfy Edie, but Hope couldn't bear to contemplate it. 'I don't want to rush any of this and, honestly, I'd like to have you to myself for a while.'

Before all hell breaks loose, she thought.

'I understand. I do,' Patrick insisted. 'Of course, I'll wait. But for me . . . this isn't so much about your past, more about who I am. When I started looking for you, I had no idea of the feelings it would release. It's so hard to explain.'

'You don't need to.' Hope bit the inside of her lip to

210

stop herself crying. She was ecstatic at being reunited with Patrick, but she couldn't help feeling that she had lost all control of her life. What on earth was going to happen next?

Patrick leaned forward. 'It'll work out. I know you're scared, but don't be.'

'I just need a little more time.'

'I know.' He came round to her side of the table, put an arm round her shoulders and kissed her. 'I really don't want to complicate your life. And it would be great to meet Paul in the meantime. I'm away for the next week, but how about the one after that?'

'At the weekend, maybe? I've a dinner to do on the Friday but Saturday or Sunday could be okay? Lunch perhaps? I'll ask Paul, and then confirm.'

'Thank you. I'm pretty sure we could do that. I'll check with Clem too and get back to you. It's okay if I bring Clem, isn't it? I'd love you to meet her.'

'Of course. I'd love that.' She sounded jollier than she felt.

She would ask Edie and the girls too. She was nervous about their meeting, but perhaps having everyone there would make it easier. And if both Patrick and Paul thought it was a good plan, then she would go along with it. They were all acting out of a sense of self-preservation in their different ways. The week's delay would be a good thing, however. Paul usually needed time to process things and work out what he wanted to do. And what about Edie? She would have to be told the whole story, as uneasy as Hope was about revealing her own vulnerabilities. In any case, it was settled now. Everyone was going to be in the know; she had no control over their reactions.

She leaned into Patrick's arm. 'And I will contact your father. Promise.'

20

Another afternoon, but this time not another hotel room. Edie stood by the plate-glass windows of the eighteenth-floor apartment in the Barbican tower block and surveyed the cityscape.

From here, she could see all the landmarks from St Paul's to the Gherkin to the tall square tower of the Tate Modern. Above, wisps of cloud smeared the sky, presaging the end of the heat wave. She wore nothing but her prettiest, briefest underwear that she reserved for Daniel alone. In her hand, she held a glass of pink champagne.

It was the sleekest, most minimal of apartments she had ever been in – all white, even down to the polished concrete floor. Daniel was running a bath – a beautiful black oval bowl that looked as if it was carved from stone – which stood alone in the middle of the bathroom. The tap was set outside it, arching over one end, making plenty of room for two. The scent of the bath oil drifted her way. Blackberry and bay?

She unclipped her bra and slid her pants to the floor, before joining Daniel. From his place in the bath, he held out the champagne bottle. She let him fill her glass, then lowered herself through the bubbles into the hot water. This was nothing like the quick shallow bath she was used to at home. She usually shared the bath with one or both of the children. The last time, with Hazel, the baby had pooed in there and they'd had to jump out immediately, showering themselves down, drying off with towels hard from hanging out in the sun. She eyed the soft and fluffy white towels on the shelves here.

'Is this luxurious enough for you?' Daniel ran his toe up her leg.

'It's heaven,' she murmured. 'Whose is it?'

'A friend of a friend. He's selling it, but has said I can use it until the deal's done.'

'He's selling it? Why?' The idea of giving up such hedonism seemed an appalling loss. She gazed out of the window again, seeing the buildings of London way below them. Up here she could almost forget her responsibilities – almost.

'He's got a place in the country that his wife likes but costs a fortune, so he's downsizing in London.'

'Couldn't you take it on?' Edie immediately realized what a daft suggestion that was. He had his own family commitments too.

'I wish I could, but at least we have it for now. Better than a hotel. And we're safe here.'

She sipped her champagne.

'No one knows we're here. No one can see us. No one has an idea about what we get up to. By the way, I've been meaning to say, I don't think we should have lunch together again. On our bench in the square, I mean.'

'Has something happened?' She was immediately alert, anxious that their relationship might be threatened.

'Not really. But someone mentioned they'd seen us and asked who you were, and that alarmed me.'

'What did you say?' Panic gripped her. She put her glass on the little table at the head of the bath.

'That you were a friend working in one of the other chambers, of course. But he said he'd seen us more than once and was there anything in it?'

'Will he say anything? Could it get back to Maggie?'

'I shouldn't think so. It was just male banter but it's better not to take any more risks. We both have too much to lose at the moment. If we want to be together long term, we must manage this the best possible way.'

The water felt suddenly cooler now. Edie climbed out of the bath and wrapped herself in a ginormous towel that was every bit as soft as she had imagined.

'Don't be like that.' Daniel covered himself with the foam.

Edie padded barefoot into the living room, leaving damp footprints on the white flooring. 'You've got me too anxious.' She heard the splash of him standing up and getting out. He came up behind her. She twisted round to see him with a towel tied round his waist then took a couple of steps backwards.

'Don't spoil the time we have together,' he said. 'So we won't do lunch again. We'll just meet up here as often as we can.'

'I've been so careful to cover my tracks ... I don't want us to get caught out now. I want us to be in control of this.'

'We won't be caught.' He gave her that look that made all her resolves weaken. 'We have this place. No one else will see us now.'

'Let's sit down.' She gestured to the L-shaped sofa. 'I want to tell you what's been happening.' She wanted him to understand the seismic changes that were shaking her world. She didn't mind if he didn't talk about Maggie, his wife, or their boy, Finn. She only wanted to know what he chose to tell her about them, but she did want to share the extraordinary appearance of Patrick in their lives, so he understood the pressures on her.

'Actually, there's something I want to talk about, too,' he said.

'That makes me nervous.' Her hands were squeezed tight together.

He leaned towards her. 'Have you thought about what I said? About the future. About how long we can go on like this. About whether we really want to.'

Her stomach turned over. 'Of course. I've thought of little else when I haven't been at work. Although I've also been distracted with family drama too.' She went on to tell him what she knew about Hope and Patrick.

'I can imagine. That's some story.' He paused. 'I wish you'd leave Paul and the girls.'

'I'm tempted, you know I am, but I'm not sure. It's such a big step.' She reached for his hand.

He looked down, frowning. 'There's time for you to decide.'

216

'Could you? Leave Maggie and Finn, I mean.'

He screwed up his face. 'Yes, I could. Yes, it would be hard – of course I don't want to hurt them – but I've thought about this a lot and it's what I want. I love you, Edie, and this arrangement isn't enough for me.'

This was the momentous conversation she had wanted to have, yet was scared of having too – so much hung on it. She was quaking inside as she reached for the right reply. 'I've always loved you. You know that. This is beginning to tear me apart.'

'What a mess,' he said, sighing.

'We should never have split up.' The pressure to make a decision was greater than ever, but she didn't feel brave enough to make it.

He put his arm round her. 'But we did. We thought it was for the best at the time, but it so obviously wasn't.'

The music caught Edie up in its rhythm, the beat pounding through her as she swayed and twisted in its thrall. Opposite her, Ana was as abandoned, arms flailing, eyes shut as she gave herself up to Lizzo's 'Juice', too. This was how it had been when they were both single. They would often go clubbing together all night and spend holidays in Ibiza, where they slept on the beach all day and raved in the clubs till dawn. They had been inseparable, one watching out for the other, having fun then returning to the serious world of work. The contrast between the two was what kept them going.

As the song came to its end, Edie was sweating. She

walked to the table by the dancefloor where she had left her drink. She hadn't even heard the name of the cocktail she was drinking. All she knew was that it was cold, long and lemony with a hit. Ana was right behind her, reaching for her Cosmopolitan.

'Great party.' Edie looked around her at the fifty or so people who had gathered to celebrate Ana's birthday. She was pleased she'd been able to execute the practical things that meant it had happened in the way her friend wanted it.

'If you hadn't stepped in, we wouldn't be here, so thank you.' Ana enveloped her in a sweaty, slightly drunken embrace.

'My pleasure. I'm loving it.' Edie pulled back from her friend, ready to carry on dancing.

'Where's Paul?'

'Dunno.' Edie hadn't seen him since she hit the dancefloor at least half an hour earlier. She'd asked him to come with her, but he refused. 'You know I never dance,' he'd said. So, unable to refuse the call of the music, she'd left him to amuse himself.

They both looked round to see him at a table on his own, a half-empty pint in front of him. He looked thoroughly miserable, not even trying to enjoy himself.

'I suppose I'd better go over.' As she spoke, he glanced up and saw them looking in his direction. He beckoned Edie over.

The opening chords of The Weekend's 'Blinding Lights' resonated through the room. 'Oh no! I love this one.'

She signalled back to him with one finger, mouthing, 'One minute.'

Back in the zone, everything melted away again. No Paul, no Daniel, no daughters, no dilemmas – just the music that wove around and through her, filling her head and lifting her soul. When it ended, she reluctantly made her way across the room to her husband, the weight of her preoccupations settling back on her shoulders as she approached him.

He stood up before she could take a seat. 'I think we should go. Work tomorrow. And we need to relieve Celine.'

'Oh, come on, don't be so responsible. She's only got to walk next door and it's not even midnight. I'm having fun for once.' She could hear herself behaving like a spoilt child and hated herself for it, but the music was a mind-numbing drug she didn't want to abandon. She couldn't expect him to understand.

'Well, I'm not.' He picked up his pint and swallowed the last dregs. 'Let's go, please. I've sat here watching you dance for nearly an hour.'

'That was your choice,' she protested. 'You could have joined in.'

He raised his eyebrows. 'You know me better than that.' His glass hit the table with a crack. 'Why have a party on a weekday?'

'Because it's her actual birthday. You know that.'

He had been in a grump ever since she had got home late from work. He'd taken the brunt of Hazel's latest tantrum over a lost furry rabbit which Edie found under a cushion

219

within minutes of walking into the house. And then, by the time she'd got ready, he was annoyed they were going to leave later than they'd agreed, which meant they'd get home late too.

Matters weren't helped when they arrived at the party and Ana had swept them off to meet some of her friends they didn't already know, who Paul decided quickly that he didn't like. 'Trustafarians,' he'd muttered under his breath. 'Tory voters.'

'You don't know that,' Edie objected, irritated by his attitude. 'They're Ana's friends so the least you could do is try.'

By the time he demanded they leave, she could see he was drunk and cantankerous – exactly the person she didn't want to spend the night with. However, it seemed prudent to agree, apologize to Ana, who was understanding, and go.

As they waited to hail a cab, Paul put his arm around her, leaning on her for support as his beery breath reached her nose. She moved away from him. 'Don't. You've ruined the evening.'

'Me?! That's rich. I didn't notice you refuse the food or drink – both of which were delicious by the way. Or turn down any invitation to dance. You had a perfectly good time.'

'Yes, but I was always aware of you sulking in a corner.' She held her coat tight round her against the cool night breeze. This was the Paul she had little time for; the Paul who judged people too quickly, who didn't share her love of parties and all they involved. Since they had got married, he had changed into a domesticated animal who enjoyed his home comforts more than going out.

'Don't let's fight,' he said, opening the door of the black cab that had drawn up beside them.

She sat beside him, slipping back and forth on the shiny leather seat when they turned corners, quietly fuming that he'd dragged her away. Why was she giving in to him? He had ruined the success of the evening as far as she was concerned. She would have to apologize to Ana properly. Having helped organize everything, she was expected to stay till the bitter end. At the same time, she knew this would blow over – occasions like this always did – although they marked the existence of something deeper that was wrong in their relationship, she was sure. She suspected Paul saw that too. There was only so long that things could be swept under the carpet before they finally emerged, full of resentment and rage.

Once they had said goodnight to Celine and she had gone home next door, Edie headed for the stairs. 'Coming to bed?'

He yawned. 'Yes, definitely. I'm sorry if I spoiled your evening,' he said, though his tone suggested he was anything but.

'That's all right. Probably leaving then was for the best.' Not what she thought at all. Now she was at home she was thinking of Hazel waking early, the next day's commitments. 'I've got a busy day tomorrow.'

And with that, together they went to bed.

*

The next day, Edie made sure she got home in time for the children's supper. She sent Jen home, put on some water for pasta and pulled a courgette and tomato sauce out of the fridge. The girls were fractious and difficult, Hazel with a cold and Betty with exhaustion after nursery.

By the time Paul returned from work, the floor round the highchair was spattered with yoghurt and the contents of Hazel's plate. In the meantime, Betty had been put on the thinking chair (a practice Edie had read about online and adopted), screaming her protest.

Judging by the smell of beer on his breath as he kissed her hello, Paul had been to the pub on the way home.

'You all right?' she asked. They had barely spoken since the previous night.

'Let me help,' he said, picking up Betty and calming her. She wiped Hazel's tray and then the floor, holding back from saying that the whole point of the thinking chair was that neither of them should remove Betty until time was up. Objecting would only make things worse between them.

'I finished the book case finally. Then Rick called me and asked if I'd meet him after work.'

Edie had met Rick a few times, someone who had been on the same City and Guilds course as Paul when he took up woodwork. They had kept their friendship going ever since.

Edie fetched a flannel for Hazel's face. 'You didn't let me know you were going to be late.'

He looked as if he didn't know whether to laugh or cry.

'You're one to talk. Look what happened last night and countless other times.'

She lifted Hazel out of the highchair. He was right. She often did get home late. 'Is something else wrong? Tell me.' He couldn't possibly have found out. Remorse pulled at her. 'Are you still angry about last night?'

'Of course not. I was unreasonable. You're allowed to enjoy yourself. I'd just like you to get back when you say you're going to be. The girls would like it, too.'

'But you know that sometimes I have to stay late. The job's unpredictable.'

'But sometimes it feels as if you don't care, as if you've got some other agenda.'

Edie felt a clutch of fear. He was so much closer to the truth that she would like him to be. She immediately leapt to her own defence. 'Of course I don't. How can you even say that? Are you taking it out on me because you're upset about your mother?'

'Don't be ridiculous! I just—'

'Come on, baby.' She squeezed Hazel, who immediately reached for her hair and pulled hard. 'Ow!' She pulled the baby's hand away and said to Betty who was all smiles in Paul's arms. 'Betty! Martin's reading you a story in a minute.'

'Again?' said Paul.

'You know he FaceTimes every other Wednesday.' She was doing her best to be patient.

'Then perhaps I'll go out and do a spot of dead-heading.'

Martin rang at seven on the dot. Edie sat on the sofa with

223

the girls, Hazel with her bottle of milk and her toy rabbit, Betty with a sippy cup of milk on the coffee table next to the pile of books with Edie's iPad open on the top of it.

'So, what's it to be, kidlets?' he asked from the other side of the screen.

'Peppa Pig!' Betty leant forward.

'Please,' prompted Edie. 'She's obsessed with those books.'

'Please!' Betty obliged.

As the screen switched to show the pages of the book and Martin began to read the story, Edie was able to separate herself. She thought about Paul and what he had said. She had laid her own trail too carefully for him to have found out about Daniel, unless . . . unless Hope had said something. Hazel wriggled in her lap, her milk finished and her eyes drifting shut. Betty was still rapt and asking for a second story. Martin brought up one of the Meg and Mog books Nora had kept from when his girls were babies.

Who was Patrick really? Edie thought. And why the mystery about his father? What was Hope hiding?

Martin came to an end of Meg and Mog and Betty, having lost interest well before he finished, said goodbye and went off to find Paul. By this time, Hazel was sound asleep in Edie's arms. The feeling of her tiny relaxed body and her milky smell gave Edie such a rare feeling of contentment that she didn't want to move. Then she realized that Martin had asked her a question and was waiting for an answer.

'I'm sorry?' Edie came back into the present. 'What did you say? I was miles away.'

'Just asking how everybody is. Nothing important. Is Paul there?'

'He's in the garden. He needed some thinking time.'

'Why? What's up?'

'I don't know. I imagine it's to do with Patrick.' She froze. The name just slipped out without her thinking. But this was Martin, she quickly reassured herself. Hope and he were married all those years, so he must know all about him anyway, whatever Paul thought. She was hardly breaking a confidence if she talked to him.

'Who?' His face creased in puzzlement.

'Pat—' She froze. Clearly, Martin didn't know who the hell she was talking about.

'Patrick, you said,' he completed the name for her. 'Who's that?'

'No one,' she said quickly, trying to summon up a neat way of getting out of the conversation.

'Edie, come on. You might as well tell me. I'm Paul's dad.'

She felt the heat rising up her face. 'I don't think I should.'

'Well, I'm not going to push you, but if he's upset, I'm concerned of course.'

Edie hesitated. If she told him, perhaps he could help Paul by fitting in the missing pieces. Having broken the confidence once, it was somehow easier to do it again.

'Hope's first son. He's turned up.' From the confused look on Martin's face, she immediately knew that she had made a big mistake.

'What do you mean?'

'I assumed you knew. I'm sorry.' She reached out to end the call, knowing he was unlikely to let her go. 'I must put the girls to bed.'

'Hey! You can't walk away now.' She had never heard him be so stern. 'At least explain. Is this some sort of joke that I'm not getting?'

'No, but I . . .' For once, her quick-thinking barrister's brain let her down.

'But you what? Shouldn't have said anything?' He had moved closer to the screen so she could see his face in miniscule detail from the hairs in his nose to the mole by his mouth. 'But you did, and I need you to explain. Hope doesn't have or hasn't had any other children as far as I know.'

'You're right, I shouldn't have said anything. Paul asked me not to breathe a word, and now I feel dreadful. I assumed you knew.' Perhaps she could persuade him not to say anything.

'You'd better tell me as much as you can.' Martin crossed his arms over his chest, protecting himself. Edie saw on the screen the door opening behind him and Nora coming into the room.

'Hey, Edie,' she said. 'How are you?'

'Not now, Nora.' Martin was sharp, but Nora just raised her eyebrows and backed out of the room, shutting the door behind her. 'Edie?'

'Can we do this later? Not when the girls are here.'

Betty was back and busy turning the pages of the Peppa Pig book, but Edie knew that wouldn't amuse her for long.

'Edie!'

There was no way round this. She would have to speak out. And maybe it would be for the best, she told herself. 'I don't know much. Only what Paul told me.' She gave him the most abbreviated version of what Paul had said.

Martin was silent, his face impossible to read. 'I see,' he said at last. 'Thanks. No wonder Paul's upset.'

'Please don't tell him or Hope I told you. They'll kill me.'

'I doubt they will, though I know you and Hope don't get on too well. I saw that when I was up with Amy.'

Edie was taken aback. She had no idea it was quite so obvious. 'Well, we don't always see eye to eye, it's true. But Paul's devastated by all this, and I'm worried about him. Maybe if everything's in the open, he might find it easier to accept.'

He shook his head. 'One thing I would say to you is, if this is anyone's business it's Hope's, not yours. I've no idea who this man is, but there's only one person I'm going to discuss him with and that's Hope, not you. I'm sorry, Edie.'

Once she'd got the kids into bed, she began to make a risotto for supper while Paul finished what he was doing in the garden. Eventually, he snuck up behind her and kissed the back of her neck. 'I'm sorry. Mum had just phoned, and I took it out on you.'

'Oh yes? What did she have to say?' She was still reeling from her conversation with Martin. Should she tell Paul she'd spilled the beans or leave events to play out by themselves?

'She's asked if we'd go to lunch there to meet Patrick. What do you think?'

227

'Whatever you want. Perhaps if you meet him, it will be easier. Think positive. A brother.'

Paul kissed her. 'You're right. I'm so glad I've got you on my side.'

Edie couldn't even look at him.

21

Hope was in the garden weeding when her mobile rang. She took it out of her jeans pocket to see who was calling. Martin. She didn't particularly want to talk to him but knew he would persist if there was something he wanted to say. She might as well answer now or he'd be phoning all night. She wouldn't tell him about Patrick yet, though. She would hear what he wanted and save her news for when she felt up to it. Perhaps they had heard about Amy's application to Saint Martins. Or was it too soon for that?

Martin barely waited for her to say hello before he began. 'Is there something you want to tell me?'

Her stomach turned over. That stroppy tone of voice meant trouble.

'Er, no. You're the one calling me.' She sat down under the pergola, looking back down the long London garden to the house. The doors were open so she could see the kitchen quite clearly as Bloater strolled inside looking for food.

'Oh come on, Hope. Edie's told me everything.'

'About what?' she said stupidly, because of course she

knew. Despite her request for secrecy, Paul must have told Edie. How could he?

'Someone called Patrick.'

'Oh.'

'*Oh?* Is that all you have to say?'

How angry he sounded, as if he still had some sort of sway over her. But then, once you've had a child together, an ex-husband never really is an ex, she reflected. They stay in one's life forever. For better or for worse.

'What do you want me to say?' Her mind was racing. She wasn't prepared for this at all.

'Who is he? Your son? He's older than Paul, so where was he all the time we were married? Whose child is he? My step-son, presumably.' He stopped for breath. 'Why haven't you ever mentioned him?'

'It wasn't meant to be like this. I was going to tell you everything myself. Everything. But I really don't want to discuss him over the phone. It's too hard and too personal.'

'When then? If not now, when? I need to know what's gone on. We were married for Christ's sake. Didn't that mean anything?'

'Of course it did. But you're being unreasonable. We're not married now.' She made a split-second decision. 'Tell you what. I'll come down.'

'Down?'

'I'll come to Cornwall.'

She would clear her diary, ask Vita to cover for her. It was the only way.

'Down here?' He sounded astonished. 'When? I'll have to explain to Nora.'

'Of course. I'll come tomorrow.' If only she had told him first. If only Edie had kept her mouth shut. He would never understand why she hadn't been completely open during their marriage, but she owed it to him to try to explain as best she could now. This conversation was likely to be even more gruelling than those surrounding their break-up.

'I'll get the train to Truro. Will you meet me?'

'Jesus, Hope. What is this? How you're going to justify not telling me you already had a son, God knows. Why the hell didn't you?'

'I'll explain when I see you. At least I'll try to but I honestly think it would be better face to face.'

He grunted but her answer seemed to satisfy him. 'How's Paul taken it?'

She could still see Paul's face as he absorbed the facts. 'Shocked at first but now he wants to meet him. He's excited too, I think. It's hard to tell.'

'I bet. He must be spinning, like me.'

'They're meeting next week, so I'm hoping he'll come round.'

'What to? The fact that his mother's kept a secret that could have changed all our lives years ago? *All* our lives. You don't just *get used* to something like that.' She hated how he could be so righteous sometimes. 'Remember how much I wanted another child? At last I know why you didn't. You already had one. Who's his father? One of the lads, I suppose?'

She remembered the friends Martin had grown up with well. Tom, now an artist; Josh, a fisherman; Phil, who used to own a garage in Redruth; and Sam, who she thought still worked on the King Harry Ferry. That summer after the boys left school in Truro, they had all hung out together with her and her best friends, Pam and Sheila. A summer of loafing about, going surfing, barbecues on the beach, beers in the pubs. What a time that had been.

'I'll explain everything tomorrow. Promise.'

The train was on time, leaving Paddington just after eight and pulling into Truro at twelve-thirty. All the way there, she felt as if a stone was sitting in her belly, becoming heavier the nearer she got to her destination. Unable to concentrate on reading, she stared out of the window at the changing countryside, from meadows and woods to the red sandstone of Dawlish to the wide riverscape at Portsmouth as they crossed the heavy iron bridge to Saltash. All the familiar landmarks were bittersweet reminders she was coming home again, back to the place where she had grown up and eventually married, where she had experienced the best of times and the worst.

Finally they were in Cornwall. She thought about how to explain the deception that had always lain at the heart of her marriage to Martin. Occasionally, she slid off at a tangent to worry about what Vita was getting up to in her absence. She had left in such a hurry that she hadn't time to leave her usual list of instructions. Fortunately she didn't have a class or a booking for that evening, and she could draw up her shopping lists on the train for later in the week. Not that she'd even begun to do them; she had so much else to think about as she journeyed back towards her past.

The train pulled into St Austell, the stop before Truro. She watched families piling off the train racing with their luggage to the taxis sitting in wait. Not long now. It was years since she'd made this journey, but she was reminded of all the times she had, not least the time when she returned from London after Patrick was born, traumatized and broken. She began to tidy up the sandwich she hadn't eaten, the book she hadn't read, the notepad she hadn't written on and put her coffee cup in the litter bin.

Standing outside Truro's station, she immediately noticed the change from the stuffiness of a London summer. Here the air was clear and fresh; she could almost smell the sea. Seagulls shrieked overhead as she gazed about, looking for Martin. Always late.

After about fifteen minutes, a battered old Land Rover turned off the road and pulled up in front of the station. Martin was at the wheel, ruddy from the sun, open-necked old shirt with sleeves rolled up. What was left of his hair was blown about. She got in, arranging her feet round the bag of dog food on the floor in front of the passenger seat. 'Can I put this on the back seat?'

'No room,' said Martin. 'Take a look.' Sure enough, the back seat was covered with bedding plants and orange Sainsbury's plastic bags stuffed with shopping. 'Promised

Nora I'd get some things for her. She's prettying up the garden.' He rolled his eyes to suggest that it was a ridiculous pursuit.

Was that intended to hurt? She had spent years working on their scrubby back yard to make it something to be proud of. An unexpected wave of nostalgia hit her.

'I booked us in for lunch at the County Arms. We're going straight there. Okay?'

'Lovely.' But the thought of food made her want to throw up.

The tension in the car was palpable. Neither of them spoke as they drove the short way to the pub. To their relief, Martin took the last space in the pub car park. He confirmed their booking in the bar before they walked down steps into the garden and found their table on the edge of the lawn, a little apart from the rest. At least he had ensured they could have some privacy. He greeted all the staff as if they were long-time friends and quickly ordered himself a beer while she opted for a lime soda. She didn't want anything to blunt her thoughts. She hadn't bargained for the blazing sun, though, and wished she had brought a sun hat.

'You look well. I'll say that.' Martin looked at her in that appraising way he had as if she was one of his heifers at auction. She was glad she'd dressed down for the journey, jeans and patterned vintage shirt; simple with nothing to criticize.

'I'm fine, thanks. Obviously a little shaken by what's happened.' She looked down at her hands and laced her fingers together.

'So ... are you going to explain?' He was in one of his pugnacious moods, difficult to gauge. 'Or should we order first? I'm going to have the fish 'n' chips.'

'I'll have the soup.' She wouldn't be able to swallow more than a mouthful.

He went inside to place the order. When he returned, he plumped himself down on the bench opposite her. 'So? Who is he?'

'Martin, don't. There's no need for you to be like this. I've come all this way to explain and that's what I'll do.' Whatever she had done, she was not going to be steamrollered by him.

'I'm sorry.' He drank from his pint. 'Thank you for doing that, at least.'

There was no time left. She had to tell him everything.

'I had him while you were at college. After you'd decided you weren't coming home. Remember those promises we made about remaining true? But then you discovered there was another life and other women you wanted more than you wanted me.'

'I thought we'd been through that years ago. I was a young man then just enjoying life. I came back in the end, didn't I?'

'Yes! But years later! And while you were away, I was free to make my own decisions about my life too. I had no idea you'd be back.' She pictured him walking into the bar of the Rising Sun when she was meeting her long-time friend Pam for a drink. It was as if he'd never been away. She had only been back in Truro a short time herself, brought back by her father's last illness. His heart had given up a few weeks after her arrival, but at least they'd had the chance to spend those last weeks alone together. Even then, she hadn't told him the truth about why she'd left home in the first place. What was the point? It would only have upset him. Too late for her to make any kind of amends. Now she wondered whether she should have. At least he'd have known about Patrick. She had denied him that knowledge and the opportunity for his forgiveness. But things seemed so different, then.

Immediately she had seen Martin in the bar, standing with his mate, Tom. The lads she had been with in the interim receded, even her boyfriend of the moment. When Martin turned to see her there, a smile had lit up his face and the years rolled away.

'Yes, it was a long time, but I was getting all that growing up out of my system.' His constant excuse. 'Gave you a chance to do the same thing, obviously.'

'Oh, please. Don't.' She'd heard it too often.

'God knows what you'd been doing. I thought that you'd told me everything there was to know about that time ... but turns out I knew nothing at all.' He took a long draft of his beer and put his glass back on the table, turning it as he watched the foam trickle down the inside. 'Our whole life together was based on a lie. I thought I knew you better than anyone, but no ... that's what I can't get over. Maybe that's what really drove us apart in the end.'

'You know that's not true. This isn't all about you! It's about me too. Don't you see that?'

His gaze was stony, unforgiving – so unlike the Martin she had once loved, so unlike the Martin she had last seen with Amy in London. 'Are you going to tell me what happened and why you never told me about my stepson?'

'My God! I'm trying to. That's what I've come for. If only you'd stop getting at me with your hurt pride.' She leaned back as the waiter placed their food in front of them. The aromas of tomato, coriander and garlic, usually ones that would have her reaching for her soup spoon, made her want to retch. She pushed her plate to one side.

'Not hungry?' Martin obviously wasn't having the same difficulties as he took his first mouthful of fish and chips. 'Can't say I'm surprised.'

'Can we do this without the unnecessary sniping? You're making it much more difficult.'

'Yes, please.' He looked at his watch, still the one he was given by his parents on his eighteenth birthday. 'I've got to be back by five.'

'And I have a train to catch.'

'You're going back this afternoon? Why don't you stay overnight with Pam?'

'I've a class tomorrow morning. This day is about you and me. I don't want anyone else involved.' The train journey would give her a chance to wind down before she got home.

'Then you'd better get on with it.'

She took a small spoonful of soup. Garlicky, sweet with tomatoes – perfect, but that was enough. She put down the spoon. 'So ... after you'd left for college, I discovered I was pregnant.'

'You didn't waste much time. Who was he?' His fist clenched and unclenched. 'Or were you two-timing me all along?'

'Of course not. Let me tell this my own way. Please.'

The pub garden was filling up with people having lunch and she didn't want a scene.

'All right. Go on.' He took a deep breath.

She had worked out on the train exactly what she had to say, and how to say it. 'Basically, I was scared. Really scared. Didn't know what to do. In the end I had to turn to Mum.

'She refused to consider an abortion. I was so naïve, I didn't even know where I would go for one. I was afraid of going to the local doctor in case he talked. I couldn't tell my friends; I had no idea how to look after a baby. I was still at school, as you know, and worked in a café at nights. I barely had the means to support myself, never mind a child. I had nothing. I felt completely trapped, terrified and didn't know where to turn.'

'But what about the father? Couldn't he have helped? Where—?' Her sudden glare silenced him.

She swallowed. 'I didn't tell him. I couldn't. I thought it would ruin his life.' She spoke with such regret, but it was the truth. 'Mum was the only person who knew – ever.'

Martin looked as if he was about to say something. His relationship with Hope's mother had always been awkward. Despite charming most women, she was one he had never

238

been able to crack. Hope's parents were hostile to him, believing their daughter was too young to have a committed relationship. Their religion had dictated the way they lived their lives and they were scared of letting their daughters loose in the modern world.

'Mum organized everything.' She described the single mother and baby home, the hardships she suffered there, the fear of the future, and the unspeakable pain and distress of losing Patrick. She was unable to hold back her tears as she began to explain how she tried, over the following years, to piece her life back together. 'I've told him that I never forgot him, and that's true. To begin with, every time I saw a baby in a pram, I'd wonder where he was, what he was like. I can't explain to you how terrible that was. I understood why bereft women snatch babies, but I believed that I had done the best I could for him. Isn't that what we're meant to do? The idea was to give him a life he could never have had with me. I didn't *know* that he got it, but I had to believe he did.'

'But I would have helped you. You could have told me when we married. I would have understood. Maybe we could have got him back.' He was softening now, thank goodness.

'We couldn't. He'd been legally adopted. I had no rights over him at all.'

'You still should have told me.' He spoke so quietly that she couldn't tell whether he was sad or angry.

'I see that now. I wish I had.' She closed her eyes.

'Was it Tom? Or Phil?' He named his two closest friends.

'The father?' She shook her head.

239

'Sam, then? Jake?'

'No.'

His expression showed his relief. He sighed. 'I don't think I could bear it if he was one of them. My closest mates, even now.'

So that's what he was so concerned about.

'Well, he wasn't.'

'Tom always had the hots for you, you know. He'd drive me mad talking about it. I always wondered when I left whether the two of you might get together.'

'Not a chance. Not with him. You must have known I'd never buy into that rocker vibe. The slicked-back hair, leathers, greasy fingernails – no thanks.'

They both laughed gently, then Martin's face grew serious.

'Hope! Just tell me.'

She hesitated. This was the moment she had dreaded for so many years, but she'd come too far to turn back now.

'I know I should have told you years ago, but you have to understand how hard it was. I only did what I thought was best for everyone.'

'Hope . . . please.'

She took a deep breath. Now or never. 'It's you.'

His eyes widened as he stared at her. 'What?'

'You're Patrick's father.' The release she felt at having told him was outweighed by her fear of his reaction.

'Jesus!' He rubbed his temple, bewildered. 'You're joking?'

'No.' She watched him as the news sank in.

'A son.' He was disbelieving. 'My son, and you never told me. How could you do that? Why would you?'

'I've tried to explain.' There was no point in going over and over what had happened. If she had known what was going to happen forty years later, perhaps she would have told him. But who in this world was blessed with the gift of foresight?

'You mean, I've another son I don't even know?' He rubbed his forehead.

'Yes. I'm so sorry. I thought I was doing the right thing by all of us and then, as time went by, it became impossible to say anything.'

'You should have told me you were pregnant in the first place.'

He was getting angry again, threatening.

'And what? Made you come home and resent me forever?'

'That wasn't your decision to make. You should have given me the choice.'

'I know. I see that now. But I've tried to make you under-stand how it was. Yes, I should have told you right at the beginning, but I can only tell you what was going through my head at the time. Telling you eight years later wouldn't have helped anyone. You still wouldn't have been able to see him. I genuinely thought I was doing the right thing for everyone, however different I wished it could be.'

Martin rubbed his hands into his face. The anger seemed to have seeped away. Hope could see only incomprehension.

'Jesus, Hope. Don't you see what you've done?' He shook

his head. 'You've betrayed him and me and Paul. I honestly don't know what to think. I'll just be a minute.' He got up to go to the Gents, leaving Hope an opportunity to take a breath of relief. The worst was over now.

When Martin returned, he seemed to have some of his stuffing back. 'Tell me what he's like, what he does.'

'He's married, a lawyer. Come and meet him with the others next week when they come to lunch. The idea terrifies me, but I think you should. I'd like you to be there.' She invited him before she thought about what she was saying.

'I'm not sure.' He stared up at the sky as if expecting an answer to be given to him.

'I'm so sorry.' Her eyes stung with tears. She couldn't imagine what he must be feeling. So many emotions must be teeming through his head.

'Stop saying that!' He wouldn't look at her.

'I just wish you hadn't heard it from Edie, of all people.'

'I'm glad I did. At least she's someone I can trust. When were *you* proposing to tell me about *my* son. Or weren't you?' His anger was back.

Heads turned at his raised voice.

'Of course I was. I wanted to pick the right moment because I was scared of what you'd say. Still am.'

'Scared? I should think so.' He leant back, a hand pressed to his forehead. 'I need to take this all in. I want to meet him. I want to know all about him.' He shook his head in disbelief. 'You've deprived me of *my* son, *our* son, of the knowledge that he exists. How could you? My God! Who are

242

you? All these years you've kept him from me.' He stood up and suddenly laughed. He looked down at her for a moment with such derision that she flinched. And then he was gone. Up the steps and away. She heard a car engine turning over, then saw the Land Rover roaring out of the car park, leaving a plume of dirty exhaust behind.

22

Paul glowered at his plate of food, his face set, furious. 'I asked you specifically not to tell anyone, but you couldn't resist, could you? For someone who's supposed to know how to keep other people's secrets, you're unbelievable.'

'I'm sorry. It was an accident. I—'

'An accident? You've succeeded in driving a bloody great wedge between my parents. You've no idea how long it's taken them to get to where they are today after the divorce. After your little conversation with Dad, Mum had to go down to bloody Cornwall and explain. He was beside himself, and she's in bits.'

'I don't really see what the problem is.'

'Because it's a huge secret to have kept to herself. Dad feels betrayed, that their whole married relationship was based on a lie. He's totally upset. And so am I.'

'But they're not married anymore, so why does it matter so much?' Edie was genuinely baffled.

He froze, knife and fork held in mid-air. 'For God's sake! What don't you get? That was Mum's story to tell, not yours. Even divorced, they have their own relationship. You and

I aren't part of that. This has made everything much more difficult for her.'

'I don't see why. But honestly, it just slipped out. I didn't mean to say anything and then I had to explain.'

'Edie! You deal with families every day. I'm amazed you're not more empathetic.'

'I can't afford too much empathy, actually.' She heard how self-important she sounded so added, 'If I became emotionally involved with every case I deal with, I'd be a wreck.'

'Well, you should have stayed out of this one, too.' Paul remained unforgiving. 'Mum wanted to tell him everything in her own time and in her own way. It was her right to do that.'

'Then let's hope she gets round to telling Patrick's father too, whoever he is.' She was unused to Paul getting so heated.

'That is none of your business either.'

'I'm your wife, aren't I? Suddenly the girls have got a new uncle and we'd all like to know who he is. I'm part of your family, however much I may sometimes wish I wasn't, so it *is* my business.'

There was an awful silence as Edie wished she could take back what she had said. 'I didn't mean that.'

'Didn't you?' He clattered his knife and fork down on the plate and stood up, his chair scraping on the floor. 'Well, you sure know how to make a guy feel good about himself. You'll know about him soon enough when we go to Mum's next weekend to meet him. But the least you can do is apologize to her first.'

'Is that an ultimatum?' She didn't have much appetite for eating humble pie with Hope.

'If you don't, you're not the person I think you are.' He gathered up their plates. 'I've suggested she pop over this Saturday. I'll take the girls out to the playground or something and you can straighten things out between the two of you. If we're going to meet Patrick, I don't want all this to be in the way.'

She pulled a face. 'Must I? Couldn't you just tell her how sorry I am?'

'No.' His anger over what she had said had made him intractable.

'At least leave the children behind. I get that you don't want to be here, but she'd love to see them.'

He raised his eyebrows, sceptical. Lately she had discouraged contact between the children and his mother whenever she could. 'No. You're having a serious conversation. You don't need the distraction.'

Which was of course exactly what she did need. 'All right. You stay here then and I'll meet her in that café, Every Last Crumb.' The place was always busy, so there couldn't be any kind of scene. Not only that, but it would be easier to walk away.

Edie deliberately arrived at the café off Upper Street early and chose a table tucked into the far corner of the room. She ordered herself a chai latte and blueberry muffin and looked around her. A couple of young lovers were leaning towards each other over their brunch, noses almost touching. An older woman nursed a coffee and the Saturday papers, pen hovering over a crossword. Four young women had gathered, talking about a party two of them had been to the night before. A man sat with his coffee, staring into space, ignoring his dog, a Westie who was focused on his owner's croissant, hopeful. In the background was the intermittent hiss of the coffee machine and the chatter among the staff.

Hope soon pushed open the door. Spotting Edie, she walked over. Her mother-in-law's purposeful stride suggested she meant business – but Edie quickly reminded herself how most judges in court were more intimidating. She could handle this. 'Hi. Can I get you a coffee?'

'I'll have a flat white, thanks. Nothing to eat.'

This new no-nonsense Hope might be rather likeable, Edie thought, as she signalled to the waitress and ordered. Forget the niceties. She had come to hear what Edie had to say and then she would be off again. Her expression was stern, unforgiving. Edie tried her old trick of looking directly into her eyes, as if she were an opponent in court, but Hope didn't look away as anticipated. There was no sign of weakness. Instead, she held Edie's gaze, waiting. Edie, long used to this sort of tactic in her career, wasn't fazed.

'Look, Hope. I'm sorry I spoke out of turn.'

Hope tipped her head to one side, expressionless. 'Really?'

'Yes. When Paul told me about the situation, I wanted to help him. He was so upset.'

'To help?' She removed her clasped hands from the table so the waitress could put down her coffee.

'Paul was upset understandably, and I thought Martin must already know, so that was why I—'

'It didn't occur to you that you might be meddling in things that had absolutely nothing to do with you?'

'It wasn't like that. I was talking to Martin and it just slipped out.' That sounded feeble coming from an advocate who spent her working day thinking about what should and shouldn't be said.

'Despite Paul explicitly asking you to keep it under your hat?'

Hope not giving an inch threw Edie, but she was determined not to let it show. She had handled much worse in court. 'Martin's one of the family and he knows you better than most. First of all, I assumed he knew, and secondly, I thought he would want to help you and Paul.'

'That doesn't sound as if anything "slipped out". It sounds quite deliberate to me.'

The sharp taste of spices in her latte caught in Edie's throat. She coughed. 'Well, I . . .'

'What?'

'Hope, I'm trying to apologize. Please let me. I understand that what I've done has annoyed you. I'm sorry.'

'Actually, Edie, you've done far more than just annoy me. The plan I had, to talk to Martin in the right way at the right time, was completely upended. And now Martin's and my relationship is badly damaged, if not destroyed. This really has nothing to do with you.'

It was time to hit back.

'It has, Hope! If something's to do with Paul – and this is – then it's to do with me, too. We're married – a team. He feels incredibly let down by you.'

There was the tiniest flicker under Hope's right eye. But then it had gone. 'Edie, I . . . Oh, never mind. Thank you for the apology. I appreciate it, but please will you stay out of this now?' Her expression softened. 'Tell me, how are the girls? I'd love to see them.'

'You will next weekend.' If Hope could be difficult, so could she by refusing to succumb to her hint that she might see them before that.

'I can't wait. I should go now.' Hope was on her feet, her face set.

'See you next weekend!' Edie called to Hope's retreating back.

Edie waited until the children were finally in bed after an exhausting struggle. Paul was slumped in a deckchair outside, scrolling through something on his phone. She went out to join him with two mugs of tea.

He glanced up at her. 'Thanks, darling.' He'd been notice-ably less distant since she'd agreed to meet Hope. All she'd told him of their meeting so far was that she'd apologized.

'I'm glad.' Paul had said. 'She'll come round.' Not that he looked particularly sure of it.

Judging by Hope's reactions, Edie had the feeling her apology to Hope might actually have made things worse, but decided against saying so. She took the deckchair beside him, stretching out her limbs, feeling the welcome warmth of the sun. 'The roses are wonderful this summer.' The roses were Paul's pride and joy, tumbling over the trellised walls. Velvety deep reds contrasted with creamy whites and pale pinks, with subtle, distinctive scents that invaded the garden.

'Mmm.' His eyes were closed, the frown he'd worn so often over the last week or so smoothed out.

'You know, I've been thinking.'

'Always dangerous.' He opened one eye and they smiled at the old, shared joke.

Was this the moment?

'No, seriously. I've been thinking about Patrick.'

'Edie.' There was a warning note in his voice. 'I asked you to leave it alone.'

'That's what your mum said, but I—'

'Look, she's dealing with it her way and I'm taking my lead from her. Whatever her reasons, and whatever I feel about the whole thing, please just leave it be.' He propped himself up so he could drink his tea.

'Let me just say this then.'

He groaned. 'Must you?'

'I'd really like to know what you think.'

'Go on.' He sounded bemused but pleased.

She wouldn't stop until she'd had her say. 'While she and I were talking, I had a feeling . . .'

'Your famous sixth sense.'

'If you like. There's something she's still not telling us.'

'I know – who Patrick's father is.'

'But why is that such a massive stumbling block?' There was something Hope wasn't saying, and Edie's forensic mind was itching to know what.

From the baby monitor, there was the sound of Hazel whimpering. 'I think that's our peace over!' She turned the screen so he could see. The baby was moving about in her cot.

Paul stood up. 'It's so humid, no wonder she can't sleep. I'll go.'

He was obviously relieved to have an excuse to get away from the conversation. As she watched the screen, she saw him fumble for Hazel's dummy and replace it with a long 'Shhhhh.' Hazel's arms flailed outside her summer sleeping bag and then she quietened down. Edie sighed with relief and leaned back to enjoy the last of the sun.

The next she knew, Paul was standing beside her. 'You were sound asleep. I didn't want disturb you so I got on with a salad for supper.'

'I must be more tired than I realized.' She sat up, stiff from the position she'd been sleeping in.

'I haven't seen this before!' He held out the bra that she'd worn when she last met Daniel. The underwear she'd bought exclusively for him.

'Where did you find it?' Her pulse rate was rising.

'In our bedroom.' He held it up by its straps – the blue lace seen at its sheerest. 'I like it.'

Paul was more used to her maternity bras and the M&S comforts she usually wore. She thought fast. 'I thought our sex life could do with a bit of spicing up.'

'Really?' Hurt crept into his voice.

'Not that there's anything wrong with it. I just saw that set and thought I'd ring the changes.' Another lie. She grabbed it from him and scrunched it up in her hand.

'Of course. You're not having an affair, then.' He smiled as if he was making a joke.

But was he joking? He didn't sound accusatory, but better to take no chances.

'Seriously? Don't be ridiculous!' This was way too close for comfort. She took his hand. 'Even if I wanted to, when would I find the time? I'm a hardworking care-worn mother of two – hardly affair material.'

'Well, you look as gorgeous as ever to me.' He kissed her gently. She couldn't help thinking of Daniel's intense, arousing kisses in contrast.

'Were you going through my things?' Surely he wouldn't be spying on her.

'I was looking for that little fan to cool Betty down and it was in the top drawer.'

She remembered getting undressed one evening after seeing Daniel and stuffing the bra there in a hurry when she heard Paul coming up the stairs.

'You're really not having an affair?' He sounded suddenly vulnerable.

She dropped his hand. 'Don't be so bloody suspicious. If you can't trust me, then what's the point?'

'Of course I do.' He kissed her forehead. 'I was joking.'

'Funny kind of joke, but good.' She walked into the kitchen where he had laid the table, lit candles and opened a bottle of expensive fizzy water. 'This is beautiful.'

'I'm sorry, Edie. This whole business with Mum and Patrick has rattled me.' He brought the salad to the table and poured them each a glass of water.

'I'm not surprised. It's been such a shock.'

'I feel like my life's been completely upturned. I don't really expect anyone else to understand but it's as if everything I knew as fact has been altered and I'm having to see Mum and my childhood in a completely new light.'

'You can't know anyone entirely.' If Edie had learned anything at the Bar, it was that. She'd seen it time and time again. 'Not even yourself.'

'But to keep a child secret. That seems almost perverse.' He frowned.

'All sorts of people keep all sort of secrets for different reasons. Family secrets, especially. I deal with them all the time in court. People are afraid of exposure, of hurting other people, of ruining their own or someone else's life.' And she knew that better than anyone.

'I suppose.'

She helped herself to salad. 'Oh, definitely. I've got to do some work tonight. I'm meeting new clients tomorrow and must be prepared.'

'Par for the course.' He sighed. 'Now you're back at work, we spend so little time together.'

'We're together now.'

'But we're always thinking about what we're going to do next. What if we have another child? Then what?'

'You know how I feel about that. It's not going to happen.' She thought she had shut that idea down ages ago.

'You say that, but wouldn't you love a boy as well?'

'I'm sorry, but no – I wouldn't. We went through this before we had Hazel. We've two healthy children, that's enough.'

'Maybe you'll change your mind.' He reached for her hand across the table.

'Maybe.' There wasn't a chance in hell, but that didn't need to be spelled out tonight.

23

Hope was left badly shaken by her trip to Cornwall. Perhaps, after Martin had absorbed the initial shock, he might begin to appreciate what had happened from her point of view. She didn't expect forgiveness, but she still hoped for some sort of understanding.

On the other hand, she was grateful that Paul had persuaded Edie to apologize. Their meeting had been short and certainly not that sweet, but the air had been cleared at least. She would have loved to have gone back with Edie to see the children, but she could see she was going to be made to work for that.

For the next couple of days, she operated on autopilot. She had taught groups of people how to make wholemeal bread and Chelsea buns enough times not to have to worry about it. And cooking for the weekend freezer fills was straightforward. She tried not to imagine what her family might be thinking of her.

The following day, while batch-cooking lasagne, Hope considered her position. Paul and Patrick believed they were half-brothers; they both wanted to know who Patrick's father was and Patrick actively wanted to meet him.

She put the dough through the machine to make the pasta sheets. Vita said she should use pre-packed pasta, but there was something so soothing about the process of making it fresh. Besides, Hope swore her lasagne tasted better because she made it herself.

Martin wanted to meet Patrick. How was she going to tell the boys the truth about their father and engineer the meeting so that the least hurt was caused? And when?

She chopped and mixed and fried. The smell of tomatoes, peppers, onions, garlic and mince rose from the pan on the stove until it was ready to be layered with the cheese and pasta in the separate foil dishes, ready to bake.

By the time she pulled the last lasagne from the oven and it was cooling, she knew what she had to do.

The first person she needed to talk to was Vita. Five minutes later, they had arranged to go for a swim together the following morning.

The second person was Patrick. She was put through to his voicemail, so she left a message confirming their lunch with Paul and Edie.

She put aside the lasagne to cool, ready for delivery the next day. Then, once the cleaning had been done, she poured herself a glass of wine and went out into the garden. Only then did she make her third crucial call to Martin. He picked up immediately.

'Martin, it's me.'

'What do you want?' It was as if he was talking to a stranger, but what else had she expected?

'Just to remind you that I'm going tell Patrick and Paul about you next weekend.'

'Is that a good idea?'

'I'm not sure what's a good idea anymore. I thought I was doing the right thing so long ago, and look what's happened. Anyway, I'm phoning to say I'd like you to be there. I know you must be busy but . . .'

'I'm harvesting. I don't think I can get away, however much I'd like to.'

'Well, the invitation's there. Listen. I can't tell you how sorry I am for how much I've hurt you, but I hope you can spare a thought to how it's been for me.'

'You want *my* sympathy?! This was your decision.'

'My mother had a big part in it.'

'Your mother died a long time ago, Hope.' He wasn't giving an inch.

'Right. So, I'll go ahead without you. Let me know if you change your mind.' As she ended the call, she felt a swell of emotion that came with the disinterring of her past and the memories that came with that.

The following morning, after fulfilling the freezer deliveries, she went to meet Vita. No fancy members' club for them, but the West Reservoir Centre where they had friends who swam summer and winter. Hope had always liked the place because of the vast body of water, only a tiny fraction roped off for swimmers, fringed by an urban landscape of factories, high-rise buildings and cranes but also by trees and wildlife.

Outside the main building, sailing boats were pulled up on shore. On the water, a couple of kayakers were heading out towards the middle, completely in sync, stroke for stroke. A totally different scene from the Hampstead Ladies' Pond.

They stripped down to their swimming costumes, left their clothes in the changing area, and pulled on their obligatory red swimming caps.

'Round the square? Or into the middle?' said Vita.

'Round the square.' Hope followed her friend down the wooden walkway into the water where she flinched with the shock of the temperature. 'God! It's much colder than I thought it would be.'

'Wuss!' And Vita was off, a very sedate breaststroke taking her to the first of the buoys that marked their route. Hope swam in her wake, once the initial shock had worn off. The repetitiveness of movement, the cool on her skin, the reflections of the sun revived her as she pulled herself through the water. By the time they were back on the decking, she was feeling happy and refreshed.

Once dressed, they headed to the café, where they got a table overlooking the reservoir and settled with two flat whites and a slice of carrot cake to share.

'So, what's happened since I last saw you?' said Vita.

'How long have you got?' Hope went on to pour out the most recent developments and her feelings about the whole situation. 'The worst thing is that neither Martin, Patrick nor Paul can understand *why* I kept the secret. Martin and Paul feel that I robbed them of their family, which I guess I did, but ...' She pulled a tissue from her bag and blew her nose.

'From their point of view, I get it,' said Vita. 'But they really should try to see it from yours. You were young, immature and reliant on your mum, who's always sounded quite ...'

'Forbidding? Straight-laced? Religious? Oh yes, all of those. She was only doing what she thought was best.'

'Best for both of you, probably. And best for that gorgeous man, as it turns out. He is gorgeous, you know.'

Hope couldn't help a smile at the thought of Patrick. 'I guess so.'

'And from what you've said, he's had a good life.'

'That's what he's told me so far. There's so much more to learn about him.'

'Take your time. Let everyone get used to the situation and to each other. This is a huge thing.' She tucked into Hope's half of the carrot cake. 'What I can't understand is what possessed Edie to tell Martin.'

'She spoke without thinking. At least, that's her version.'

'Or she was just stirring it. She's trained to think before she speaks, isn't she? I don't entirely trust your daughter-in-law.'

'Don't say that! I can't bear to think of Paul being married to someone untrustworthy.'

'You can't protect him now. He's a grown-up. Remember, I've seen four children grow up, leave home and start their own families. You put the graft in for years, you just have to hope it's enough in the end. For the moment, you should concentrate on Paul's new brother.'

'Oh yes, he's real enough.' Hope pulled off her sun hat and ruffled her hair that was damp with sweat. 'I feel like our story together is just starting, or rather re-starting. But the amount of upset it's caused. It's never like this on the TV. Everyone hugs and kisses and music plays. Do you think they're like that when the camera stops rolling?'

'God knows. Maybe they've all been better prepped than you. You're having to deal with your own shock as well Martin and Paul's, don't forget.' She took a swig of coffee. 'Another piece of cake before we go?'

Only a week till her two sons would meet for the first time. Hope had work to occupy her, but otherwise how would she fill the time till then? Her mind was constantly jumping ahead. What if Paul and Patrick didn't get on? What if they did, but ganged up against her? All the worst-case scenarios presented themselves, especially in the middle of the night.

On the Sunday, Paul called. Her stomach immediately flipped.

'You around tomorrow afternoon? I thought I might bring the kids round.'

'Great! I'd love that.' So she was going to see them after all. She experienced a sudden burst of joy at the prospect. 'What about Edie?'

'She has something else going on.' He sounded awkward. 'She might stop by on her way home.'

Of course, Paul would want to talk more about Patrick, now he'd had time to assimilate the idea of him. But she could handle that. Anyway, the girls would demand most of their attention. But he must be feeling more positive towards her if he was bringing them. She wouldn't have time to make a cake, but there were chocolate oatie biscuits that Betty would love. She smiled to herself. Less than twenty-four hours to go.

When Paul arrived with the girls the next day, Betty dashed in and Hope squatted down to her level, braced for the lunge. How good it felt to have the little girl in her arms again, and this time her arm was out of plaster. Paul was carrying Hazel and, when Hope stood up, passed her over.

'Oh, my beautiful girls, how are you?'

'Gwanny! Look!' Betty flourished her backpack. 'Stickers.'

Hope could see a see-through pencil case full of sticker sheets and the corner of a book. 'Let's go down and find a good place on the table where you can show me.' She leaned forward to kiss Paul over Hazel's head. 'Lovely to see you.'

'And you, Mum.' He held her arm for a moment. 'I know I've already said so, but I'm sorry I told Edie your secret. I shouldn't have.'

'All it did was force me to have a conversation with your father that I was putting off. Probably a good thing, really.' But had it been? Martin's and her relationship would never recover. She was almost certain of that. Perhaps that didn't matter so much in the great scheme of things, but they were bound by their two sons, forever.

'And Patrick's dad? Have you told him yet?'

'Yes, I have.' She shivered, despite Hazel's warm breath against her cheek.

'And . . .'

'B'oater.' Betty was already halfway down the stairs when she stopped and pointed.

Hope laughed. 'Yes, Bloater. He's been waiting to see you.'

The cat took one look at Betty and headed for the cat flap, knowing the sort of attention the child would inflict on him.

'Come.' Betty held out her hand to Hope who took it.

'Better do as she says! Tea? We can talk about it later.'

In the kitchen, she brought out the box of chocolate oaties. 'Orange juice? Biscuits?' Betty raced up to Hope, excited, as she prised off the tin's lid.

'Actually, Mum, I have these.' Paul produced a pack of something. Hope could see the word 'organic' from where she was. 'Edie gave them to me, to make sure they didn't have anything with too much sugar. It makes them go wild! And could you possibly give Betty some water, rather than juice?'

'Sure.' She put the lid back on the box. She would drink the orange juice she'd defrosted herself. This was not the moment to start another argument about the girls' diet.

The afternoon passed without another chance to have a proper talk with Paul. Hope became so involved in creating a wonderland of sticky fairies, unicorns and rainbows that she barely noticed time passing. She was about to start reading to Hazel when the doorbell rang.

'You stay there. I'll get it.' Paul headed towards the stairs. 'It's probably Edie.'

'Me see!' Betty rushed ahead of him.

Hope kept turning the pages of Peppa Pig, pretending to be involved with the supermarket story while loving the comforting bulk of Hazel in her arms.

'Look, Mummy! Stickers!' Betty was back. And sure enough, Edie was right behind her.

'Have you had a good time, darling?' She addressed Betty, not Hope.

'Hello, Edie, good to see you.' Despite their last meeting, Hope felt uneasy in front of her.

'And you, Hope.' Edie was obviously feeling the same way. 'Let me see, Bets. What have you done?' While Edie clucked over the picture she was being presented with – all Hope's own work – Hope finished Hazel's story then passed her to Paul. She watched the little family in front of her, enjoying their closeness with the children, though there seemed to be some tension between Paul and Edie. They didn't speak directly to each other once.

'Is something wrong? Between you and Paul I mean?' she asked Edie when Paul had left the room to change Hazel's nappy.

'What do you mean? We're fine.' She spoke hastily, as if there was something she wasn't saying.

But she looked pale, Hope thought. It must be tough having two young children and a demanding full-time job. With a jolt of sympathy, she asked, 'Coffee?'

Edie grimaced. 'No thanks. Weirdly, I've completely lost the taste for it.'

'But you're usually such a coffee junkie like me.' Hope picked up the plates she and Paul had used for their slices of cake. 'Don't worry. The girls had the biscuits Paul brought. What about you? A slice of cake?'

Edie shook her head. 'I couldn't. I haven't been feeling so great for the past couple of days.'

Hope studied her, remembering how Edie had suffered at the beginning of her pregnancies with each of the girls. She couldn't be. Not again.

'You don't think there's a chance you're pregnant?' The words were out before Hope had thought about how they would land.

Edie's face registered shock at the question, then the shutters came down. 'No, absolutely not.'

It was Hope's turn to be shocked by the finality of Edie's answer. But her daughter-in-law's face made her think that perhaps she was closer to the mark than Edie was confessing.

24

Pregnant! She couldn't be.

The moment Hope suggested it, Edie realized with horror that there was a faint possibility that she might be. Having just had Hazel, she had imagined it was nigh-on impossible for her to get pregnant so quickly again. She and Daniel had been too hasty, too passionate, too slapdash on the contraception front. The combination of urgency and need made her hot just remembering the occasion. She had been ignoring the symptoms, kidding herself she had an upset stomach, that her tender breasts meant her period was due. But, no, no, no! She couldn't be pregnant!

'No,' she had said firmly. 'Absolutely not.'

Hope's chin dipped. So what? Edie didn't want Hope's approval. In that moment, she came to the realization that, if the worst had happened and she really was pregnant, she wouldn't go through with it. She just couldn't.

'Are you quite sure?' Hope pressed her. 'You look—'

'Yes, I'm sure. Thanks. Quite sure.'

'Everything okay?' Paul breezed back in with Hazel and handed her to Hope. 'That's better.'

'Yes,' said Edie. 'I was just saying how much we're looking forward to meeting Patrick next weekend.' Edie forced herself to smile.

'Look, Daddy!'

Betty had found a colouring book in her bag and was concentrating ferociously on getting the colours somewhere near the lines.

'Shall we go outside?' Edie asked Hope. 'Your garden's looking amazing.'

Hope looked surprised at Edie's unusual interest. 'Sure. If you'd like to.'

Outside, Bloater was sitting on the terrace, looking longingly through the window towards his favourite chair placed too close to where Betty was sitting.

They walked past him and down the path that took them to the little pergola at the end, Hope reeling off a list of plant names as they went – something Edie always found indescribably uninteresting and forgettable. She preferred her own sort of gardening, which involved watching Paul's efforts. She didn't need to know what each plant was called in order to enjoy them. They reached the wrought-iron table and two chairs and sat down with Hazel on Hope's knee.

'Is there something special you wanted to say?' asked Hope.

'Yes. I want you to promise me you won't mention what you said in there to Paul.' She could see him inside, bent over with Betty.

'So, you *are* pregnant?'

'Maybe, but I sincerely hope not.'

'Is it Paul's? I'm sorry but I've got to ask.' Hope looked back to the house as she spoke but was distracted by Hazel, reaching up to yank the thin gold chain she wore round her neck.

'Hope! How can you?' But it was the question Edie hadn't dared ask herself. 'Hazel, no. Do give her to me.' She stretched out her arms and took her daughter.

Hope looked at her at last, unflinching. 'Because I worry about what you've been doing behind Paul's back.'

The weariness in Hope's voice annoyed Edie. After all, she and Paul were adults now. They ran their own lives and should be able to do that without the interference of his parents. Besides, who was Hope to judge an unwanted pregnancy?

'You're not really in a position to judge me, are you? Besides, I told you that was all over.'

'You did say that.' On their way down the garden, Hope had dead-headed a dahlia and was picking off the petals, one by one. 'Was that the truth, though?' She passed the flower to Hazel to demolish.

Edie's cheeks were burning as she put Hazel on the ground, conscious of Hope's eyes on her. Her daughter reached her arms up to Hope.

'It could be another Betty or Hazel,' Hope said, lifting Hazel on to her knee. She kissed Hazel's head, her eyes half-closed in pleasure.

Edie watched her mother-in-law play 'One little piggy went to market . . .', reducing Hazel into giggles, stretching out her pudgy hands in appeal for more.

'How could you resist another one of these?' And Hope began the game again, counting off Hazel's toes.

'I've only just gone back to work. We need my salary. I love my job. I can't have another baby now. I just can't.' Edie was aware this was a conversation she should not be having with her mother-in-law, of all people. Despite doing her best to stay in control, Edie's chin wobbled.

But when was the last time she and Paul had had sex? The previous month, perhaps. They both fell into bed exhausted every night and were at work or on duty with the children when not. Ana had once said to her, 'You've got to find a way back together. Use it or lose it. That's what happens.' And they were in danger of losing it. Perhaps they already had. Whereas she and Daniel had been having wild, uninhibited sex whenever they could.

She had been so wrong to think that she could love Paul and Daniel at the same time. She saw that now. But if she dumped Daniel now, she would always know that her life could have been better. These were the thoughts she kept coming back to. She only had one life and had to make of it what she could. But, of course, the girls. What of them? Could she deprive Paul of them? Could she deprive herself?

There was no question of her having another baby. If only she had admitted the signs to herself sooner, then Hope would never have noticed and she could have made her decision quietly and alone.

Hope paused her game with Hazel. 'Have you talked to Paul?'

'No, and that's why I brought you outside, to ask you not to until I've found out for myself. Then I'll decide what to do.' Her insides felt as if they were melting.

'You will tell him though, won't you?' She raised an eyebrow. 'You're probably thinking of what I went through, but this is very different. You have each other and the girls. I had no one.'

This was exactly what made Edie so mad – Hope's apparent confidence that her way was the right way.

'You're not really in a position to tell me what to do.'

'I'm not telling you anything.' Hope locked eyes with Edie. 'I'm just thinking about you both.'

'No need. We're okay on our own.'

Hope's face fell at the rejection.

'You made your decision and look where it got you.' Edie couldn't stop her anger bubbling over.

'Yes, I chose life over death. But the situation was different. If you are pregnant, you can give this baby a family. I couldn't.'

'My body. My choice. Nobody else's. I'm sorry, Hope, but this really isn't anything to do with you. I wish you hadn't said anything.'

'But I did.' She put Hazel down on the grass. 'And I have a view.' She was sounding stronger.

Edie had enough and stood up. 'Paul!' she called. 'We should go now. The kids will want their tea soon.'

'They can have something here.'

But Edie didn't want to listen to another word. The sooner

she could escape her mother-in-law's house the better. She was desperate to get home, get the kids to bed, take a pregnancy test and straighten out her head. Thinking about it, she already knew alienating Hope would be an own goal. She couldn't justifiably cut off her children's grandmother, especially when she was so useful. Besides, she wanted to be there on Saturday for the big family reunion. She turned back to Hope, who was looking pale herself, older than her years, as if everything was suddenly all too much for her. The pang of sympathy she felt for her surprised Edie.

'I think we should go before all havoc breaks loose. You know what they're like when they're tired. Perhaps next time?' She hoped Hope would understand she was offering a truce.

Hope lifted her head to look at her. 'I'd like that.'

'Let's try to keep things level between us, shall we?' Edie said quietly. 'Neither of us wants any more trouble than we've got.'

Hope looked at the ground where her foot was noodling away at a weed between the flagstones. 'You've made things very difficult but, all right, I won't mention this to Paul – no. You know that, if you are, I think you should keep it, especially if he's the father. But I'll leave you to work it out.'

Edie understood what she was really saying. *You spoke out of turn to Martin, but I'm going to show you how to behave by not breaking your confidence to Paul.* Hope's fall-back position was always to head to the moral high ground where a touch of passive aggression often came in handy. Perhaps she had inherited that from her mother, who had such a big role to play in Patrick's existence and adoption. Edie's own mother, Mary, was singularly useless as an advisor on the practical aspects of life. As a result, Edie had been self-made; all the decisions she had taken had been hers alone. And she wasn't one for looking back and regretting. What was the point? You had to deal with the here and now in the best way possible then move forward.

In the kitchen, Betty was helping Paul tidy up. He watched Hope following Edie up the garden. 'What have you said? Mum looks absolutely exhausted.'

She assumed her most innocent face. 'Nothing at all. I think everything's all got too much.'

He went outside and put his arm round Hope. 'You okay, Mum?'

Edie saw how Hope lit up as he guided her back to the house. Mother and son, together.

'I'm fine. I wish life could just get back to normal. And I'm nervous about next week when you'll all meet.'

'I think we all are, but we can be civilized. Can't we, Edie?'

Edie forced herself to laugh along with him. 'Yes, of course we can.'

That night after supper, Edie took a long bath, not too hot because it was a sultry summer night, but comfortingly warm and with the window open. She looked down the length of her body, her stomach still not as flat as she would like and her breasts showing the tell-tale veining that she'd told herself was the result of her last pregnancy. Of course, it wasn't. What she certainly hadn't been ready for was throwing up before breakfast and then once at work during the previous week.

When she got out of the bath, she rummaged in one of the drawers and found an old pregnancy test that she had been going to use when she conceived Hazel. She had been so desperate not to be pregnant then, she had bought eight test kits. After four positives, she gave up and stuffed the remaining four into the bathroom cupboard. She unboxed one of them now and peed on the stick, once again praying for a negative result, and waited. She didn't have to wait for long. To her horror, as she watched, a blue line appeared in the control window. Although she realized after the last time that testing again was pointless, she couldn't resist. Two more tests later, she knew for sure. She was pregnant. Now what?

Eventually, she climbed into bed and arranged her favourite green and orange cushions behind her. Sinking back into them, she allowed herself to close her eyes and continue the thoughts that had been running through her mind all evening. She needed to slow them down, order them and make some sane decisions. That was how she'd run her life to date – at least until Paul came along. In fact, he rarely disagreed with her unless he felt unusually strongly about something. He loved her and was proud of her but wasn't afraid of standing up to her when the moment called for it.

But she couldn't help reminding herself of that missing sexual spark. She had told herself many times to be satisfied with what she had got. But Edie had grown up watching her mother take precisely what she wanted from life. She had learned at the knee of a world-class self-server.

And if Edie knew anything, it was that she did not want another child, whoever's it was. To satisfy herself, however, she had to go through the possibilities and probabilities.

So, what if the baby was Daniel's? Whatever her decision, about the baby, she didn't think she would ever tell him. He had his own family, his own child. Unless ... She thought about what he had said to her. He wanted a future for the two of them together. Could there be? The hurdles already seemed impossible, but now there was this new one – her pregnancy.

And if the baby were Paul's? They would have a family of three children. She would have to go through another maternity leave, pretending to be happy and fulfilled when she would be feeling frazzled and stretched way beyond her limits. She could only imagine the frustration, the boredom, the embarrassment, having risked the support of her chambers, and most importantly her clerk. She would never get moved on to the really big cases that she so longed to be involved in. Nor would she be voted on to the various boards that would give her exposure and advance her career. How would they survive financially? Paul had work, he was expert at what he did and was satisfied by it, but he was never going to earn big bucks. Even if they both longed for a third child, they would need the income she brought in more than ever. But might the baby be Paul's? The odds were against it.

She thought of his mother and of her story. Hope had a baby when she couldn't support one and look what had happened. She'd lived the following decades harbouring her secret. Perhaps she was unsure who the father was too and that's why she was being so slow about telling them the truth. But at least Hope had agreed with her mother that they had done the right thing in the circumstances. Hope was lucky that her decision had gone well for her baby. Things could have turned out very differently. Of course Hope would want her to have this baby partly because it might be Paul's, her grandchild, but also perhaps subconsciously as a way of making up for what she had done to her own.

Whatever the considerations, there wasn't one convincing enough to make Edie change her mind. She would make an appointment with the doctor tomorrow and not tell Paul. Not ever. Nor Daniel. She was aware of the irony of her lumbering herself with a lifetime's secret in the same way Hope had. They were more alike than either of them thought.

She tossed the cushions on to the floor, turned out her bedside light and snuggled down under the duvet. Downstairs, she heard the sitting room door close and the security chain rattling on the front door as Paul locked up for the night before coming up.

His footsteps on the landing told her he was checking on the girls before coming to bed. Then their door opened and he tiptoed across the wooden floor to the bathroom. She listened to all the usual noises, keeping her eyes tight shut throughout.

'Edie?' He was whispering as he turned on his bedside light before dimming it. 'You awake?'

She groaned as if she was on the brink of sleep. The last thing she wanted was him touching her in case he noticed any changes to her body. The sooner she dealt with the problem the better.

'Okay. We can talk in the morning. G'night.' He kissed her bare shoulder, leaving her to replay her thoughts one last time.

Breakfast the following morning was as it should be for once. Instead of the usual chaos and rush, Betty was up and dressed in good time, Paul wasn't in a hurry and Hazel was as cute as a button. As they talked about what their days held, Edie realized how many people would think she was blessed in her life. She watched Paul with the kids; he was so good with them, as always. Every now and then, they'd catch eyes over Betty or Hazel's head as they helped their daughters and they'd smile. That morning, the connection between them was back. Edie felt chastened, but her resolution held.

'I wanted to talk to you about Mum last night,' Paul said. 'But you were out for the count.'

Just at that moment, Hazel splashed her open hands into her cereal, sending milk and Weetabix cascading over Betty's dress. Betty screamed, knocking her drink on to the floor, before grabbing the tray of Hazel's highchair and shaking it.

'Let go,' said Edie, her fantasy family dissolving in front of her eyes.

'No. Naughty Hazel.' She took Hazel's wrist and held it tight.

'Let her go!' This time there was no doubting the command.

Hazel's little smiley face wobbled as she looked uncertainly between her sister and mother. Her bottom lip turned down and her eyes brimmed with tears as Betty's grip tightened. There was a moment of quiet before the storm as she opened her mouth to give a loud yell and the tears overflowed.

Edie prised Betty's hand off her sister's arm, letting it go so it banged the edge of the table. Betty immediately joined in the cacophony.

'Are you in a hurry?' Paul asked over the noise.

'Not really. Why?' He was obviously asking her to wait so they could talk about Hope.

'Because I ought to get going. Sorry to leave you, but we've an onsite meeting at half past eight.'

'Jen'll be here soon,' she reassured him. 'You go. I can manage.'

For the next half hour, Edie wiped, cleaned, comforted and changed so that order was restored before Jen arrived to take over.

'Morning!' Jen was her usual cheerful self, pink hair pinker than before. 'What's been going on?' she immediately started clearing up the spilled Weetabix and milk that Edie hadn't got round to. 'Five minutes and we'll be off to nursery. Betty! Can you find your shoes?'

'I don't think she needs to take anything else,' Edie said.

'They did ask for some spare clothes. But don't you worry. I'll sort them out.' She went over to the laundry basket which contained everything she had folded last thing the day before.

'Thanks. I don't know what I'd do without you.' Edie began the transference from mother to barrister in her head. She didn't have to worry about what went on at home for now. Someone else would deal with it.

Jen beamed and went to help Betty with her shoes.

By the time Edie left the house, she was already worn out. Another baby? There was just no way. She reached for her phone and made the doctor's appointment before giving herself time to change her mind.

25

So, Edie might be pregnant ... again.

When Hope wasn't worrying about what would happen when Paul met Patrick and Patrick met Martin and they all learned the truth, she now had something else to worry about. She was aware she had prompted the conversation with Edie and that Edie had asked for her discretion. What did that say about their marriage? That any cracks weren't healing at all. Hope had only ever wanted what was best for Paul, and by 'best' she meant whatever made him happy. That's why she had never voiced her concern about him changing his career path from economics to woodwork. He was good at what he did and, most importantly, was fulfilled by it. She had taken a similarly creative path herself, so understood how financially precarious it could be. He seemed to be establishing himself, but whether he would ever earn the sort of money that might support the sort of lifestyle Edie preferred was in question. Edie was right in saying they needed her salary. But ... she seemed to love him, or at least had when they married. That had been so obvious then. Hope couldn't work out how or why that had changed – except, of course, for this other man. Paul was still the same person when he was with her, but had Edie changed him?

'Not your business,' Vita had said when she tried to discuss the matter with her. 'Take a step back. It's their marriage, not yours.'

She was right, of course. But how hard it was to do in practice. Even though Paul was a grown man, he was still her son and she worried about him. She couldn't bear the idea of him being made unhappy by a rift in his marriage. Worse was the thought of what would happen to his children if he and Edie ever split up. Not that that had been suggested. At the same time, of course, Hope had plenty more of her own making to concern her as she considered how her own life choices would impinge on the other people in her family.

She knew Paul would always take first place in her heart. How could it be otherwise when she had spent so much of her life bonded with him? She felt only regret and sadness thinking about how she could have had the same bond with Patrick. And now, here was Edie possibly with similar dilemmas.

She thought back to her own mother, remembering the moment she confessed to her. Hope had been in tears upstairs, anticipating her mother's shock and disapproval, but she had no choice. There was no one else she could ask to help her. Eventually, she came down to the kitchen where her mum was making apple snow for pudding. Her dad had yet to get back from work.

'Mum?' Her voice had seemed to come from somewhere outside her body.

'Mmmm?' Her mother stopped whisking and looked up. 'What's up, pet?'

Hope could feel the tears on her cheeks as she explained her predicament. She would never forget her mother's expression as its normal warm, amiable self grew serious. She groped for a chair back, pulled the chair out and sat down at the kitchen table.

'How could you? What will Father O'Driscoll say? And our friends?'

All her mother was concerned about was what other people thought. For a second, Hope almost laughed.

Her mother scowled. 'You're bringing disgrace on to the family and you laugh?'

She had never seen her mother so angry, made more so when she refused to tell her who the father was. Rightly or wrongly, she always knew she didn't want to drag him into it.

'Go upstairs and leave me to think how we'll deal with this.' Her mother's shock spilled over into her practical side. This was an inconvenience and a potential scandal that she would have to deal with. There was no one else. She knew that as well as Hope did.

And now, years later, the shoe would be on the other foot if Edie was pregnant. The irony. Except she didn't have the control or authority that her mother had over the situation. Nor should she. What she had learned, if anything, was that these decisions shouldn't be made by an outside agency but by the person involved alone.

Hope's week was busy enough to keep her mind occupied for most of the time. Both her cookery classes on Tuesday and Thursday were full. She had batch cooking for two freezers to do with a small dinner party to cater for on the Friday night. And then came Saturday – the day of The Lunch. Patrick had been in touch to confirm he and Clem would be there. She knew Paul and Edie would. Martin had not changed his mind.

She had invited everyone for one-thirty, so she had plenty of time to prepare. Getting the food ready was one way of allaying her anxiety. She wasn't doing anything complicated, not wanting to detract from the occasion. Poached salmon, potato and tomato salads, bread, cheese and raspberries. She chose the flinty Sauvignon that she knew Paul and Edie liked and some bottles of craft lager for Patrick. As she put the bottles in the fridge along with a jug of water, she wondered what the others would be feeling. Would they be as apprehensive as she was? Despite being tired after the dinner party she'd catered for the previous evening, she had lain in bed for a long time unable to sleep, reliving the moment Patrick had been taken from her, questioning her motives for telling no one about him, remembering her mother and the way she had refused to discuss the subject ever again.

What if they had opened up to each other? Would there have been forgiveness in that? Would her mother have expressed curiosity about her lost grandchild? She had set the example of silence and Hope had blindly followed, sharing some of her mother's shame. Her mother seemed to feel none of Hope's terrible sense of loss. A distance had opened between them that was never closed.

In the morning, the weather looked warm but uncertain, so she laid the table inside while leaving the doors to the garden wide open. By twelve o'clock everything was ready, so she threw herself on to the sofa upstairs and waited. The novel she was trying to read provided no escape at all, so she ended up staring into space, her thoughts picking up where they had left off during the night.

She almost leapt out of her skin when the doorbell rang. She stood, waited a moment, closed her eyes and took two deliberate deep breaths to compose herself before going to answer it. This was it.

Standing on the doorstep were Paul and Edie. Edie was holding a soundly sleeping Hazel.

'Can I take her upstairs?' she whispered. Without waiting for an answer, she went ahead to put her in the travel cot in the spare room. Betty was lugging her backpack, which seemed to be filled with the entire contents of her toy box, so Hope picked it up for her and led the way downstairs.

For once in their lives, Paul and she had nothing to say to each other. He must be as nervous as she was.

'It'll be all right,' she murmured, despite not entirely believing that.

'You think?'

'I hope,' she said. 'Betty, why don't we take your bag to

your table?' She indicated the Betty-sized table that she'd pushed back against the wall. 'I've got her some new stickers and paper for after lunch.' That at least might occupy her for a while if things got emotional.

Betty ran over to Bloater and grabbed his tail. 'Cat.'

'Better to leave him alone. He doesn't like that much.' Hope removed her granddaughter's hand from the long-suffering animal who made a discreet but speedy exit upstairs. 'Drink?'

'I'll have a water. Thanks, Mum,' said Paul. 'I'm driving.'

Before she had a chance to fill the glass, there was a second ring at the doorbell. They both tensed, but Hope was quick to pull herself together. She had to keep on top of this gathering for as long as she could. If she seemed at ease, the others would feel better.

'I'll go.'

She opened the door to find Patrick with his arm around a pretty young woman, blonde curls up, slim and smiley. She put out her hand. 'Hi, you must be Hope. I'm Clem.'

'My wife.' The pride in Patrick's voice was touching as he leaned forward and kissed Hope on both cheeks.

'The others are here.' *Could you die from a racing heart?* Hope wondered.

As they came in, they coincided with Edie coming down the stairs. 'Phew! She's gone down again.' She stared at the newcomers.

'Patrick, this is Edie.' Hope stepped in quickly.

'Yes, and this is Clem,' he said, turning to his wife.

Hope noticed Edie taking them in with a slight frown. Patrick – tall, tanned, sportsmanlike in shorts and shirt. Clem – shorter than Edie, her face rounder, her clothes less showy. Edie could make a pair of jeans and a white shirt look world-class, whereas Clem's summer dress was pretty but ordinary. On the other hand, her smile seemed entirely warm and genuine without any kind of agenda. Hope was glad she was there.

'I've been looking forward to meeting you.' Edie ran down to the basement ahead of them. 'Paul! They're here.' She sounded as if she was introducing a new act at the circus. Hope could throttle her. She had wanted to be the one making the introductions.

'It'll be okay.' Clem put her hand on Hope's wrist. All Hope could do was smile back, grateful.

'You lead the way,' said Patrick.

When they reached the kitchen, they found Paul and Edie, side by side, Edie's arm threaded through her husband's.

'Patrick and Clem, this is Paul and Edie.' Hope felt a wave of relief close over her. It was done.

'And this is Betty,' Edie said, gesturing. Her daughter turned to see who she was being introduced to, then went straight back to her colouring in.

'Hi, Betty. What are you doing?' Clem went to squat beside her. 'That's so good. Who's this?' The atmosphere in the room relaxed a little.

Patrick held out his hand to Paul. 'Good to meet you.'

Paul stirred himself to take the hand, detaching himself from Edie. 'Likewise.'

Patrick closed his other hand over their clasped fingers. 'I've looked forward to this moment ever since I knew you existed.'

To Hope's relief, Paul smiled.

'Once I'd got over the initial shock, I have too.'

Then, quite suddenly, the two brothers embraced, the only sounds in the room being the pats on each other's back and the scrawling of Betty's crayon.

Hope felt tears in her eyes at the sight of her two sons together – for now, at least.

'Drinks, anyone?' Her wavering voice betrayed her emotion, but she managed to provide something for everyone without any spillages.

'Shall we take our beers into the garden?' To Hope's pleasure, Paul took Patrick towards the pergola. She just heard him say, 'How on earth did you find Mum?' And Patrick began to reply.

Edie seemed to understand the need to let them talk alone, so stayed in the kitchen. 'Can I help?'

'I think it's all done, thanks.' The last person she wanted to talk to at that moment was Edie.

'You must be wondering what I've done about . . .' Edie lowered her voice as she followed Hope into the garden. Hope cut three roses and faced her daughter-in-law.

'Of course I am, but this really isn't the time.' Hope was only interested in seeing her boys get to know each other. The sound of laughter came from the end of the garden.

'I tested and was negative. So, nothing to worry about.' She looked back to check that Clem couldn't hear them.

'Are you sure?' Hope noticed the flash of annoyance that crossed Edie's face and regretted the question. She didn't want to be the repository of Edie's secrets. She'd hoarded her own for so long. 'We'll talk later.' She returned to the kitchen to put the roses in a small vase for the middle of the table.

Clem got up from Betty and joined them to claim her glass of wine. 'She's adorable.'

Edie laughed. 'You wouldn't have said that if you'd seen the fuss we had getting her dressed this morning. She was determined to wear her Disney princess outfit and wellies.'

'I wouldn't have minded if she had,' said Hope mildly.

'Oh, you would.' Edie was definite. 'It's all ripped and muddy. She wore it to a party last weekend and it's hardly been off her since.'

'Even so.' But Hope could see that her contradiction of Edie was an irritation.

Edie neatly dodged the issue and began her interrogation of Clem.

'How did you meet Patrick, Clem?'

'Well-meaning friends introduced us four years ago. Matchmaking, but it worked.' She looked down the garden towards the two brothers. 'What about you two?'

'Paul's a brilliant carpenter and furniture maker. He came to do some work for me.' She smiled. 'So, just chance.'

'Why don't you both sit in the garden? I'll keep an eye on Betty and put the lunch on the table.' Hope was glad to have a moment to regroup alone while the others got to know each other. But when would be the best moment to broach the subject of the boys' father? She swallowed. The question was hanging over all of them. Now they were here, she was relieved Martin had flatly refused the invitation. She wanted to be in control of how her story was told and received.

She soon had lunch on the table, so called everyone in.

'I'd better check on Hazel,' said Edie.

'Let me come with you,' said Clem. 'I'd love to see her.'

Hope was left with Paul, Patrick and Betty. Was this the moment, when their wives were out of the room, before they brought the subject up themselves? Or would they see that as too exclusive? Perhaps they'd prefer the support of Edie and Clem when the time came? Deciding to delay for a little longer, she began to serve the salmon. All the plates were full by the time Edie returned, holding a red-faced, bashful Hazel, who hid her face in her mother's neck.

'Paul, could you get the children's lunch for me?' Edie gestured in the direction of the backpack Paul had carried in with them.

'Won't Betty eat salmon?' Hope had imagined she was catering for everyone.

'I don't think so. Too rich.'

Edie put Hazel in the highchair and began feeding her what looked like pureed fruit from a Tupperware box that Paul had extracted from the bag.

'Wouldn't you like to warm that up?' Hope suggested. 'It'll only take me a minute.'

'She prefers it cold.' Edie spooned in another mouthful.

Just as the doorbell rang, Hazel knocked the spoon on to the floor, scattering her mouthful underfoot.

Hope ran upstairs and opened the door.

'Martin!' She was stunned to see him on her doorstep. 'What are you doing here?'

Her ex was standing there spruced up in a decent pair of chinos and a short-sleeved checked shirt. Nora's influence had clearly travelled as far as his wardrobe.

'I thought I'd come to lunch after all.' There was no smile, no gesture of warmth. 'Hope the invitation's still there.'

'Why didn't you call me?' She tried to compose her racing thoughts. What now?

'In case you changed your mind and said no, of course. Nora and I thought it was better if I just turned up. Desperate measures.'

Desperate, indeed. 'You deserve to be turned away.'

Did she have the balls to refuse to let him in? His arrival meant the whole afternoon would be completely different from the one she had planned. That sense of losing her way, losing control, was back.

'I've come to see my sons.' The way he looked at her showed they were a long way from mending bridges.

She put her finger to her lips. 'Shhh.' She didn't want them to learn the truth through an overheard snippet of conversation.

'You still haven't told them?' His eyes registered surprise. 'So much the better. It turns out this is quite a timely visit after all.'

'Martin, please.'

'Please what? Aren't you going to ask me in?' He put his hand on the door as if he thought she might try to close it.

'I don't want this to become unpleasant. They're getting on well at the moment.' She stepped back to let him into the house.

'There,' he said. 'Thank you. Still got that I see.' He was pointing to a picture on the wall – a tree with foliage made of hundreds of different-sized hearts. He had bought it for her on a wedding anniversary. She'd always loved it, despite their differences. Oh God! What had happened to them both since then?

But she knew the answer to that. The affair. That was what had divided them. Something else she had spent years trying not to think about. She had been working in a local restaurant when things between her and Martin had become difficult. He was stressed over the farm and their precarious finances; she was made frustrated and resentful by his lack of communication over the difficulties. When a new chef working at the restaurant started flirting with her, she responded. It had given her a sense of self-worth that Martin didn't provide anymore. But if she hadn't had that brief fling, they would probably still be together. She had paid for that mistake, watching Martin as he rebuilt his life so successfully and happily with Nora.

'Your face!' he said. 'Don't look so petrified. I'm not here to make things difficult. But I do want to make sure the record's absolutely straight.'

She moved to stand in his way. 'Are you sure about this? You could come back after lunch? Then I could tell them in my own way, and you could come in then as a crowning surprise.'

His expression and the shake of his head told her that wasn't going to happen. The two of them side-stepped into the living room, where they sat down on the sofa facing the fireplace. Bloater lay snoozing on a chair, having found an escape from Betty's tail-pulling.

'Well, as you've come all this way, you'd better join us.'

'Thanks.' He visibly relaxed.

'But please can we play it my way? I'd like to tell them after lunch when they've had a chance to get to know each other a bit better.'

'Agreed. I'm just pleased to be here.' He ran his finger down the arm of the chair as if he was testing out the grey linen.

'I know you're angry and hurt and I'm truly sorry, but I really did think I was doing the right thing for everyone.' *Except for me*, an inner voice whispered. *Except for me*. 'I realize now I was terribly wrong and I regret that.'

He looked at her long and hard.

'Mum! What's up?' Paul shouted up the stairs. 'Are you coming down?'

'Sorry, on my way,' she yelled back. 'So . . . shall we do this?' The invitation sounded far more confident than she felt.

'Yes, let's,' said Martin, more forgiving. At least, that's how she chose to interpret him.

They went downstairs together, him a few steps behind her. The others at the table turned to see who was coming. Their upturned faces were a picture of pleasure (Paul), surprise (Edie) and mystification (Patrick and Clem).

'Dad!' Paul was first on his feet, Edie close behind. 'I didn't know you were coming. This is great. Mum, you never said.'

'Your mother is a woman of many secrets,' said Martin, embracing one then the other. 'Good to see you both. So, you must be Patrick?'

Hope thought she detected a tremor in his voice, but beyond that he gave nothing away. He shook Patrick's hand and waited to be introduced to Clem.

'Could you move along Edie, so I can lay an extra place here?' Hope went to get a mat and some cutlery.

'What a surprise, Martin,' said Edie. 'We weren't expecting you.'

'Hope and I made a very loose arrangement,' said Martin. 'Last-minute decision. I had something else to do up here, as it happened.'

Hope wanted to hug him. He did understand something of what she was going through, and was trying to help her after all, however difficult for him. Meanwhile, she could see he couldn't take his eyes off Patrick.

They made their way through the meal, chatting about Patrick's life as he brought everyone up to date. Then he started asking questions of everyone at the table. When Edie revealed with a touch of pride that she was a barrister, Patrick cocked his head in interest. 'Working around Lincoln's Inn

Fields?' He clicked his fingers. 'Of course, that's where I've seen you.'

Edie blushed. 'Really? I don't think I've seen you there, have I?'

Patrick had an amused glint in his eye. 'I sometimes have work round there, and I've seen you having lunch a couple of times in the gardens.'

'Can't imagine how. I very rarely do that.' Just for a moment, Edie looked uncomfortable.

Patrick shrugged. 'Maybe I'm wrong. Sorry.'

'Patrick's hopeless with faces, aren't you?' Clem laughed. 'Remember when you mistook that poor old woman for your ex-headmistress? She was so confused.'

'I hope you didn't think I was one of your teachers,' said Edie.

'You're far too young for that,' said Patrick, smiling.

Hope gathered up the pudding plates with Clem's help. Edie was trying to persuade Hazel to eat a pink puree (raspberry?) with little success. Her bib and her mouth were covered with spat-out dribbles of whatever it was.

Hope had a sudden urge to say, 'Shall I try?', but supressed it. Besides, the time was approaching when she would have to say her piece. Martin had given her the occasional look when an appropriate gap had come in the conversation, but he had let her stick to her plan. She took orders for coffee and tea and brought them to the table. When everyone had what they wanted, Martin dinged his glass with a spoon and looked at Hope. 'Hope.'

She thought she might vomit as her stomach lurched over.

'Are you all right, Mum?' Paul's usual solicitude made her feel worse, but they were all watching her, waiting.

'Yes, I'm fine, thanks.' She swallowed. 'I have got something to say to you all and I'm grateful Martin's let me do this my way.' She put her hand on the pulse that was thumping at her throat. Everyone's attention was on her. 'The thing is . . . well . . . you all know that Patrick didn't just come looking for me. He came looking for his father, too.'

There was an audible intake of breath from Edie, but Hope was most aware of Patrick, who was entirely focused on her, holding tight to Clem's hand.

'You all know my own story. I've tried to explain as best I can what happened and why I kept Patrick's existence secret. But, Patrick, you want to know your father too. I hope you'll understand my hesitation up until now when I tell you that your father's sitting at this table.'

There was a stunned silence.

'Dad?!' Paul spoke first. 'Is this a joke?'

'No,' said Martin quietly. 'I knew nothing about it. Nothing about Patrick. Not until your mother came to see me in Cornwall and told me the truth.'

'Mum?' Paul sounded lost.

'It's true,' said Hope, her voice faint now.

Patrick, whose face had paled, smiled uncertainly. 'Really? Is it really true?'

'I can see the likeness now,' said Edie.

More than anything, Hope wanted to go upstairs and

leave them to it, but she couldn't. Martin dinged his glass again.

'I know that must have been hard to do, Hope, having kept this secret for so long. But the truth's out now and I believe we can all make a new start.' He went round to Patrick, who was also on his feet, and they hugged hard, chest-to-chest.

Paul sat and watched them, his cheeks ashen with shock.

Edie got up and went to the drinks fridge and pulled out a bottle of champagne. 'We should have a special toast to the new brothers – the new family,' she cried.

Hope wanted to strangle her for her tactlessness. Couldn't she see how conflicted her husband was – and in how much pain?

'But, Mum, I don't understand,' said Paul. 'Why didn't you tell me? Or Dad? We're a family.'

'What I've told you is the truth. Dad left for college before the baby – Patrick – was born. I didn't tell him I was pregnant; I didn't want to ruin his life. By the time we met up again and started going out together years later, Patrick was already adopted and living in a family of his own. Do you see?'

There was a pop as the cork flew out of the bottle.

Hope took the stickers and paper she'd bought for Betty from the side and gave them to her.

This was going to be a long afternoon.

26

'You should have seen them all.' Edie paused her dishing up of the crab linguini. 'Gob-smacked doesn't do it justice. Although, I have to say, I wasn't really surprised.'

Ana was providing the sort of audience that Edie loved – enthralled and shocked. 'But what happened then?'

'Hope tried to explain away how it all happened. A teenage fling. A controlling Catholic mother. Martin disappeared for about eight years. Then, it was somehow too late to row back. Imagine.'

'I can't,' said Ana, helping herself to salad. 'See what a tangled web we weave . . . and all that.'

Edie eyed her, more aware than ever of the irony in all this. She and Daniel were meeting in a couple of days, work allowing.

'But what about Hope? How was she?'

'Obviously desperate for the three of them to understand what she had been through and why. But it's hard for them, and actually I think it's hard for her too. Oddly enough, I feel quite sorry for her. And thank God times have changed and women are allowed more control over their own bodies.'

Her own procedure had been quick and efficient, with nothing but minor side effects. Once she'd had the pregnancy confirmed, after the blood tests were cleared, she was given two pills. One she took immediately. Not too arduous, although she had felt a bit sick. The following day, she whacked back a couple of ibuprofen then opened the second package in the pack. It was only following the instructions to place four pills between her gums and her cheeks for half an hour before swallowing them that she questioned what she was doing.

This was a baby she was getting rid of – perhaps another Hazel or Betty. Just as Hope had said. Even so, she quickly talked herself out of any regret or sadness. This was a practical decision, she told herself, made over an inconvenient group of cells. It was much simpler if her mother-in-law believed the test had been negative.

Within a couple of hours the cramps and bleeding had begun. Paul was out with the girls so she was able to lie in bed with a hot-water bottle till the worst was over. All she had left to do was take another test three weeks later to make sure – and make sure her contraception was more efficient in future.

Thankfully neither Paul nor Daniel were any the wiser after the procedure, and nobody need know about it now.

'And did they understand?'

'Hard to tell. Patrick and Clem were delighted, of course. He was happy to have found the family he'd come looking for, and she was pleased for him. Martin was very emotional – thrilled, I think. Imagine meeting a child you didn't even know you'd had for the first time. The only person who was completely thrown was Paul.' She reached for the bottle of Pellegrino and poured them both a glass. 'He feels massively let down by his mother; can't understand why she never told him.'

'But how could she, without telling Martin, too?'

'I had to hear her for myself to get a real sense of it. Being sent off to a mother-and-baby home does sound horrendous; harsh conditions and no respect. Nowadays it would have been a simple termination, I expect.' Edie pictured Patrick. Would the collection of cells, as she preferred to think of her short pregnancy, have become someone like him? Better not to go there, she thought.

'What can you do for Paul though?'

'I don't know. He'll have to come to terms with it somehow himself. I'm not sure there's anything I can do.'

'What a mess,' Ana linked her fingers and stretched both arms into the air above her head. 'I'm sorry for them.'

Edie felt full of regret. Hope's story made her own decision to have an abortion all the more real, and strangely intolerable. The baby might have been Daniel's, with his sandy hair and lazy smile. Or Paul's. A brother for Betty and Hazel.

Might-have-beens. The paths not taken.

'I'm off to the Opera House this evening,' said Ana. '*Swan Lake*. Should be a wonderful evening.'

Edie was relieved to have a change of subject. 'With?'

'No one you know. A guy I met through work. He's a photographer, fun, but there's nothing more to it than that.'

Her friend's eyes gave her away. 'Ana?'

'Well, maybe there's a bit more, but we're just enjoying it. You know.'

Edie did know. That excitement was what she had now with Daniel again. Fun. As she hankered for Ana's freedom, a life free of nappies, broken nights and screaming, she thought of her affair with him. Seeing someone every now and then wasn't real, just like Ana's relationships weren't real. They didn't require the daily commitment, the effort involved in thinking about someone else's needs as well as your own. But she and Daniel could have that. He had said so. They just had to decide to take the plunge.

Edie reminded herself how much she loved her children. What was difficult was not the girls themselves but the limitations, the boredom and repetitious nature of everything that came with children. Everyone said things got better, but she couldn't imagine it. She had never made that really close bond that other women talked about. And Paul needed the chance to find someone else to give him what he wanted. They weren't the match they had once thought they were. The insight hit her like a lightning strike.

As she swithered between what she had and what she wanted for the umpteenth time, Ana interrupted her train of thought. 'What are you thinking?'

'Oh, marriage. Your life against mine.' She couldn't help the despair in her voice.

'You shouldn't compare. They're just different. That domestic bliss isn't something I'm ready for yet. Maybe one day, but I can't imagine it.'

Edie's voice choked up. 'I'm just not a natural mum.'

'What?' Ana sounded genuinely astonished. 'Don't say that. You're great with them.'

'No. Paul's great with them, but I'm impatient and grumpy a lot of the time and I don't love them enough.'

She couldn't remember ever admitting her true feelings about motherhood out loud. With the admission came the dawning realization that being a mum really wasn't what she wanted. Other women might be fulfilled by it and want to stay at home, but she needed more. At least, she had a career. If she just kept working to keep herself stimulated and her brain ticking over, perhaps she would cope with motherhood as well, but increasingly she doubted it. Especially not with Daniel in the wings.

'Well, you've rather landed yourself with the kids, so you'll have to come round to it. I read somewhere that not everyone bonds immediately. It takes time.' Although she didn't sound understanding, Edie recognized the sympathy in her voice.

'It's been two years.' Edie groaned. 'Sometimes I feel as if I've lost who I am. I'm okay when I'm at work, but that's sandwiched between bouts of domestic purgatory.'

'I don't believe it's that bad. Come on! You'd never leave them now you've got them would you?'

When Edie didn't reply immediately, Ana's eyes widened. 'You would?!'

Edie didn't answer because, to her horror, tears were stinging her eyes. This emotional vulnerability was not part of the person she normally was with Ana, so she resisted it.

Ana got up and came over to sit on the arm of her chair and put her arm round her. 'Oh, Edie. It's Daniel, isn't it? I knew you weren't telling me the truth when you said it was over.'

'I'm sorry. I thought I was doing the right thing by not involving you.' Edie sniffed as she wiped away a tear. 'I've made a terrible mistake. I should have never married Paul. Even I knew at the time, deep down. Daniel was still in the shadows.'

'You loved Paul,' Ana said with confidence. 'I remember watching you two dancing at your wedding. Daniel wasn't in your head then. I saw how you looked at Paul, and how he looked at you.'

'We had a good few years. He was such fun, and we were proud of each other, but everything's changed. *We've* changed. I thought I wanted a family – one that wouldn't be anything like my own but one of the happy ones that all my friends seemed to have. But I was wrong. Wrong to want it, I mean. I didn't know what I was letting myself in for. Also, I didn't know I was going to meet Daniel again or that I'd still feel the same about him. I didn't know.' She buried her head in her hands. 'What a mess.'

For once, Ana was at a loss for words.

'And now he's talked about us being together,' Edie went on. 'Really together, I mean.'

'But you wouldn't, would you? I mean, the girls. What about them? You know what this means better than anyone.'

'I know, I do. But I've only got one life. I look at my own mother and see someone who would have preferred a life without children. I should have taken notice. I don't want to end up like her, living a lie because of other people's opinions.'

'You won't. You've put so much energy into forging your own career. She never had anything like that.'

'Only because she didn't have to work for Dad's approval. That's what I've been doing all the time – wanting Dad to be proud of me, to notice me. Even though he's been dead for years now.'

'Jesus, Edie! You can't break up your family.'

'You don't know what it's like. This is impossible. I don't want the girls to grow up feeling like I did. Unloved. Unlovable.' Tears ran down her cheeks.

'Oh Edie. You shouldn't feel that. It's obviously not true. But leaving them would be a huge step that would harm so many people.'

'Maybe they'd do worse with me as their mother?' She felt despairing. 'I'm not like other women. I thought I was but I'm not.'

'And Paul? He adores you.'

'He deserves a chance to find someone else. Don't you think?' She put her head in her hands.

'This is ridiculous.' Ana got up and went out to return with a bottle of wine and two glasses. 'We need this. You've

301

got a lot of hard thinking to do. I can't do it for you, but I can listen.'

Eventually she went home, pleading tiredness and an early start, leaving Edie to wait up for Paul. She settled down in front of the TV where she was making her way through the back series of *Mad Men* while Paul was out, because he hated the slick, whisky-swigging admen of the Fifties and their domestic dramas. She had almost reached the end of an episode without taking in any of it when the front door slammed in an I'm-a-bit-pissed-but-I'm-back way.

Paul's face was flushed when he came into the living room and threw himself with a groan onto the chair where Ana had been sitting earlier.

Edie reached for the remote and turned off the TV. 'How was Patrick? Did you have a good time?'

'Yeah.' He propped himself up. 'Actually, I like the guy.'

'Good.' She was genuinely pleased that they might get on. 'Brothers in arms.'

'I always quite wanted a brother when I was a kid. Now, I've got one. He's interesting. Successful, but it hasn't gone to his head. He mentioned again that he'd seen you in the gardens at work.'

Edie pushed herself up into a sitting position. She'd forgotten in the heat of what had followed that Patrick had said he'd seen her. 'Hundreds of people go there. He's probably mistaken someone else for me,' she said, grasping at straws.

'You're a very memorable woman, you know.' He sat

forward, elbows on knees and head steadied on his hands to study her.

'Don't, Paul. I hate it when you do that.' She raised her hand in front of her face.

'Do what? I'm only looking at my beautiful wife.' He stuck his tongue out at her. 'Can't I do that?'

'It's more of a leer than a look.' She pretended to shiver in disgust. 'I'm going to bed.'

'Stay here and have a beer with me.' He held out his hand.

'No, thanks.' She took it, interlocking fingers. 'I'll only regret it tomorrow. I do want to hear about Patrick, but only when you're sober.'

'Then, I'll come up with you.'

'No, you stay and have your beer.' The thought of the drunken fumbling that was bound to follow didn't appeal to her one bit. With luck, she'd be asleep before he joined her. But she'd go to sleep thinking of Daniel and how she could untangle herself from this mess.

The bubble in which Edie and Daniel's new relationship existed had burst after Hope had come across them together in the park, and then in the restaurant. And now Ana knew Edie, her closest friend, had lied to her about the affair continuing. Thankfully, she didn't harbour any resentment but understood and wanted to try to help Edie find the right way out of her predicament.

Edie had given Daniel an abbreviated account of what had happened, but what she really wanted to talk about was something that had been nagging away at her since Paul had returned from his drink with his brother.

'How could Patrick have seen me and remembered me from the Fields?'

'I'd remember you.' Daniel was lying on his back on the bed, loosely covered by a sheet, sounding drowsy.

'No, you wouldn't. We're just two in a million in that square. Don't you think that's weird?'

'Mmmmm. Not really. Come here.'

She slid across the bed so that she was pressed against him, his arm around her, her head just below his collar bone, hearing his heartbeat, where she belonged. 'It's bothering me, though.'

'Maybe he's seen you in court.' His arm tightened round her.

'Then, he'd say so.'

'What's his name again?'

She sighed. 'Don't you ever listen to anything I say?'

He laughed. 'You know I do, but when we're here we've better things to do.' His free hand moved between her legs.

She moved away. 'I'm not just a body, you know.' She couldn't help being reminded of the abortion. Would it have been Daniel's child? She would never know.

He sat up, frowning. 'What's the matter with you today?'

And she would never tell him. Or perhaps, one day, she would.

'I'm trying to explain to you. There's something odd about all this and I can't work out what. Anyway, his name's Patrick.'

'Patrick what?'

'No idea. I don't think anybody's told me.'

'Guy who owns this flat's a Patrick.' He got up and wandered over to the bathroom. She heard him pee and then the shower start before he returned to get a towel. 'Patrick something.'

'Very helpful. Can I go first?' Now the afternoon was almost over, it was time to leave.

'Sure.' He picked up a property magazine and arranged himself on the bed, relaxed.

In the shower, she reflected on the coincidence of the owner of the flat having the same name as Paul's brother. The arm moving the lathery sponge over her body dropped to her side. But what if there was no coincidence?

She exited the bathroom a few minutes later, a bath sheet wrapped round her and tucked under her arms. She was half laughing at her thought. 'How funny it would be if the two Patricks were the same person.'

'Not a chance. This Patrick's just got married and has decided to give up city life for a life rotting away in the country. Clem must have persuaded him. I mean no one in their right mind ...'

Edie stared at him, aghast. 'Clem?' She could hardly get the word out. 'Is she a lawyer too?'

'No idea. I don't really know them. Sandy's a mutual mate who tipped me off that we might be able to borrow the flat.'

She felt sick. 'Does he know about me?'

He looked sheepish. 'I've mentioned you to Sandy, I think. I must have because he knows we're here.'

'But not by name?'

'Of course not.' He looked up from his magazine, puzzled. 'What are you . . .' His expression cleared. 'What? You mean you think they're the same person?'

'Paul's brother's wife is called Clem. She works in the theatre.'

He burst out laughing. 'I don't believe it! How could that happen? We obviously can't come here again then.'

But Edie hadn't finished. 'Is that why he recognized me – because he's seen you with me in the Fields? I mean, would he have recognized you? Remember, he also saw us that time when he and Hope were in Giovanni's.'

Daniel thought for a moment. 'It's possible. He sometimes comes up to chambers. He might have seen us together. But loads of people have. It's no crime to have a sandwich with a colleague.'

'But if he joins up the dots?' The fluttering inside her was pure panic taking flight. 'Why didn't he say to me that he knows of you? The fact he didn't must mean he suspects something.'

Daniel patted the air, as if to calm things down. 'There's no need for this. If it's him, I'm absolutely certain he won't say anything. He knows the score. We're not the first people to have an affair!'

'But he's Paul's brother! He may feel he has to tell him.'

Daniel grabbed the end of her towel and spun her out of it. 'Try not to think about it. May never happen.'

As he showered, Edie got dressed. She put on the wisps of underwear she'd saved for him, pulled up the stockings one by one, then slid into her black skirt and white shirt. By the time Daniel was out, she was ready to leave.

'You're in a hurry,' he commented.

'I just want to get out of here.' She was seriously rocked by her new knowledge. What with Hope and this, she had the sense of things spiralling out of control, and she didn't like that one bit.

'Have you thought about what I said?' He began getting dressed. White shirt, black suit and tie. 'Will you come and live with me? It's what I want more than anything.'

Their eyes met.

'Have I thought about it? Of course. I can hardly think about anything else. But we'd hurt so many people.' And yet . . .

'I know. But as far as I'm concerned, you're my number-one concern. It won't be easy at first, of course it won't, but we'd be happy together and we both know that's true.'

'Stop it! We can't.' Her thoughts were taking her to a place where she wanted to be, but couldn't go.

He pulled on his socks and shoes before standing up and wrapping his arms round her. She felt herself melting into him. The thought that she might have aborted his child made her shiver.

'Are you all right?' he asked, concerned.

'Just thinking about us. Our future.' The secret she would keep from him.

'We love each other. That's all that matters,' he said into her ear. 'Yes, it'll be difficult, but we can make it work.'

In that moment, how Edie wanted that to be true.

27

'We should go away,' Vita said. 'Just you and me and a beach somewhere. Or a spa. Just to give you a break from all this.' She took the puff pastry out of the fridge to make vol au vents for the Pritchards' Seventies-themed anniversary party the following day.

'You know I'm not that sort of person.' Hope paused in weighing out the ingredients for a black forest gateau.

'Not what sort of person? The kind who likes beaches and spas, or the kind who won't take an exit from the shit that life's throwing at them?'

'The first.' Hope was emotionally wrung out, but having Vita on her side at least helped her keep sane. Now her secret was out, she felt equal relief and anxiety as to how everything would shake down. In fact, the afternoon of The Lunch hadn't lasted as long as she'd anticipated. Paul had shepherded Edie and the girls out of there as quickly as he could, clearly unable to deal with the situation. Hope could only pray that he would eventually come to some sort of understanding and forgiveness but, at the moment, in his eyes, she had betrayed him and Martin.

Paul had taken her to one side just before they all left. 'You've rewritten our past, don't you see that? What I thought we had wasn't what it was at all, and you're not the person I thought you were. I had a brother all that time. Dad had a son.'

Those words had repeated themselves to her in the days that followed.

How could she argue? She hadn't allowed herself to be her real self since the day Patrick was taken from her. She understood that for the first time now. For years, she'd had to shunt him and the pain that came with the memory of him as far to the back of her mind as was possible. That stifling of the truth must have made her a different person to the one she might have been without it.

'Have any of them been in touch with you yet?' Vita was cutting puff pastry circles with a circular cutter.

Hope looked up from the sponge mix and shook her head, recalling Edie's smile as she had said goodbye. 'I'm surprised it's Martin,' she'd said. 'Poor thing.'

Whether she meant poor Hope, or Martin, or Paul wasn't clear, and Hope didn't care. If Edie thought she was gaining ground where Hope had lost, she should think twice. Hope wasn't going to give up the little piece of Paul she still had without a fight.

Martin was another matter. She hadn't heard from him since he left the house with Patrick and Clem, who had offered to give him a lift to Paddington. Hope had considered asking him to stay, but had quickly realized how unwelcome that invitation would be. They had been no nearer any kind of rapprochement than they were after her visit to Cornwall. But what did she expect? She had to cling on to one thing – what she had done, however misguided, she had done for the wellbeing of Patrick. *But*, said the dark angel on her shoulder, *was that really the only reason? Were you frightened of what Martin would say or do if he found out afterwards? Might he have left you? And taken Paul with him?*

Being governed by fear was incapacitating, but Martin could be an unforgiving man. She had to hope that eventually he would come to understand her.

'So,' said Vita, cutting out holes in half the pastry circles and stacking them on the whole ones. 'If I can't drag you away for a few days, then what about one day of escape? Just one. A day of relaxation and pampering somewhere fancy. It might make you feel a bit better.'

Hope thought for a moment. She appreciated the suggestion, but neither would make her forget her family was imploding. 'You know what I'd really like?'

'What?'

'A long walk.' Hope could see herself striding out in the countryside, the sun on her face, the wind in her hair and the feeling of physical satisfaction that exercise gave.

Vita's face fell. 'Really?'

'Mmm. If I'm lying around being pummelled, the same old thoughts will just keep going round and round. If I'm actually doing something physical, I might just forget for a few hours.'

Vita shrugged. 'Your wish is my command.'

'I'll find a route with a place to have a good lunch halfway round. Will that do?'

'It's a deal,' Vita said. 'Now, where are the mushrooms to make this filling? And why a Seventies party, for God's sake? Of all things!'

That Sunday, they caught the train to Teynham, where the walk began. Through the village of Conyer they reached apple orchards and finally the Swale estuary. The tide was out so they walked along the sea wall beside brown mudflats with sea birds wheeling in the vast expanse of sky. On the opposite side was the almost equally featureless Isle of Sheppey. The place was deserted apart from the occasional dog walker or birdwatcher hung about with binoculars, trudging along to their next sighting.

For Hope, fresh air was the tonic she needed. The bleak flat landscape suited her mood. This was nothing like the landscape she was brought up with in Cornwall, but being outside did remind her of her childhood spent on beaches or roaming the countryside. Free.

'I feel like the Red Queen in Alice,' said Vita. 'Running as fast as she can, but always staying on the same spot. I swear we've been going for forty-five minutes, and we haven't got anywhere.'

A quirk of perspective meant that as hard as they walked, they never seemed to be getting anywhere nearer their goal.

'Turn around.'

Looking behind them, it was clear that they'd covered quite a way.

'See.' Hope put out her arms and spun round. 'We're making progress even though it doesn't look like it. It's a weird optical illusion.'

'Like life, really.'

'Deep! But yes, you said it. Water?' She pulled a bottle from her backpack.

'Nah. I'm saving myself for my glass of lunchtime wine. Where would I pee in the meantime?' There wasn't a bush on the sea wall. 'So, are you going to tell me what's happening with Edie? Have you kissed and made up?'

Hope looked at her, eyebrows raised. 'As if. She wasn't pregnant after all.'

'Do you believe her?' Vita stopped to stand with her hands on her hips.

'That's what she told me. I can't really challenge her.'

'True. Well I'm glad for everyone's sake.'

'You know how she feels about her job, and how incredibly hard she works so it's as well.'

'Is the affair going on?'

'She says not. ' Hope felt utterly helpless. 'But Edie comes first in her world, so who knows what the truth is.'

'Poor guy. The two women he's closest to—'

'Don't say it,' Hope interrupted. 'I know. Looks like we've both betrayed him.' She returned the bottle to her backpack.

'That wasn't what I was going to say.'

Just then, a rabbit darted up on to the sea wall and

ran ahead of them before returning into the long grass lower down.

They started walking again.

'But it's true. At least that's what he thinks I've done. And that's minimizing it. Edie doesn't help.'

'She's scared of you.'

Hope laughed. 'Hardly.' The thought of Edie being frightened of anyone was ridiculous. She could be one of the most intimidating women Hope had met, despite their thirty-year age gap.

'But you know so much about her. She must be scared you'll tell.'

'I just have!' Hope laughed. 'Even though I shouldn't have.'

'Not me; Paul.'

'Do you think I should? Think about how upset he'd be. Isn't it better to leave him the dark. After all it is over.'

'So she says.'

'Oh, don't. If there's one thing I do know, it's how to keep my mouth shut when it matters. And I think it does.' They looked at each other and grinned. 'Though now of course, I'm wishing that I hadn't known that. If only Mum had been another sort of person. If she hadn't drilled it into my head how shameful it was to be unmarried and pregnant, things could have been so very different.'

'No point even going there.' Vita squeezed herself through a kissing gate. 'Do you think Martin will forgive you?'

'Who knows, and I'm really sad about that. After all we've been through, after my fling and the divorce, we'd got to a much better place. I've just screwed the whole thing all up again. I can't blame him for being so angry. If I were him, I would be too.'

'Don't be so bloody understanding. Sounds to me that he behaved like a total prick back in the day. The least he could do now is try to understand. He met your mum and he knows perfectly well what the prevailing opinion of the time was. You've suffered every bit as much as he's suffering now. More. What else were you meant to do when Patrick contacted you?' Vita was always ready to stand up for her friend, and Hope had never been more grateful.

'I could always have told him I didn't want to see him, that I didn't want to upset my family. Some people do that. I'm glad that I didn't, but a little bit of me wishes I had. Just not to upset the status quo, I suppose. All that I'd achieved on my own.'

'But you didn't, and that's all there is to it.' Vita's robust acceptance of the facts made Hope feel stronger.

'Yes, but I'd spent years in silence believing it was better for everyone that way, so why didn't I just keep it like that?'

'Because you're you. You wanted to find out the end of the story.'

'At the expense of everyone else.' She stopped to retie her shoelace.

'I don't think so. I hate to resort to cliché, but time is a great healer. Things will change. You've just got to be patient while they absorb the shock.'

'I wish I had your faith. Patrick's coming over next week at least.'

'Focus on him for the moment.' A few drops of rain had begun to fall. 'Where is that pub?'

Patrick came round on Wednesday evening for a drink after work. Hope had been counting the hours. Even if she had lost Paul for the time being, she had found Patrick, and every hour with him brought new discoveries.

He gave her a bunch of deep orange and yellow freesias and watched as she cut the stems and arranged them in a narrow blue vase. She put them on the table between their two places.

'How's Clem?'

'She's well. As overcome as I was to meet Paul and Martin.' He stood braced with his hands on the worktop. 'I've seen Paul since, by the way.'

This was news.

'Yeah, we've had a drink. He's a good guy, but you already know that. I'm finding it hard to think of him as my brother still.'

'I wish lunch had gone better.' She had her back to him as she opened the fridge for the chilled almond soup.

'I'm glad Martin made the journey though. I know it was all a bit sticky, but my questions are answered now and the circle's closed. I'm sorry Paul was upset by what happened.'

She didn't say anything, concentrating on taking the olive focaccia out of the oven. The faint piney smell of rosemary rose to meet her.

'Actually, I wanted to talk to you about him. Shall I take

these out?' He picked up the knives and forks on the worktop ready to lay the table outside.

'Yes, please. You must tell me what you think of the soup. I'm considering putting it on one of the menus.'

'Let's sit down. Can I help myself to a beer?'

'In the fridge.' She took out a tray carrying the bowls of soup and the bread and sat down, ready to talk. She was nervous but surprised to sense his own nervousness, too, as he pulled out a chair and sat opposite her.

'So, what was it you wanted to say?'

He looked uncomfortable, frowning. 'It's difficult, Hope. I feel as if I've known you all my life and yet, obviously, we hardly know each other at all. And then, of course, Paul's my brother, and that makes me doubly concerned. So, I'm really not sure whether I should say this or not.'

'Try me,' she suggested. 'You know I can keep a secret.' Usually. She hadn't kept Edie's, but that was a discovery not a confidence, she told herself.

'Do you remember I said that I recognized Edie?' he said. 'That I'd seen her before.'

'Of course. You'd seen her in Giovanni's. I meant to thank you for not saying so.' She tore off a piece of the focaccia and bit into the soft, fragrant bread.

He followed suit. 'It's worse than that.'

'Worse? What do you mean?'

'I think I've also mentioned that I've a small flat in the Barbican. I'm going to sell it once we've properly settled in the country but it's still quite useful if I have to stay over for work or we're in town for a party or dinner or something.'

Hope nodded, wishing he'd get to the point.

'But sometimes I lend it to friends if they need to stay a night in London.' He cleared his throat, embarrassed. 'One of them, Sandy, asked me if a friend of his could use it. Someone I've met but would hardly say I know.'

'So?' Why was he telling her this?

He twisted his wedding ring around his finger, looking embarrassed. 'I'm not exactly over the moon about this, but the guy's having an affair and needed somewhere discreet to go because her family was getting suspicious.'

Hope couldn't move. She had a horrible feeling she knew where this was leading.

'I didn't think what he did was anything to do with me. His life, his mess. The flat was there, out of use most of the time. It was no skin off my nose . . . or so I thought.'

'It's Edie, isn't it?' Hope spoke almost in a whisper.

'You know?'

'Not know. Suspect. The man in Giovanni's with her. Remember?'

'Honestly? I didn't clock who she was with. I was more focused on meeting you. I thought Edie looked faintly familiar, but I couldn't place her. And he was sitting behind me until we moved. But Sandy had pointed them out to me a couple of times in the Fields when they were having lunch together, and then again recently. They were having sandwiches on a park bench.' He smiled, spooning up some soup.

'She's certainly very striking, but when you meet someone out of context, you don't always recognize them immediately. Now, I'm absolutely certain it was her.'

Hope put her head in her hands. 'Shit. I knew it wasn't finished.'

'You knew about it?'

'I knew something had been going on with another man. I suspected it still was, but she promised me it was over. Just a brief flirtation that was done with as soon as it had started, she said.'

'Does Paul know?'

'No. At least I don't think so. He adores her and I'd be surprised if he suspected anything.' She broke off a piece of bread. 'I really don't get it. Why would she do that to him?'

'Should we say anything?'

We.

Hope looked at him. Patrick was ten years older than Paul, greyer, more self-assured, more worldly, but still like him, with Martin's nose and wide-set eyes. He'd only known their family a few weeks, and yet he was prepared to involve himself in something that could provoke a huge family drama. That was astonishing. She was suddenly grateful to have him on her side. Perhaps, together, they could do the right thing by Paul. At last, she wasn't so alone.

'To Paul? Or to her?' she asked.

He cocked his head to one side as he considered. 'I'm hardly in a position to throw a spanner in the works. I'm practically a stranger.'

'No, you're not. Not now.'

'If I were him, I'd hate to find out about this and then discover that my family had known for months or even years without saying anything. I think I'd find that a betrayal in itself.'

'He already thinks I committed two betrayals, keeping you a secret, and then not telling him about Martin being your father. I don't want to be responsible for another one. We'll never recover.'

He looked thoughtful. 'Going back to that, I do understand why you did what you did. I'm going to try to make him eventually see things from your point of view, if I possibly can. When I decided I wanted to find you, I didn't stop to consider the effect my turning up might have on you and your family. That was thoughtless.'

'If you had considered then you might not have done it at all – and that would be terrible.'

'You think that now. But if I hadn't written you would never have been any the wiser.'

'And I'd never have met you. And I'd never have felt what I did when I told them about you. Although it wasn't what I'd planned, it was a tremendous relief.'

'You mean you were forced into it by Edie talking to Martin?'

'You heard about that?'

'Paul told me. Edie's obviously a pretty headstrong woman.'

Hope laughed. 'You could say that. She does what she wants. Yes. We never really hit it off from the start. I try, and perhaps she does, but the two of us aren't a good fit.' She started gathering the plates up and went into the kitchen to get the wooden platter of meats and cheeses that she'd arranged for their main course. She put it on the table with a small bowl of tomato salad.

'Why do you think that is?'

Hope paused to think. 'Edie's very self-sufficient and ambitious – not that that's a bad thing. Her work comes first. She knows how she likes things done and it irritates her if I disagree. When I try not to that only seems to make things worse.'

'Perhaps I could say something to her, if not to Paul,' Patrick said doubtfully. 'I mean, I hardly know them.'

'No. I don't want you all falling out even before you've got to know each other better. I don't want you to fall out at all.' At the same time, having him to support her decisions over what to say, and when to say it, was an unexpected blessing.

'We'll see.' He helped himself to lunch. 'By the way, Nora's asked me and Clem to go down to Cornwall for a long weekend.'

'Has she?' Hope tried not to show how unsettled that made her feel. She worried that Patrick and Clem might prefer being with Nora and Martin over being with her.

'You don't like her?'

'It's not that I dislike Nora. But, look – let me tell you what really happened between your father and me. Martin and I split up over a brief, meaningless affair I had with someone I worked with . . . it meant nothing. A terrible, stupid mistake.

When he found out, he asked me to leave, so I did. I moved to a cottage in Polzeath, not too far away, still hoping we would build bridges. Instead, he got together with Nora and never looked back. But I was miserable for a long while. So, I still have some residual resentment towards her, I suppose.'

'That must have been hard.'

'Yes, it was. But we've moved on since then and I really should get over it.'

'Look, if us visiting Martin makes you unhappy, then we won't go. We'll take things more slowly.'

What had she done to deserve such a considerate son? 'No. You must go and get to know them. He's your dad after all.'

He reached across the table to take her hand. 'Thank you. And, in the meantime, I'll think about whether I can do something for you about Edie.'

28

How could Edie find out whether Patrick had said anything to Paul about Daniel and her using his flat? Ask him, was the obvious answer . . . but also impossible. Paul's behaviour towards her hadn't changed, which suggested he was still oblivious. But for how long would Patrick keep quiet?

During the day, she focused on the case in hand. She had to be at her best, as ever. Her early start had taken her to Chelmsford County Court, reading the expert report that had been sent through overnight on the train journey, working out her cross-examination in the light of it. She was acting for a woman who claimed to have been abused by a violent husband. She also alleged he had begun to threaten the children. Exposing the private life of this well-off but dysfunctional middle-class family to the court was emotionally draining for all concerned, but in the end justice found a way. Edie's client was awarded temporary sole custody of the kids with another date to be fixed for a second hearing.

By the end of the day, Edie was tired but, on the way back to chambers, her personal concerns returned. Was Patrick merely biding his time until the right moment presented itself to denounce her? By the time she had to go home, she had persuaded herself this must be what was happening. Why had she been so reckless? Passion was a dangerous thing: on the other hand, that was exactly what she liked about it.

'We should ask Patrick and Clem over for a meal. You ought to get to know them better. What do you think?' Edie said later that evening, over supper with Paul.

She had decided on this strategy as being the only way to get close enough to Patrick to find out what he'd done – or meant to do. She didn't have his phone number, and asking Paul for it without a reasonable excuse would seem odd.

'No, it's too soon,' said Paul, toying with his fish pie, separating out the prawns. 'I'm not ready to start behaving as if we're blood brothers. Not yet. I'm still getting my head round the whole thing.'

'But you are blood brothers,' she pointed out. 'And you did say that you liked him.'

'But it doesn't mean I want to be his best mate.' A ping prompted him to pick up his phone.

'There is a happy medium though.' She tried not to get impatient.

'Not at the moment, there isn't.' He started thumbing a reply to the message.

'What's wrong?'

'I just don't want to have to think about him or Mum or Dad. There's still a part of me that wishes none of this had happened, if you want to know. Why couldn't Patrick have stayed in his own life and not come crashing into ours? I liked things the way they were.'

'But, surely, it's better that he has.'

'Of course it's not. Look what it's done to us. Nobody's speaking to each other, everybody's in a state. It's an almighty mess.'

She had been so preoccupied with her own dilemma that Edie hadn't realized just how upset Paul had been by Hope's revelation. 'I know it's hard, but it really will be okay. Hope made a decision a long time ago without imagining its ramifications years down the line. That can happen to any of us. Then it's hard to confess. Frightening even.'

Paul's eyes suddenly brimmed with tears. 'I can't believe it though. I thought Mum and I were completely solid, especially since the divorce.'

Edie's found her patience being tested. 'But, even if you're not, that's no reason not to get on with your father and Patrick. Neither of them have done anything wrong. You can't blame Patrick for wanting to know his real parents, and he's not taking anything away from you. He's not making a grab for Hope and Martin. He seems quite happy with the family that brought him up. You don't need to feel threatened.'

'Threatened?' The idea had clearly never crossed his mind. 'Why would I be?'

'I thought you might be worried she'll give him the attention you're used to having.' It was a concern she'd only just imagined Paul might have, but it might make him see his mother in a more negative light for once.

He looked at her as though she was mad. 'That wouldn't happen,' he said, flatly.

'She might want to see more of him to make up for the lost years, and then if he and Clem have their own family . . .' Thinking out loud, she then let the thought hang there for both of them to consider.

'What are you doing?' She had his full attention now. 'Why are you being like this?'

'I'm not being like anything.' She put her screwed-up napkin on the table, realizing she had gone too far. 'I'm just thinking about you. I'll clear up.'

He stood up, too. 'By the way, that was Marcus saying he was in the Kings Head with Brian. You don't mind if I join them for a pint, do you?'

A drink with old friends would probably do him good, and give her time to unwind. 'You go ahead. I need to prepare a position statement for the morning.'

'I won't be late.'

The truth was, she knew he preferred the company of his mates, with whom he could spend an unthinking evening of banter. He didn't want to navel gaze alone or with her. It was too hard for him to confront and talk about his emotions. She loaded the dishwasher and finished clearing the table before heading for the living room. She picked up her work bag from the bottom of the stairs and took it with her.

After about half an hour, she stopped trying to read, kicking herself for not thinking of the obvious before. What about Martin? He must have Patrick's number. Within seconds, she was calling him.

'Edie? Do you know what time it is?' He sounded as if she might have woken him up. She checked the time – only ten o'clock.

'Is it too late? I'm sorry.'

'May not be too late for you in the big city, but down here we farmers have an early start.'

'I'll ring back.' Setting off on the wrong foot wouldn't get her what she wanted.

'No, no. We're here now.' There was the sound of him moving round as if he was sitting up in bed. 'What is it?'

There was no point in pretending with a few niceties, at least not at this time. 'I was wondering if you'd give me Patrick's number. We want to ask him and Clem to supper.'

'You're phoning to ask me for that *now*?' He groaned, presumably as he swung his legs out of bed, because then she could hear his footsteps on the wood floor. She could picture him walking down the corridor and downstairs, switching on the light at the top of the stairs and making his way to his disorganized office, such a contrast to her own.

'Hang on a minute. Right, here you are.' He read out the number as Edie jotted it down, pleased with the success of her plan, and thanked him.

'I liked him,' she said, feeling she had to say something.

'Me, too, but I'm still reeling. I can't get over what's happened.'

'I know. It's terrible.' Was that being too condemnatory?

'It's just sad, Edie. Sad she felt she couldn't tell me she was pregnant all those years ago and sad that, as a result, none of us had the life we might have had.'

'That's what I meant,' she said, backtracking. His remarkable measured response had a whiff of Nora in it, she suspected. She had always taken him as someone less forgiving, but actually he was trying to see Hope's side of things. This family was full of surprises. Her mother or father would have walked away from the problem. Or they would have locked it up and never referred to it again.

'Of course you did.' Was he being sarcastic?

'I should go, Martin. I'll see you on FaceTime with Betty and Hazel in the week.'

'Now I'm up, I might as well have a word with Paul.'

'He's gone to the pub. When's he back I'll tell him to give you a buzz in the morning.'

When she had done her work and was considering going to bed, the front door opened and Paul came in. 'Sorry if I was snippy earlier,' he said, depositing a kiss on her forehead. 'Rough day at work. I had to go back to the wardrobe in Finchley because one of the doors was catching. And all this stuff with Mum's been getting to me.'

'I know.' She would phone Patrick from work the next day, where she could be sure no one would overhear. For the moment, she would do what she could at home to smooth things over. However, the question still remained . . . what was she going to do? Her indecisiveness was eating away at them, and Daniel wouldn't wait forever.

The following day, she had a chunk of the morning in chambers – answering emails, chatting to her clerk and organizing admin. At midday, she caught the train to Guildford where she was appealing for child support from a husband who could well afford what he was trying to wriggle out of paying. On the journey, she tried calling Patrick.

He didn't answer. He'd be at work too, of course. She left a brief message asking him to call her.

By the time she got home, she was thankful to find that Jen had fed and cleared up after the children and had them bathed and ready for her.

'Here you are, Edie.' Jen was carrying Hazel and with the other hand shepherded Betty towards her mother. 'Betty, show Mummy what you got at nursery.' Edie felt rather like a Victorian matriarch being presented with her offspring for half an hour before bed. The only difference being that she put them to bed herself and got up for them at three or four in the morning.

Betty held out her arm to show off a red plastic heart bracelet. 'Look!'

'That's gorgeous. What's it for?'

Betty obviously didn't really know so Jen chipped in. 'For helping someone who'd fallen over in the playground.'

'You are good, Betty.' Edie kissed her daughter. 'Thanks, Jen. Have you had a good day?'

'Great.' None of the day-to-day grind fazed her in the way it did Edie. 'This one's been a poppet all day. Everything's done. Washing's put away. They ate all their supper and I think they'll sleep well tonight.' She kissed both girls, handed Hazel over to Edie and let herself out. She never hung around once Edie or Paul returned home, unless she was staying to babysit, something Edie was grateful for. She didn't want Jen as a best friend, just a first-rate nanny.

Both girls were warm and snuggly as they settled down for story time. Hazel was on Edie's knee, blowing a raspberry while Betty chose a story. It should have been a delightful moment in the day, but Edie just wanted to be left alone.

'Look, Mumma.' Betty held up a hair clip shaped like a brightly coloured parrot, at the same time almost dropping her chosen book.

'That's lovely,' said Edie, her heart sinking at the idea of reading *The Smeds and the Smoos* yet again. 'Who gave you that?'

'Jen.' She climbed on to the sofa beside Hazel so Edie could put an arm round her.

Edie bent to kiss her apple-scented younger daughter on the top of her head and was rewarded with a wide but dozy grin. Given her bottle, Hazel started sucking quite happily, clutching her rabbit tight.

Edie was on the second book of the evening, having followed *The Smeds and the Smoos* with *Elmer's Parade*. Hazel had drifted off, and Betty was losing interest.

'Hey, kids.' The door opened and Paul came in.

Betty leapt from the sofa and raced up to him.

'Daddee!'

Her shout made Hazel stir.

'Shhhh!' said Edie.

'Sorry,' Paul whispered. 'Come on, Bets. Let's go to the kitchen, leave Mummy to put Hazel to bed.'

Edie's little family bubble was burst, but she was pleased to be able to put down Hazel on her own, so she waited till the two of them had cleared off and crept up to bed with her youngest daughter, careful not to wake her. Of course, the moment she put her in the cot, Hazel's eyes popped wide open, so Edie had to begin the more and more frustrating rigmarole of shushing and lulling.

When at last she came down, Paul had put Betty to bed and was in the kitchen with a bottle of beer.

'You okay?' Edie said, casually busying herself with making a start on their supper. Her mobile pinged from the worktop. Paul picked it up and glanced at it before holding it out to her.

'Who's "D"?'

Edie stopped cutting up tomatoes, racing through possible explanations. She read the part message on the home screen of her iPhone, feeling as if the temperature in the room had dropped to freezing. She had always been so careful, never left her phone lying around . . . ever. Except for this one time.

> The flat isn't an option open to us any longer.
> Shall I book our favourite hotel?

She deleted it immediately – as if that would stop Paul having seen it and doing any harm. Too late.

'So?'

'So, what?' She pretended a nonchalance she didn't feel at all.

'I asked you who D is?'

Edie's mind was racing. 'Dinah.' She picked up her knife again. At least she'd had the foresight to shorten Daniel's name on her phone, just in case.

Think. Think.

'You've never talked about anyone called Dinah. Who is she?' Paul looked puzzled.

'A friend of Ana's I met recently. We got on so well that we thought we might all three have a couple of days away together. Just a quick break.' Convincing improvisation was a talent she had developed at work.

She turned away from him to put a saucepan of water on for the pasta.

'You never said.' He obviously wanted to believe her, but was unsure. His fingers tapped a rhythm on the counter.

'Nothing's been set in stone. We just had the idea.' She hoped the panic she was feeling didn't show on the outside but his stare was disconcerting.

'Why are you being so odd?' His head tipped to one side but his gaze never left her.

'I'm not.' Whatever she said came out sounding stilted, her voice pitched wrong. 'I was going to tell you tonight. Do you mind?' She was making it up as she went along, her mind working quickly.

'If you're going away, what about the girls?'

'Hope would come over to help you. Jen too.'

'When we're in the middle of all this family rumpus? How can you even suggest that? We should be pulling together now, not pulling apart.'

'I'm not pulling apart. I didn't think I needed to put my plans with Dinah and Ana on hold because of what's happening in your family. But okay, I will. I'll tell her that it's not going to happen.' And then there'd be no way Paul could be suspicious.

'You will?'

'Of course. I didn't realize you'd mind so much.' She started frying the onions and garlic.

His face relaxed. 'Thank you. I don't like the idea of you going away just now.'

Had she persuaded him? She couldn't tell for sure, but it seemed so.

Too many people knew about the affair now, Edie realized, and Paul had just come so close to finding out. The look he gave her reminded her of what she could be throwing away. Paul really did love her, and Edie was tired of trying to manage the affair and its potential fallout. She knew where her responsibilities lay and must stop vacillating. This wasn't fair on anyone. She would talk to Daniel when she next saw him, in whichever hotel he chose. Just one last time. And she would end it, although the thought of living without him was too devastating to contemplate. She didn't trust herself to go through with it.

'What do you think I should do?' asked Paul.

Edie dropped the fusilli into the boiling water and tipped the tomatoes into the pan with the onions, grateful he had changed the subject.

'About Hope?' She paused to think. 'Talk to her.'

'I don't think I can. Not again.'

She didn't like seeing him looking so careworn.

'But you must. Tell her what you're feeling, but listen to her too. Listening can be just as therapeutic as talking.' Hope might be able to give him what Edie couldn't at that moment.

'You think that'll work?' A new note of optimism entered his voice.

'Perhaps. It's what the therapists advise all the time.' She bent to pick up the toys scattered on the floor. Paul's problems were Paul's; she couldn't solve them for him.

When her phone rang, she was quick to pick it up and look at the name of the caller. 'It's Patrick.'

'Really?' he said, surprised. 'What can he want?'

'Shall I ask them over, then?' She moved in the direction of the door, not wanting to have this conversation in front of Paul.

'If you really want to, I give in. But how does he know your number?' He went round to where she'd been standing and took over chopping the parsley for her.

'He must have got it from Hope.' Edie went to the living room where she could have the quiet conversation she wanted. Having established Patrick and Clem would come for supper, she attacked her other problem. 'I was wondering whether you'd talked to Paul recently.'

'Not since we went to the pub, no,' he said, his voice smooth in her ear. Did he know what she was really asking? 'I was going to call him.' So, almost certainly, Paul didn't know a thing. She felt herself relax as the weight lifted from her shoulders. 'Why do you ask?'

She realized that she couldn't bring herself to tell him directly. But, as it turned out, she didn't need to.

'If you're worried about me telling him about my flat, don't be,' he said.

'What do you mean?' Protesting her innocence was hard and pointless.

'I mean that I know about your arrangement with Sandy's friend. Paul's my brother, but I don't want to be the one who tells him what's going on. If anyone does, it should be you. See you next week.'

29

Hope had been surprised and relieved to hear from Paul suggesting she come over for tea. He said that he wanted to talk, and that Edie would be out with the girls. She was pleased to have another opportunity to put things right between them.

'Just explain the whole thing to him again,' had been Vita's advice. 'He probably didn't take it all in the first time. Now he's had time to absorb it, he might listen properly.'

They had been prepping ahead for a dinner they were catering for the following day, and were taking a break for lunch, sitting inside watching the rain fall. Summer was almost over.

'I hope you're right,' she said, but Hope didn't feel confident.

'I know how hard this has been for you, but things will improve. Martin and Paul will come to understand better what you did. It'll just take time. And meanwhile, you've all this work to distract you.'

However unhelpful Vita's advice was in theory, it was true; work *was* helping Hope get through.

When Sunday came round, Hope was nervous but ready for the fray. Paul answered the doorbell so swiftly it was as if he'd been standing by the door waiting for her. 'Mum.' He hugged her stiffly before pulling away. 'Betty's party's been cancelled so the girls and Edie are here after all. A friend's coming over with her daughter. I thought we might drive out to Epping Forest for a walk instead. What do you say?'

'That would be lovely.' This was something they'd done together for years on the occasions they wanted to talk about something – before Paul met Edie. Once there, they would be surrounded by ancient woodland with only a distant hum of traffic in the distance. It crossed her mind that she was being pushed out of the house without a chance to see her granddaughters, probably at Edie's insistence. Although she was disappointed, she decided not to show it. Instead, she closed the top of her bag so he couldn't see the *Frozen* comic she'd brought for Betty and the knitted mouse for Hazel.

'We'll come back for a cup of tea after and you'll see the girls then.' He read her mind as he led the way to his car.

On the drive, they kept off the subject of Patrick, talking instead about Betty and Hazel and what they'd been up to, which was one of their favourite topics of conversation. By the time they were on the M11, any awkwardness had thawed between them, although Hope was only too aware that The Conversation still loomed. Just as they took the Debden turning towards Loughton, Paul said, 'I'm thinking about giving up my work.'

This was completely out of the blue.

Hope was astonished. 'You're not serious? But you love it, and you're very good at it.'

'I need a more reliable income for Edie and the girls.'

'Is that what Edie thinks?' She wondered whether his wife had finally grown tired of being the breadwinner and had delivered some kind of ultimatum. She wouldn't put it past her. But Hope knew how much Paul loved working with wood and, despite her initial reservations when he decided to follow such an unpredictable career, she wanted him to do whatever made him happy.

'I can't expect Edie to carry us on her own. It isn't fair.' His eyes were fixed ahead on the road as he circled a small round-about, turning right towards the centre of the forest.

'But has she prompted this?'

'No! I haven't spoken to her about it yet. I want to have a plan when I do. I don't want to present it as some sort of whim, with no idea how to put it into practice. She won't like that.' He turned right into the small car park, parked and led the way through some scrub onto the wide downward path that took them towards a stretch with a view across open forest. Nothing was said until they reached the top of the next hill, where they were surrounded by ancient beech trees.

'What are you going to do?' said Hope.

'Retrain, I think.'

'But you love what you do,' she protested again, stepping aside to let a couple of mountain bikers ride by.

'I do. But I could still have my own workshop on the side while I earn more doing something else.'

Just then, a deer ran out from their left and crossed the path right in front of them, disappearing into the forest.

'Wow! Look at him go,' Paul exclaimed.

They stared after it.

'Would Edie want that, though?' Hope didn't want to drop the subject, but to get to what lay behind Paul's thinking.

'You know what? I think she rather wishes she'd married a higher flyer now instead of a lowly craftsman earning virtually nothing beside her.'

Hope tried to put her arm around him, but he stepped to one side.

'Hey! Come on! But she knew who she was marrying. She chose you.'

'People change, circumstances change. I'm old enough to know that.' He kicked a stone that skittered ahead of them. 'Perhaps we're both different people now.'

They hadn't talked so intimately for a long time, and she was touched he was sharing all this with her. They might not be discussing Patrick's appearance in their life, but this was every bit as important to him. She couldn't help wondering whether there wasn't something else underlying his sudden decision to change direction.

'So, what are you thinking of doing?'

'An MBA.' He kicked at another stone.

'Business!' She couldn't help her surprise. 'Really?'

He turned his head to give her a small smile in acknowledgement of her badly hidden surprise. 'I know. But I thought I might as well make use of what I've learned so far. I'm thinking of applying to the London Business School for a two-year course. I wanted to know what you thought.'

'Two years?' She stood to one side as two bicyclists panted

their way up the hill. 'Can you afford it?' How much of a mother she still felt.

'Well,' he hesitated. 'I was going to ask you if you'd help me out. Dad has said he will, and I'll apply for a scholarship. It would only be a loan,' he added hastily. 'I promise I'll pay you back.'

'I don't know,' she said, disappointed that he'd gone to Martin first. 'How much do you need?'

The sum he mentioned shook her, but she would do what she could to help him achieve the life he wanted. His life and those of her granddaughters were what was important now, and his following the career he wanted would be part of that.

'Are you sure this is what you really want to do?'

'No. But it might make things easier with Edie. I need to talk to her first, but before I do that I want to know that I can somehow raise my own finance. I don't want to have to lean on her anymore.'

'She is your wife.' Her eye was caught by a grey squirrel that jinked through the trees and up a tree trunk, pausing halfway up to look around, tail twitching. 'Partners often support one another financially until they both get on the right track.'

'I think she might be having an affair.' He came out with it, just like that.

She stopped dead. 'What makes you think that?' He would be destroyed if he discovered that was true, especially coming so hot on the heels of her own revelations. One betrayal after another. She dreaded the hurt he would suffer and the inevitable fallout. But should she tell him what she knew? She hesitated. Were secrets really always better out in the open? If Patrick was able to influence Edie perhaps Paul need never know about her betrayal. Perhaps it wasn't too late for the two of them to get back on track. Would Hope telling him be more destructive than helpful?

'I saw a text. I could tell she was lying about who it was from. She looked so uncomfortable, though she was trying hard not to. That just made it worse. I'm not sure what to do or how to make her love me more.' He stuffed his hands in his pockets.

'Oh, Paul. I don't know what to say.'

This was the moment to say what she did know. But, seconds later, she had missed the opportunity.

'You don't have to say anything, but I've got to tell someone I know can keep a secret.' He gazed at the ground, slowly shaking his head.

Another secret. Hadn't they had enough?

'Do you know who with?' She pictured the man in the restaurant, smart and moneyed.

'No. But the message came from someone signing themselves "D" about some hotel arrangements. She said the D stood for Dinah, a friend of Ana's, and they're planning a weekend away together. She's never mentioned it before, and I've never heard her talk about a Dinah. She was so obviously struggling for a story. Anyhow, that's all I know. I can't believe that she'd do it though, especially now we've got Betty and Hazel.'

'Perhaps you've got it wrong.' But, of course, she already knew he hadn't.

'It's as though she's changed gear with me, and I don't like it. She's pleasant but distant at home and so tied up in her work again. Perhaps she'll realize how much I care if she sees me trying to make changes for her sake. Perhaps she'll come back to me.'

She felt the gruelling weight of his distress. She heard Vita: *Take a step back.*

'I don't know. I've just got this feeling. So you mustn't mention this to her. Promise?'

She nodded. 'I promise.'

Her knowledge weighed heavy but before saying anything, she wanted to ask for Patrick's advice now he was involved too.

They continued through the forest along a path lined on either side with more majestic beech trees, a cloudy sky above them. After a prolonged silence, they began to talk about anything and everything that didn't lead back to Edie or Patrick and Martin.

After a while, he told her about Betty receiving a prize at nursery for attendance. 'The one thing she can't do anything about.' He laughed.

'I remember you winning a prize for English. You were supposed to be given a choice, so you asked for something special – was it *Mr Nice*, that autobiography of some drug lord? But they insisted on giving you *Great Expectations*?'

'Biggest disappointment of my school life.' He pulled a face.

And so they continued, swapping reminiscences and stories of his children. Hope began to feel that their relationship was getting back on the same familiar footing as before. But what was she to do about Edie's secret? She hoped Patrick would help her.

It wasn't until they were in the car and back on the motorway that Paul finally brought up the subject of Patrick. 'We've met a couple of times now and we get on okay. But what I still can't understand is why you didn't tell Dad and me about him, especially Dad.'

Hope looked out of the window as the traffic rushed by. 'Everything we've done together as a family was real. Of course it would have been different if Patrick had been there, or you'd known about him, but that just wasn't possible. And Martin and I both loved you more than anything. Nothing can change that.'

'Did you ever think of him? On birthdays, Christmases – times like that?' Did he hope she'd deny it?

She took a deep breath. 'Look, let me try and explain again. All of it. From the beginning.'

To her, the story sounded tired. Yes, she almost certainly would never have said anything if Patrick hadn't made the first move, and, yes, she had thought of him, and not just on special occasions, but every day of her life. Yet, somehow she'd been able to compartmentalize him so he was nothing to do with the life she was leading – quite how, she had no idea.

By the time they pulled up outside the house, Hope could see Paul was struggling with it all over again. He couldn't have completely forgotten the closeness they'd had on the walk. So much bound them together, including the way they'd supported each other when she and Martin split up. When she had finally arrived in London, she didn't want to lean on her son or interrupt his new life, but Paul had helped find the house she still lived in, while she and Vita set up *Booking the Cooks*. He had kept in touch with her pretty much every week to check on her until he was satisfied she was standing on her own feet.

'Cup of tea?' Paul interrupted her thoughts.

'I'd love to see the girls,' she said, realizing Edie might not welcome her but – what the hell? 'I won't stay long.'

She followed him to the front door. As Paul turned his key in the lock, she could hear the yelling going on behind it.

'Daddy! Daddy!'

By the time the door was open, Betty was standing there, looking thrilled to see him. He swung her on to his hip and kissed her cheek.

Nothing made Hope happier than seeing Paul with his daughters. There was a special pleasure in seeing how much he loved them, and the pleasure they gave him in turn. She followed them down to the kitchen, listening to Betty chatter on before she was put down and dashed off.

'Hope!' Edie obviously hadn't been expecting her.

'I asked her in for a cup of tea,' said Paul, 'and to see the girls.'

The atmosphere was decidedly cool. The tension ricocheted between them, but Hope was determined to stick it out long enough to see her granddaughters. She hoisted Hazel out of her bouncy chair and on to her knee.

'Look what I've got for you.' She opened her bag and pulled out the mouse.

'You shouldn't have,' said Edie.

Hope ignored her disapproval. Why shouldn't she spoil her grandchildren every now and then? Wasn't that what grandparents were for?

'Me?' Betty said.

'As a matter of fact . . .' Hope pulled out the *Frozen* comic. Betty grabbed it. 'Mummy, look!'

'Betty! What do you say? Hope, you can't bring them presents every time you see them!'

'She's right, Mum, you shouldn't spoil them,' Paul added.

Hope was torn between bursting into tears and banging their heads together. Suddenly, she was almost shouting. 'Why not? Why bloody not? They're my grandchildren. Isn't that what I'm *meant* to do?'

They were both taken aback by her outburst.

'We-ell,' said Edie. 'I'm not sure—'

Betty looked concerned for a moment, then brought the comic to Hope.

'Look, Gwanny. Read.' She had the pages open at a comic strip about Anna and Elsa that Hope gratefully began to read. After the conversation with Paul in Epping, Hope wanted to wrap the two little girls in a protective embrace and shelter them from any storm that might be coming their way. This was all she could do – be there for them.

The atmosphere in the kitchen continued to be strained. Paul barely exchanged a word with Edie and, once he'd made the tea, he excused himself to go to his shed. 'Something I want to finish off. Won't be long.' It was as if he couldn't be in the same room with his wife in case he did or said the wrong thing. Hope sympathized.

When he'd gone, Edie sat down with Hope and the girls. Of course, Hope remembered, Granny couldn't be left alone with them in case there was another accident.

'So . . .' Edie began, then stopped.

'Paul suspects you're having an affair.' Hope spoke quickly, mindful they didn't have long. She returned Hazel to her seat.

'Er . . . I don't think he does.' From the way Edie hesitated, Hope knew she was lying.

'Edie, he's just told me. I didn't tell him what I know, because I think you should. If you won't, I will.' Should she go as far as telling her what Patrick had said?

Edie looked up from the *Frozen* comic, frowning and furious. 'Not in front of the girls!'

'I'll make it brief. We both know they're too young to understand.' She refused to be deterred. 'So . . . Now Paul suspects, shouldn't you put him out of his misery and tell him what's been going on?'

Betty had lost interest in the comic and wandered off to put her toys 'to bed', wrapping them in napkins from a kitchen drawer. Hazel was quite happy in the seat being bounced gently by Hope's foot.

'You would say that. You're his mother.'

'Edie, careful! Yes, I am, and I care about him. Look at it from my side – I know you've been having a flirtation. You told me it was over, but is it really? I've heard otherwise. You can't treat him like this. He deserves better.'

Edie's face flushed. At least she had the grace to look guilty. Betty had abandoned her toys and was over at her play kitchen clattering pans and plastic vegetables.

'I don't know what to do.' Edie sighed, surprising Hope with a rare burst of emotion. 'Honestly? I don't expect you to understand. I've known Daniel – the man you saw me with – for years, since long before I met Paul. I thought I was over him and I certainly never expected to see him again. We met again quite by chance. This is so difficult for me.'

Hope absorbed this new piece of information with disbelief. 'However difficult it is for you, you've got to understand that Paul comes first for me.' She wished he had never met Edie at all.

'Don't I know that. He always has.' Edie's burst of aggression was uncalled for.

'Then, you'd better make up your mind what you're doing before you do any more damage. You're married to Paul, and you have these two beautiful children. What about them?'

Edie bowed her head. 'I know,' she whispered. 'Don't you think I know?'

'You can't take them from Paul.' Imagining her grandchildren divided between their parents with the possibility of another man taking Paul's role some of the time led Hope to think of what she had done to Patrick. However happy the family life he had, it hadn't been with hers – and that was her responsibility to bear. There was nothing more she could say. Upsetting Edie any more in front of the children would achieve nothing. She had said her piece. The rest was up to them. After a couple of minutes, she stood up. 'I'd better go. I'll just pop out and say goodbye to Paul.'

The agony she saw in Edie's face was hard to see, but she couldn't help her. Instead, she hugged her tight for a moment in a spontaneous gesture of sympathy.

'You must sort this out. For everyone's sake. If you don't, I will.'

'I will.' Edie's voice quavered but she kept herself in check as Hope left the room to cross the garden.

Through the window of the shed, Hope could see Paul sanding a wooden bowl that he'd obviously turned himself. He turned as she opened the door. 'Sorry to leave you. I wanted another go at this bowl. Isn't it beautiful? Walnut. The tree came down in a friend's garden. I'm giving it to Edie. It's a surprise.'

The desperation in his voice and the longing to please his wife almost broke Hope's heart. She touched the bowl, the dark grain with subtle hints of black and blue, its surface silken. 'It's beautiful. I'm off. I'll see you all soon.'

They kissed each other.

'Thanks, Mum. I feel better for talking with you.'

'You need to talk to Edie,' she said. 'I'm sure everything will work out for the best. Try not to worry.' But as she walked back down the garden, the family's future looked more uncertain that ever.

30

Edie was brooding as she brushed Betty's hair. Heart or head – which should she follow? In an unguarded moment, she had said too much to Hope and completely alienated her. Somehow her mother-in-law had found out what was happening so Edie was on her own now and had to make up her mind before Hope said anything. She felt as if a net was closing in around her. The decision had to be made. Paul or Daniel. Responsibility or love. The choice was impossible, but she had reached a critical point.

One moment, she wanted the security and the sort of love she had in her marriage with Paul and their girls. Tedious as caring for them might be, now she was back at work with Jen picking up on the worst of the drudgery, she could begin to imagine things getting easier as the girls got older. Perhaps it needn't be as limiting as she had felt when trapped at home with Betty and Hazel twenty-four hours a day. She knew there were plenty of women who relished being a full-time mum, but that definitely wasn't for her. Her career was what gave her the satisfaction she needed, and it was incredibly demanding. She was pretty sure Paul didn't fully appreciate just how much.

Working long days made being a good wife and mother almost impossible. Everyone else took up the slack and she saw far too little of her own children. What Daniel was offering was a clean slate. A new start. But a start that would be marred by access arrangements for both of them. Each of them would be involved in the other's children's lives. They would have limited time with their own children. How would their lives work together? Their days of sitting in bars and clubs, flirting and chatting, were over now. It was time to get serious.

Edie was brooding as she tidied up downstairs. She went up to check on the girls. In the light of the roundabout lamp, she could see that Hazel had wiggled her way to the top of the cot and squished herself into the top corner, Bunny clasped tightly in her pudgy hands while continually sucking on her dummy. In Betty's bedroom, the little girl was sprawled in her own cot, her favourite baby blanket over her face, thumb on the silky part of the label. They both looked so innocent and peaceful. Neither of them with any idea of what might be about to engulf them.

Downstairs, she poured herself a glass of white wine and went to sit on the roof terrace that led out from the back of the sitting room on top of the kitchen extension. From here, she had a perfect view of the neighbours' gardens and was in earshot of most of their outdoor conversations. They may as well live together during the summer, she knew so much about the colours Zoe and Ted were divided over for their bedroom, about Rosie and Seb's disagreements over the drinks party they were giving next week. But tonight, she was the only one out there. It was silent except for the sound of birds and occasional distant traffic. She leaned back against the pineapple-print cushion, stretched out her legs towards the sinking sun, and closed her eyes.

First, she imagined telling Paul that their marriage was over. Then she imagined telling Daniel their affair was over. She tried to picture their reactions and what she would feel herself in each scenario. She tried to see the girls, and how they would react. Afterwards, she considered Daniel. They hadn't even discussed how they would be together, where they would live, how they would manage their separate families, the sacrifices that would have to be made. Her life going forward with Paul was all too clear.

Her phone pinged. Annoyed her time out was interrupted, she ignored it, but then had second thoughts in case it was her clerk texting about the next day's workload. She picked it up.

It wasn't James. It was a text from Daniel.

> We can't meet again. I'm so sorry. Not on our
> bench for lunch nor at any other time. You
> don't know how much it hurts to have to say
> this. I've had to give my word. D

What?! She read it again, but the words remained stubbornly the same.

His word? Who to? His wife? How could she have found out about them? Whatever, he couldn't just end their affair with a short text and no explanation, not after everything he'd said to her. She recognized a certain irony in the situation, given her own attempt to do the same thing only months earlier. But they were in a different position now. She would take her lead from him and kick back. There was far too much they had left to discuss. What had happened to change his mind? How she longed to see him. With that burst of longing, came the certitude that she wouldn't take this lying down. Not without a proper explanation, a proper discussion.

She deleted his text and quickly typed a reply.

> Daniel! You can't end it like this. Why? After
> everything you said. I thought you wanted us
> to be together? Can we talk? Please

Tears came to her eyes as she once again considered the magnitude of leaving Paul, the impact it would have on so many people. She had been considering ending her affair with Daniel after one last time together, so why did she mind so much when the decision was taken out of her hands? He'd made it easy for her. But that wasn't what she wanted. She should leave him, and yet she wanted to see him, make love and talk. Her fingernails rapped against her phone as she waited for his reply. 'Come on.'

As if he heard her, the phone pinged.

> We really shouldn't. I'm sorry.

He sounded almost scared. Something must have happened. She read it once again and deleted it, her eyes welling with tears as she wrote.

> I need to talk to you. Please

> OK. When are you next in chambers? I'll meet
> you in Red Lion Square

She called up her diary. She had a couple of days travelling to cases in various parts of the south-east, but Friday looked as if it would be in London. She had an advocacy meeting in chambers in the morning.

> If you can do Friday, I'll meet you then.

At that moment, Paul came and joined her, a bottle of Corona in his hand. She put her phone away immediately, her stomach churning as guilt, longing and Hope's ultimatum battled for her attention.

'Would you like another glass of wine?' He fetched her one and they sat together on the terrace, companionable now. But the question *What Next?* hung over her. Just chatting would be hard now she knew his suspicions. But she couldn't say anything to him until she'd spoken to Daniel.

'What have you been doing?' she asked, barely able to stay out there with him.

'Thinking.' He reached across and took her hand.

'Anything come of it?' Her hand remained limp in his.

'Yeah. Mum and I had a good talk this afternoon. However difficult I'm finding it, I'm trying to understand better what she was going through. I guess Dad was a bit of an arse, off at college, shagging around. No wonder she didn't want to make him come home and be a father. She's right, too – he would have resented it forever.'

'Are you going to say something to her?' This was so much easier than talking about what mattered so much to both of them. Putting the moment off.

'Yes, to Mum *and* Dad. I want them to know that I'm beginning to understand. Mum will be pleased but Dad will kick off. I can't imagine him ever forgiving her for not telling him about Patrick.' He tipped his head back for a swig of lager.

'Surely that's his problem, not yours.' But her mind was not on his problems. It was on Daniel. There was nothing else she could think of, however hard she tried.

What could have happened to persuade him to end their affair so abruptly?

As Edie entered the square, she looked for Daniel. The benches round the central circle were all taken, along with the green metal tables and chairs grouped outside the modest hut serving food. She walked to the eastern end of the square, grateful for the shade afforded by the sycamores and the tall surrounding buildings. She found a bench close to the bust of Bertrand Russell, sat down and waited.

She didn't have to wait for long.

Daniel entered from the west side of the square, spotted her and, with a wave, crossed over. He was spruce, as ever, in his dark suit and tie, hair newly cut, brisk and purposeful. Everything Paul was not, she thought.

'You're here.' He looked pleased to see her but so apprehensive. They couldn't touch or kiss in case they were seen, however much she longed to.

'I brought a sandwich for you.'

She pulled out the sandwiches she'd bought from Prêt on her way there. She knew his favourite – the classic super club.

'Thanks,' he smiled. 'That's thoughtful. I'll do coffee from the café in a minute.'

'Just thinking ahead.'

He started unwrapping his sandwich straightaway.

'What's happened?' She couldn't bring herself to unwrap her own hummus and chipotle wrap. 'Why would you end it after everything we've said?'

He stopped and looked up at her. 'For your sake. Someone knows about us using the flat and I've been warned off. It really is all getting too close for comfort.'

'Paul's mother told me he thinks I'm having an affair. She knows about us, but she's promised not to tell him as long as I do.'

He closed his eyes for a moment. 'This is getting worse. Too many people know. I don't want to upend your life any more than I have already have. Or indeed mine. If you don't want to be with me, then I think we have to break up. It's getting too precarious for both of us.' He tapped his fingers on the arm of the bench, impatient.

She needed to hear him say he wanted her, that he loved her.

He bit into his sandwich, eating it in silence, then said, 'I don't want us to stop. I want us to be together. You've been in my life for so long now, and I can't imagine it without you.'

'I feel exactly the same.' That's all she could say, aware this was the moment of truth, the commitment she could not undo. Leaving Paul would rupture her family every bit as badly as Hope's secret had ruptured hers.

But it was the truth – at last.

'Are you saying you *will* leave Paul for me?' His face was alight, the sandwich forgotten. 'Are you?'

She felt giddy with anticipation. 'Yes. Yes, I will.'

Forgetting all their previous caution, he flung his arms round her. 'At last. I can't imagine my life without you in it. I've always loved you, you know.'

'I don't want to lose you either.' For a moment she was oblivious of their surroundings. 'I love you, too.'

They separated, and looked at each other.

'Together?'

'Together.' She was overwhelmed by joy. He squeezed her hand hard, then brought them back to earth with a bump. 'So, what do we do now?'

After Daniel had fetched a couple of coffees, they remained on that seat for the next three-quarters of an hour. They were too absorbed to notice any of the people walking past. As they talked, Edie became more and more certain that she was doing the right thing – not just for her, but for Paul and the girls. She told herself they deserved someone better than her. Paul would manage, find someone else, while he and she would co-parent. They would be reasonable. She would not fight with him, but negotiate an arrangement that would suit them both. The more she and Daniel discussed their situation, the more she was convinced this was right.

Eventually, when they left to go back to their separate chambers, they had made a plan. Carrying it out would cause terrible immediate pain to everyone involved, but it was the only way forward if they were to have a future together. Worlds would be overturned, but in time, they would find new orbits. Everyone would get used to a new orientation, and perhaps their happiness would eventually enable the happiness of others.

Two days later, when the girls were in bed and she and Paul had eaten supper, Edie suggested they have a nightcap in the living room. Her hands were shaking, her heart racing. She couldn't imagine how she would survive this. Paul had done nothing to deserve what was about to happen to him. The wooden bowl he had given a couple of days earlier, specially turned for her, showed how much he loved her. He might suspect she was having an affair, but he had no proof or any idea of how serious and longstanding her relationship with Daniel was. The thought of telling him had been torturing her since Hope had said she must, made worse since she had left Daniel in the square. All weekend they'd been together with the girls and she had been pretending . . . pretending. Also snatching moments to have conversations with Daniel to confirm their plans. How could she let them all down?

She was about to show herself how.

Daniel and she had agreed that they each would tell their partners together on the following Sunday evening. Then they would move into a hotel, followed by a rented flat, while everything was sorted out and until everything had settled down. It would in the end, because these things always did in one way or another. Jen would make sure the girls were okay. So would Hope.

Edie was praying that once Paul's initial shock and anger – she was prepared for all that – had died down, they'd be able to work out a way of co-parenting Hazel and Betty. She was determined not to go the way of the rich vindictive clients she so often dealt with who forgot about the wellbeing of their kids in their desire for revenge. Paul, at heart, wasn't like that. In time, he would be ready to listen.

Paul sat on the sofa, obviously taken aback when she took the chair nearby him instead of plumping down beside him. He looked tired and grey, slumped, as he had since reading Daniel's text, as if his stuffing had been ripped out. Her timing couldn't be worse; it was one thing on top of the other, but circumstances were driving them now and decisions had taken on a momentum of their own. He looked down at his hands, waiting for her to say something. Did he have an inkling of what was about to hit him?

Edie sat up straight, drawing on every ounce of self-control. She wanted to make this as easy as she could for him, but that was not going to be possible. A sip of wine and a deep breath.

Paul looked up expectant, unhappy.

'Paul, darling Paul. There's something I have to tell you . . .'

31

Hope set off early to meet Patrick in one of the fancy restaurants behind Kings Cross. He'd suggested they meet there and booked a table, so all she had to do was turn up. She glanced down at her belted vintage tea-dress, red with gaudy flowers. It was a statement, if ever there was one. *Notice me, I'm not over yet.*

Their table was outside, so she was able to sit in the sun, watching the world go by. So many people enjoying the brilliant September weather, walking up to the canal or back down to the station, everything overshadowed by the cranes towering into the blue sky. Summer dresses, ice creams, sunhats, smiles – London at its most relaxed. An Indian summer. Eventually she saw Patrick walking briskly from the station. He was dressed smartly in a suit with the jacket slung over his shoulder, shirt collar open, and he looked uncannily like a young Martin. Even more so than Paul ever had.

He kissed her on the cheek and pulled out the other chair. 'I'm so sorry. Train was delayed. Have you a coffee?'

She hadn't, so he ordered for them both. Eventually, they were settled. She was pleased to be with him. Although there was so much she knew about him, there was so much more that she wanted to know, so much that would take a lifetime to learn. She knew she couldn't keep firing questions at him like the Inquisition. The story of his life must be allowed to unroll gradually as they got to know each other.

'I'm sorry to drag you down here,' he said. 'But there's something I wanted to tell you and it feels better doing it face to face.'

She had a moment of panic, imagining the worst – that he had decided to withdraw from her and her family. He'd found them and that was enough. His curiosity had been satisfied and he didn't want any more contact because his heart lay with the family who had brought him up instead. The dramas that had recently overtaken them had been too much, and he wanted no part of them anymore. She took a sip of her flat white and braced herself for the worst.

He cut one of the pastries in half and put one piece on a plate for her. 'Well, two things really. We talked about Edie, remember?'

'Of course.' She couldn't imagine what he could have to say about her daughter-in-law that merited a trip to Kings Cross.

'I'm afraid I've been a bit underhand.' He grimaced. 'I told Sandy to tell Daniel that he couldn't use the flat again, and if he didn't stop seeing Edie, he would tell his wife.'

She was astonished. 'You did that? But that's blackmail! What happened?' Hope was equally impressed and shocked by his guile.

'Apparently, he was so convincing that Daniel agreed, begging him not to say anything. Although it was really none of my business, it struck me that it was just that one thing I could do for you and Paul, so I did.' He immediately looked apprehensive.

'But that's really wonderful,' she said. 'Thank you.' Edie thwarted might not be an easy person to live with, but that was a bridge to be crossed later.

'Is it?' He allowed himself to smile at last. 'I was worried you might think I was interfering. I had to think twice before I said anything.'

'Neither Paul nor I could have done it, so I'm glad. And, of course, Paul will never know.' Despite him suspecting the affair, perhaps there was a chance that Paul's marriage would be saved after all, and nothing needed to be said. She might not ever have an easy relationship with her daughter-in-law after all this, but in future she would leave Edie well alone and just try to rub along when they had to. Hope knew so much that she wished she didn't about her. For the first time, she saw a similarity between their two predicaments. A lifetime secret as a result – all so as not to hurt the person they loved.

'That's right,' said Patrick. 'Not from me, anyway.'

'What was the second thing?'

He brightened. 'I wanted you to know first ... Clem's pregnant! She's gone to see her dad to tell him. We wanted to tell you both at exactly the same time. You're going to be a grandmother again.'

She leapt to her feet and hugged him. 'What fantastic news. I'm so pleased for you both. When?'

'Another six months to go. We didn't want to say anything until we knew it was definitely happening – didn't want to tempt fate. We're not finding out whether it's a girl or a boy, so that'll be another surprise. Clem's wondering if you'd like to come and visit us – she wants your opinion on the baby's room.'

'I'd love to.' How wonderful that she was going to be included. This was much more than she had a right to expect.

Her phone buzzed in her pocket. Probably Vita about the job they had that evening, except Hope had prepped everything and would have plenty of time to finish off when she got home. 'Do you mind if I just check, in case it's a work emergency?'

'Of course not.'

But it wasn't Vita. It was a message from Paul asking her to call him. She would do so on the way home. How pleased he'd be to have Patrick's news too. A cousin for Betty and Hazel.

'This is so exciting!' Also, the first time she had felt so pleased about something for ages. Meeting Patrick and introducing him to the family had been circumscribed by so many other feelings that the pleasure had been diminished. But this was something else.

'I hoped you'd be pleased.'

'More than you can know.' This baby would be a chance for them all to start again and would bring so much joy to them all. Even Edie. Surely.

They had their coffee, then Patrick wanted to get home so that he could spend the rest of the day with Clem. Hope remembered how once, a long time ago, it had been like that with Martin. She couldn't help wondering what he was up to at that moment. Was he coming round to understanding her actions? She suspected not. That sort of generosity of understanding and forgiveness did not come easy to him. Not immediately, at least. She would have to get used to the idea that their relationship was probably over. At least he left it knowing what had happened so many years ago and had met Patrick. Truth, then, if not reconciliation. He and Hope could have their separate relationships with their two sons, if not with each other anymore. Hope had attempted to contact him, but had failed. He hadn't returned her call or her email. Patrick had assured her that he and Paul would try to make him see sense, but she had very little hope that would work.

As she walked back along the canal, past the narrowboats – some better maintained than others with bright paint and roofs of potted plants – she got out her phone to call Paul. He answered immediately.

'Mum!' She could sense from the break in his voice that something was wrong.

'I'm sorry. I was having lunch with Patrick. Clem's pregnant! Isn't that wonderful news?'

Paul choked out a 'Yes', but nothing more.

'Are you all right?"

'She's leaving me.' He was crying, she could make it out now. Her happiness at Patrick's news dropped away.

'What do you mean?' She'd believed that Patrick's inter-vention had ended the affair. How stupid she felt. How sad for Paul.

He blew his nose. 'Exactly that. I was right about her having an affair. She's hooked up with a guy she knew before me. Her first love. Daniel. They've been seeing each other since Betty was born.' He gasped for air. 'She's leaving today; feels the quicker the ties are cut the better.'

Hope felt punched in the gut. 'So soon! What about the girls? Can I come over and help?'

Advising Edie to come clean might not have been the right thing to do. Had she forced her hand? Made her decide before she was ready?

'Come later, when Edie's gone. She's packing. Jen's been here this morning and she's told me she'll stay on with them and help with the transition so I can keep working. Not that I feel much like doing anything.'

'Bless her, but can you afford her now? Can I help?'

'Edie's going to keep on paying her. When she told me last night, she had it all worked out. She wants the girls to stay here with me.'

Hope gasped. 'She's not taking them?' Her first selfish reaction was that at least she wouldn't lose them too.

'No. She loves this guy, and she loves her career, so she's leaving to live with him. He's another barrister. She says she'd like to have the girls every Wednesday night and every other weekend. Can you believe that? Her own daughters. It's all so calculated.'

'No, I can't.' It might be all worked out, but that didn't mean it wouldn't hurt Edie terribly. Hope knew exactly what that felt like. But what about Paul? While Edie got the life she wanted, how would he manage with two small girls to look after? What about the girls themselves? 'I'm coming over.'

'No, Mum, don't. Please. You'll only make things worse.' His distress was awful to hear.

'Where are you now?'

'In the shed, trying to straighten my head out.'

'And the girls?'

'Jen's got Hazel and will pick up Betty from nursery and take them to the park. We decided it was better that they didn't have to say goodbye to Edie today. Jesus! I can't believe this is happening.'

'Nor can I.' She was crying too. Although she had known there was a faint chance something like this might happen, she had trusted the girls would keep Edie with Paul. How would Paul juggle his work or his studies if he went through with that idea now? How would he ever get over this? All she knew was she would be there to help him in any way she could.

'How can she do this, Mum? How? I thought she loved us.'

'I don't know,' Hope said, carefully. 'She's not someone who makes snap decisions. And you say she's known this guy for ages so she must have been thinking about it for some time.' She wondered whether Patrick's intervention had provoked this fork in the road rather than helped. But there was little point in dwelling on what had happened. The affair had been going on for a long time and there was nothing anyone could do to turn the clock back. Once Edie's mind was made up, trying to stop her would be like standing in front of a steam roller. Impossible. 'You'll have to focus on the girls so this affects them as little as possible, and I'll help you as much as I can.'

'As little as possible?' His voice rose to a shout. 'Their mother's leaving them. How can they not be affected?'

'Okay, I'm sorry. Look, I'm walking home at the moment. I'll come round as soon as you'd like me to. Just call me. Any time at all.' What she wanted to do was to dash round there and make things better for him, despite knowing there was nothing she could do to alleviate his pain. However, she respected his request for her to stay away for the moment, said a tearful goodbye and continued her way home.

What was the saying? 'You're only as happy as your unhappiest child.' So, this was what that felt like – utterly inconsolable.

As soon as she got through her front door, she threw herself on the sofa and burst into tears. She and Paul had been through so much upset recently. How would they survive this, too? It felt as though they were suddenly confronted by a new mountain to climb, and they hadn't yet reached the foothills. How could Edie take such a drastic decision? She hadn't found motherhood easy, as Hope knew – but this! Hope knew what it was to give up a child. She couldn't imagine what must be going through Edie's mind, the struggle she must have had in coming to this decision.

How would Paul cope? Her thoughts remained with him as she gradually pulled herself together and went downstairs into the pro kitchen. Vita would be here soon, and they'd have to finish off, as far as they could, before going round to that evening's booking – an anniversary dinner. She hadn't the heart for it, but when she was phoned by a woman who wanted to surprise her husband but had three children and no babysitter, she couldn't say no. She'd kept it simple but impressive – scallops, ossobuco and tiramisu. None of it would pack or transport itself, so she had to get on with it.

She texted Vita and told her she didn't need to come.

> I'm on top of it and can manage on my own.
> Enjoy your evening instead. Honestly.

The truth was, she would prefer to do everything on her own at that moment. Having something to do kept her occupied, but she didn't want to talk about what was happening until she had processed it herself and spoken properly to Paul. This proposed arrangement for Edie to see the children in such a limited way troubled her. The worry was that Edie would have second thoughts, then turn and use her barrister skills and connections to take the children away. Whatever she said in the heat of the moment could so easily be overturned given time and a change of perspective.

She sighed. The previous few months had been so fraught with secrets, betrayal and high emotion. What on earth were the next few going to bring?

32

One year later . . .

'Granny, look at me!' Betty called from the swimming pool. She was standing on the steps into the shallow end, ready.

Hope hauled herself up to a sitting position to watch her swim unaided towards Paul, who was encouraging her, tanned and relaxed after being in Amorgos for ten days. A different holiday, a different Greek island.

'That's brilliant.' Hope clapped her hands from the sun lounger, watching Paul slip the child's armbands back on so they could go deeper in the pool and splash around with the white unicorn float toy. He collected Hazel from the steps, where she was sitting in her ring, splashing her hands in the water, waiting for him.

'Come on, little one. Let's swim.' He swooshed her towards Betty.

Raising her hand to shield her eyes against the sun, Hope squinted to her right where Clem sat in the shade with Dylan, her third grandchild. He was sitting up on the terrace, surrounded by cushions from indoors, beaming at anyone who came near. After a grouchy, sleepless start in life, he'd become an amiable little boy whom they all adored.

Patrick was inside, cooking.

Family. That's what this holiday was all about.

The door to the kitchen was open, but the shuttered windows of the house were keeping the sun out, so the interior remained as cool as possible. A fig tree stood to one side, its green fruit just beginning to ripen in the sun, a couple of hibiscus bushes trumpeted red flowers and bougainvillea draped purple and red over the wall. Cicadas shrilled in the background, perhaps from the gnarled olive trees that grew around the garden. The view beyond the swimming pool spread across the rooftops of the neighbouring villas, down to the port town of Katapola and the glittering sea beyond. A safer walk to the sea than the one Hope had embarked on the previous year. But she had been careful not to repeat her accident. This time she really was needed to help out from time to time.

She stretched out, feeling the warmth of the sun on her body, happy at last.

'Aren't you coming in, Mum?'

'Sure. If you want me to.' Nothing gave her greater pleasure than joining in, but she was aware that sometimes she should wait to be invited. After all, they were Paul's children, not hers. She had to remember that and keep those boundaries, however tempting it was to comment on what he fed them or how long Betty watched his iPad or any one of those things that differed so much from when she had been bringing him up. If she had learned anything from Edie, it was that.

The water was a heaven-sent relief from the heat, and she swam slowly over to Paul and the girls, relishing every moment.

A little later, there was a shout from the house. 'Grub's up. Come and get it!' Patrick was on the edge of the terrace, wearing an apron over his shorts. The outdoor table was spread with an array of cold meats and cheeses, grapes and oranges, a bowl of pasta for the kids, and a focaccia loaf made by him. He had turned out to be quite a whizz in the kitchen, and Hope was delighted to have the onus removed from her this once.

Paul and Hope marshalled the kids out of the pool, dried them off and followed Clem up to the table that stood under a pergola thick with vines, their dark grapes hanging above them.

While they ate, Paul's phone rang. He pulled a face but answered it immediately. 'Betty, it's Mummy on FaceTime. Come here. Hazel – you, too.' He addressed the screen. 'You've caught us at lunch, but it doesn't matter.'

Hope felt faintly uncomfortable being present. She never knew whether to say hello to Edie or whether to move away. Their relationship, such as it was now, was awkward at best, neither of them knowing how to relate to the other. So nothing much had changed but, whatever Hope felt, Edie was the mother of her granddaughters and always would be. They needed to make a good relationship for the girls' sake and for Paul's.

'I can ring back.'

Edie's voice made Hope nervous, although by this time it really shouldn't. Edie had stuck to her word. She really didn't want her daughters except on the most part-time basis and was prepared to pay for the cost of any childcare to help Paul, maintaining that she wasn't cut out to be a mother. Hope still couldn't come to terms with a woman abandoning her children for a life she wanted more, as hard as she tried to understand the rigours of Edie's profession and the lure of the man she had always loved over her son. But she had to follow Paul's lead and if he could get along well enough with Edie, then she must too.

'How is she?' asked Patrick when the call was over. He had a relaxed attitude to his ex-sister-in-law and behaved as if their separate living arrangements were the most natural thing in the world.

'She looks well,' said Paul. 'Busy as always.'

Hope was always surprised to hear Paul talk so calmly about her. His initial devastation had been taken over by a practicality and calmness that was impressive and reassuring as he got on with his life. 'It is what it is,' he'd say although she could hear the underlying sadness sometimes.

'Where are they living now?'

'They've moved out of the flat that was too small when the girls visited. So they've bought a house in Kentish Town, so not too far but far away enough!' He grinned.

That was the first time Hope had heard him joke about the situation.

'But she and Daniel are taking the kids to Italy after we get back, so Freya and I will be able to have some time to ourselves.'

Clem caught Hope's eye and they exchanged a quick smile. They were both harbouring hopes for Paul's new relationship with a fellow mature student he had met at the London Business School a few months earlier.

'I want to make a card for Mummy.' Betty jumped from her seat.

Paul turned off the sound on his phone and replaced it face down on the table. 'No, Betty. Not now. Sit down and eat your pasta.'

She sat down and spooned up a mouthful. She looked up at him, eyes wide. 'After this?'

'Let me finish my lunch and then we will. Promise.' Paul stroked her cheek. Then he turned to Hazel who was busy feeding herself with her fingers. 'Well done, Hazel. Keep going.' The little girl beamed at him through the layer of tomato sauce that coated most of her face and hands.

'So, that's getting serious then?' Clem asked, spooning some mushed-up vegetables into Dylan's wide-open mouth. She, Patrick and Hope all speculated behind Paul's back about the significance of their relationship. They had all heard her name but none of them had met her yet.

'Give us a chance,' said Paul. Despite the tan, they could see him colouring slightly. 'We're taking it as it comes.'

'Have you introduced her to the girls yet?' Patrick poured out the home-made lemonade for them all.

Hope sat back and listened. These were the questions she'd never dare ask. Paul knew how keen she was for him to settle down with someone new, but would brush off her questions, never giving anything away. He didn't want her interfering. His priority was giving the girls the best and most stable life he could and forging a career that would enable him to do his bit in supporting them.

'They've met her as a friend,' said Paul, looking faintly embarrassed. 'That's all. I don't want to muddle them.'

'I think that's fair enough,' Clem said. 'Take your time. It's early days.'

'I do think they've got used to Edie and Daniel though.' Paul could talk about his ex-wife and her lover without sounding resentful or angry. Hope often wondered what he really felt now. Once, perhaps, he might have told her, but they had both learned to give the other space. He didn't want to worry her, and she had to accept that. More than that, she had to trust him.

She was proud of the way he had so quickly moved forward into the next stage of his life. Edie was always going to play some part, so it was better to accept the status quo, if they all could. At least there were no secrets in the cupboard anymore. As for Paul, he seemed to be coming to terms with the situation. Having his girls was what had got him through and given him a reason to get up every morning. Hope helped out when he asked her and, of course, Jen had made so much possible.

Hope looked round the table, happy with what she saw.

The last year had been turbulent but her new, revised family had survived and were looking forward to a different future.

And Martin and her? Their relationship would probably never recover, but they had discovered they could share their sons and families without needing to be close. Something she had never imagined could happen. They had arrived at a good place. They were peaceful with each other, which left her free to consider other things.

In fact, she was even thinking of trying a new dating app Vita had found and pressed her to join. Hope was beginning to think that perhaps she was ready to have someone for herself in her life again. Something in her had changed. She was ready for a new chapter.

Acknowledgements

Firstly, to the mothers of my own wonderful grandchildren in whom I've been so lucky.

This was my lockdown book and, as such, I found it particularly difficult to write. I have many people to thank for helping me get it to a publishable state. Clare Alexander, my indomitable agent and friend. My trusty editor Clare Hey and her phenomenal team especially Louise Davies, Sara-Jade Virtue and Jess Barratt. Eagle-eyed copyeditors Karen Ball and Victoria Godden – how I needed you both and your invaluable suggestions. Roma Ferguson for her advice on the life of a family law barrister – any mistakes are unquestionably mine. Julie Sharman and Elizabeth Buchan and other dear friends for listening when I moaned. And, as always, Robin and my family without whom nothing would be achieved.